An Immoral Code

AN IMMORAL CODE

Caro Fraser

ORION

Copyright © Caro Fraser 1997
All rights reserved

The right of Caro Fraser to be identified as the author
of this work has been asserted by her in accordance
with the Copyright, Designs and Patents Act 1988.

First published in Great Britain in 1997 by Orion
An imprint of Orion Books Ltd
Orion House, 5 Upper St Martin's Lane,
London WC2H 9EA

A CIP catalogue record for this book is available
from the British Library

ISBN 0 75281 169 X (hardcover)

Typeset at The Spartan Press Ltd,
Lymington, Hants

Printed in Great Britain by
Clays Ltd, St Ives plc

For all long-suffering lawyers –
in particular, Jim and Richard

Chapter One

Charles Beecham could see the postman from where he sat at his desk, next to the stone-framed window. He knew that he himself was screened from the postman's gaze by the tumble of fading jasmine and honeysuckle leaves which partly obscured the window, and for this he felt both secretly relieved and ashamed. He was reminded of early days in his marriage to Hetty, when his heart had contracted at the sound of letters flipping on to the doormat, and at the awful sight of those cheap brown envelopes containing bills and reminders and letters from his bank manager. Even worse were the ones which Hetty had concealed, or mislaid under a jumble of overdue library books and children's belongings on the hall table. Hetty was gone. Those days were gone. But, twenty years on, the guilt and dread of financial indebtedness had returned with a vengeance.

The envelopes were no longer cheap little brown things. They were long and white, franked in the City of London, and the paper on which the demands for money were written was thick and expensive, the demands themselves elegantly phrased and gentlemanly. Just as a struggling young polytechnic lecturer in a terraced house in Maida Vale had deserved nothing more than scrappy, terse final demands for mean little sums in double figures, so it befitted a middle-aged man of independent means, living in intellectual tranquillity in his snug eighteenth-century house in the Wiltshire countryside, to receive demands from Lloyd's of London for sums that ran into tens of thousands.

He heard the flap and clink of the letter box, and watched the postman as he made his way down the long, stone-flagged path, brushing past the clumps of lavender that grew beneath the mulberry tree. It was irrational, of course, to live in the fearful

1

assumption that each delivery of post might contain yet another reminder from his members' agents that there were overdue calls for which they had yet to receive settlement. But when one owed money, when the yearly demands from Lloyd's were relentless and overwhelming, one lived in a perpetual state of anxiety and guilt. Gone were the days when he would stroll carelessly into the hall and stoop to pick up the mail, confident perhaps of another royalty cheque, or a letter from his agent confirming the sale of television rights to his latest work. Those might still come, Charles Beecham might still be a familiar name to the elite who cared to watch his documentaries, or buy his books, but the comfortable living which his occupation as a historian and academic had once provided him had long since been eclipsed, obscured by the fiasco of Lloyd's.

Joining Lloyd's had seemed the right thing to do at the time, back in the mid-eighties, when his finances had taken that wonderful upward swing. He no longer needed to pay money to Hetty, who had remarried some stockbroker, and the children were both past school age. His elder brother, a childless bachelor, had recently died, so that he had inherited the modest country house in which he now lived, together with a tidy little fortune tied up in gilts and treasury bonds. He had been able to give up lecturing, and to use his new-found leisure to write a series of books, which were well received. He had become established as a popular historian, and his boyish good looks, his blond curling hair, had made him a natural for television. His first BBC2 series, on the history of the Mogul empire, had been a success, and the familiarity of his face ensured that his subsequent book on the history of Assyria sold widely, and a further television series followed. Successful and reasonably wealthy, he had every reason to believe that membership of Lloyd's would bring advantages in terms of both money and status. He remembered all the enticements which had been spelt out to him – making one's capital work twice, setting off losses against taxed income, an unbroken seven-year record of profits – and how he had been told that an investment of £100,000 could net him yearly returns of £15,000 or £20,000. Now, seven years later, his boyish good looks were fading slightly, and the golden hair was greying, but he was still attractive, his books still sold well, and his latest documentary attracted a healthy audience. The nice amount of additional annual income which he had been told Lloyd's would bring him had, however, never manifested. Disaster after disaster had hit the market, and now he was the embittered recipient of regular demands for money which he could no longer pay. It had never been meant to work that way. Lloyd's should have brought him in money, instead of draining him of it. And there was no way out. He glanced round at the comfortable room in which he now sat, at the carefully collected pieces of furniture, the shelves of books, and then out at the rambling garden surrounded by warm, worn brick walls, and wondered how soon he would manage to sell the house. It had been on the market for five months now.

The sound of the telephone interrupted his meditations and he reached out to pick it up. When he heard Freddie Hendry's voice, he sighed inwardly. At least, he thought, whatever bitterness he might feel about the Lloyd's business, it hadn't sent him barmy, like poor old Freddie.

'Beecham?' barked the voice.

'Freddie,' sighed Charles. 'How are you?'

But Freddie did not bother with preliminary pleasantries. 'Look, Charles, we're going to have to rally the troops over this time-bar point. That ass Cochrane has been writing letters to everybody, and I can see we're going to have to canvass support against the rest of the committee. Now, what I propose . . . '

But Charles did not listen to the rest. He just sat, the receiver against his ear, waiting for Freddie to finish. He wished, oh, how he wished, that he had never been talked into going on this committee. Charles and Freddie, along with a couple of thousand other unfortunates, were on the Capstall syndicate, number 1766, one of the worst-hit syndicates at Lloyd's. Alan Capstall, a flamboyant Lloyd's underwriter whose successes in the seventies were legend, had managed to underwrite a series of run-off policies involving asbestos and pollution risks which exposed his Names to liabilities of horrific, undreamt-of proportions, and had triggered the beginning of Charles Beecham's financial disaster. Of course, the Capstall syndicate was not the only Lloyd's syndicate to be adversely affected by the negligent underwriting of spectacularly bad risks. Other syndicates – Outhwaite, Merrett, Gooda Walker – had all suffered calamitous losses. The Capstall syndicate Names had banded together to form an action group with the aim of taking legal proceedings against Alan Capstall and the members' agents. With all the enthusiasm of grievously wronged litigants, they formed a committee to oversee the matter of the litigation, and Charles Beecham, as a prominent figure, had seemed an obvious choice as a committee member. People liked the idea of having someone on the committee who was something of a celebrity. Besides, at forty-two, Charles was relatively youthful, compared to many of the Names, and it was felt he might inject a certain amount of enthusiasm and energy into the project.

Now, as he listened to Freddie Hendry's dotty ramblings, Charles felt anything but enthusiastic. When they had launched the case a year ago, his energies had been fuelled by outrage at the disaster which had befallen him, by a bitter sense of complete betrayal by an institution which he had regarded as impregnable. But the warmth of those feelings had gradually been cooled by tedious months of painstakingly slow litigation, and by the increasingly apparent eccentricities and fixations of his fellow committee members. He was still keen to pursue the litigation – anything to avert the financial nightmare which threatened to ruin his life – but he wished now that he did not have to be in any way involved in the co-ordination of the thing. It seemed that all the energies of the committee were taken up with internal wranglings and petty vendettas against their chairman, a harmless and well-meaning man by the name of Snodgrass. Freddie Hendry was one of the worst of the lot, forever ringing Charles and other members of the committee, and sending endless faxes to Nichols & Co, the solicitors, and even to Godfrey Ellwood and Anthony Cross, the counsel retained by the action group to fight their case.

' ... did you see that article in the *Sunday Telegraph*? Perfectly obvious that Capstall is a complete crook, and worse besides. I rather think they're bugging my phone now, Charles. That happened a lot in 1981. And another odd thing. Chap came up to me three times in Wimpole Street the other day and asked me the way to Grosvenor Square. Three times! Same chap! It reminded me of the time when I was in Regent Street, couple of years after the war, actually on my way to Garrard's ... '

'Freddie,' interrupted Charles, 'I'm afraid there's someone at the door ... I'll have to go ... Yes, yes – I understood all of it. Perfectly. Well, maybe we should just leave all that to counsel. They are the experts, after all ... No, I don't imagine that

4

Godfrey Ellwood is related to the Ellwood whom your cousin knew in M16 . . . You get those letters out. Super. Bye.'

He heaved a sigh of relief as he put the phone down, then sat motionless in his chair, wondering if he should go out and look at the mail lying on the mat in the hall.

In the living room of his small Bloomsbury flat, Freddie Hendry put the phone down and rubbed his chin. He sometimes wondered if Beecham appreciated the urgency of this whole thing. All very well for him to sit there in the country with his history books, doing his bit towards co-ordinating and so forth, but what they needed at a time like this was spirit, people prepared to fight their corner.

Freddie rose slowly and went through to the kitchen. It was small and spartan, with just the few basics – pots and pans, some crockery, a kettle, tea in a caddy, powdered milk, cereal, some tins and packets of food. He hadn't really cooked much for himself since Dorothy died. Just the odd bit of spaghetti on toast, cold tuna . . . he rather liked those Batchelor's Cup a Soups, particularly the pea and ham. Poor Dorothy – what would she think if she could see how he lived now? Of course, it had been the Lloyd's business which had finished her. She had never got over losing the house in Hampshire, seeing everything sold, leaving all their friends. When they had been forced to move into this poky little flat, that had been the end for her. Freddie muttered to himself, baring his teeth and jerking up his salt-and-pepper moustache as he did so, as he engaged yet again in one of his imaginary diatribes against Capstall. Capstall the smooth-talking charlatan, the crook, the swindler who had abused the trust of his syndicate members, who had cynically underwritten those asbestos risks when the evidence of mounting asbestos claims was there for all to see.

With a hand that trembled faintly, Freddie poured boiling water on to his powdered soup and stirred it carefully. He took it back through to the living room, which was sparsely furnished with a few handsome remnants of furniture from the Hampshire house. Silver-framed pictures of his two grown-up children and their families adorned the mantelpiece, and in the grate stood an old, inefficient gas heater. From the landing outside, beyond the faceless front doors of countless apartments whose inhabitants Freddie did not know, came the distant sound of the lift doors

5

opening and closing, then the whine of the mechanism. It was a bleak sound. On days like this, with the autumn melancholy setting in and long hours to fill, Freddie had to try hard to stave off the loneliness. At least this litigation gave him a sense of purpose. This was probably the last fight he would fight in his life, and by God, he was determined to win it. He sat down beside the telephone and fax machine and set his mug of soup carefully next to it. Freddie had got the fax machine from a second-hand office equipment place, and he regarded it as indispensable to his work as a committee member. It seemed to him vital that he should be able to transmit his thoughts as quickly as possible to those in charge of the case. Ideas often came to him in the middle of the night, and at a time when phones would have rung unanswered, Freddie could sit in his dressing gown, feeding in handwritten pages.

He sipped his soup and wiped his moustache, staring at the pale October sky through the window. What should his next line of campaign be? He must muster more support for his views over this time-bar point. Cochrane and his quislings mustn't be allowed to get away with what they were doing. Basher Snodgrass was far too weak to be the committee chairman. Freddie had sent three faxes to Godfrey Ellwood on the subject of the time bar in the past two days, and he had the feeling Ellwood hadn't paid them much attention. Freddie suspected him of approaching this case too cynically. Well, he would try that junior of Ellwood's, Anthony Cross. The boy looked far too young to be handling such important litigation, let alone to be a barrister, but everyone assured Freddie he was tremendously good. Maybe he would pay more attention. Freddie took another sip of his soup, picked up his pen and pad of A4 paper, and began to write in his steady, sloping hand, marking the first page for the *urgent* attention of Anthony Cross, 5 Caper Court, the Temple, London.

In the buildings of 5 Caper Court, all was not as tranquil as it should normally have been on a Friday morning. True, to the eye of the idle clerk passing by on his way from Fleet Street to King's Bench Walk, or to any barrister glancing in at the windows as they hurried through Serjeant's Inn to Middle Temple Lane, the picture was ostensibly that of one of the most select sets of barristers' chambers in the Temple going diligently about its work. Shirtsleeved barristers toiled over briefs and books, computers and word processors hummed and winked reassuringly, figures came and went, and all seemed testimony to a composed little world where the fees were fat and the opinions eminently learned. Among the figures which came and went, however, one moved with greater rapidity and fluster than was normal within those sedate walls.

Felicity Waller thought she would burst into tears if she couldn't have either a fag or a good swear – right now. Why couldn't Anthony look after his own effing files? She was a clerk now, not a bleeding secretary, and this stupid Lloyd's Names case of his was driving her demented. If she had to find yet another frigging Capstall file for him – and there were 208 of the bleeding things, and more to come, apparently – she'd scream.

She tapped up the wooden stairs of chambers at furious speed in her heels, swearing under her breath, and knocked briefly on Anthony Cross's door before entering in a flurry of lycra and bad temper. Anthony Cross, one of the more junior barristers in 5 Caper Court, but presently made self-important and irritable by the cares and complexities of the case in which he was involved, was in a state of temper fit to match his clerk's.

'Well?' he demanded, straightening up from a swamp of documents. 'Have you found it?'

'No,' replied Felicity shortly. 'Wherever you think that file is, Mr Cross, it is certainly not downstairs.' She marched over to a stack of lever arch files that had come to resemble a small stockade.

'Don't touch those!'

Felicity ignored him and began unbuilding the stockade. Half-way down, she reached in behind and triumphantly pulled out a dog-eared blue cardboard wallet, thick with papers. She held it out to Anthony without a word, but the ominous tilt of that formidable bust and the set of those pursed lips told him that he had better search his own room thoroughly another time before setting Felicity off to scour the building for his files. Although she had started as a lowly typist at 5 Caper Court a year ago, Felicity possessed all the streetwise talents necessary for a good barrister's clerk. Henry, the chief clerk, had recognised this and made her his protégée a few months ago. Felicity was determined that the members of chambers should appreciate her new status, and not carry on treating her like a complete dogsbody. Clerks generally received respect, and Felicity wanted some of it.

7

'Thanks,' muttered Anthony, his hauteur somewhat dented by this incident. Then he added, 'Sorry,' and shot a look of such charming apology from those great dark eyes of his that Felicity melted, as she usually did after getting into a temper with Anthony. Only inwardly, however, and only slightly. She still had plenty of work to do and not much of the morning left to do it in. Leaving Anthony's room and turning to go downstairs, she bumped into Leo Davies returning from a conference with counsel in Hare Court, overcoat on and papers tucked beneath his arm. He smiled as he saw Felicity's face.

'Our young Mr Cross been giving you grief, then?' he asked, adopting Felicity's idiom, which was something he enjoyed doing, in a middle-aged way. He felt a sort of paternal responsibility for her, since he had got her the job here. She had been his wife's secretary once, but had lost that job, through no fault of her own. He was glad Henry had made her a clerk, was pleased to see her doing well. He enjoyed, too, the way that her micro-skirts and generous expanse of cleavage enlivened the sombre atmosphere of chambers.

She glanced at him, thinking, as she always did, that you could forget Anthony's dark, pretty good looks, and give her Leo any day. His voice had a light Welsh lilt, which Felicity thought very sexy. And that chiselled face, the silver hair, the blue of his eyes, reminded her of Terence Stamp. She could die for Leo. 'Don't, Mr Davies,' she sighed. 'You'd think this Capstall case of his was the only one in the world.'

'You are seeing an up-and-coming junior in the heady throes of his first really big case. It's like a love affair. You have to make allowances.' Leo fished in his pocket for the key to his room. 'By the way, have we got a date for that Driscoll hearing yet?'

'Yeah, we did. I can't remember it off-hand, but it's in the book. I'll look it up.'

'Thanks.' She clattered off downstairs, and Leo, about to go up to his room on the next landing, paused, glancing at Anthony's door. They hadn't really had much to do with one another over the past few months. Just the odd snatch of conversation over tea, and whatever exchanges their work might necessitate. But apart from that, Anthony had been careful to avoid Leo unless there were other people around. Leo could understand it. There was no real resolution to that whole sorry mess, which had begun with

8

Anthony falling in love with Rachel, and had ended with Leo marrying her. Surely by this time he must have grown to accept the situation – whatever he imagined the situation to be. Leo wished that he could take him out, explain it to him over a drink. But he didn't really understand it all himself. And Rachel? What did Rachel, alone in her big, beautiful house with her baby, think was going on?

Leo hesitated, then raised his hand, knocked on Anthony's door, and went in. Anthony was sitting at his desk, flicking through the file which Felicity had found for him. He had loosened his tie and unfastened his collar, and his dark hair was rumpled from where he had been running his fingers through it in concentration. As always, the sight of Anthony's vulnerable, frowning face, caught unawares at his work, had a powerful effect on Leo. He wished that he could study Anthony in that pose, gaze at his youthfulness for a long moment. But the moment passed. Anthony cleared his throat and said, 'Yes?' His voice was distant, preoccupied, as though the intrusion was slightly unwelcome. Leo could remember times when it would not have been so.

'I just wondered whether you fancied lunch round the corner. If you're nearly finished, that is.' Anthony looked back at his papers, saying nothing, and Leo added, in a slightly gentler tone, 'We don't seem to have talked to one another properly in a long time.'

Anthony looked up. 'I'm afraid I've still got rather a lot of work to do,' he said. It was true. Next Wednesday they were in the House of Lords, and there were still documents which he had not read. 'Sorry,' he added, his voice stiff.

Leo paused, his hand on the doorknob, then nodded. 'Right,' he said. 'Some other time.' He closed the door, and Anthony sat listening to the sound of his feet on the stairs as Leo made his way to his room. He did not resume his work. He sat staring at the far corner of his room, at the stacks of documents. He remembered how he had sat in this room five years ago, when he had been Michael Gibbon's pupil and new to 5 Caper Court, and had listened for Leo's feet on the stairs, hoping that he would stop and look in. He had always been able to tell Leo's footsteps; they were more rapid than the others. His heart used to beat painfully if the footsteps passed the room and went on upstairs. He could feel his heartbeat beginning to slow now. The sight of Leo always affected him in this way. Nothing about him ever grew stale or too familiar.

9

His presence was always electrifying. But then, Leo seemed to have that effect upon most people. Look at Rachel.

Anthony swivelled round in his chair and stared out at the grey autumn sky above the roofs of the Caper Court buildings. Of course, it was nothing to do with Rachel. Anthony had been in love more than a few times, and he couldn't pretend that he hadn't got over it by now. Naturally he had. Well, he assumed he had – he hadn't seen her since just before she and Leo got married, and that was nearly a year ago. Admittedly, he had been steering clear of women since then, but that was largely to do with the burden of this Lloyd's case, and the amount of work he had to put in. No, it was not Rachel. It was not even the fact that she had married Leo. Rather, it was that Leo had married her. That he had married anyone. Anthony thought back to the times that he and Leo had spent together, times when his friendship with the older man had seemed the most passionately important thing in the world. That was where he felt betrayed. He rubbed his hands over his tired face and turned back to his work, gazing unseeingly down at the papers before him. So why hadn't he said yes just now? Why hadn't he just gone for lunch with Leo, let him work his old magic, maybe make things as they had once been? God knows, he missed his company. Anthony sighed. It was because, he told himself, that now Leo was married all that was over. It should stay that way. What was the point of resuming a friendship which seemed to produce nothing but pain? He put his elbows on the desk and propped his head between his fists, and stared down at the page in front of him:

> ... a line slip is a device whereby a broker places 100% of a maximum limit for pre-defined classes of business, and is then able to cede risks to this line slip upon the approval of the rate and terms by the first two subscribing underwriters without having to see the remainder of the underwriters subscribing to the line slip.

He read this sentence over and over until it made sense, and Leo's visit had faded from his mind. Five minutes later, Felicity came in with a few pages of paper.

'This fax just came in for you. It says it's urgent, so I thought I'd bring it up.'

'Thanks,' said Anthony. He picked up the first page and recognised the name of the sender. It was the daft old geezer who had been deluging Godfrey Ellwood with missives. Anthony groaned. Now it was obviously his turn. With a sigh, he began patiently to read Freddie's fax.

In his own room, Leo chucked his papers on to the bare surface of his desk and sat down, still in his overcoat. He sighed and leaned back wearily in his chair. There had been a time, on Fridays such as this with the weekend ahead of him, when his life had been his own, the next two days an expanse of time in which he could do as he pleased. He made a wry face as he thought of all the things which it had once pleased him to do. It had been those very things – the lovers, the rent boys, the occasional enjoyable ménage à trois in his country home, the pleasurable, careless dissipation of his private life – which had threatened, a mere twelve months ago, to wreck his career, to blight his prospects of taking silk, of moving on in his profession as a barrister. In this most proper of worlds image was all. At the time, salvaging his respectability in the face of growing rumours had seemed like the most important thing in the world. Yet how might it have been if he had not married Rachel? Leo often wondered this. But it was too late for wondering now. He hadn't intended to marry her. Not at first. She had been just a good-looking young woman, a solicitor from one of the big City firms, and he had hoped that the fact of having her as his girlfriend would be enough to scotch the rumours which might have wrecked his prospects of becoming a QC. The fact that Anthony had been in love with her had not mattered. Of what significance was that, compared to his own career? Then Rachel had got pregnant, and the rest was history. He had married her, and there she was at home now, waiting for him, with their child, a weight in his heart and in his life.

Leo sighed and looked up across the room at the familiar, warm rectangular shapes in the Patrick Heron painting which hung on the wall opposite. He remembered purchasing the picture at the Redfern Gallery eight years ago, as well the two Tabner drawings which hung next to the bookcase, with some of the money he had earned from a large case. It was his habit, if a case was particularly lucrative, to buy himself a painting, or a piece of sculpture, by way of reward. It harked back to his time as a boy in Wales, when he would reward himself with extra sweets, or a comic, if the money from his gardening jobs exceeded the amount designated for his savings account. Gazing at the picture, then at the drawings, it occurred to Leo that this room in chambers was now the only place in the world which was utterly, absolutely his own.

His mind returned to Rachel. She was going to say something to him soon, he knew. He could see it in her eyes. It was merely extraordinary that she had not said anything before. Where did she think he went on those nights when he did not come home? She never asked. Her silence was astonishing, unsettling. In many ways, he had hoped that there would be some sort of confrontation before now, that the issue might be resolved. The issue of their respective lives, and of where they went from here. He thought of his infant son, Oliver, and a certain guilt touched his heart momentarily. He did not want to be like his own father, did not want to desert his son and leave a painful space in his life for ever.

He sat motionless for a moment, toying with the crimson ribbon tied round the papers on his desk, then picked up the telephone and rang Rachel to tell her to book a babysitter, that they would dine out that night.

Chapter Two

Rachel Davies put down the phone and glanced down at the baby in his carry-seat. She had just been bringing him and the shopping from the car when she had heard the phone ringing. She decided that she might as well leave him where he was; he was quite warm next to the radiator, still asleep, tendrils of blond hair clinging damply to his forehead, tiny fists loosely curled. She wondered idly, as she pulled off her jacket, how long his hair would stay blond. Not for long, she supposed, since she and Leo were both dark. Or Leo had been, before his hair had turned prematurely silver some time in his thirties, giving him a distinctive and dashing look. Just the kind of thing a successful QC needed, thought Rachel wryly, taking the shopping through to the kitchen. Of course, she had not known him then, in his dark-haired days. And if she had, if she had known everything about him she knew now, would she have married him? Probably not. Ah, but that wasn't the correct question, she told herself, spooning instant coffee into a cup and gazing across the large and beautiful garden of their Hampstead house. It wasn't a question of marrying. Would she have fallen in love with him? And the answer was yes, of course. She would have fallen in love with him at twelve, or twenty, or seventy-seven. He had just happened to be forty-four at the time, and she twenty-six. In the space of a year she had met and married him, had his baby, and yet she now realised that she scarcely knew Leo at all.

She began to sort out the small amount of shopping, then glanced around the kitchen to see if there was anything to be done, any little domestic chores to while away the time until Oliver's lunchtime feed. But Mrs Floyd had left everything spotless and smelling lightly of Sainsbury's Germ-clear. She had even watered the geraniums, Rachel noticed, and now the distant sound of her ever-efficient hoovering could be heard from the upstairs rooms. Rachel often wished that Mrs Floyd wasn't quite so thorough, and sometimes that she didn't exist at all. But Leo had insisted, telling her that she couldn't possibly do all the housework in so large a house, with Oliver to look after as well. But Rachel enjoyed housework. Even when she had been working as a solicitor in a large, high-powered City firm, one of her special pleasures had been to polish and dust and keep her flat trim and pretty and tidy. Had it been a pleasure, or just therapy? Well, whatever, she missed it now. She missed activity, if the truth be told. She missed people, the constant hum of machines, office chatter, telephones, work to be done, people to see, meetings, clients . . . She sipped her coffee and looked critically at the autumn garden, at the large expanse of lawn which disappeared behind an elegant curve of Leyland cypresses, and wondered if there was any work that she could do out there. But they had a gardener who came once a week, and, anyway, Rachel had little experience of gardens and their contents. This one was dauntingly large, its beautiful mysteries carefully planned by a previous owner. Much as she enjoyed its seasonal beauty, Rachel scarcely felt as though it belonged to her. She might as well have been the second Mrs de Winter, and these the gardens at Manderley. Some other, cleverer person had designed it all, had understood it and coped with it. It was much the same with the house, which she and Leo had bought five months ago. Certainly, she had had a hand in choosing colours and furniture and fabrics, but Leo had done most of it – his taste was so unerring, his experience greater than hers. She had felt it difficult to cope with the size of the rooms, had little idea of proportions, of the right furniture for the right space. Apart from anything else, she had found it impossible to spend money as freely as Leo did. She simply wasn't used to it. And it was his money, after all.

It was his house. It was his life. That was why she found it so hard to question it, to challenge him. She turned her gaze away from the garden and thought she heard Oliver whimper in the hallway. But there was only silence, and the sound of Mrs Floyd bumping about with the squeeze-mop in the bathrooms above. Rachel stared at the table, at its polished surface and the bowl of fruit carefully arranged in its centre, and remembered the first night that he had not come home, when they had still been living in his mews house in Mayfair. She had been heavily pregnant. She recalled the deathly sensation of that realisation, as she woke in the morning, that he had not come back, that she had been alone all through the night. Some odd shadow had fallen upon her, and it had never lifted. She had known he was probably with another man, or some boy. In spite of everything he had said, all his assurances, she had known it instantly. It was something to do with the feeling that his absence gave her – could absence have a quality? His had, that morning.

Rachel slid her thin fingers through her dark, shining hair and put her coffee cup in the dishwasher. Even the interior of that was sparkling clean. Well, she had known about his life before she married him. She had gathered enough about the men and women who had shared his bed, so she had had no right to demand change. Or even to expect it. But she had hoped.

When he had returned home in the evening after that first night's absence, it had not been mentioned. The envelope from the Lord Chancellor's office had been waiting for him, telling him that he had been made a Queen's Counsel, and that had eclipsed everything else. He had been too pleased, and she had had to share his pleasure. She had sensed his relief at the distraction which it provided from his absence. The thing had never been referred to. That had been her first mistake, Rachel told herself. If she had said something then, if there had been some frankness between them, then perhaps things would not be as they were now. It had taken just seven months, during which Leo had regularly failed to come home, for their relationship to have reached a point where the matter of this concealment dominated it. They had mundane, domestic conversations – about his work, about the baby – they made love, they shared one another's interests, but the thing which was most important was not spoken about. Where Leo went, and what he did, on those nights when he did not come home to her.

From the hallway came the thinnest of wails, resolving itself into a spate of hungry cries, and Rachel, like someone brought back to life, broke free from her thoughts and went to fetch her son, deciding that she would, she must, say something to Leo tonight.

As they sat that evening in the restaurant, Rachel watched and listened while Leo chatted in easy Italian with the owner, and marvelled at his ability to charm whomever he met. Not that Leo exercised his charm without discrimination. She had begun to notice, over the past year, that he only used it on people who were, or might become, important or useful to him. She sipped her wine and remembered the first time she had met him. There had been no deliberate exercise of charm then. That had come later. Why? What had made her suddenly seem useful, or important? Perhaps that was unfair. Maybe he had really fallen in love with her. The past few months had given her a critical detachment, and she wondered now.

She glanced up at the restaurant owner, thinking that perhaps this conversation had gone on a little too long. Would he rather talk to this man than to her? The owner glanced at Rachel, realising her thoughts, and moved away, laughing at Leo's last remark.

'You haven't eaten much,' Leo remarked, glancing at his wife's plate. 'Salad?'

'I'm not terribly hungry.' She realised that she felt faintly panicky at the prospect of raising the unspoken subject, too tense to eat. But she had drunk two glasses of wine, and they fortified her resolve not to let the evening pass without discussing it. He was telling her something about a conference he had had that morning, but she realised she had to seize the moment, and interrupted him.

'Leo – '

He stopped talking and looked up, struck by the urgent tone of her voice. 'What?' When he looked directly at her like that, with his intense, blue gaze, his handsome features frozen in surprise and anticipation, her resolve almost wavered. She was desperately afraid that this might precipitate something awful, a row, or worse, perhaps. And because she was still in love with him, dependent upon him for all her emotional needs, the thought terrified her. Perhaps it was better just to leave it alone. But the detached, reasoning part of her told her that she must continue.

She sighed, and then said, 'Oh God, you must know what I'm going to say. What it is I want to talk about. Properly.'

She looked up, and he was still staring at her intently. He put down his fork and drank some of his wine, then poured them both some more. Again he looked at her, and at last he said, 'Yes, of course I do. We should have talked about it long ago.'

She was thrown by the assertive, brisk tone of his voice. What had she expected? Evasion? That was not Leo's nature. He was too clever a lawyer not to know that to attack is the best form of defence. Which was what he was doing now, she assumed. Only it wasn't an attack – more a sort of assumption of control. She found it fascinating. He began to speak again. 'To be honest, I'm amazed you've let it go so long without saying anything.'

'Where is it you go?' she asked softly, her insides starting to dissolve in panic, as she realised that this was all going too fast for her, that she had never intended to reach this point without some sort of protective build-up.

He took a reflective sip of his wine, and there was a long silence. Then he said, 'I go to see a friend. His name is Francis.' He did not look at her, and she knew suddenly that he detested this, that he wanted to get it over as briskly and in as businesslike a fashion as possible.

Rachel took a deep breath. 'Is he your lover?' she asked. She knew the answer, had known all this for months, but when it came, the truth was still unbearable.

'Yes.' He looked up at her at last. 'Yes.' He tapped the table lightly with his fingers, apparently in irritation, but she knew him, knew that this was a sign of embarrassment. Suddenly he shook his head. 'It is incredible. I used to come home in the evening the next day, and you'd be there, feeding Oliver, or getting supper ready, whatever, and I would think, "She has to ask me this time."' He paused and gave a smile that was not really a smile. 'You never did.'

'Why didn't you say something – ask me?'

'What – why you never said anything? I didn't care, frankly.'

The words numbed her. That he should not care was the possibility that terrified her most. 'About me?' Her voice was almost a whisper.

He looked across at her. When she was like this – apprehensive, dark eyes wide – her loveliness always moved him. There was something fascinating and fragile about her that almost pushed him to hurt her. 'Of course I cared – care – about you. I mean, I didn't care that you didn't ask. It seemed better, easier.'

'I can't believe we're having this conversation,' she said, shaking her head slightly. 'We have been married for a matter of months, and you're telling me that you have had a lover all along. A man. And you say that you care about me.'

Leo crumpled up his napkin in exasperation. 'Rachel, you must have formed your own conclusions about where I was. The fact that you never asked me shows that. You knew when you married me how it might be. I'm too old to change. I make no apologies for that. And,' he added, 'I'm too tired for any rows.'

She looked down at the tablecloth. 'I don't want to row, Leo. I want to understand.' She pressed her fingers against her forehead. 'I want to know why – if you need to do this, if you need to lead this kind of other life – why did you marry me?' She looked up, the puzzlement on her face quite genuine.

He paused, then drew a small leather case from his pocket and took out a slender cigar. 'Because you were pregnant.'

'You tried to persuade me to have an abortion.'

She watched as he lit the cigar carefully, tilting one of the candles on their table towards him. 'But I changed my mind.' He looked at her levelly. 'And I loved you.' He did not add that he had, at that time, badly needed something to give his life an aura of respectability, something to remove the taint of rumour regarding sexual scandals in his past life which had threatened to prevent him being made a QC. A wife had been just the thing. And there had been Rachel, beautiful, intelligent, and conveniently willing.

'Loved?'

'I still love you.' Her eyes met his, and she wanted to believe him with every fibre of her being. 'It's just,' he added softly, drawing on his cigar, 'that I need more.'

There was a long silence, while she considered all of this, feeling slightly dazed. She could make nothing of it. 'What am I meant to do?' she asked at last, looking up at him.

'Do?' He smiled, then shrugged. 'Whatever you want to do. There are no rules.'

She met his gaze, and the expression in his eyes seemed fathomless. As so often before, she felt there was no way in which she could reach him. It was a situation in which she felt completely helpless. She could not make threats or issue ultimatums – it would get her nowhere. What he had just said was true. For Leo, there were no rules. He might say he loved her, but he loved no one enough to allow them to dictate his life. That she knew. Any other woman would probably leave a husband who was behaving as Leo was. But she was too much in love with him for that. Before she had met him she had not thought herself capable of feeling anything for any man. It was Leo who had taught her not to be afraid. He had rescued her from many things. Maybe it was because he was so amoral that he could understand men and women so completely, and betray their trust utterly. No, she knew she could not go – but what kind of life were they to lead together if she stayed?

'I think I'd like to go home now,' she said quietly.

'Very well,' said Leo. He glanced at her curiously as he signalled for the bill. He had wondered how she would react when all this was out in the open, and he was still not sure what she was thinking. He knew that the answer would come in the next few hours.

When he came into the bedroom, loosening his tie, Rachel was lying against the pillows, feeding Oliver. Her eyes were closed, and her nightdress was opened to the waist. Oliver lay at her breast, lightly and rhythmically stroking her skin with a tiny fat hand as he sucked. Leo watched them. He always found the sight vaguely erotic, her body open to the child; the blissful mutual absorption of mother and baby made him feel excluded, tantalised him.

He took off his tie and threw it over a chair, unbuttoning his shirt. Then he lay down next to Rachel. Oliver, sated, eyes still closed, moved his head away slightly from her breast, exhaling a little bubble of milk. Rachel opened her eyes and looked at Leo. He gazed at her and traced her lips with his finger, then slid his hand down to caress her. This was the moment. If she was going to say, 'Don't touch me, don't ever come near me again,' she would say it now. But she said nothing.

'Put him in his cot,' murmured Leo. Wordlessly, she picked Oliver up and went through to the nursery. Then she came back and lay back down next to Leo, and let him kiss and draw her body against his, enveloped by a sense of passion that nothing could extinguish, not even the worst of his actions.

Two hours later, while Leo slept beside her, Rachel still lay awake, staring into the half-darkness. With an odd sense of detachment, she wondered why the events of the evening had not made her weep, why the pillow was not wet from her sobbing. Wasn't that the natural reaction? But crying was easy. It was for small griefs, not for something as shattering as this.

19

It was clear to her that she must do something. If this was to be her life – with Leo or without him – then she could not allow herself to depend on him any longer. The last few months had been an illusion. She had even thought, in a blind and stupid way, that they might have another baby. At the thought of this she tried to laugh, but it sounded only as a whimper of pain. Life would not be the safe and certain thing she had once hoped for. The first thing to do was to regain something of herself, her old life, and prepare herself for eventualities. She would go back to work. Nichols & Co were holding her job open for her for her period of maternity leave, and that expired in a fortnight's time, when Oliver would be six months old. In that instant she made her decision. Tomorrow morning she would ring her senior partner and tell him. She would have no compunction about spending as much of Leo's money as might be necessary to find the best nanny possible. Then, when she had recovered something of her independence, she might feel strong enough to make whatever decisions had to be made about the future.

She turned and glanced at the outline of Leo's sleeping face. How could he be so at peace with himself, so untroubled by his actions? What was it like to live inside his mind? And why did all that he had told her this evening not make her hate him? If anything, the realisation of how tenuous her position was made her love him all the more helplessly. At that moment Oliver's thin, waking cry broke the silence. Rachel sighed and pushed back the bedclothes. Before she got up to go to the baby, she leaned over and kissed Leo lightly on the side of his head, without knowing why, and felt, for the first time, like weeping.

Chapter Three

Anthony arrived in chambers on Monday morning to discover that he had been loaned the services of Camilla, the pupil of one of his colleagues, Jeremy Vine, while Jeremy was on holiday. They were services which he felt he could happily have dispensed with. Camilla was fresh from Bar School, and had struck Anthony from the first as being a typical bluestocking. She was quite pretty, with reddish chestnut hair that was constantly falling in her eyes, but she was astonishingly untidy, wearing baggy black suits and crumpled white blouses, and heavy black shoes. Most women at the Bar managed to make the regulation black and white outfit into something passingly feminine, but not Camilla. She blushed a lot and always seemed to be bumping into people and things, but she made up for all of this by being supernaturally bright. She had been Jeremy's pupil for three months now, and the other members of chambers were rather impressed by the fact that, as the first female barrister ever to be admitted to the hallowed precincts of 5 Caper Court, she was managing to handle its most arrogant and work-driven member pretty adequately. Jeremy was famous for his vanity, his loquaciousness and his unpopularity with judges, but it had to be admitted that he was very able, and seemed set to become the chambers' youngest QC next year, when he would be just thirty-seven. He expected Camilla to work as hard as he did, but she was robust and energetic and stood the pace.

'Only Jeremy thought that I should keep busy while he's away, you know,' said Camilla, smiling radiantly at Anthony and following him into his room. It was common knowledge in chambers that Camilla was hopelessly in love with Anthony. Even Anthony was aware of this, and he returned her shining gaze with a rather dismal smile as he unwound his scarf and dumped his papers on his desk. Camilla stood before him, hands clasped behind her back, ready to do his bidding. It was rather like having an eager puppy waiting for one to throw a ball, reflected Anthony. He looked around at the mess of documents, and then glanced at her thoughtfully. Actually, maybe she could be quite useful. 'Tell you what,' he said, 'we've got a hearing in the House of Lords on Wednesday. You can help with that.'

She nodded. 'What's it about?'

'It's this Lloyd's Names case I've been involved in for a few months now. Do you know anything about it?'

'Not really.'

'Right,' said Anthony, sitting down and feeling quite magisterial as he recounted the facts of the case to Camilla. 'Our clients are all members of the Capstall syndicate, which unfortunately is one of the long-tail syndicates at Lloyd's. Do you know what one of those is?'

Camilla, with her double first from Oxford, didn't like to profess ignorance in any area, but here she was forced to. 'No,' she admitted.

'Well, a syndicate is a group of Lloyd's investors, and a long-tail syndicate is one specialising in insuring long-term risks, like latent disease and pollution, which might result in claims years after the insurance was written. Now, Lloyd's syndicates operate a three-year accounting period, and when a syndicate's accounts are closed at the end of that three-year period, one of the decisions which the underwriter has to make is the amount of internal reinsurance to close. It's called an RITC. It's the amount required to reinsure any outstanding risks, and it's the amount the Names on one year pay to the Names on the next year to take over liabilities. Sort of selling the risks on, if you like.'

'But if you have a syndicate specialising in latent disease claims, like Capstall's, how can you assess the amount of reinsurance to close? I mean, how can you possibly know the extent of future claims?'

Very quick on the uptake, thought Anthony, with a flicker of admiration. 'Precisely. On long-tail syndicates, like Capstall's, the amount of RITC has to be judged very finely by the underwriter, because the Names on the new year may be different from those on the old years. So if the RITC is too low, the Names inheriting the risks lose out, because the premium's too low to pay the claims, but if it's too high, the old Names lose out by having paid too much. Now, run-off contracts, which are what Capstall was writing, are similar to RITCs, but whereas RITC is an internal syndicate transaction, a run-off is an arm's-length policy written by another reinsurer. Our fellow Capstall wrote a load of run-off policies in the eighties, as a result of which the Names were exposed to massive claims arising out of asbestos and pollution actions, mainly in the States. And the Names' argument is that Capstall was negligent when he wrote all those run-off contracts, because he completely failed to make adequate provision for the latent disease claims which were looming, particularly asbestosis. Which is why they're trying to recover some of their losses by suing him.'

'But I don't understand how he could write those run-offs. It must have been obvious to anyone the kind of risks he was running. Why did he do it?'

'A variety of reasons. Premiums were high and potential profits must have appeared good. Plus, he probably took the view that such claims as might be made would only arise over a very long period, and in the meantime profit would pile up on the investment income. Unfortunately, it didn't turn out that way.'

'But as an underwriter surely he had a duty to investigate the risks he was assuming on behalf of the Names?'

'You would have thought so, given the amount of concern there was in the market at that time about asbestosis, but he seems to have been too lazy, or too arrogant. Or both. When you get a reputation as a high-flier, a risk-taker, you tend to live by that code. He's a character – flamboyant, daring, all that stuff. Not exactly a man of prudence and caution. Anyway, you know the motto of Lloyd's – *Uberrima Fides*. The utmost good faith. That seems to have been conspicuously lacking here. Now,' sighed Anthony, 'the asbestos and pollution claims are literally piling up in the American courts, and the courts are using any device they can to get at the insurers. Our Names are the poor suckers who have underwritten those risks. They've already paid out a small fortune in claims, and God knows how many more demands will be made on them. Most of them hadn't a clue what kind of risks Capstall was underwriting.'

'If you're a Lloyd's Name, your liability is unlimited, isn't it?' said Camilla.

'Quite. Most people didn't appreciate the dire implications of that, even though they were told it when they became members. The fact is,' sighed Anthony, 'a lot of our Names were suckered into joining Lloyd's. I feel a bit sorry for most of them. They had no business becoming Names. But they'd heard that there was nice, easy money to be made, and decided they'd like some of it.'

Camilla was thrilled to be having her most sustained conversation with Anthony so far. She was happy just to sit and listen to him, to watch him. She found something romantic in the fact that Anthony didn't come from the same background as the other people in chambers – people like Roderick Hayter, Cameron Renshaw, and Jeremy, who had all been to public school and Oxbridge – but had struggled to become the excellent barrister he now was, with a brilliant career ahead of him. She had heard that his mother was a primary school teacher, and that he'd only just managed to get by on scholarships and hand-outs when he'd first started. As Anthony swivelled around in his chair, talking about run-offs and under-reserved risks, Camilla gazed at his lean, tall, figure, at his expensively cut suit and silk tie, and marvelled.

'What's the hearing on Wednesday about?' she asked, forcing herself to concentrate on the case in hand and trying not to gaze too fixedly into Anthony's wonderful brown eyes.

'It's a preliminary point, but pretty much a vital one. Capstall's lawyers are saying that there's no duty of care owed by Capstall to the Names. We say there is, and that there's also a parallel duty in tort. We won at first instance in front of the blessed Sir Basil, but lost in the Court of Appeal.'

'Do you think you'll win in the House of Lords?'

Anthony grimaced. 'God, I hope so. Because if we don't, our claim is finished before it even gets off the ground. At any rate, Godfrey Ellwood – he's our leader in the case – seems fairly sanguine. But you can never be sure about these things.'

'So what can I do?' asked Camilla, preparing to throw herself into the task of learning everything there was to learn about reinsurance and the complexities of Lloyd's underwriting. She wanted very much to demonstrate to Anthony how able she was.

Anthony smiled. She really was rather sweet. 'Well, you can start by putting all those files in date order, and then you can photocopy these three bundles. Not very exciting I know, but very useful.'

She nodded, gazing apprehensively at the heaps of documents which lay stacked around Anthony's desk. Oh, well, at least she was doing it for Anthony, which made it worthwhile. And maybe he would let her come to the hearing. She could sit in the House of Lords in her wig and gown – she didn't think the thrilling novelty of appearing robed in court was ever going to wear off.

'How'd it go?' asked Felicity two days later, as Camilla puffed into chambers behind Anthony, bearing bundles of documents, her cheeks red from the cold air and the excitement of having been in the House of Lords. She had sat next to Anthony, feeling pretty important, even though she'd had nothing to do except carry things in and take notes. Anthony hadn't had much to do either, since the leader, Godfrey Ellwood QC, had done all the talking, but she could see from the way that Ellwood spoke to him, asked his advice in an undertone while the other side's counsel was on his feet, that Ellwood respected his views and regarded Anthony as important to the case. For Camilla, it had been bliss just to be so near to him, to smell the wondrous faint scent of his aftershave, to watch the way he held his pen, crossed his legs, yawned . . . all for two whole hours.

Felicity was able to gather this much just by glancing at Camilla's face, and added, 'The hearing, I mean.' Felicity had already been the recipient of Camilla's shy coffee-break confidences regarding her hero.

'Oh, fine! Ellwood is really brilliant. We're bound to win.'

'I'm delighted that you think so,' remarked Anthony, flicking through his mail and handing a couple of things to Felicity. 'If you're right, I'll buy you a drink to celebrate as soon as we get the judgment.' He strolled off to his room, and Felicity grinned and arched her eyebrows meaningfully at Camilla.

A week later, it turned out that Camilla's confidence had not been misplaced. Godfrey Ellwood rang Anthony at the end of the day to tell him that the House of Lords had found in their favour.

'Our clerk brought the judgment up a moment ago,' said Ellwood. 'I think this calls for a small celebratory drink, don't you?'

'Absolutely,' agreed Anthony, recalling his promise to Camilla.

'Shall we say, the Edgar Wallace at six?'

'Fine.' Anthony hung up and went in search of Camilla, anticipating with a certain kindhearted vanity her pleasure at being taken for a drink by him. He found her in the clerks' room, with Felicity and Henry, the head clerk, gossiping the end of the afternoon away. Deciding that an enigmatic approach might boost Camilla's ego, he gave her his best mysterious smile and simply said, 'How about that drink, then?'

As he left with Camilla, Henry shot a questioning look at Felicity. '*Really?*' he asked.

'Don't be daft! Anthony? He's just at that age when it does his ego good to have an adoring young thing in tow,' replied Felicity, in her twenty-three-year-old wisdom. She shook her head as she thought of Camilla. 'Isn't love beautiful?'

Henry said nothing. Felicity had been at 5 Caper Court for just a year. Henry, who was only thirty, but had been made head clerk when the old clerk, Mr Slee, had retired with heart trouble, had wrestled uncomfortably with his feelings for her throughout that time. She had just been another typist at first – nice, admittedly, with her curly brown hair and infectious laugh, but in the beginning he had been too busy keeping chambers' business flowing smoothly and cultivating an air of knowing authority to pay much attention. But there was something about Felicity that was irrepressible. She had enthusiasm, took an interest in everything and everyone, and refused to be intimidated by the loftier senior members of chambers. For those reasons, when Henry had realised some months ago that he needed an assistant, if life at 5 Caper Court was not to descend into chaos, he had promoted Felicity to the post. This had not gone down well with the word-processing sorority, but that didn't trouble Felicity. She had taken to her new job like a duck to water. She had the right blend of savvy and common sense, she was energetic, and she was good with people – all the right qualities for a barrister's clerk. What she lacked in organisation she made up for in quickness of thought and tongue, managing to negotiate good fees for the barristers and taking no nonsense from solicitors. In any event, Henry often thought that the typing pool was better off without her, since her spelling and secretarial skills left much to be desired. Admittedly, she did not possess that quality of polished deference which was the hallmark of the old school of barrister's clerk, like Mr Slee, but Henry realised that that was probably becoming a thing of the past, in these days of high-tech and egalitarianism. She handled the members of chambers firmly and with cheeky good humour, and they liked her for that.

But, in addition to his appreciation of Felicity's practical and intellectual merits, Henry had rapidly grown aware that feelings of an altogether more lyrical kind stirred within him. He was an unremarkable young man, of medium height, with thinning dark hair and a pleasant, oval face, softly spoken and mildly jovial, but he possessed a passionate heart. Such girlfriends as he had tended to be mild-mannered, unexciting girls of his own type, but in Felicity, with her volatile ways and raucous spirit, he felt he had met the woman of his dreams. She was unpredictable, often vulgar, and occasionally bad-tempered, but Henry had discovered that he loved all of these qualities, just as he loved her shocking pink angora sweater and her black lycra micro-skirts. But he felt she was far beyond his reach. He knew all about her turbulent life with her boyfriend, Vince, and felt he could never compete. Felicity obviously adored Vince. Besides, Henry was keenly aware of the conventions of chambers, and knew that the fact that he and Felicity worked together in a professional capacity precluded any possibility of romance. He consoled himself with this notion, telling himself that if they had not worked together, things might be very different. Henry accepted that his feelings must stay unrequited, but they remained to trouble him every working day.

In response to Felicity's observation about love being beautiful, Henry merely sighed and replied in a mutter that he wasn't so sure about that.

By the time Anthony and Camilla arrived at the pub, Godfrey Ellwood was already there. He was a tall man, almost completely bald, with a leathery face and a sharp sense of humour. As a QC, Ellwood was renowned for his energy, for throwing himself wholeheartedly into cases, especially those in which he believed. The Capstall case was one of those. Whatever cynicism he might possess regarding the fate of those Names who had gambled greedily and lost, he was thoroughly convinced that Lloyd's had failed the bulk of its members miserably, and that fortunes had been made by a few at the expense of the many. He regarded Capstall, the underwriter, as an overweeningly ambitious and irresponsible man who had written some of the most spectacularly bad risks in the market purely in the hope of long-term gain, at the expense of the Names on his syndicate. Ellwood's personal convictions had entirely infected Anthony, his junior, and not since he had first helped Leo Davies on a case a few years ago had Anthony felt so inspired and enthusiastic. Ellwood managed to make him feel that they were acting for the little man against the mighty, that in taking on Lloyd's they were challenging an institution whose lofty disdain for its members was no longer tolerable. Those agents, underwriters and auditors who had been so dismissive of the threat of litigation three or four years ago now knew they had real cause for concern. This victory in the House of Lords, although only a stepping-stone, was a significant achievement, and Ellwood was in an ebullient mood when he greeted Anthony and Camilla.

'We've cleared that hurdle in no uncertain terms, eh? What'll you both have? Julian says he'll be down to join us shortly – got some speed and consumption claim to finish . . . ' They took their drinks over to a table, and sat discussing the case. Gradually the pub began to fill up, a few more people joined them, and by seven o'clock the place was crowded and smoky. Camilla, who knew from experience that more than two gin and tonics made her face permanently pink, sat nursing the remains of her second drink and shooting rapid, admiring glances at Anthony. She liked to think that working with him on this case had formed a bond between them, that she shared part of the glamour of this success. She was totally happy. Glancing around the pub, she suddenly saw a familiar face, a girl who had been in the year below her at Oxford, and with whom she shared several mutual friends. Proud to be seen in such distinguished company as that of Godfrey Ellwood and Anthony Cross, she gave her a little wave.

On the other side of the room, the blonde girl returned her wave unenthusiastically. She was alone, still waiting for her friends, and she did not particularly wish to be accosted by Camilla, who was looking pink and rather pleased with herself. They hadn't met for some months, but she recalled that on the several occasions when she had been in Camilla's company she had found herself distinctly bored. There was something desperately nice about her, and she tended to be too keen on talking about law. But Camilla had turned away now, so she assumed she was safe. The girl, who was dressed in tight jeans and boots and a white polo-neck sweater beneath a denim jacket, in contrast to Camilla's dusty black suit and high-necked white blouse, took a sip of her drink and ran her eye curiously over the people Camilla was sitting with. Typical crowd of barristers. Then she saw Anthony, and her gaze halted. She had never seen him in here before, of that she was certain. She would have remembered. At that moment, Anthony rose from his seat and came over to the bar with some empty glasses. He set them down on the bar not far from the blonde girl and fished in his wallet for a ten pound note, and she gave him a long, discreet glance, enough to take in his tall, elegant figure, the handsome face, the rather girlish brown eyes. He glanced across and caught her eye, and they looked at one another for a significant fraction of a second. Then the barman said something to Anthony and he looked away again. She watched as he took the drinks back over to the table, sitting down next to Camilla and saying something to her which made Camilla smile with pleasure.

Perhaps Camilla wasn't so boring after all, thought the blonde girl. The company she kept certainly wasn't. Smoothing back her hair, the girl moved over towards Camilla, setting her face in a surprised smile.

'Camilla!' She bent and kissed the air next to Camilla's warm cheek. 'How amazing to see you! Do you mind if I join you for a moment until my friends come? It's a bit busy at the bar.'

She drew up a chair and sat down between Camilla and Anthony, and the others at the table edged their chairs round to make room for her. She glanced around, her eyes not meeting Anthony's, but aware that he was looking at her.

Camilla was momentarily flustered, then said, 'Oh, everyone, this is Sarah – Sarah Colman, a friend of mine.'

There was a general murmur of 'how do you do?', and then the conversation resumed. Camilla, who had been pleased enough to wave to Sarah at a distance, was less sure that she wanted her attractive friend muscling in on this exclusive little circle. Still, there she was, lovely as ever, with that knowing smile. She'd often wondered why it was that Sarah, who was a year younger than she was, always managed somehow to appear older. But at least on this occasion Camilla could steal a march on her, since Sarah was still only at Bar School, a mere novice, and could not boast of such sophisticated experiences as appearing in the House of Lords with Godfrey Ellwood, QC. Camilla quickly let it be known what was being celebrated, and Sarah smiled with only the mildest condescension. 'Aren't you clever? But now tell me, who did the real work while you were taking notes?' And her cool glance fell on Anthony, whose face at that moment turned in her direction.

'Sorry?' said Anthony, uncertain whether he'd been addressed or not.

'I was just asking Camilla whether you'd been involved in the case she's been telling me about – I'm sorry, I don't know your name.'

'Oh!' exclaimed Camilla in mild embarrassment, 'Sarah, this is Anthony Cross. I'm sort of working for him while my pupil-master's away.'

Anthony stretched out his hand and Sarah took it. Camilla saw him smile at Sarah in a way that he had never smiled at her, and felt her heart lurch in fear and anguish. 'How do you do?' said Anthony. 'Yes, I'm Godfrey's junior in the case.' He glanced at Ellwood, then looked back at Sarah. 'Are you at the Bar?' he asked with interest.

'Not yet,' she replied. 'I don't sit my Bar finals till next summer. But I'm hoping to specialise in commercial work – if I can get a pupillage, that is.' She smiled significantly at Anthony as she raised her drink. '*You* wouldn't know of anyone who needs a pupil in a year's time, would you?'

Anthony laughed, and ran his fingers through his thick brown hair. Camilla knew that mannerism – oh, how well she knew it and how much she adored it. She knew that it was something Anthony did when he felt himself either distracted or flattered. She wished he would not do it now. She watched as he looked up at Sarah, who was finishing her drink.

'Well,' said Anthony, who was not unaccustomed to being flirted with, 'I'll certainly try to think of someone.' He glanced at Sarah's empty glass. 'Can I get you another drink?'

'Thank you,' said Sarah, and he took her glass and went to the bar. Sarah widened her eyes as she smiled innocently at Camilla. 'What a nice man,' she remarked, and then glanced around while she waited for Anthony to return to the table. She loved the suspenseful excitement of encountering someone new and attractive, and there was the added zest of putting Camilla's nose out of joint.

Camilla, who now felt thoroughly resentful, managed to blurt out, as Anthony came back to the table, 'I hardly think you'll have much trouble getting a pupillage, Sarah, since your father's the Recorder of London.' She had intended this to signify that Sarah got by on connections rather than ability, but Anthony merely looked at Sarah with increased interest as he set her drink down.

'Really? Of course – Colman. I thought the name was familiar when Camilla introduced you. Actually, I appeared before your father a couple of weeks ago . . . ' He carried on talking to Sarah. Camilla, who was sitting on the other side of him, could not help feeling excluded. She could not join in their conversation without raising her voice and making Anthony turn back in her direction, and she had an unhappy feeling that he might not be much inclined to do that. She nursed her glass and sat quietly pondering the situation. It wasn't fair that she should feel at a disadvantage, but she did. She should feel superior to Sarah, who was still a student, after all, but it suddenly seemed to Camilla that, far from being superior, her own position was invidious. In Anthony's company, in Ellwood's company, she was on the very lowest rung of the hierarchy, a mere pupil. Sarah, however, was not yet part of the pecking order. Anthony did not regard her in any particular light, and Sarah could afford to behave with him exactly as she chose. At that moment Sarah laughed, a very clear, pretty laugh, meant to be heard, and Camilla glanced at her balefully. She suspected that Sarah, even when she had to go through the rigours of pupillage, was unlikely to feel any of the inferiority which she herself felt towards other members of chambers. Camilla sipped morosely at the lemony dregs of her gin and tonic.

'I'd have thought that you might have had enough of lawyers without becoming one yourself,' said Anthony. The tilt of his chin as he drained his glass gave his glance an unconsciously seductive air.

'Mmm. Depends on the kind of lawyer one meets,' replied Sarah. 'Anyway, these things often run in families, don't they? What does your father do?'

Ah, the question, thought Anthony. The idle, potent question that hummed throughout drinks parties and over restaurant tables and in crowded hallways at parties wherever people under thirty gathered. It marked out the middle-class, aspiring child so surely. No one ever asked, 'What does your mother do?' That would give no indication of status, of family background or connections, of

31

whether the family house was large and in the country, or small and in the suburbs.

'He's an artist,' replied Anthony.

'Really? Would I know his work?'

'You might. Chay Cross.' Anthony's voice was diffident, but he still expected the customary reaction when people learned who his father was. The high-minded might seriously regard his father as one of the foremost abstract expressionists of his day, but to Anthony he would always be a superannuated hippy, possessed of only a modicum of talent, who had happened to get lucky by suckering the gullible artistic elite.

'You're joking!' Sarah smiled in amazement at Anthony. 'I wouldn't have guessed.'

'We're not at all alike,' replied Anthony, hoping that he was not going to have to talk about his father and his work for very long. Both subjects bored him. He was much more interested in finding out more about this extraordinarily pretty girl who had materialised from nowhere. She had an assuredness, a knowingness that he found oddly exciting. Suddenly he met her eyes again, and saw in them an expression which aroused in him a kind of instant desire, such as he had not felt in a long time. There was an intensity, a sexuality, about her gaze that made him feel for a few seconds as though no one existed in the room apart from her. It was an extraordinary, quite dizzying sensation, passing almost immediately. Then he saw her glance towards the doorway and smile.

'My friends have just arrived,' she said, and raised her glass to finish her drink. Anthony glanced momentarily to his left and saw that Camilla was now engaged in the general conversation and unlikely to overhear him.

'Are you spending the whole evening with your friends? I mean, do you have plans for later on?' he asked quietly, just as she was about to rise. He hoped his voice sounded casual, but was astonished to find that his heart was thudding. He had never known any girl to have such an instantaneous effect upon him. He wanted suddenly to be able to leave with her now, go somewhere, anywhere.

She leaned down to pick up her bag and murmured, 'I'm afraid I do.' She paused and then added, 'But I'll be here at the same time tomorrow.' It was the briefest exchange, overheard by no one, but at that moment Camilla had turned and caught the faint intensity of the moment, like an animal with a scent. She stared at Anthony, and then Sarah raised her head and smiled at her. 'Lovely to see you again, Camilla. Got to go, I'm afraid.' Her eyes did not meet Anthony's again as she left the table.

Chapter Four

It was after ten when Anthony arrived at chambers the next day, and Henry put his head round the door of the clerks' room just as he was heading upstairs.

'Godfrey Ellwood's chambers have rung three times already. You'd better speak to him as soon as you can. Something's up. I'll get him for you.'

The phone was already ringing as Anthony came into his room, and he picked it up straight away, still tugging off his coat and unwinding his scarf as Godfrey Ellwood came on the line.

'Have you heard what's happened?' demanded Ellwood, clearly furious about something.

'No – what? I've only just got in,' replied Anthony. 'Don't tell me it's something in the judgment – '

'God, no, the judgment's fine! But I'm being asked to withdraw from the case.'

'What? Why?' Anthony was aghast at the thought of losing his leader at such a critical juncture.

'According to Fred Fenton at Nichols and Co, it's because I acted for a firm of accountants called Bessermans in some case three years ago.'

'I don't follow.'

'Marples and Clark, the auditors – you know, one of the defendants in the Capstall case – apparently took Bessermans over two years ago. The other side are now saying that there's a conflict of interest, that I can't act against Marples and Clark. One sees their point, of course, but it makes me bloody angry, after the months of work and preparation.' Ellwood was trying to contain his temper, aware that he was powerless to do anything.

'This is awful,' said Anthony. And it was. Godfrey Ellwood had been a guiding spirit in the case so far. Anthony, as he tried to digest this staggering information, felt as though he had been cut adrift. 'Do you have any idea who they're going to replace you with?'

'Not a clue,' sighed Ellwood. 'It's a bloody mess. I'm just sick and depressed by the whole thing. And no doubt our ever loyal instructing solicitor, Fred Fenton, will use it as an excuse for a discount.'

'I can believe it,' said Anthony unhappily. When they had finished speaking, Anthony hung up and sat back in his chair, pondering the possibilities. This would mean a new leader would have to be instructed, and they would be back at square one. Worse than that, there was a hearing coming up in two weeks' time on another preliminary matter, involving a time bar, and any new leader was going to have his work cut out to read all the papers by then. The action group committee weren't going to be best pleased when they learned about Ellwood. They had staked all their faith in the brilliance of their leading counsel, and now he was being booted out only months before the full hearing. Anthony covered his face with his hands and groaned. When word of this reached Freddie Hendry, a positive torrent of faxes would doubtless be unleashed on 5 Caper Court.

The officers of Nichols & Co stood in Bishopsgate, not far from St Mary Axe, affording an excellent view of the soaring chrome and glass tower of the new Lloyd's building. The coffee pot, Fred Fenton called it. Fred was a twenty-seven-year-old solicitor who had been with Nichols & Co for six years, and as he now stood in the office of his colleague, Murray Campbell, waiting for Murray to get off the phone so that they could discuss this latest catastrophe to befall the Capstall case, he cast a malevolent gaze through the window at Richard Rogers' monstrous edifice. He now loathed anything to do with Lloyd's of London. When he had been assigned to this case six months ago, he had been quite excited at the prospect of becoming involved in such an enormous piece of litigation. Now he wished that that dubious honour had been bestowed upon any other assistant at Nichols & Co except himself. He slept, ate and breathed the Capstall syndicate and its miserable history, and longed for a return to days filled with a variety of different pieces of work, instead of the dragging weight of this great albatross of a case.

Murray, a tall, overweight Scot in his late thirties, put down the phone at last. 'Sorry about that. Now – this business with Ellwood. We'll have to find another leader pretty damned quick, someone who's not already involved with some other piece of Lloyd's business, and someone bloody good. Any ideas?'

'One or two,' replied Fred. 'I had originally thought of Mark Dempster, at 4 Essex Court – ' Murray nodded approvingly. '– but from what his clerk says – and this is only reading between the lines, mind – there's a chance he could be made a judge within the next six months, and then we'd be scuppered twice.'

'Quite. To lose one leader may be regarded as a misfortune, but to lose two . . . ' Murray sighed and rubbed his chin. 'Who else, then?'

'Well, neither Eric Wilson nor Leo Davies has anything major going on at the moment.'

'Davies only took silk a few months ago, didn't he?' asked Murray. He got up, hitching his trousers, and began to pace the room slowly.

'Well, yes, Wilson is a bit more seasoned, and he's first class, but I reckon he's not so good on his feet as Davies. There's no one better in a courtroom than he is, and that's important in this case, especially when it comes to cross-examining Capstall and the other side's expert witnesses.'

Murray paced silently for a moment, then he nodded. 'Fine. Let's give him a go. He's in the same chambers as Anthony Cross, anyway, so that helps. Give his clerk a ring.'

At that moment the door opened, and Mr Rothwell, the senior partner, looked in. 'Thought I'd just tell you two that Rachel Dean – rather, Rachel Davies – will be rejoining us in a couple of weeks' time.'

Murray raised his eyebrows. 'Return of the Ice Maiden, eh? Funnily enough, we were just talking about her husband. Ellwood's had to drop out of the Lloyd's litigation, and Fred was suggesting Leo Davies as a replacement.'

'You could do a lot worse. I'm sorry to hear Ellwood's been dropped. What's all that about?'

'Conflict of interest,' said Fred.

Rothwell shook his head. 'Shame. Anyway, thought I'd pass on the news about Rachel.'

When the door had closed, Fred remarked, 'That's a bit of a

surprise. I mean, she had the baby only a few months ago. You wouldn't have thought she'd bother coming back to work, given the amount of money her husband must be coining.'

'A very chauvinistic attitude,' replied Murray with a grin. 'She wants her own career – doesn't want to waste away as a bored, rich housewife. And very creditable. She's an excellent lawyer.'

'Oh, granted,' said Fred. 'She just always struck me as the type who'd be happy at home with her babies.'

'Who knows about women, Fred?' said Murray, seating himself at his desk again. 'Anyway, you'd better get on to Leo Davies's clerk before someone else does.'

'Mr Davies will want a brief fee of two hundred and fifty thousand, and a refresher of two thousand a day,' said Felicity crisply.

At the other end of the phone, Fred Fenton sighed. It was pure extortion, the amount these silks demanded. 'Look, this isn't some multinational corporation here. These Names can't just chuck it about. Call it two hundred thousand for the brief fee, and a daily refresher of a thousand.'

Felicity smiled. She never thought of it as money – it was just big numbers, and a bit of difference splitting. 'You can't get the best for peanuts,' she reminded Fred, then thought for a few seconds. 'Tell you what – two hundred and thirty thousand and twelve hundred refresher.'

Fred hesitated. He hoped Davies would be worth it. 'All right,' he said. 'You'd better contact Ellwood's chambers and ask them to send the papers over.'

'Right ho,' said Felicity cheerfully, and put the phone down. At that moment Leo came into the clerk's room in his shirtsleeves and dropped some letters in the outgoing mail tray.

'What are you smiling about?' he asked morosely. 'You're always smiling.'

'I just like to brighten your day up, Mr Davies. Actually, that was Nichols and Co asking if you'd like to be instructed as leader in the Capstall case. Godfrey Ellwood's had to stand down. And I checked your diary and said you'd love to. How about that?'

Leo regarded her thoughtfully. 'Mmm. Well, now. That's rather interesting, isn't it?' His manner was casual, but Leo felt an inner excitement such as he had not felt in a long time. To replace someone like Godfrey Ellwood in a case of this magnitude was something of a challenge. He'd had plenty of decent work since becoming a QC, but this could be landmark litigation. This could make his name in a very big way.

'I'll ring Brick Court and ask them to send the papers round, shall I?'

'Yes, you do that. Though I imagine Anthony's got any amount of stuff – we don't want to duplicate too much.'

As he made his way upstairs, Leo reflected on Anthony's likely reaction to this news. Given the way he'd been actively avoiding Leo's company for the past few months, he might not exactly relish having Leo as his leader. They would necessarily be spending a lot of time together from now on. Leo suddenly realised how much he genuinely liked that prospect. Since he had met Rachel, Anthony's company was something he had missed. He had long ago learned to suppress the physical and emotional attraction he had once felt towards him, had taught himself to think of his feelings as those merely of friendship and not love, but he would never be able to deny the pleasure which he took simply in being with Anthony, talking to him, watching him. And he knew that the pleasure was mutual – had been mutual, before Rachel. If it was a kind of love which existed between them, Leo did not believe events could entirely extinguish it. They would see.

He saw Anthony in the common room at teatime that afternoon, and realised from his demeanour that he had not yet heard the news. Leo approached him, setting down his cup next to Anthony's and dropping into an armchair opposite him. Anthony, who had just picked up a copy of the *Evening Standard*, gave Leo a glance and a smile that seemed half-cold. He turned his gaze to the paper.

'You've got a new leader in the Capstall case,' said Leo, and stirred his tea, watching with mild pleasure the way that Anthony's languid expression suddenly sharpened with interest. He stared at Leo.

'I hadn't heard anything. How do you know?'

Leo paused for a few seconds, sipped his tea. 'I know, because Nichols instructed me this morning.'

Anthony sat staring at him for a moment. 'I see,' he murmured. 'I see.' He nodded, then looked away. Leo, as he regarded him, had no idea what he was thinking. There had been a time once when he had been able to read every emotion in the younger man's face, but this was a more mature, guarded Anthony, one who, as his success as a barrister grew, had cultivated a certain hauteur. Only occasionally was Leo able to glimpse the boy beneath the cool exterior. Anthony looked back at Leo again, his expression cold. 'I'm rather surprised that Fred Fenton or Murray didn't mention it to me first – I mean, before they instructed you.'

Something in Anthony's tone made Leo feel a sudden flash of anger. He put down his cup. 'That is a quite extraordinary remark.'

'Is it? I don't see why you think so.' Anthony was about to pick up the newspaper again, but Leo laid a detaining hand over it.

'Anthony, for better or worse, I have been instructed as leader in this case. Now, if you don't like it, you can always ask to be taken off it. I can think of many excellent juniors whom I would be happy to see in your place.' As he spoke, Leo found himself wondering how this hostility had suddenly sprung up between them, when only a few hours ago he had supposed this might provide an opportunity for them to renew their friendship. Clearly that was not how Anthony saw it.

Anthony gave a faint smile. 'I'm sure you can. How about Leslie Curtis, that pretty blond chap in 4 King's Bench Walk? Just your type.'

The restraint upon his temper which Leo had assiduously cultivated over the years very nearly snapped at this. But not quite. He smiled quickly in response, and glanced away. 'My dear boy, in that regard, I can think of no one who could possibly exceed your own attractions. No, I was speaking more in intellectual terms.' Anthony flushed. There was silence for a few seconds, and then Leo sighed and said in neutral tones, 'Look, it's going to be impossible for us to work together if things are to go on like this. Whatever is wrong between us, we have to straighten it out.'

Anthony struggled for a minute to maintain his cold demeanour, and failed. 'Christ, Leo . . . ' His voice was almost angry.

'Come on,' said Leo, glancing at his watch. 'It's quarter past four. Never too early for El Vino's. Let's go for a drink and sort this out.'

'I've got too much – '

'Forget it,' Leo cut in. 'Whatever it is, it'll wait. This is more important. Besides,' he added, 'it's Friday.' He stood up and put his hands in his pockets, looking down at Anthony. For a moment Anthony hesitated, then, with a reluctant sigh, he rose, dropping the newspaper beside his empty teacup, and followed Leo out.

They walked together in silence through Serjeant's Inn and passed through the side door into the dim interior of El Vino's, Anthony aware of some emotion at work within him which he could not quite define. Was it fear? Apprehension? As they sat down together at a corner table in the near-empty bar, Anthony watched Leo ordering a bottle from the waitress, and then suddenly realised that what he felt was a kind of excitement. Excitement, fear, pleasure – all these things mingled together. And relief – relief that after all these months they would be able to talk alone, and frankly. Then Anthony realised that he had no idea what he was going to say to Leo. Nor what Leo might say to him.

The waitress brought a bottle of chablis and two glasses, and Leo lit a small cigar. He glanced at Anthony. 'Are you hungry?' he asked. Without waiting for his answer, Leo turned to the waitress. 'A round of smoked salmon sandwiches, please,' he said.

When she had left, Leo poured them each a glass of wine. Still Anthony said nothing. He sat regarding Leo, waiting. Leo sipped his wine in silence for a moment or two, drawing on his cigar occasionally, staring thoughtfully at the table. Anthony knew, from all the times he had watched Leo in court, the way in which he would keep his gaze averted from a witness for long, suspenseful seconds, that Leo was carefully formulating whatever it was he had to say. But now he could afford to take longer than he ever did in court. At last he looked up at Anthony.

'I think,' said Leo slowly, 'that the best thing that you can do – the best thing for all of us, the best thing for this case – is to try to find some forgiveness for what I have done. For whatever there is in the past that has made you feel towards me as you do now.'

Anthony took a long drink of his wine. 'I don't know that that's possible,' he said.

Leo sighed and sat back in his chair. 'Anthony, you do genuinely bewilder me. Is it Rachel? Is it that you were so in love with her that you still feel like this? I don't believe so.' He leaned forward again, stroking ash from the tip of his cigar against the rim of the ashtray. 'I have seen you in love.' Anthony looked up at him sharply, his face suddenly vulnerable and young. 'You fall in love easily, and you recover easily. I know.' His gaze held Anthony's. 'I don't believe it has anything to do with Rachel. So tell me – what is it? What have I done that is so unforgivable?'

There was silence for a moment, and Anthony poured some more wine, then drank to fortify his nerve. He shook his head. 'I don't know that I can say this. It's beyond me. I simply don't think I can.' Leo said nothing. Anthony drew a deep breath, then looked up at Leo. 'Do you remember that evening just after you had announced your engagement, when we had drinks in chambers?' Leo said nothing, merely lifted his chin slightly as he drew on his cigar, his eyes fixed on Anthony's face. Anthony looked down at his wine glass, twisting the stem between his fingers. 'I'd had a bit to drink, I know, but I stopped you just as you came out of chambers afterwards – '

'I remember,' said Leo, and nodded.

Anthony looked up at him. 'Do you remember what I said?'

'Yes,' said Leo. This was a dangerous conversation, he realised. He had no idea where it might be leading and, scrupulous lawyer that he was, he did not relish that kind of unpredictability. He took a sip of his wine, then met Anthony's gaze. 'You asked me if I loved Rachel more than I had loved you.' In the brief silence they regarded one another intently.

'And did you mean what you said in reply?' asked Anthony quietly.

Leo looked away and pondered this, and for an instant Anthony saw a lost, hollow look pass across his face. Then it was gone. Leo nodded. 'Yes. Yes, I meant it. I have never loved Rachel as much as I did you.'

Anthony shook his head slowly. 'That's it, you see. That's all.'

Leo gazed at him sadly. 'Anthony, I would make you my lover tomorrow, if you wanted me to. But you don't – and it's not possible, anyway.'

Anthony sighed. 'That's not what I meant. It's just that you – you have been so important to me . . . and – and I feel as though I have somehow . . . ' He struggled for words. ' . . . somehow lost you.' He paused. 'And you know something else? I sometimes wonder whether I even like you. I mistrust you. I mistrusted you when you married Rachel, because I didn't believe in what you were doing.'

This touched an instant nerve in Leo and he looked quickly away. 'That has nothing to do with you.'

'I know,' sighed Anthony. 'It's just – so many things don't add up. I once thought I understood you, the kind of man you are.' He shook his head. 'Now I don't.'

41

Again Leo sat thinking for a long moment before speaking. 'Whatever has happened,' he said at last, 'I want you to understand that I have – I always will have – a deep affection for you. Nothing can alter that. I would never do anything willingly to hurt you.'

'And Rachel?'

Leo took a deep breath, then glanced at the bottle. It was half empty. He poured the remains into their glasses. 'Anthony, don't judge me. I will not permit anyone to judge me. Just accept what I say. After all the things that have passed between us – ' His memory flickered back to a moonlit room, to an embrace which he had thought promised so much, and ended in nothing. '– the least we can do is remain friends.' He paused, and added softly, 'Don't you think?'

Anthony stared for a long time at his wine glass. 'Yes. Yes, I know you're right. I suppose it's because things have changed, and I wish they hadn't. Something like that. I don't know . . . ' He raised his eyes and Leo smiled at him. Slowly Anthony smiled back. The waitress arrived with their sandwiches.

'You'd better start eating those,' said Leo. 'No point drinking on an empty stomach.' He glanced at the waitress. 'Another bottle, please.' He looked back at Anthony. 'Now, you'd better start filling me in about this case of ours.'

It was half past eight when Anthony left El Vino's. Although he had switched to mineral water an hour ago, when Cameron Renshaw and Michael Gibbon had joined them, he was conscious of feeling pleasantly tipsy. The chill of the October air felt fresh, bracing, after the smoky fug of the wine bar. He crossed the cobbles and went through the cloisters into Caper Court, letting himself into chambers with his entry pass. He went upstairs, conscious of the silence of the empty building, and flipped on his light. As he put together some papers for the weekend, Anthony was aware that his conversation with Leo had left him feeling happier than he had been for some months. The tension between them had been unsettling, and it was a relief to be able to resume a friendship upon which he had relied so much in the past. He paused, looking down at the Capstall file in his briefcase, and realised that he was glad that Leo had been instructed as leader. There was something sure and certain about Leo which gave him confidence. He wondered what Freddie and Charles Beecham and the rest of the committee would make of him. Then as he closed his briefcase a flash of recollection blotted out thoughts of Leo and everything else. He had suddenly remembered the girl from the pub last night, Sarah. She had said she would be there this evening. He glanced at his watch. Twenty to nine. Damn, damn! he thought. God, he had spent most of the morning thinking about her, and had then completely forgotten. There probably wasn't much chance that she'd still be there. Hastily he grabbed the rest of his things and hurried out of chambers, locking the door behind him.

As he crossed Hare Court he slowed his pace – if she was still there, he didn't want to arrive breathless. Very uncool. And from what he remembered of her smile, her voice, her astonishingly sensuous glance, Miss Colman was very cool indeed. He paused outside the pub door, telling himself that she must have left long ago, if she had ever turned up, then went in. The place was packed with Friday evening drinkers, and he stood for a few moments, casting his eye over the various groups of people, trying to look casual and unconcerned. She wasn't there. He would have seen her immediately if she had been. Disappointed, he turned away and was halfway through the door when a hand touched his arm. He turned, and there she was, smiling at him.

'Hello,' she said. 'You're late.'

He was surprised by how intensely relieved he was to see her. 'I thought you might have gone.'

'I was just about to.'

He glanced around. 'You don't want to stay here, do you?'

She shook her head, still smiling, still looking at him. God, he thought, there was some very strange chemistry at work here – just looking at her brought back all the feelings from the previous night. He held the door open and she went out ahead of him. They stood together on the cold pavement, she in a long black overcoat and the boots from the night before, her silky blonde hair spilling on to her collar, which she turned up against the chill.

'Where shall we go?' she asked.

'Let's see . . . there's a wine bar in Chancery Lane that's usually fairly quiet.' She nodded, and they walked together up to the traffic lights, and crossed over.

'Actually,' said Sarah, 'I didn't get to the pub until eight thirty. I didn't think you'd have waited. I was just going to have one drink and go.'

'I'm glad you stayed. I got caught up discussing a case.' They reached the wine bar and he opened the door for her. He had been wondering what he was going to talk to her about, and decided this was as good a subject as any. 'The leader in our Lloyd's litigation has had to bow out of the case, so they've instructed someone new. I had to go over the nuts and bolts with him.'

They found a booth at the back of the wine bar and Sarah slid into the seat, while Anthony fetched her a glass of wine from the bar and an orange juice for himself. When he came back she had taken off her coat, and he saw that she was still dressed in her tight-fitting jeans, although this time her jumper was blue cashmere, cut provocatively low. Anthony tried, as they talked, not to let his eyes wander to the milky curve of her breasts as they rose and fell beneath the soft wool of her jumper, but it was difficult.

'So you've lost your brilliant leader – that bald chap who was with you in the pub last night?' said Sarah, tucking a strand of blonde hair behind her ear and sipping her wine. Anthony studied her face, noticing that her eyes were the same pale blue as her jumper, and that her nose was small and straight, her eyebrows and lashes darker than her hair. Very pretty, he thought, but with an indefinable extra ingredient that made her remarkably sexy. Perhaps her smile, which was secretive, as though she was laughing at some inner, private joke.

'Ellwood. Yes. Still, the solicitors instructed someone else today – someone from my chambers, actually, and he's very good. So maybe it won't be a major spanner in the works.'

'Who's that, then? We law students have to keep up with the great names, you know.'

'Chap called Leo Davies,' said Anthony, his gaze lingering helplessly on the way the slender gold chain round her neck grazed her soft flesh every time she breathed.

When she heard the name Sarah's gaze did not flicker. She nodded, then sipped her wine. So this beautiful young man knew Leo, did he? Well, well. She suddenly thought of the previous summer, the weeks that she had spent at Leo's country house with James, the things the three of them had done together, and she smiled slowly.

'What?' asked Anthony, returning her smile.

44

'Oh, nothing,' she said, wondering what Anthony would think of his new leading counsel if she were to tell him how well, and in exactly what ways, she knew Leo. He would be horrified probably. Leo was so careful, so discreet, that no one at the Bar would ever guess the kind of person that lay behind that brilliant, cultivated image.

Anthony gazed at her, fascinated by the secrecy of her smile, and suddenly realised what it was about her – it was an animal quality, something almost feral. He had no wish whatsoever, he realised, to go on talking about this case. Or about anything. He stretched out a hand and stroked the back of hers lightly with his thumb. Even this slight contact was astonishingly exciting. He reached out with his other hand and pulled her gently towards him, leaned forward, and kissed her for a long and exquisite moment.

Then he leaned back in his seat. 'I've been thinking about doing that since I first saw you,' he said, slightly breathless.

'I know,' replied Sarah, and he recognised from the softened, sensuous look of her face that their minds were moving along exactly the same lines. 'Listen,' she said, 'I can think of much cosier places to get to know each other than this wine bar. Why don't we just get a taxi back to my place?' she asked.

Anthony nodded, a little dazed. 'Yes. All right.'

As they left the wine bar, Leo was coming out of El Vino's with Michael.

'Shall we share a cab as far as Charing Cross?' asked Michael.

'Fine,' said Leo. Michael raised a hand to hail a passing cab, and Leo glanced across the road to see Anthony with a blonde girl, walking away up Fleet Street. For a moment he thought there was something vaguely familiar about her, but he couldn't think what. Dismissing it from his mind, he climbed into the taxi with Michael.

Chapter Five

Freddie Hendry woke early – far too early. It always happened these days. The older you got, the less sleep you needed, that was a fact. He could wish that it were not so. He loved sleep, he loved the cocoon of nothingness, the dreams that so pleasantly distorted reality, that allowed him to be with Dorothy again, or to be stumbling happily through nonsensical patchwork landscapes of the past. Nothing in life was so kind as sleep. He hated especially these early parts of the day, when the light through the curtains was greyish and depressing, and the trilling of the waking starlings in the street outside merely shrill and repetitive, quite unlike the varied music of birdsong in the countryside. He was aware, too, of an unpleasant, feverish restlessness that told him he had drunk too much whisky the night before. He knew he should not do that, but some evenings it all grew unbearable, and whisky blunted the wretchedness, made him feel as though the blood coursing in his veins was young and vigorous, not sluggish and old. Then in the mornings he would repent it.

He looked at his watch, propped up on the bedside cabinet, willing it to be past seven, at least. Six fifteen. He groaned and lay back on his pillow, his furred tongue probing and licking his toothless upper gums. He would lie awhile and wait for the water to heat up, then have coffee and an early bath. That would fill in a good deal of time. And then he would switch on breakfast television. He disliked it, didn't really take it in at all, but the colour of bright, lively faces and the sound of voices gave him the illusion of company. Then he would tidy up a bit, write some letters, maybe even do a spot of shopping, though there wasn't really anything he needed. That would fill in the hours until lunchtime, and after that he would drop in at the library and then set off for the tube and travel into the City to the offices of Nichols & Co. That was to be the high point of the day. This afternoon they were to meet their new leading counsel – some Welsh fella, Freddie had forgotten his name. He trained his eye on the spidery cracks on the ceiling, feeling quite invigorated by the prospect of meeting this new man. It had been one hell of a blow losing Ellwood, but lately he had ceased to pay attention to many of the important points which Freddie made to him in his faxes. Simply took no notice. Now this new chap, he could make him listen – here was an opportunity to get some really sound ideas across.

Already formulating in his mind the things he would say to their new leader, Freddie turned over and stretched out a hand to the tumbler on the bedside cabinet, fishing with his fingers for his slippery upper dentures.

At two o'clock that afternoon Charles Beecham was pacing impatiently up and down in the hallway of his house, listening to the sound of voices on the floor above him, waiting for the estate agent and his clients to finish their meanderings. This was the second time they'd been here, and the estate agent knew that he had an appointment in town; Carstairs would start to fret if Charles didn't pick him up on time. Charles glanced at his watch, then heard feet slowly descending the stairs. He fixed his slightly self-deprecating, minor celebrity smile on his face.

'Please don't think I want to rush you in any way, but I'm afraid I have an appointment in town . . . ' He let his voice trail away, knowing that the woman would take up the thread with vigorous apologies; he could tell, from the experience of recent years, that she found the fact that he was a media personality rather glamorous.

'Oh, Mr Beecham, forgive us. We really mustn't keep you. It was so kind of you to let us pop round again at short notice. We do like the house so very much – don't we?' She turned to her husband, who nodded in a vague way, not looking at Charles. She wanted the house, Charles could tell, but the husband didn't like the price. They were in for some hard bargaining.

By the time they had gone, it was nearly two thirty. Charles drove as fast as was safely possible to Brian Carstairs' place some thirty miles away. Brian and his family lived in a small, boxlike house on an estate which had been built ten years ago, an unattractive sprawling, modern development on the edge of Andover. The houses might have looked smart and new once, but now they looked shabby, too close together, the gardens too small. Charles did not have to wonder how Brian and his wife coped with three teenage children in a house that size; he knew all too well. He sighed as he drew up and glanced across at the house, reflecting that in his own case he had been relatively young, with his life ahead of him. For Charles and Hetty it had been the beginning. For Brian, this was very nearly the end.

As he had predicted, Brian was waiting for him anxiously. He was a small, spare man in his late forties, with a head that seemed a little big for his body, large, sad, intelligent eyes, and thinning dark hair. Twenty years ago he had been a salesman, selling plastics. Ten years later he had gone into partnership and started his own plastics and polythene manufacturing business. Six years later he and his partner had sold it for nearly three million. That was when he had gambled on Lloyd's, never thinking he could lose. Now, four years later, it was all gone, thanks to Alan Capstall. He and his wife had been forced to sell their six-bedroomed house with its swimming pool, extensive grounds and paddock, the children had been taken out of private school, and they had moved to this dreary semi. Brian spent most of his days applying for sales jobs which he would never get, which went to a younger, more dynamic breed of man – the kind of man Brian had once been.

Charles saw him watching and waiting behind the net curtains of the small front room, and when he opened the door to Charles a few seconds later, he was ready to go, his large briefcase in his hand stuffed with documents, relevant and irrelevant. For once he looked alert and almost cheerful. The committee meeting in London gave his day some point, his life some focus.

Brian's wife, Alison, watched from the doorway as they set off down the path. Charles, raising his hand in a faintly embarrassed gesture which was intended to be both greeting and farewell, was glad he had not had to stop and talk to her. She had a beaten, miserable quality about her. He imagined that she blamed Brian daily, and vocally, for their reduced circumstances.

In the car, Brian talked nervously and excitedly about the meeting at Nichols & Co, about their new leader, the ramifications for their case. Charles, as he drove, observed that the skin around Brian's fingernails was red and sore, and that Brian picked fretfully at it during silences.

'How are the children?' asked Charles, trying to steer Brian away from his interminable rant about the case.

Brian nibbled briefly at his fingers before answering. 'Not good. Paul is having a hellish time at his new school. Sophie used to go around in tears about losing her pony, but now she's coming home late for tea, we don't know where she is half the time, who she's with . . . Anna doesn't seem too bad . . . Anyone can say what they like, Charles, but money makes a big difference where children are concerned. I mean, we've had to uproot them from everything they've known – naturally they resent it, and me. I'm to blame.' He frowned, picking at an obstinate little tail of skin. 'Alison bloody nearly tells them that. You would think, after eight months, that she'd stop going on about how she always had doubts about Lloyd's, she never thought it was a good idea . . . '

Charles gave a wry smile. 'Everyone says that. Everyone's wise after the event.'

They drove in silence for a while, then Brian suddenly burst out, 'What I find impossible to live with, day in, day out, is the sheer arrogance of those bastards who ruined me in the first place. I'm not complaining about the losses on properly managed syndicates. It's the fact that I have to shell out for the malpractices of that crook Alan Capstall, and he's still got his debenture at the opera, and his companies, and his two homes and expensive cars. And those stuffed shirts at Lloyd's – people thinking they can get away with murder . . . '

Charles murmured something neutral, and glanced discreetly at the clock, realising with a sinking heart that Brian would probably go on like this for the rest of the journey.

'So, tell me about this committee. Describe them all,' said Leo. He and Anthony were sitting in a cab in slow-moving traffic on Holborn Viaduct, on their way to the offices of Nichols & Co.

'Well,' said Anthony, 'there are seven of them. The chairman is a chap called Basher Snodgrass, some retired Air Force chap who became a Lloyd's broker after the war. He knows what's going on and he's fairly innocuous – they voted him in four months ago because they couldn't stand the last one they had, Verney. They booted him out at the last AGM, and a right shambles that was. We held it in the Mansion House, and everybody just kept shouting. Not very edifying, the spectacle of hundreds of Lloyd's Names bellowing at each other, or at Verney, or anyone else who happened to be handy. Anyway, Snodgrass is the chairman. Then there's a chap called Beecham – actually, you may know him. Or his face, at any rate. Charles Beecham. He does those historical documentaries on Channel Four. He's got one on the Crusades at the moment.'

Leo nodded. 'I know the one. Good-looking chap, waves his hands about when he talks.'

'That's him. He's fairly pleasant, actually – compared to the rest, that is. Well, not that they're *un*pleasant. Just a bit . . . tiresome. Then there's a Mrs Hunter. Got some strange Christian name that I can never remember, like Hyacinth, or Hermione. She seems to be on the committee by virtue of the fact that she's lost more money than anybody else. Mind you, it still doesn't seem to have made much of a dent. Her late husband owned oil tankers. She's rolling in it. But you know how it is – the more they have, the more they hate to lose any.' He glanced out as they passed the Royal Exchange and turned into Threadneedle Street. 'Let's see – who else . . . ? There's an American by the name of Cochrane, and he's worth a fortune, too. He's all right, but he's very argumentative, blames his lawyers whenever things go wrong.'

'Quite right, too,' said Leo with a smile. 'That's what they pay us for.'

'Then there's a fellow called Carstairs – fairly retiring type, does all the minutes and the secretarial work. And, of course, there's Freddie Hendry.' Anthony sighed. 'I think this Lloyd's business has actually sent him a bit mad. Or else he's going senile. He's an ex-colonial type, worked in the civil service out in Bermuda, then came back here in the late seventies. He'd made quite a tidy fortune in investments, and then he and his wife lost everything at Lloyd's. She was a Name, too. She died a year or so ago, and according to Fred Fenton he's not been quite right since then. He's quite fanatical about the case – it's life or death to him. But he's not like Cochrane or Mrs Hunter. He's completely broke. So's Carstairs. Anyway, that's your committee.'

'Right,' said Leo, as the taxi turned into London Wall, 'let's see what they make of me.'

*

By the time the meeting was an hour old, Leo had succeeded in securing the confidence of each member of the committee and charming them entirely. It made Anthony smile to watch him at work, the way he smoothly allayed their suspicions, quelled their fears, boosted their morale, and showed them that he had spent long hours thoroughly acquainting himself with the most minute details of the litigation so far. Like patients with a doctor, these people had put their entire faith in Godfrey Ellwood, who was ten years Leo's senior, and Leo was conscious that he had a hard act to follow. Moreover, the meeting made Leo aware of something that he had not fully realised until then – the extent to which these people relied on him. It shone from their eyes as they listened to him detailing the next steps to be taken in the case. Their faith in the justice of their case was unshakeable, and they wanted to believe that Leo would triumph on their behalf. Leo, who had a cynical view of the folly and greed of these luckless Names, was slightly taken aback by the earnest nature of their trust in him. It emerged from their discussions that, while they might regard their solicitors as flawed beings, there could be no question of their leading counsel having feet of clay.

'Now, about this time-bar point,' said Freddie Hendry, stabbing at the tabletop with a gnarled, slightly shaky finger. 'What do you think the chances are that the other side might succeed?' He regarded Leo with the eye of one demanding an oracular vision.

'There is always a possibility that the Court of Appeal will go against us, but I don't see how they can support the finding of the judge at first instance,' replied Leo. He glanced at Anthony and smiled. 'Mr Cross has constructed a very attractive, if rather complex, argument to say that the letter the other side rely on doesn't amount to a confession of negligence, and I think – I hope – the court will find for us.'

Cochrane, the craggy American, sighed. 'Jesus, they better. Otherwise – well, we're done.' There was a heavy finality in his voice. 'We've all lost hundreds of thousands – some of us stand to lose everything if our claim dies on its feet now.'

Leo glanced round the circle of faces, at the anxious shadow which passed over each one. What kind of reassurance could he possibly give? The truth was, he had little sympathy for any of them. He might be prepared to devote all his energies to fighting their case for them, but there it ended. They had all invested in

Lloyd's in the hope of making easy money, and they had foundered on the rock of their own greed. That was the way he saw it.

'All I can promise you,' he said, 'is that I shall do my very best.'

At half past six the discussions drew to a close, and Murray Campbell invited them all into a side room where bottles of wine and glasses had been laid out. This had the effect of turning the business meeting into something of a small social gathering, and Anthony found himself trapped in a corner with Mrs Honoria Hunter, obliged to listen as she recounted the history of her misfortunes at Lloyd's. He glanced over to where Leo was talking to Fred Fenton and Charles Beecham, and hoped that Leo wouldn't want to go back to chambers and go over this afternoon's work. When Leo got into a case, he worked all the hours God gave, and social and domestic considerations were cast to one side. Anthony, however, had arranged to see Sarah this evening, and had been thinking about her all afternoon with an intense physical longing.

' . . . and you know, they say we should have realised what we were getting into, but frankly, Mr Cross, when I joined Lloyd's it was mainly to have somewhere new to lunch. One has to trust one's agents and underwriters, and so forth, or where is one?' Anthony nodded as she talked, and let his mind wander back to that moment when Sarah and he had begun to tear one another's clothes off, laughing and kissing at the same time. The recollection was extraordinarily erotic, and its physical effect on him obliged him to shift his stance as he listened attentively to Mrs Hunter.

On the other side of the room Fred excused himself to fill glasses, leaving Leo and Charles Beecham together.

'I think we all feel a lot better after talking to you today,' Charles confided to Leo. 'Losing Ellwood was something of a blow. I suppose it must be rather daunting for you, stepping into his shoes at this stage.'

Leo smiled and surveyed Beecham's boyishly attractive features. He had found himself glancing at the man occasionally during the meeting, and wondering. There was something faintly effeminate about him, about his mannerisms, his blond, curling hair. 'I doubt whether you found me particularly reassuring,' he replied.

'On the contrary,' said Charles. Leo returned Charles's smile and wondered whether he was right, whether he could really read an unmistakable sign of interest in those grey eyes, or whether the chap was just naturally friendly. He felt stirrings of excitement. Absurd, and distinctly bizarre, to be attracted to one's client. Dangerous, too. But just the kind of situation which Leo relished. Not that there was any question of developing anything at present. Yet it added a distinct spice to the proceedings, to consider the possibilities. At that moment Anthony, who had made his escape from Mrs Hunter, approached them.

'I'm going to head off now, unless you need me,' he said to Leo.

Leo glanced at his watch. Please, thought Anthony, don't say you want to go back to chambers to go over things. But Leo merely nodded and said, 'Fine. I'd suggest discussing matters tonight, but I've got some things I have to do.'

Relief swept Anthony. In under an hour he would have her in bed, and be able to relive every incredible second of last Friday night. 'Right,' he said, 'see you tomorrow.'

During this exchange Charles Beecham had turned away to reply to something which Freddie had said to him. Standing alone, Leo let his gaze rest speculatively on Charles's lanky figure for a moment. Then his thoughts turned to this evening, the appointment he had to keep, the thing he had to do. He felt a heaviness, a longing for it to be over and done with. He finished his glass of wine, gathered his papers together, said goodnight to those who remained, and went down in the lift. In the taxi on the way to Islington, he tried to rehearse what he was going to say, but found it impossible. It was bad enough having to do this, without working out beforehand how to. But the thing had gone on long enough. It had been an amusing diversion at first, but now it had grown stale and Leo was bored. It had to end.

He found Francis in the middle of cooking a meal for them both. The table in his small living room was carefully laid, dark blue linen napkins and tablecloth, white plates, shining glasses, candles ... Francis always went to such trouble. But it was his nature to attend meticulously to detail. In this he reminded Leo vaguely of Rachel. In fact, they were rather alike. Although Rachel was dark and Francis fair, both were slender, hesitant, hiding their vulnerability beneath cool exteriors. Leo recalled how casual and indifferent Francis had seemed when they first met. But that pose had been dropped long ago.

Leo stood in the middle of the living room, surveying the table, only half-listening as Francis talked to him from the kitchen about his day, something about an argument he had had with some women from the personnel department. He looked up as Francis came through from the kitchen, still talking, a glass of wine in either hand.

'Francis, I can't stay,' he said abruptly.

Francis halted, seeming to sway slightly as he handed Leo his wine. Leo took it, but did not drink. He could tell from the look in Francis's eyes that Francis had read the expression on Leo's face and understood instantly. Leo knew he should feel wretchedly guilty, but such feelings had been expunged from his repertoire of emotional responses long ago. When it came to Francis, and all the other young men like him, it was purely a matter of sex. They could dress it up with candlelit dinners and pretences of shared affection, but for Leo it was nothing more, nothing less. This had been simply an affair of a few months, and now he was ending it.

'You haven't taken off your coat,' said Francis faintly, and watched as Leo set his untouched glass down carefully on the table.

'I told you – I can't stay.'

Francis gazed at Leo's handsome, impassive face and tried to find some trace of compassion there, but saw none. He tried to smile. 'Not even for dinner? I cooked . . . '

Oh God, thought Leo, not tears. 'Francis,' he said, 'whatever was between us is over. I never pretended that there was anything in it – it was you who built up the – the – ' For once, the normally articulate Leo was lost for words.

'The romance?' supplied Francis. Leo said nothing. 'The friendship? How can you deal with people in this way, Leo, pretend that there are no feelings?'

'I didn't say that,' replied Leo. 'It's just that we don't have the same kind of feelings, and those that I had are gone. I'm sorry.'

'No, you're not.' The young man's voice was slow and soft.

No, thought Leo, I'm not. He looked away. 'There's no point in saying anything more. I have to go.' He turned, opened the door, and left.

Francis watched as Leo closed the door behind him, and listened to his feet on the stairs, descending unhesitatingly, their sound dying away. How very final and brutal, thought Francis. He leaned against the table, looking down at Leo's wine glass. For a moment he imagined himself sweeping away the carefully laid plates, glasses and candles with one movement of his arm, hearing the satisfying crash and observing the ruins of his carefully planned meal lying shattered on the floor. It would have been a fitting gesture, something to complement the devastating effect of Leo's announcement. But Francis knew that it was not in his nature. Instead he sat down on one of the chairs, put his face in his hands and wept.

When Leo got home, Rachel was in the kitchen, Oliver sitting in his baby bouncer alternately waving and sucking a wooden spoon. He began to kick even more vigorously when he saw Leo. Rachel murmured hello without turning round, and as he glanced at her, it occurred bizarrely to Leo that he could simply go through the same routine that he had just done with Francis, and end it all. I can't stay. It's over. There is nothing between us. But that wasn't true. In this case, it simply wasn't true. He bent down and picked up Oliver, marvelling at the slight compactness of his body, and kissed the fat, silky folds of his neck.

'Mmm. You are one good thing I have done in my life,' he murmured, and Oliver dribbled happily on to the collar of Leo's suit. He carried him over to where Rachel was stirring some pasta and kissed her lightly on the side of her face. She did not turn round. Look at us, thought Leo, a happy nuclear family. He went over to the fridge and took out a chilled bottle of wine with his free hand. 'White all right?' he asked.

'Yes, fine,' said Rachel.

Leo set the bottle down and then flew Oliver above his head, making him laugh, and swooped him towards Rachel, who smiled and kissed him in mid-flight. She glanced at Leo, who was making Spitfire noises at Oliver.

'You're in a good mood.'

'Am I?'

The large kitchen table was already laid, and Rachel put out the pasta and salad in dishes. Leo put Oliver back in his baby bouncer and Oliver immediately started to howl. When Leo gave him back his wooden spoon, Oliver flung it at him. Rachel fished in a drawer and brought out an egg whisk. 'Give him this.'

'Is he all right with it?' asked Leo, handing it to Oliver, who was instantly placated and started to gnaw the egg whisk, goggling at Leo.

'He's fine. Come and sit down.'

Leo opened the wine and sat down opposite Rachel. She had both elbows on the table, the tips of her fingers pressed together, and was staring at the table. Leo knew that attitude. Here comes something, he thought, and felt an odd sense of panic.

'I have something to tell you,' said Rachel. As he poured the wine, Leo was suddenly conscious of the warmth and security of his kitchen, of the little unit within it, and of the threat that her words seemed to contain. He thought for an instant of Francis, and for the first time felt a flash of pity for him. Or was it for himself?

Seeing that he was not going to say anything, that he was simply waiting, Rachel sipped her wine and went on. 'I'm going back to work. I've arranged it with the office. I start in two weeks.'

Leo felt a curious sense of relief and anticlimax, and his feelings impelled him to a burst of honesty. 'I thought for a moment,' he said quietly, 'that you were going to tell me you were leaving.'

'I don't think that's an option,' replied Rachel. 'Not right now.' She helped herself to salad and passed him the bread.

What did she mean by 'not right now'? wondered Leo. He supposed it meant that she had formed some notion of going, eventually. Did he want her to leave? In some ways. In some ways she cluttered his life, obscuring its former easy enjoyment, and in some ways she was his life, she and Oliver. For no particular reason he thought of Charles Beecham, of how once the prospect of any relationship with another man would have been simple and excitingly pleasurable. Because of Rachel, and the need for evasion and lies, it couldn't be, not now. I am simply not used to making sacrifices, thought Leo. I am too old. He glanced at Oliver, who gazed back at him steadily and trustingly as he kicked and sucked his egg whisk.

'I have something to tell you, too,' he said, looking back at Rachel.

'Oh?'

'The affair I told you about – I've finished it.'

She said nothing for a moment, broke her bread into pieces and chewed it rapidly. Then she said, 'Oddly enough, I feel rather sorry for him – whoever he is.'

Leo grimaced at this, and then laughed. She looked at him in surprise.

'Do you know,' he said, 'I can't think of any other woman capable of saying that, on being told that her husband has just discarded his homosexual lover. You are truly extraordinary.'

Rachel smiled faintly. He didn't realise that she had already decided that it didn't matter whether he had affairs or not. She might love him, but now it was simply a question of biding her time. 'Don't you want to know what arrangements I've made for Oliver when I start work again?' she asked.

'Yes,' said Leo, picking up his fork, realising that he had hardly even taken in what she had told him earlier. 'Yes. Go on. Tell me.'

Chapter Six

From the bed, Anthony watched Sarah as she stood at her dressing table, putting on eye makeup. She was wearing only a short blue silk camisole and, as she moved, her blonde hair grazed her naked back, the curving flesh of her legs gleaming in the low light. Exhausted though he was from making love to her, there was a sensuality, a vulnerability about her pose that made him wish she would stop what she was doing and come back to bed.

He yawned and folded his arms behind his head against the crimson pillows. 'Do we have to go to this party? I really don't feel like it, you know, and I have to be in chambers early tomorrow to go over a few things with Leo.' He yawned again.

Sarah smiled at him in the mirror. 'Leo, Leo, this wonderful Leo ... He plays the tune and you dance to it, don't you? What's the big attraction?'

Anthony glanced up at her a little sharply, and Sarah realised that her words had touched him on the raw. She smiled again, and brushed more mascara on to her lashes with deft strokes. It amused her to think that Anthony had no idea that she and Leo had ever been just as intimate as she and Anthony currently were. More so, in some ways, if one took into account Leo's odd predilections. She wondered if he and Leo had ever been lovers. It seemed unlikely, judging by Anthony's character, but one never knew what lay beneath that apparently straightforward and simple exterior. It wouldn't be like Leo to pass up someone quite as delectable as Anthony. Then again, they did work in the same chambers, and Leo liked to draw a very clear line between his public and his private life. She knew all that from experience.

'We're in the Court of Appeal next week,' said Anthony. 'You know that. It's only three days away, and it's vitally important that we win this point – '

'Oh, everything's so *vitally* important with you, Anthony!' mocked Sarah, imitating his tone. 'You're so serious!' She dropped her makeup and returned to the bed, leaned down and kissed him. Then she drew away and looked at him speculatively. 'I know what you need,' she said.

'What?'

'Something to pep you up.' She smiled and went into the bathroom. She returned with a small mirror and a little cylinder of tissue paper, twisted at either end. She sat down on the edge of the bed and untwisted one end, pouring a trickle of white powder in a careful line on to the mirror. Then she fished in her bedside drawer for a piece of paper, rolled it into a little tube and held it out to Anthony.

'There you are,' she said, flicking back her blonde hair from her shoulder.

Anthony looked up at her. He didn't take the paper from her.

'Is that coke?' he asked.

Sarah smiled. 'Of course it is!' she said, and waggled the little tube of paper at him. 'Go on.'

He shook his head. 'No, thanks.'

'Come on. It won't kill you. Just make you feel a bit zappier.'

'Sarah, I'm a barrister. I don't do drugs,' replied Anthony indifferently, then added, 'And if you have any ideas of being called to the Bar, you shouldn't either.' He turned away from her, pushing back the sheets and leaning over the other side of the bed to grope on the floor for his underwear.

She shrugged, bent down and snorted up the line of coke, holding her hair away from the mirror with her free hand. Anthony watched her as he stood up and began to button his shirt. She glanced up at him, wiping a finger beneath her nose and sniffing. 'Oh, don't look like that! That reproving, censorious look!' She laughed and picked up the mirror.

'I'm not looking like anything,' replied Anthony mildly. 'I just don't see why you need it.'

His tone irritated her. 'Oh, why does anyone need anything?' she snapped at him. 'Why do you need bottles of wine in El Vino's? It's no different, you know. If anything, it probably does you less harm.'

'Christ, you sound like my father,' sighed Anthony. 'Come on, if we're going to go to this thing, you'd better get dressed.'

There was something in his voice that made her feel defensive, as though she had been put in the wrong. The balance between them had tilted, and Sarah did not like it. Deciding to make amends, she came round the bed and put her arms about him.

'We could stay in, if you'd rather. Get a takeaway, go back to bed, watch a movie . . . do lots of interesting things.' She kissed his throat where his shirt was still unbuttoned.

Anthony looked at her, and realised that his mood had been altered by the small incident of the cocaine. It was not that he disapproved, it just didn't interest him. He generally thought less of people for doing it, although he knew that was unfair. Whatever it was, he no longer had any desire to stay in with her. He felt that the pleasant intimacy of the past hour had been dissipated, and they might as well go to the party.

'No,' he said, 'I'd rather go out.'

At the party, Sarah compensated for her dented ego by behaving with carefree ostentation. She drank too much, smoked a couple of joints just to show Anthony that she didn't care, and danced in a manner bordering on indecency with a good-looking Italian in snakeskin shoes which Anthony thought were the last word in rotten taste. He saw her as he wandered through from the kitchen with a drink, and watched, leaning against a wall. The music was heavy and insistent, the room was darkened, and someone had set up some fairly ineffective strobe lighting. Most of the people, it seemed to him, were in their late teens or twenties, and he felt he did not belong. He was too accustomed to spending time with people older than himself, and to moving in a more sophisticated world, to enjoy this kind of thing much. He preferred dinner with friends, or agreeable drinks parties where people could talk without having to shout over an insistent din, and drink and eat without being choked by cigarette smoke and jostled. There wasn't any food here, either, except for a few sad little rectangles of cold pizza and some cheese cubes on a tray in the kitchen, and Anthony hadn't eaten since lunchtime.

The music stopped and Sarah came over to him, smiling and out of breath. 'What about getting out of here and going for something to eat?' he asked.

'Why? Aren't you enjoying it?'

'I'm rather bored, if you must know. I didn't even enjoy this kind of thing much when I was a student.'

'God, Anthony, you must have been born middle-aged! Why don't you dance with me?' Some slow music had started up and Sarah put her arms around his neck and started to move sinuously against him. As they danced, Sarah suddenly noticed Camilla. She had just arrived and was talking to some people in the doorway. She looked a bit better than usual, thought Sarah, although that top she was wearing made her tits look enormous. At least she'd brushed her hair. Sarah smiled into Anthony's shoulder. It was just a matter of timing, waiting until Camilla had seen them. She chose her moment, saw Camilla turn and glance in their direction, and she raised her mouth to Anthony's and kissed him at some length, running her hands over his buttocks as she did so.

Camilla hadn't realised that Sarah would be at the party – she hadn't seen her since that evening in the Edgar Wallace. But there she was, looking unmistakably lovely. Then suddenly Camilla recognised the man whom Sarah was kissing, and her heart contracted with pain. It must have started that evening, when she introduced Sarah to Anthony in the pub – they must have been seeing each other for three weeks. So like Sarah, thought Camilla, trying to look away and pay attention to what someone was saying to her. Any man she wanted, she got. It had been like that at Oxford. She slept with whomever she chose, and although Camilla had always been brought up to believe that that was the way you got a bad name for yourself, it never seemed to affect Sarah. She wasn't seen as an easy lay, but as someone who knew what she wanted and just took it. Camilla wondered whether Sarah and Anthony slept together, and this prompted a painful image which she immediately tried to push from her mind.

The music ended, and Sarah glanced innocently in Camilla's direction. 'Oh, look, there's Camilla,' she said brightly.

'Really?' asked Anthony, turning. Because she was Jeremy's pupil, Anthony always thought of Camilla as a sort of schoolgirl, and he didn't really expect to see her at parties. It was ridiculous, he realised, considering she was twenty-two. Seeing Anthony looking in her direction, Camilla lifted her chin and smiled. Anthony, with Sarah at his side, crossed the room to talk to her.

'Hello,' he said. 'Nice to see you out of office hours.'

Camilla could feel her face flushing, and wished that it was something she could prevent by exercise of sheer self-control. But she couldn't.

'Hi,' she answered. 'I didn't expect – that is . . . I didn't know you knew Lesley – I mean, you know, the girl whose party it is,' said Camilla, wishing she could appear self-possessed and cool. She had so often fantasised about meeting Anthony by chance in some social situation like this, somewhere where she wouldn't be wearing her fusty black suit from chambers, and could dazzle him with an as yet unseen image. And here it was happening, and she still felt awkward and naive, and Sarah stood smiling at his side.

Anthony, a little surprised at the shyness of her manner, suddenly realised that she could have had no idea that he was seeing Sarah, and he felt a momentary awkward unhappiness. He had been unable to ignore the obvious fact that Camilla had something of a crush on him, and with mild conceit he acknowledged that it must be difficult for her to accept that he was going out with one of her friends. He was about to offer to fetch her a drink, when Sarah remarked, 'That's a pretty top. From Next, isn't it? I've got one like it, but of course, you have the figure for it.' The remark sounded entirely innocent, but Camilla felt instantly self-conscious, envious of Sarah's fashionable, boyish figure.

She could think of nothing to say, and so merely replied, 'I'm just going to put this in the kitchen,' holding up a bottle of wine which she had brought. She smiled uncertainly at them both and turned away.

'Poor old Camilla,' murmured Sarah. 'You'll always find her in the kitchen at parties.'

'I don't know why you say that,' said Anthony. 'She looks very nice – quite fanciable.' And, indeed, he had been surprised at how pretty she looked. Very nice legs. He realised that he never really thought of her as being female – pupils tended to be ciphers, and their place at the bottom of the pecking order in chambers prevented them from having properly developed personalities, so that one scarcely thought about them much at all. The tone of Sarah's remark made him want to defend Camilla, because he liked her.

Sarah laughed. 'Am I supposed to feel jealous?'

'You?' said Anthony. He kissed her and realised he was still hungry, and that it was getting late. 'Let's go and get something to eat.'

Quite content to have rubbed Camilla's nose in the fact of her relationship with Anthony, Sarah agreed. Anthony got their coats and waited in the hallway while Sarah said protracted, air-kissing farewells to friends. Camilla was trapped in conversation in the kitchen with a short, sweaty criminal barrister who had pursued her all through Bar School year, and to whom she had not the heart to be unkind. She glanced out and saw Anthony leaning against the front door, patiently waiting for Sarah. He yawned and then looked in her direction. Their eyes met, and he smiled at her, then raised his eyes heavenwards. She smiled broadly back, happiness spreading throughout her whole being at this word-less, conspiratorial exchange. Maybe he wasn't in love with Sarah, really. And, anyway, the fact that he could share his impatience with Sarah's luvvie leave-takings showed that he regarded her as a friend, a proper friend. She was still smiling as she turned back to the persistent young man and his account of his recent success at Snaresbrook Crown Court.

Anthony and Sarah found a cheap Italian restaurant a few streets away. Sarah was a little drunk from the party, and by the time she and Anthony had shared a bottle of wine over a plate of pasta, she had that languorous, utterly relaxed hunger that only sex could satisfy. Anthony paid the bill, and as the waiter disap-peared she smiled at Anthony and said, 'Why don't we go back to my flat and start where we left off? I feel incredibly randy just looking at you.'

'I'd love to, but – ' sighed Anthony, '– I have to go home and get some sleep before tomorrow.' His mind was already focused on the work that he and Leo would have to do the next day, and he was in that singular, purposeful frame of mind where not even Sarah's provocative charms could touch him.

'Oh, come on,' she said, leaning her head on her hand. 'You can sleep at mine. Afterwards, that is.'

The table at which they were sitting was small, small enough for Sarah to reach a hand below the table, take one of Anthony's, and slide it between her thighs. The restaurant was practically deserted, and Anthony had not the strength of will to draw his hand away, and as his fingers stroked the damp warmth of her crotch his insides dissolved, and his good intentions almost deserted him. Then he thought of how he would feel the next day if he didn't get enough sleep, how his inability to concentrate would irritate both himself and Leo. He took his hand away and shook his head.

'I'm going home.'

Sarah's desire to be made love to now combined with a fierce wish to have her own way. She was not accustomed to being turned down in this manner, and for such a reason.

'You mean I'm not as important as a piece of work? Not as important as your wondrous Leo, and his good opinion?' she asked, her tone sullen.

Anthony had turned away to look for the waiter, anxious to retrieve his credit card and leave. Now he turned back to her, looked at her without expression, and said simply, 'Not right at this moment, no.' He did not intend to be rude. But she had asked a question, and he gave a short answer. He knew that his offhandedness had something to do with the fact that she had spent a small part of the meal bitching about Camilla, which he hadn't liked, and also with his own growing sense of fatigue. He looked impatiently round for the waiter again.

'If he's so important to you, I'm surprised you don't sleep with him as well,' snapped Sarah, then added, 'Or maybe you already do.'

Anthony froze, but said nothing, and at that moment the waiter returned with his card. When he had gone, Anthony, without even glancing at Sarah, said, 'Listen, I don't need this. Why don't you just go home and sleep off your bad temper? Or maybe you could take some more coke to cheer yourself up.' The slight contempt in his voice roused a kind of impotent fury in her. She rose, snatching her coat from the back of the chair.

'Don't bother to find me a taxi,' she said, her voice icy. 'I can do it myself.' And she left, a gust of cold air blowing in through the swing doors. Anthony sighed and slipped his credit card into his wallet, then put on his coat, musing on her extraordinary volatility. It hadn't been evident when they first met, but now they were getting to know one another a little better, certain raw truths were beginning to surface. He stood thoughtfully for a moment or two, then left the restaurant, turning up his collar against the cold air. He glanced up and down the pavement. She was nowhere in sight, and he realised with guilt that he felt faintly relieved.

The following morning at half past seven, Anthony locked his car and made his way across the cobblestones to Caper Court. The Temple was still deserted, the stately buildings silent, not yet filled with the industrious bustle of clerks and barristers going about their day. From a distance came the hum of early traffic in Fleet Street, and somewhere a City church clock chimed as the sun's first watery rays parted the faint mist which lay over the lawns of Inner Temple Gardens and hung in the bare branches of the trees lining King's Bench Walk. Anthony surveyed his tranquil surroundings, aware that his spirits were lower than they should be. The business of Sarah had been preying on his mind. He had thought about her as he drove into work, having changed his mind about ringing her first thing to apologise. He had nothing to apologise for. He had been seeing her for three weeks now – not long, certainly, but long enough in his books to know that he would never love her. That depressed him. Anthony had a natural propensity for falling in love, and an insatiable liking for the tenderness and intimacy which it brought. Last night had made him realise that there would be none of that with Sarah. She was not tender. She was not, he thought, particularly kind. She was wonderful in bed, and he often wondered where she had acquired certain of her more inventive techniques, but he did not think of her company as restful or easy. What had started off as a purely physical attraction had failed to turn into love, or even affection, and Anthony knew that once he began to tire of sleeping with her the whole thing would become worthless. It had happened to him so often before, and it disheartened him to know that the pattern was repeating itself yet again.

He passed through the archway and under the two small cherry trees which grew in the courtyard, and let himself into chambers. From thinking about Sarah in this way, he found his thoughts straying to Rachel. She had possessed a gentleness and openness of heart which Sarah so singularly lacked. Perhaps that was what had attracted Leo to her. Although Anthony had reconciled himself to the business of Leo being married to someone with whom he himself had once been in love – whom Leo had effectively taken from him, in fact – he still could not think of her without a faint sense of pain. It was just as well he hadn't seen her for months, although for some reason the fact of having Sarah in his life made him think of her more often than before. Possibly he could not help making comparisons. Then again, at least Sarah had never shrunk from him physically, the way Rachel had. As he mounted the stairs to his room, he recalled the embarrassment and clumsiness of those encounters. They were a far cry from Sarah's expert and ardent caresses.

He knew that Leo was already in chambers, having seen his car in the car park, and decided to make them both a cup of coffee before they got on with the day's work. He went through to the little kitchen and found the sink was half-filled with scummy water and stacked with unwashed mugs, not a clean one in sight. Cursing Felicity, Anthony drained the sink and ran fresh hot water, into which he squirted a little detergent. Glancing around at the small, grubby space, he decided that Roderick was right. These chambers were cramped, they were outgrowing them. They were taking on two new juniors in a month's time, he himself was thinking of taking on a pupil next year, and there simply wasn't going to be enough room for everyone. Sighing, he took the two cups of coffee up to Leo's room.

Leo was sitting back in his chair with his feet on the desk, a file of papers in his lap. He looked up over his half-moon spectacles as Anthony came in.

'Good man.' He took his feet off the desk and leaned forward to take the mug from Anthony, then yawned. 'I've just spent an hour reading through the statements of some of our Names.'

'Why? You don't have to, you know. Leave that to the solicitors.' Anthony settled into one of the chairs opposite Leo's desk and sipped his coffee.

'Wrong, Anthony. It's one thing to stand up and say that our Names had no knowledge of how bad affairs were in 1985, and so could not have been expected to make a claim, but it's quite another to believe it. It's quite interesting getting a perspective on just how much some of them knew, and how little others did. Mrs Hunter, for instance –' Leo flipped the pages of a blue-backed document with his thumb '– comes across in conversation as someone who joined Lloyd's without having the first idea what she was going into. In fact, she probably read and understood the annual accounts and Capstall's letters more thoroughly than most of the businessmen on this syndicate. She's pretty sharp.' Leo dropped the documents on to the pale polished surface of his desk and picked up his coffee. 'And of course,' he added after a moment, 'it's useful to get an idea of the kind of people one's acting for. Greedy fools, largely, so far as one can see.'

'That's a bit hard,' said Anthony. 'You have to have some sympathy, surely.'

'Oh, I don't know,' said Leo. 'I accept that Capstall made some absolutely disastrous decisions, that he simply turned a blind eye to the way asbestos claims were piling up in the States. I suppose, when he started to write these run-off policies, he hoped that the claims would only arise over a very long period and that he could make a profit in the meantime from investment income. That was rash in the extreme. But these people went into Lloyd's with their eyes wide open. No one lied to them. They understood perfectly well that their liability would be unlimited.' Leo picked up the papers from his desk and flipped through the pages. 'Listen to this. " . . . I was reasonably aware from the early eighties of the working of the Lloyd's market and I understood the concept of unlimited personal liability." And again, "The concept of un-limited liability was explained to me when I joined Lloyd's. I treated Lloyd's as an investment and believed my agents were good, efficient and honest."'

'Well, there you are,' said Anthony. 'Every one of them thought Capstall knew what he was doing, that anything he did would be in their best interests. That's why they all feel as they do. They put their trust in Capstall – in the institution of Lloyd's, if you like – and they were let down in ways that they never expected.'

'Then they were simpletons,' said Leo dismissively, and drop-ped the papers back on his desk. 'Each and every one of them thought it was a way to make easy money, and I have no sympathy for people who are prepared to gamble not only their own futures, but those of their families as well.'

'Oh, come on,' said Anthony, growing a little heated. 'It's one thing to say that they went into it with their eyes open, but no one told them the real truth. You yourself accept that the scale of the asbestos claims was foreseeable as far back as the seventies, that there were really serious problems facing the market by the eighties. But nobody told these people that. All those managing agents and members' agents were only interested in getting their commission and recruiting as many people as they could. Half of the people they brought into the syndicates had no business being Lloyd's Names. Look at that poor sod Carstairs, for in-stance.'

'So you're saying that the Names are right to blame the underwriting agency for recruiting them when they weren't suitable? I'm sorry, Anthony, it doesn't work that way. People have to take responsibility for their individual decisions. No one forced them to join Lloyd's. It was explained to them that their liability was unlimited. They knew they could lose everything.'

'What? You think that the members' agent sat down with Brian Carstairs and said, "Listen, Brian, old man, when you join Lloyd's, there is a real chance that you will lose everything you have in the world. Within five years your nice country house could be gone, your BMW, all your expensive possessions. Your children will have to be taken out of their exclusive private schools and sent to the local state ones, there may be no money left for them or for your grandchildren, and there is a real possibility that you and your wife will be reduced to penury." Do you think anyone said that to him? No, someone sat him down at the end of a nice boozy lunch, gave him a glass of brandy, and said, "Brian, this is your chance to make a nice bit of extra income, make your money work twice. Look at all the other lucky chaps who've joined Lloyd's, the money they've made over the years! Look at this unbroken seven-year profit record, consider how good it will sound to your friends, being able to say you're a Name at Lloyd's! Here, have another cigar, Brian." And then some pipsqueak solicitor would come in and mumble a few words at Carstairs about unlimited liability, and that would be it!' Anthony had begun to pace around the room, stirred by what he felt was the injustice which his clients had suffered. He stopped, and saw that Leo was smiling at him.

'Anthony, you are still as naive and passionate as you were when I first met you. Maybe that's a good thing.' He sighed. 'But you won't convince me. Capstall's a scoundrel, and I will do my best to make sure he, and the members' agents, and the managing agents, and the auditors, and anyone else we can rope in as defendants, are made to account for hazarding our clients' money in a quite unjustifiable fashion. But I won't shed a tear if we lose. Maybe Names were suckered into joining Lloyd's. But they were suckered through snobbery and greed, not because they weren't told about asbestosis.'

Anthony sat down again. 'Maybe when you get to know them a bit better – I mean, all right, some of them were a bit stupid, but they didn't deserve to finish up destitute.'

Leo shrugged. 'You call that destitute, do you? Where I come from, they'd call it being well off. These people have still got their cars, haven't they? Their bank accounts? A roof over their heads? I didn't see any of our committee members looking particularly down at heel. Even poor old Freddie Hendry still manages to pay the rent on his flat in Bloomsbury and buy his Scotch. Come on, save your energies for some worthy cause. Your job is not to feel for these people, but to work for them. Let's get on with it.'

Anthony sighed. 'All right. But I still think it's better not to feel entirely dispassionate.'

'Don't you worry,' said Leo, and grinned. 'When the time comes, I will be able to convince everyone that I am utterly, passionately on the side of my clients. Even you. Just you wait till we get to the Court of Appeal on Monday.'

Chapter Seven

Freddie rang Charles Beecham at eight in the morning on the day of the Court of Appeal hearing. Charles had held a drinks party for a few neighbourhood friends the night before, in view of the fact that he had had an offer on his house and might shortly be leaving the village, and the whole thing had become rather riotous and had gone on longer than he had expected. The trilling of the phone next to his bed woke him with a horrible start from a deep, hungover sleep. He picked up the receiver and lay back, unpleasantly aware that his heart had begun to race, his head was aching, and his mouth felt like the inside of a toaster.

'Hello, Beecham? Hendry here,' barked Freddie's voice.

'God, Freddie, what is it? I was still asleep.'

'Asleep? You can't have forgotten we're in the Court of Appeal today! I've been up since five – already sent a fax to Davies just to keep him on his toes. I'm just ringing to check that you'll be bringing those documents along. The ones Carstairs said he would pass to you, since he's not coming.'

'Freddie,' sighed Charles, 'I'm sure that Mr Davies and Mr Cross have got everything they need. They don't want extra bumf from me.' He held the phone away and let Freddie's staccato protestations die on the air. Then he put the receiver back against his ear and said, 'All right, anything you say. But I won't be there till after lunch. I've got a meeting with my agent this morning. Yes, Freddie . . . No, I don't think Capstall's brother is writing articles against the Names to sell to the Sunday papers. Yes, I know he's a journalist, but I still don't . . . Very well, you do that. Yes. Bye.'

Charles clicked off the phone and closed his eyes, pulling the covers up to his chin, but knowing that sleep would not return to him now.

Freddie put the phone down and went over to the speckled oval mirror on his dressing table. He straightened his tie and flicked at the lapels of his blazer. They were a bit threadbare and shiny, he noticed, but still not too bad. When they'd won this case, he'd go and see his old tailor, get some new things made up. The reflection of his grizzled face gazed back at him, his thinning hair brushed back from his freckled forehead, his moustache grey now, the pouched skin of his cheeks lined with tiny veins. Shouldn't drink so much Scotch, he knew, but still ... Today was the day. He drew himself upright and gave his reflection a raffish smile, the kind he used to give the girls when he was young and the best-looking chap in the regiment. Then he put on his overcoat, collected his bits and pieces together, his keys, change for the tube, newspaper, pen and A4 pad for taking notes at the hearing, and, locking the door of his flat behind him, set off for the City. The sun was burning away the early morning frost and he could see a blue sky behind the chilly fog. A good omen, he thought, enjoying the dry crunch of the dead leaves beneath his polished brogues as he marched with a firm tread towards Russell Square station.

It was nine by the time he reached the Law Courts, and he knew the case would not come on until ten thirty, so he dawdled around the central hall, examining the lists of the day's cases, gazing up at the paintings of stern-faced judges and long-dead chancellors, scrutinising the people as they passed to and fro, frowning at a passing group of loud-mouthed young men in leather jackets and trainers, who talked and joked without any reverence for their dignified surroundings, their voices echoing from the high walls. For Freddie, the Law Courts were hallowed, steeped in mystery, splendid in their majesty, and it seemed to him that a respectful hush, as if in a cathedral, should be observed by visitors. He paced the chequered flagstones patiently, until, at ten past ten, he saw Basher Snodgrass come through the entrance doors, and then Murray Campbell and Fred Fenton. He joined them, and they all made their way to Court Number 71, where the hearing was to be held.

Freddie squeezed into the wooden bench next to Snodgrass, his newspaper folded on his lap, and leaned forward, gazing around the court with a faint thrill of excitement. Leo and Anthony were already seated at the front of the court, Murray and Fred behind them with a couple of assistants, and further along sat the other side's counsel, about five of them, so far as he could see, with a bevy of besuited young male and female solicitors behind them. There was much muttering and passing of paper, but this gradually died away as the usher stood up, glanced round and then, with lugubrious self-importance, intoned, 'Court rise.'

Everybody duly rose, and through the little door at the back of the court issued forth three of Her Majesty's Lords of Appeal, looking suitably stern and dignified in their full-bottomed wigs and robes, although they had been laughing and enjoying a particularly juicy piece of gossip involving a Chancery Court judge and a masseuse only minutes before. Everyone resumed their seats amid a spate of coughing, and then Leo rose, adjusting his wig and glancing down at the papers in front of him. There was a hushed pause before he spoke.

'My Lords, I appear for the appellants in this case, and my learned friends Mr Glynn and Mrs Abbott appear for the respondents. This appeal is brought against an order of Mr Justice Fry which declared that certain claims in tort by my clients, arising out of their losses as Lloyd's Names and members of syndicate 1766, were statute-barred. The respondents contend that my clients could reasonably have been expected to acquire the knowledge required for bringing an action for damages more than three years before the issue of the first writ, and rely principally upon the annual syndicate reports and accounts for 1981 to 1988 and a letter from the managing agents to all Names dated May 11th, 1984 . . . '

Anthony put his chin on his hand and glanced up at Leo, conscious of a deep thankfulness that he was not conducting this appeal. He was fully acquainted with the arguments, had helped to polish and adjust the very one upon which Leo was now embarking, but he would not have relished the prospect of standing up in front of the Master of the Rolls and Lord Justices Manfred and Howell and expounding them himself. He had plenty of faith in his own skills as an advocate, but he recognised that there were certain levels in a case where maturity and authority went a long way. Leo had both those qualities. Anthony reflected, smiling to himself as he picked up his pen to jot down a note, that Leo's prematurely silver hair must have been of considerable help to him in his career. People took you more seriously the older you got, or looked.

At the back of the court Freddie unconsciously bared his teeth in a momentary spasm of concentration and leaned forward to listen to Leo. It was blasted hard to follow the arguments, the way these legal chappies dressed things up. Davies was saying something about requiring knowledge of whether potential liabilities were capable of reasonable quantification. Well, that was one way of talking about whether any of them should have known things would go seriously wrong. But the Lloyd's agents were always sending reports, great bundles of information. You couldn't be expected to read it all and understand it. Before all this blasted business began, he hadn't had the first idea what a run-off policy was. Barely understood the three-year accounting system. You put your affairs in the hands of your agents and you trusted them to get on with it. Back in the old days, chaps at Lloyd's had been gentlemen – MCC ties, pinstripe suits. That had all changed. No gentlemen now. Just rogues and shysters. The idea of Lloyd's being self-regulating these days was laughable. Laughable. Freddie began to mutter to himself as he lost the thread of what Leo was saying, and let his thoughts wander down their usual erratic avenues. Basher Snodgrass glanced at him and sighed.

Leo was well into his stride now. He glanced at each one of the three faces on the bench before him as he spoke, noting the faint nod from the Master of the Rolls as he scribbled something down, the approving little lift of Lord Justice Howell's head as he sat back in his seat, and the encouraging angle at which Lord Justice Manfred's bushy eyebrows were set while he listened, resting his head on one hand. They had, of course, read a potted version of the arguments well before the hearing, and had already formed something of a view. Leo had a feeling that they were in sympathy with the Names. It would hardly be surprising, since every member of the judiciary probably had a close friend or relative who'd been knocked sideways by the Lloyd's catastrophe.

'My Lords,' he said smoothly, glancing round at no one in particular with his serene blue gaze, 'what are the acts which constitute the negligence of which my clients complain? It would, in my respectful submission, be incomplete to say that these consisted of the writing of the run-off reinsurance policies, or the reinsurances to close, or the certification of the syndicate accounts. These do not in themselves amount to acts of which the Names would be *prima facie* entitled to complain . . . '

At the back of the courtroom Freddie Hendry ceased to mutter, but fell into a slight doze as the proceedings in Court number 71 drifted past him.

Charles was sitting in the Regent Street offices of his film and television agent with a broad smile on his face.

'The United States? And Canada?' he asked.

His agent, a brisk young man in his late twenties, nodded. The autumn sun which streamed through the large window reflected from his glasses, giving him a blank, sightless look. 'Australia, too. We've sold the rights to the first and second series and I'm presently negotiating in respect of your current one on the Crusades. It's an excellent package, Charles. I'm bound to say I'm very pleased.'

Charles crossed his legs, shook his head and smiled again. 'So – how much are we talking about? I mean, with this Lloyd's thing, you know, money's, well . . . '

'Too tight to mention? Well, I won't go so far as to say your worries are over, but for the outright sale of the first and second series, we're talking in excess of five hundred thousand. And then, of course, there's the present series, and possibly subsequent ones.'

'I see.' Charles nodded, trying to look as though he were giving this some serious thought, but in fact trying to contain his utter, pure and delirious joy.

'I thought,' said his agent, 'that we might go over the details of the contract over an early lunch – if you're free, that is.'

Charles nodded. 'Fine. I have to be at the Law Courts this afternoon, but I hadn't anything planned before then . . . Look, do you mind if I use your phone?'

His agent picked up the phone and passed it to Charles. 'I'll just go and ask Sarah to book us a table at the Groucho,' he said, and left the room. Charles took out his address book and flipped through it, tapped in some numbers on the phone and waited.

'Hello, Mr Bryant? Charles Beecham here. About the house. I'm sorry to disappoint the Fullers, but I'm taking it off the market. I've decided not to sell.'

As he put the phone down, smiling to himself, Charles reflected that he would probably have to throw another drinks party, to celebrate the fact that he would not be leaving the neighbourhood after all.

*

It was a curious feeling, returning to work after an absence of seven months. Rachel pushed open the heavy glass doors of Nichols & Co, and saw the familiar figure of Nora, the receptionist, murmuring into her headset and flicking buttons with her long, crimson nails. It was as if she had only been away for a few days. Nora smiled and gave her a little fluttering wave, and Rachel took the lift to the fourth floor. She walked along the carpeted corridors, past the glass-walled offices, seeing familiar figures bent over desks, talking into telephones, pulling open filing cabinet drawers, all busy with their work. She reached her own room, half-expecting to find some stranger occupying it, but there it was, empty and neat as she had left it when she went on maternity leave. The shelves where her files had lain were largely empty, but that would change in a week or two. She hung up her coat, slung her bag down beside her desk and sat down in her chair, swivelling in it and looking round. She was rather at a loss, she realised. It wasn't like starting a new job, where there was someone to greet you, give you things to do. No, it was up to her to fit back in, to reassert herself. She thought back to the time when she had first joined Nichols & Co, only two years ago, with all her earnest ambitions. Then she had married Leo, and had thought that that would become the most important thing in the world. It was, in a way. Only not in the way she had imagined. She was discovering pain where she had expected contentment. She was not to be to Leo everything she had thought she might be. But at least by coming back to work she might find something of her old self, and in the process restore her badly damaged self-esteem. Or so she hoped.

Time to have a coffee, thought Rachel, and to try and dig up some work. She went to the percolator and poured herself a cup, then wandered along the corridor to Murray Campbell's room. He was always up to his eyeballs – he was bound to have something for her. But his room was empty. Then Rachel remembered that he would be in court – Leo had mentioned that morning that the Names were in the Court of Appeal that day. She sighed. That meant Fred Fenton would be out, too. She could have done with Fred's banter and jokes to cheer her up. There was something dispiriting about coming back, having nothing to do while everyone else got on with their busy day.

Turning away from Murray's room, she bumped into Roger Williams. Roger, a suave, portly individual who fancied himself as a bit of a ladies' man, was one of the more senior of the partners, and a typical City chauvinist. He had made a couple of passes at Rachel in her early days in the office, and they were not the best of friends, but now she felt almost pleased to see him.

'Good God!' he said, smiling. 'Nobody told me you were coming back! Well, well . . . Come into my room and catch up on the gossip.' He laid a hand lightly on her shoulder, and they walked together to Roger's office, Rachel listening as he chatted. Conscious of Roger's hand resting on her shoulder, she remembered a time when she could not bear to let any man – especially Roger's type – touch her. Now she did not mind. Leo had cured her – or maybe he had simply made her indifferent. She did not know.

Rachel sat in the chair opposite his desk and stirred her coffee with a little plastic spoon. 'I thought Mr Rothwell might at least have told you I was coming back,' she remarked, feeling a little hurt that the senior partner had not thought the information worth passing on.

'Darling, I've been in Calcutta for the past three weeks.' Roger folded his hands behind his head and yawned. 'Only got back yesterday.' There was a pause as Rachel stared down at her coffee cup. 'So, how's the baby? And hubby?'

'Oh, fine. It feels a bit strange, being without Oliver, but I imagine I'll get used to it.' Rachel realised she didn't want to think too much about Oliver – the pang of separation was quite acute – and she changed the subject quickly. 'So, anything you can't handle at the moment? I need some work to get myself back into gear.'

'Well, funny you should ask that,' said Roger swivelling in his chair and stretching to a shelf behind him. 'Some instructions came in half an hour ago from one of the clubs . . . let's see . . . ' Roger flipped through a slim sheaf of documents. 'We've got a vessel carrying bagged cement sitting in Bangladesh, charterers haven't paid the balance of freight, there's accrued loadport demurrage of $233,000, the owners are going spare, all the usual thing.' He pushed them towards Rachel. 'Not exactly anything major, but something to be going on with until people realise you're back. All the old favourites, like Mr Nikolaos.'

Rachel made a face. 'Don't. I can do without Mr Nikolaos and his disasters for a week or two.' She glanced at the documents.

'Freight prepaid bills, I take it?' Roger nodded. 'Right,' said Rachel, and rose. 'It's a start, anyway. Thanks.'

'Don't thank me,' said Roger, and smiled. Funny, thought Rachel, how Roger had dropped his natural lechery after she got married. Old-fashioned values, she supposed. Anyway, it made him pleasanter to be around. She picked up her coffee cup, and as she was about to leave Mr Rothwell came in.

'Ah, Rachel. I wondered where you'd got to.'

Rachel held up the papers which Roger had given her. 'Just drumming up work. From the state of my room, all my cases seem to have been poached.'

'Don't worry – I shouldn't imagine anyone's done much work on them over the past six months. You'll probably get them back fast enough,' said Mr Rothwell.

'Exactly,' said Roger. 'Just whip out the usual letter to the clients: "We have now had an opportunity of considering at length the most appropriate manner of pursuing this action . . ." They won't even know you've been away.'

Mr Rothwell leaned against the window-sill and smiled at Rachel. 'Glad to hear you're in need of work, because you and I are taking some important new clients out to lunch today,' he said. 'They're a Japanese company with a new fleet of tankers. Just be your usual charming self and I'm sure they'll put lots of lovely cases your way.'

'Sounds promising,' said Rachel. 'Anyway, I'll get on with this in the meantime.' She and Mr Rothwell left Roger's office and walked back together to Rachel's room.

'By the way,' he said, as they reached her door, 'I've assigned one of the new secretaries to you – Barbara. She's about forty, very efficient, but she does tend to come and go absolutely on the dot. She's got children. You won't be able to ask her to work late.'

'You're forgetting,' replied Rachel with a smile, 'so have I. You won't see much of me after five thirty.'

'Good God, so you have! How absurd of me! No, no – of course.' Mr Rothwell paused. 'How is Leo, by the way? I instructed him on an oil spillage case a few months ago, but it settled. Haven't spoken to him since. All well?'

'Oh, yes,' said Rachel. 'He's acting for some Lloyd's Names at the moment. Very busy.' She realised that she did not wish to think of Leo at present, and her tone was faintly dismissive.

'Right,' said Mr Rothwell. 'I'll see you in reception at about half twelve.'

Rachel went back into her room, and closed the door, feeling happier. She hadn't been forgotten. Mr Rothwell had particularly chosen her to meet these new clients, and take on their initial business. He still thought well of her. Smiling, she glanced through the faxes Roger had given her and picked up the telephone.

When he left the Groucho Club at three o'clock, Charles felt distinctly fuzzy and extraordinarily well. The glare of daylight did odd things to his eyesight as he scanned the streets for a taxi; everything seemed bright and a little fast. Really, sharing a couple of bottles of very good Pomerol was just the thing after a heavy night. It had put him right back on form. Still, it was probably just as well that he had nothing to do that afternoon except sit in the Court of Appeal for an hour or so and daydream. Daydream about those foreign rights, about the lovely great tide of money soon to be flowing into his bank account, while sales of his books soared worldwide. He was going to be the David Attenborough of historical documentaries. Still smiling, Charles hailed a taxi and asked to be taken to the Law Courts in the Strand.

In Court Number 71, the post-prandial atmosphere was distinctly lethargic. The Master of the Rolls was regretting having eaten that lamb curry at lunchtime, and Lord Justice Manfred was, as usual, having a little difficulty in focusing his attention properly on Leo's argument. Counsel on the other side were restive, gearing up for their turn, and the solicitors yawned and fidgeted as they listened. To the inattentive spectators, time in the courtroom had a suspended quality, the little play being acted out seeming to bear no relation to the busy hum of the world outside.

' ... My Lords, I would therefore submit that, on the basis of these documents, my clients did not possess sufficient knowledge to satisfy section 14A. The accounts may have shown over successive years a reinsurance to close premium which was substantially larger than the year before, but I would respectfully submit that this would not necessarily lead a Name to infer that the estimate in the previous year was wrong. I invite your Lordships to allow this appeal, and to discharge the declarations made by the learned judge at first instance.'

Leo drew his papers together with the tips of his fingers, and, with the merest inclination of his head in the direction of the Lords of Appeal, sat down. There was a general rustle and movement in the rest of the court, and Basher Snodgrass nudged Freddie Hendry with his elbow. Freddie, who had unwisely drunk three glasses of red wine with his roast beef sandwiches at lunchtime, had let his head fall forward on to his chest and was snoring gently. Now he jerked awake, and demanded to know how things were going. As he did so, Charles came through the swing doors at the back of the court and glanced around.

Leo, who had turned round in his seat to speak in an undertone to Murray, looked up and saw him and felt his heart give a little lurch of pleasure. That old, delightful feeling. He had not given a thought to the man since their last meeting at Nichols & Co, but the sight of his lean, attractive figure rekindled instantly the attraction which Leo had previously felt. His vanity made him wish that Charles could have been there earlier to listen and watch. Still.

Charles caught sight of Freddie in the back row, sitting next to Basher Snodgrass, cupping his ear attentively to catch what Basher was whispering to him. He slid into the seat next to Freddie and asked how things were going.

'Haven't a clue, old fella,' said Freddie in a loud mutter. 'Can't understand a blasted word of what's going on. Davies seems to have spent most of the afternoon talking about some woman having her breast removed.'

'That's one of the authorities, one of the leading cases,' said Basher in exasperation. 'I told you about it at lunchtime. It's germane to the question of whether or not a plaintiff needs to know that the thing they are complaining about was negligent at the time it happened.'

Freddie waved a veiny hand. 'Load of nonsense, so far as I can tell.' He leaned towards Charles. 'Anyway, Davies has done his stuff. You just missed it. The other side are on now.'

Charles caught a whiff of Freddie's cheesy breath and sat back a little. He looked down into the well of the courtroom and saw Leo incline his head to catch something Anthony was saying, then laugh. Very good-looking man, Davies, with that silver hair and those clean-cut features. Must be about his own age. Charles unconsciously touched the slightly sagging skin beneath his own jaw, stroking it, then lifted his chin.

'Well, Mrs Abbott?' said the Master of the Rolls mildly, glancing at the defendants' leading counsel. Mrs Abbott, a composed and confident middle-aged woman, rose. Leo glanced round briefly at the back of the court as she began to speak, and caught Charles's eye. Charles found himself smiling faintly, as he tended to do when he had had too much to drink and nothing to think about, and Leo, as he turned away again, was aware of a slight thrill of satisfaction.

At the end of the afternoon, when the day's proceedings were finished, a small group of people, including Basher, Freddie and Charles, stood in conversation outside the courtroom doors. Leo and Anthony came out, still in conversation with the other side's counsel, and Leo felt faintly pleased and relieved to see that Charles Beecham had not yet left.

Charles caught sight of Leo and Anthony and came over.

'How do you think it's going?' he asked. 'I'm afraid I couldn't be here this morning.'

'Oh, you didn't miss much,' said Leo with a smile. 'It all seems to be going pretty well so far. I don't think the other side are going to say anything they haven't said before. Should be over by tomorrow afternoon.' Charles nodded. 'Actually, Anthony and I were just going to have a chat about it over a quick drink. Why don't you join us?'

Charles hesitated, glancing at his watch. It was nearly five. No point in catching a train in the rush hour – he'd just have to stand all the way. Besides, he could feel his alcohol-level dropping since lunchtime. Could probably do with topping up. Then he could have an early night and get on with some serious work tomorrow. Leo looked at him, taking in the narrow boyish face, the blond, curling hair that was beginning to grey attractively at the temples. He very much wanted Charles to say yes.

Charles smiled and nodded. 'Yes. Yes, I'd like to, thanks.'

Leo glanced over at Freddie and Basher. 'I'd rather not have to listen to Freddie all evening, though, so don't mention it to them. We'll see you downstairs in ten minutes.'

Leo and Anthony went to the robing room and changed out of their wigs and gowns.

'I told Charles Beecham we'd meet him next door for a drink,' said Leo as he unfastened his collar. 'Normally I'd do my best to avoid socialising with most members of the committee, but he seems fairly decent.'

'Next door? Bellamy's?' asked Anthony. That particular wine bar was one of the favourite haunts of Sarah and her friends. He hadn't heard from her since last Thursday, when they had argued after the party, and he didn't particularly want to bump into her right now. He was still uncertain of his feelings about her, knew that she was potentially bad news, but had spells of longing for her delightful body and the pleasurable time spent in bed with her.

'I think that's the one,' replied Leo, folding his robe into his red QC's bag.

When they went into the wine bar Anthony scanned the place casually, but there was no sign of Sarah. He was surprised to feel a slight disappointment, and resolved to ring her later when he got home.

The three of them stayed in the wine bar for only an hour, but during that time Leo was at his best. He was witty, fascinating, everything he said and did was designed to captivate, and Charles thought him one of the most amusing men he had met in a long time. He felt considerable regret when, eventually, Leo glanced at his watch and said he had to go. Charles had just been thinking that it would fill in a blank evening for the three of them to have dinner together.

As Leo was putting on his overcoat, Charles said, 'If we win, I'll take you both out and buy you dinner. How about that?' He liked the idea of spending another evening in Leo's company, and Anthony was a nice chap, too.

'You're on,' said Leo. He gave Anthony and Charles a quick salute of farewell and left. As he walked briskly to the station, he smiled to himself, aware of a certain sense of accomplishment. He enjoyed using his charm and powers of fascination to his own ends.

As she hurried home to Oliver that evening, Rachel's feelings were a mixture of longing and anxiety. She had never been away from him for such a long stretch of time. She had spent the past two weeks interviewing nannies, determined to find exactly the right person, but had realised, after several interviews, that such a person did not exist. At last she had chosen a quiet, pretty blonde girl, who seemed quite mature and sensible, had very good references, and played with Oliver easily and calmly throughout the interview, sitting him on her knee and bouncing him as she talked. Jennifer had moved in the day before, and had been quite unobtrusive so far. She had a bedroom, sitting room and small bathroom on the top floor of the house, and had spent the afternoon up there sorting her belongings out. In the evening she had come down to make herself a meal, exchanging some brief, friendly conversation with Rachel, and then she had gone out in Rachel's car, to get used to driving it. Leo had been in his study working on his Lloyd's case, and had scarcely spoken to the girl, beyond being introduced. He had taken no part in the employment of the nanny, leaving the matter entirely to Rachel. This had angered her – any normal man, surely, would have taken some interest in the person who was going to be looking after his infant son for most of the day. But then, she supposed, Leo was not normal.

As she opened the front door, Rachel could hear a murmur of voices from the kitchen, and when she went through she found Oliver sitting contentedly in his high chair, puréed apple on his chin and bib, and Jennifer talking to him as she fed him. An Australian soap burbled faintly from the television.

'Hi,' said Rachel, going forward to kiss Oliver, to smell his delicious baby fragrance and stroke his fat satin hands. He dabbed apple on to the cuff of her shirt. 'How has the first day been?'

'Fine,' said Jennifer, smiling. 'We went to the park and fed the ducks, and I found that there's a playgroup at the church up the road. Quite a few nannies go there.'

Rachel felt relieved. She had worried about whether Jennifer would make friends in the neighbourhood. She was a very attractive girl, but seemed rather quiet. Rachel didn't want to think of her moping around in her room in the evenings.

'Good. I hope you'll make some friends.'

Jennifer scraped the apple mush from around Oliver's mouth with the edge of his spoon and took the dish over to the sink. 'Oh, no problem,' she said. 'You know that health club up the road? I'm going to go up there this evening and see what it's like. They've got a gym and a pool, and I might join, if it's not too expensive. I do quite a bit of aerobics.'

'Yes, I remember you told me,' said Rachel. She leaned against the edge of the table and watched as Jennifer wiped Oliver and unfastened his bib, longing to take over, for Jennifer to go out and let her have the baby all to herself. She felt something almost like jealousy as Jennifer lifted Oliver from his high chair and kissed his cheek. Then she handed him to Rachel and said, 'There. Your mum's been wanting a cuddle all day. I'll just go and run his bath.'

'Thanks. By the way, will you be eating with us this evening?'

'No, thanks. I'll have something before I go out. I don't like eating too late in the evening.'

Better and better, thought Rachel. She had rather dreaded the idea of the nanny eating with herself and Leo every evening. She was a nice enough girl, but it might have been a little awkward. Rachel took Oliver through to the living room and sank into an armchair with him, nuzzling against the soft folds of his neck, listening to his happy, bubbling noises. It had been a good day. Going back to work had been invigorating, and wooing those clients at lunchtime had reasserted her confidence. On top of that, this girl looked as though she would work out. The house was tidy, Oliver was happy, and she did not feel as guilty as she had expected.

She heard the front door open and close, and after a few moments Leo came in. He bent to kiss her, and then Oliver, and she could smell smoke from his jacket and a faint scent of wine on his breath. 'How was your first day back?' he asked as he straightened up, and turned to go and fetch the mail from the hall table.

'Good.' She thought of lunch, of the smiling, nodding Japanese tanker owners who would be putting some prestigious work her way. 'In fact, excellent. How was yours?'

Leo paused in the doorway. He thought of Charles Beecham, his laughter as he had listened to Leo talk, his slight expression of disappointment when Leo had said he had to go. He smiled. 'It went very well,' he replied. 'Things are looking very promising.'

Chapter Eight

When the hearing finished late the following afternoon, the feeling amongst the Names and their lawyers was generally optimistic. In a mood of elation Basher Snodgrass invited Freddie to have dinner with him at the Beefsteak Club, and Murray Campbell and Fred took a taxi back to Bishopsgate in fairly high spirits. As Anthony and Leo crossed the Strand through the drone and thunder of late afternoon traffic, street lights were already glimmering against the gathering dusk.

'We should get a decision quite swiftly,' said Leo. He had been vaguely disappointed not to see Charles Beecham in court that day, but he still felt buoyant from the brief time spent with him the evening before. 'I mean, Fry's decision was obviously wrong in law. Ludicrously wrong. They're bound to reverse it.'

'I hope you're right,' sighed Anthony, as they went up the steps to 5 Caper Court. He dreaded to think how it would affect the Names, especially those whom he had got to know on a personal basis, if they lost now. For Leo, he knew, the point was far more academic. He left Leo fishing around through the lunchtime mail in the clerks' room and went upstairs to his room, his bag and bundles of documents clutched about him. Camilla passed Anthony on the landing as he was trying to key in his door code.

'How did it go?' she asked.

'Pretty well,' said Anthony, grabbing at some documents which were slipping from his grasp. Camilla caught them.

'Here, I'll bring these in,' she said, and followed him into the room, tucking untidy strands of her hair behind her ear with her free hand. All afternoon she had been waiting for him to come back from court, so that she could ask him something, and now she could feel her heart beginning to thump at the prospect.

'Thanks,' said Anthony, dumping everything in a heap on his desk. 'It's a pity Jeremy works you so hard – you could have come along to the hearing. You'd have found it interesting, particularly since you helped out on the last one. Maybe I could have a word with Jeremy and ask him to let you do a bit of work with us. Then you could come to the full hearing.'

'When's that?'

'Oh, some time next year – March, probably. It'll take four or five weeks – possibly longer.'

'I see,' murmured Camilla. She hesitated, rubbing the toe of one shoe against the back of her tights, and then suddenly said, 'I was wondering, Anthony, if you'd do me a favour. That is – well, it's not exactly a favour . . . ' She could feel herself beginning to blush and wished she could stop it. She didn't normally blush when talking to men, but when Anthony gave her that sideways glance with his brown eyes, it was heart-stopping.

Anthony smiled at her. She was rather sweet, in an idiotic way. No one would imagine she was twenty-two. And why did she wear those awful suits with skirts that came halfway down her calves, and which completely concealed her rather nice figure? it might be an idea if she did something about her hair as well. It was a pretty colour, but it always looked a mess. 'What?' he asked. 'Spit it out.'

'Well, it's just that I've got two tickets for Grand Night on Thursday next week – you know, in Middle Temple. I was going with a friend, but she's had to cancel – and I wondered whether – well . . . actually, really, you know, whether you would like to come.' Grand Night was, as its name suggested, a gala affair in the Temple, a splendid dinner for which everyone dressed up, attended by the great and good of the judiciary, plus a handful of celebrated thespians who seemed to attach themselves somehow to the legal world. It was pompous, elaborate, and quite good fun for those who were seated well away from the high table and could get riotously drunk. Anthony had been once before. Camilla went on rapidly, 'I mean, it's purely – well, that is, I gather you're going out with Sarah, and things, and I don't want you to get the wrong idea. I mean, it's nothing like that. I just had a spare ticket, you see, and wondered, if you're not doing anything, whether you'd like to – but I suppose you're busy, and so on – '

Anthony, realising she could go on indefinitely in this confused vein, held up a hand. 'Whoah! Stop. Enough.' Camilla stopped and stared at him. He nodded. 'Yes, I'd like to very much,' he said. 'Thank you.' He immediately wondered whether he was doing a wise thing. It might not be a good idea to encourage her. Still, she herself had made it clear that it was purely a friendly thing, and it was useful to show one's face occasionally at these official bashes. Camilla looked mildly astonished and gave a smile of delight, a smile that lit up her eyes, Anthony noticed. She had a sort of transparency, an innocence that was in complete contrast to Sarah's opaque cleverness.

'Great!' She beamed. 'Great ... well ... I suppose you've got a lot to do. I'd better let you get on. We can talk about it nearer the time. Bye.' She left the room abruptly, leaving Anthony smiling in bemusement. Why on earth had he agreed to go? Grand Night, when they wheeled out every bencher in existence, even the ones you'd thought were dead, or looked it, at any rate. Well, he'd said yes, so that was that. He thought fleetingly of Sarah, whom he'd spoken to last night. She had been cool, but had agreed to see him tomorrow evening. He was aware that their relationship was moving on to another level, one at a remove from the utterly physical obsession which had obliterated anything else in the early weeks, and he was not entirely sure whether he liked Sarah enough to continue it. But when he thought about making love to her, the sensuous perfection of her silky body, he managed to persuade himself that he might as well let it carry on for a while. Perhaps it would be best, however, not to mention that he would be going out with Camilla next Thursday.

Camilla went back to Jeremy Vine's room, and Jeremy glanced up at her with a frown. He was a heavy-set, pedantic man in his late thirties, with a ponderous manner which made him seem older than he was. The more lighthearted, easygoing members of chambers, such as Leo, had little time for him, although it had to be acknowledged that he was hardworking and conscientious, possibly too much so. Certainly Camilla, bright and willing as she was, did not entirely enjoy working for him. He was not easy to get along with, and he had a tendency to treat her rather as a workhorse, giving her boring, repetitive tasks to do, instead of involving her with the minutiae of his cases.

'Can you take those briefs and give them to Felicity or Henry, please?' he asked, indicating his wire basket in which two briefs lay, scrawled with upside-down loops to show they were completed. Camilla, still smiling from her talk with Anthony, picked them up. 'And then,' added Jeremy, glancing at his watch and picking up the phone, 'perhaps you could look up this list of cases for me. I'd like the books, marked, on my desk first thing tomorrow, before we go into court.' He waved her away and began to speak into the phone.

Camilla went downstairs to the clerks' room, where Felicity was busy tapping at the computer screen and sipping coffee. She glanced up at Camilla and took the briefs from her.

'Mr Vine's latest efforts? Thanks. He's always late getting them back.' She noticed that Camilla's face wore an unusually glowing look. 'You look like the cat who's just had some. Tell me about it.'

Camilla glanced across the room to where Henry was busy on the phone. 'I've just invited Anthony to Grand Night – it's a sort of formal dinner in Middle Temple Hall. It's a week on Thursday. He said yes.'

'He never.' Felicity smiled at Camilla's radiant pleasure.

Camilla shrugged. 'It's just platonic, I know that. I mean, he's got a girlfriend. Someone I know, actually.'

Felicity waved this away. 'Doesn't mean a thing. Anthony's girlfriends come and go so fast it'd make your head spin.' She folded her arms and sat back, surveying Camilla with a candid expression. Gawd, she was a mess. Nice face, good cheekbones, good skin – but not so good that she could go about with absolutely no makeup, the way she did – and possibly quite a good figure. The trouble was, you couldn't tell, beneath those layers of drab clothes, and those high-buttoned blouses that were meant to be white but had gone grey with being washed too often. Felicity wondered what she was planning to wear to this thing next Thursday. She sighed involuntarily at the thought, and then her eyes met Camilla's.

'What?' asked Camilla. 'Why are you looking like that?'

Felicity shifted in her seat and crossed her legs. 'You really want to know?' she asked.

Camilla looked at Felicity's frank expression and wondered whether in fact she did. 'Go on,' she said.

Felicity leaned forward and, putting one elbow on the desk, rested her chin on it. 'The trouble is, see, with someone like

Anthony, you're going to have to try a little harder. Take my meaning?' Camilla said nothing, but glanced at Henry, who was still talking on the phone, and subsided into a chair opposite Felicity. She looked despairingly at her. 'I know you barristers have got to wear all that black stuff,' went on Felicity, 'but – well, there are ways of making it a bit more attractive. Know what I'm saying?' ·

'I look awful, you mean.' Camilla's tone was dull.

Bloody awful, thought Felicity, realising she was reaching one of those sticky conversational patches that always made her long for a fag. That was the trouble with the chambers' 'no smoking' policy, which only Leo seemed to manage to flout. It stopped you from lighting up just when you needed it most. 'No!' Felicity's voice was bright and reassuring. 'No, I didn't say that. It's just that – well, what are you planning to wear on Thursday?'

Camilla looked at her sadly. 'Well, I've got the dress I wore to my college May Ball . . . I suspect it's a bit tight now, though.'

'What colour is it?'

'Black.'

'Uh huh.' Felicity thought for a moment. 'Definitely not,' she said.

'What?'

'Definitely not your colour. That's half the trouble, see? Black doesn't suit you. Now, what you want, with your colouring, is some deep sort of colour, but vibrant. Sort of dark magenta, or dark green, something like that.'

Camilla sighed. 'I'm so awful at choosing clothes, though. I really hate it. I hate those shop assistants who come in and ask you how you're doing when you're trying to do up the zip. I'd rather wear my old college dress than shop for something new. Besides, I haven't got much money.'

'How much could you run to?' Felicity put her head on one side, already dressing Camilla in her mind. She'd have to find out what lay beneath those horrible suits of hers, though. Girl might have a waist like a sack of potatoes, for all she knew.

'I don't know. My mother offered to lend me some money to get something new, but she didn't say how much. Anyway, I said my old dress would do.'

'Well, you find out what she'll give you, and you and me will go shopping tomorrow lunchtime. You can't go to this posh do with

Anthony wearing some old black number that doesn't suit you. You put yourself in my hands, and I'll make you look fantastic. Dress, hair, the works. How about it?'

Camilla looked at her wonderingly. 'You mean you'd help me choose something? And do my hair?'

Felicity smiled, nodding. 'Yeah, and a bit of makeup. We could have you looking like a million dollars, I reckon. At least good enough to be seen with our young Mr Cross. Have you ever seen him in a dinner suit?'

'Anthony? No.' Camilla could imagine, though, how wonderful he must look.

'Well, he's something to live up to, girl, I can tell you.' Henry put the phone down on the other side of the room and came over. 'We'll go up West tomorrow and kit you out. It'll be fun,' added Felicity.

Camilla smiled uncertainly. She wasn't sure about Felicity's taste – she could be pretty outrageous. On the other hand, she did seem to know what men found attractive. She nodded. 'Yes. All right. Thank you.'

Felicity flapped a hand. 'Nothing to it. You'll see.' She watched as Camilla went back upstairs to look up Jeremy's cases, two inches of dusty hem hanging down at the back of her skirt. Felicity sighed and shook her head. Oh, well – nothing like a challenge.

'What was that all about?' asked Henry.

'Oh, Camilla and me are getting up a sort of chambers feminist group. Something quite radical – militant, even. So you lot better watch yourselves,' said Felicity breezily. She smiled at Henry. 'We're calling it the Inner Thigh Club.' She picked up the briefs which Camilla had left, put on her coat, and went out, leaving Henry looking uncertainly after her. He never knew what to make of Felicity. He had spent the past few weeks trying to persuade himself that she wasn't on his level, that she was really quite common and not worth being hung up about. His mother wouldn't have liked her, that was for sure. But that kind of thinking hadn't helped. He still found himself fantasising about her when he was doing the photocopying, or some other mundane task. She was, he suspected, on a level way above him, and there was no way of reaching her.

That evening Sir Neville Graham, Master of the Rolls, as wise and fair-minded a man as ever distinguished the senior ranks of Her Majesty's judiciary, sat nursing his varicose veins by the fireplace at White's. He was waiting for his two fellow Lords of Appeal to join him to discuss their judgment in the Capstall case, and was impatient for their arrival, having decided not to order a drink until they got there. He glanced at his watch. Ten past seven. Blast them. He longed for a large Scotch, but it was a peculiarity of his character to set up little rules and codes for himself, and then employ all his powers of self-discipline to abide by them. It had begun in his boyhood, when, at boarding school, he made it a rule not to have jam on his bread unless the second hand of the dining-hall clock was approaching an even number when he came into the hall. He still avoided the cracks in paving stones on those rare occasions when he found himself walking in London's streets, and his clerk had noticed that Sir Neville liked to have the pens on his desk arranged on the left-hand side of his blotter. He was unaware, however, that Sir Neville made it a private rule to have morning coffee at half eleven instead of eleven if the pens should perchance be arranged on the other side. Now he would not permit himself to order his drink until his colleagues showed up.

Five minutes later, when it was beginning to seem to Sir Neville that his powers of self-restraint were being quite impossibly tried, Lord Justice Manfred appeared, incongruously attired in a pin-stripe jacket and waistcoat, and leather motor-cycle leggings. He greeted Sir Neville and sat down in an armchair, and it was only the creaking of his trousers and the surprise in Sir Neville's gaze that caused him to glance down.

'Good grief!' he exclaimed. 'Back in a moment. Quite forgot.' He left the room, and Sir Neville ground his teeth, wondering if Manfred's arrival permitted him to order his drink, even though he had subsequently disappeared. He decided that, although on a strict view it might, an even stricter interpretation would require the arrival of both of his fellows, not just one.

Manfred, who was a middle-sized, energetic man with a schoolboyish face and thick grey hair, reappeared a few moments later, his legs now decently clad in pinstripe trousers. On his way through the room he halted a passing steward and ordered a drink for himself, then came over and sat down again in the armchair on the other side of the fireplace. He glanced at the empty table at Sir Neville's elbow. 'No drink? Dear me, I would have ordered you one with my own, if I'd realised.'

'I had decided to wait until you both arrived,' growled Sir Neville. His varicose veins throbbed again, and he lifted his leg slightly to ease the pain, wincing. The steward returned with Lord Justice Manfred's drink, and at that moment Bertrand Howell appeared in the doorway. He saw his two colleagues by the fire, raised his copy of the *Financial Times* in greeting, and strode over. Sir Neville sighed with relief and gestured to the steward. His mood brightened as he ordered Scotch for himself and a dry Martini for Lord Justice Howell.

'You just missed Guy coming in his motor-cycle leggings, Bertrand,' he remarked jovially to Lord Justice Howell, who glanced with mild disapproval at Lord Justice Manfred as he sat down.

'Damned silly thing, riding that scooter about town. Don't see why you can't take taxis like anyone else.'

'Penis extension, if you ask me,' smirked Sir Neville.

But Lord Justice Manfred, settling back easily in his chair and sipping his drink, merely smiled tolerantly. 'Do I detect a note of envy? Some of the most attractive young members of the female Bar strike up conversations with me on the strength of that motor bike.' He glanced at his watch. 'Anyway, we didn't come here to discuss my BMW. I've got dinner in fifteen minutes, so let's hurry this up.'

'Right,' said Lord Justice Howell, swirling his dry Martini and popping the olive into his mouth. He chewed, then popped the stone out of his mouth and flung it into the fire. 'Perfectly clear to me that the claim isn't time-barred. All the hogwash Fry came up with about the Names having constructive knowledge of their losses when they got Capstall's letter – utter tripe.'

Sir Neville glanced at Howell's drink, then at Manfred's gin and tonic, which he was sipping very slowly. He would ask whichever one of them finished his drink first to write the judgment, he decided. He certainly had no intention of writing it himself, even though he would read it out on behalf of all three of them. He always liked that bit. He glanced again with faint misgiving at Howell's drink, realising that it had arrived moments later than Manfred's. Was that strictly fair? Oh, well, rules were rules.

Lord Justice Manfred rubbed his hand across his chin. 'I go along with what you say about the letter, but there are the accounts, you know. I can't help thinking that the Names could have seen from those that the position was deteriorating year by year, and that the reserves and reinsurances were clearly inadequate.'

Sir Neville raised his eyebrows. 'Oh, I think we can work our way round that, you know. The point is, it's a political thing, this decision. I mean, we all know someone who's out-of-pocket through this Lloyd's business. What about your brother, Guy?' he asked, glancing at Manfred. This caused Lord Justice Manfred to take a sudden gulp of his gin and tonic.

'Yes,' admitted Manfred cautiously. 'He's suffered pretty badly.' Surely Sir Neville wasn't suggesting that they base their decision on whether or not they sympathised with the plight of the Lloyd's Names? That would be a little too much.

Lord Justice Howell said nothing, but nursed his Martini and thought of his sister-in-law, whom he'd had to bail out so that her boys could remain at Eton, and of several of his friends at home in Gloucestershire who were facing complete ruin.

'I have to tell you,' said Sir Neville, 'that I'd be inclined to decide this case as a matter of policy, if I had to. Those people at Lloyd's can't just be allowed to walk away from this mess, and I certainly wouldn't allow a technicality to prevent the Names pursuing a just claim.' He met Lord Justice Manfred's enquiring gaze with utter serenity, and went on, 'Fortunately, however, I don't believe we have to decide it on that basis. I regard Fry's decision as wrong in law. I believe he was unnecessarily restrictive in his interpretation of the requirements of Section 14.'

Howell took a long swallow of his drink. Down to an inch, noticed Sir Neville. He glanced at the ice cubes that cluttered the bottom of Manfred's drink. Did they count? he wondered.

'Absolutely,' agreed Lord Justice Howell. 'In my view, you can't say that Capstall's letter amounted to constructive knowledge that the risks reinsured weren't reasonably quantifiable. Fry simply wasn't entitled on the facts before him to say that the claims were statute-barred.' He lifted his chin and tossed back the remainder of his drink.

Watching him drain the glass, Sir Neville felt a faint relief that he did not have to concern himself with the issue of the ice cubes. He liked to be strictly fair, and those ice cubes would have worried him.

For a moment Lord Justice Manfred thought of expressing his reservations. Then he thought once again of those nephews of his. 'I must go along with you. I think that has to be right, as a matter of strict law.'

'Excellent,' said Sir Neville, and smiled at Lord Justice Howell. 'And since you stated your own conclusion so very succinctly, Bertrand, perhaps you would be kind enough to write the judgment for us all.'

The next morning Camilla came into the clerks' room in a state of faint excitement. 'Two hundred pounds,' she said to Felicity. 'A hundred from my mother, and the rest is my savings.'

'Excellent,' said Felicity. Her phone began to ring. 'See you at twelve on the dot.' As she picked the phone up Felicity had a heavy feeling in her heart; she hoped she hadn't taken on a hopeless cause in Camilla. Well, they would see.

As she was talking on the phone, Leo passed the door of the clerks' room, unbuttoning his overcoat, stuffing his leather gloves into his pocket. Felicity looked up and glimpsed him just as she was putting the receiver down.

'Mr Davies!' she called. Leo turned back from the stairs.

'Morning, Felicity. What news from the front line?'

'That was the registrar at the Court of Appeal. They're ready to give judgment in your Names case.'

'Really? What day did you give them?' Leo felt a quickening of excited interest, as he always did when a judgment was due.

'Well, I didn't. I mean, I would have said next Friday, but you said you were keeping the morning free in case those Indonesian people wanted a conference.'

Leo waved a dismissive hand. 'Forget them. Ring the registrar back and say Friday is fine.'

'Righty-ho.'

Leo went on up to his room, smiling. That was a good sign – an early judgment was an indication that they'd decided in the Names' favour and just wanted them to get on with the rest of the litigation. He paused at Anthony's room to tell him the news.

At lunchtime Camilla and Felicity took the tube to Oxford Circus and went into Dickins and Jones. Felicity scanned the store directory. Evening wear, third floor.

'Come on,' she said to Camilla, and they headed for the escalator.

On the third floor Camilla wandered in a state of unhappy uncertainty amongst the racks of dresses, fingering yards of chiffon and stroking folds of crisp taffeta. 'Everything costs a fortune,' she moaned.

'We'll find something,' said Felicity, peering amongst the dresses and price labels. 'What size are you, anyway?'

'Fourteen, I think,' said Camilla. 'Though sometimes I'm a twelve.'

A birdlike assistant approached them, hands folded together as if in prayer. 'Can I help you, ladies?' she asked brightly.

'Just looking, thanks,' said Felicity firmly.

Frowning in concentration, she continued to scour the dress racks, while Camilla gave up and sat down on a chair. She might as well just wear her black dress. She could see nothing here which suited her, or which she could possibly afford. After five minutes Felicity reappeared with a dress over each arm. 'Come on,' she said briskly, and headed for the fitting rooms. Camilla followed her through and stared at the dresses which Felicity was hanging up in the cubicle. One was cream coloured, made of a silky material, which fastened over one shoulder. The other was of plum-coloured velvet, with a low, curving neckline, which swept round to the back, just off the shoulder. She touched its softness.

'Try the other one on first,' said Felicity. She liked the plum-coloured one best, too, but she wanted to get the other one out of the way. Camilla gave her a nervous glance. 'Go on!' said Felicity. 'I'm on my lunch hour – we haven't got all day!'

She stood outside the cubicle to fend off any approaching assistants, and waited until Camilla reappeared. She gave her a glance. It was interesting to see that, beneath that awful suit, Camilla had a very good figure, with a narrow waist, a full bust, and pretty shoulders. But the dress was all wrong. 'No,' said Felicity. 'Try the other one.'

Obediently Camilla retreated behind the curtain, and after a few moments of rustling and zipping, reappeared. She was smiling. She knew she looked good. Even with her dark red hair straggling over her shoulders, she looked sensational. The rich colour was perfect against her creamy skin, and the fitted contours of the dress showed off the curve of her breasts and the slenderness of her waist. Felicity smiled back at her. 'Terrific,' she said.

'It does look quite nice, doesn't it?' said Camilla, with the shy satisfaction of a woman who knows how good she looks. She glanced uncertainly back in the cubicle mirror. 'Don't you think this colour is a bit funny with my hair? I've never gone for purples or reds, you know – I always thought it wouldn't look right with red hair.'

'Rubbish,' said Felicity. 'It's perfect. You're going to buy that.' She felt immensely pleased with herself for having singled out that dress, and in record time, too. They'd have to hurry to get back to chambers by one thirty.

Camilla bent her head and fumbled for the label at the side of the dress. She looked up at Felicity in despair. 'It's Jasper Conran! It's three hundred pounds! I can't afford it!'

But Felicity had thought it all out even before taking the dress off the rail. 'Yes, you can. I'm lending you a hundred. I earn a fortune as a clerk, compared to you pupils. Pay me back when you can.'

There followed a few moments of debate, which Felicity eventually won, and Camilla went back into the cubicle to change out of the dress. She reappeared in her baggy black suit, the white blouse wrongly buttoned, the velvet dress draped reverently over her arm. At the cash desk Felicity watched Camilla watching the woman smooth down layers of tissue paper between the folds of the dress as she wrapped it up. She's like a child, thought Felicity fondly. She realised that she very badly wanted Camilla to look as good as she possibly could on Thursday night. I'm a right little matchmaker, she thought, and smiled conspiratorially at Camilla as they went back towards the escalator.

Chapter Nine

A week later, Rachel arrived home late from work and found Leo slumped on the sofa, watching television, with Oliver lying slumbering against his chest. She looked across at them both from the doorway, saw Leo yawn, and thought what a cosy domestic picture it made. She wished that the truth did not have to be so different. She kicked off her shoes in the hallway and padded into the room.

'Thanks for coming home early,' she said. 'I didn't know that Mr Rothwell had arranged that meeting with these Japanese clients for six. I think he thinks it's just like the old days. I'll have to speak to him. The plan is that I should be able to leave at five thirty every night.'

'That's all right,' replied Leo. 'I'm just pushing paper around until we get this judgment next Friday.' He glanced up at her. 'Anyway, Jennifer would have done a couple of extra hours. She said so. She wouldn't have minded. What's the point of having a nanny if you can't get a bit of flexibility out of her?'

'Exploit her, you mean,' sighed Rachel, and sank into an armchair. 'She's got her hours, and I like to keep to them, if possible.' She yawned. 'Anyway, what do you think of her?' This was safe territory – domestic conversation, a means of maintaining contact without actually having to address deeper issues, such as their relationship, and where it was going.

Leo tried to pull himself into a sitting position, and Oliver stirred and cried weakly. Rachel held out her arms and Leo plucked Oliver gently from his chest and passed him over to his mother. Then he sat back down, rubbing his face with his hands. 'Jennifer? She seems very competent. I don't talk to her much, I'm afraid.'

'Why not? She's friendly enough.' Rachel stroked the blond

wisps of baby hair and kissed Oliver's damp, hot temple. He was waking up, and she would have to go and prepare his bottle in a minute.

'Is she?' Leo's expression was vague. 'She always seems rather watchful, sort of guarded, when I'm around.'

'You probably scare her. That aloof look of yours.' Oliver began to howl fitfully, and Rachel stood up with him. 'Come on, let's find you a bottle.'

'There's one in the microwave,' said Leo. 'I made it earlier. I'm a good father, if nothing else.'

'If nothing else,' murmured Rachel to herself as she went through to the kitchen. She pressed the buttons on the microwave and watched the bottle revolve, jiggling Oliver against her shoulder to soothe him. She felt depressed. She felt depressed by this charade, this appearance of humdrum, happy domesticity. They were both living some kind of a lie, each waiting for the other to do something to resolve it. If only she could turn to someone – it should be Leo, it should be Leo to whom she could turn. But there was no one. Perversely, it would have comforted her just to be able to have his physical love, but they had not made love for weeks. She told herself that this was her decision, that it was part of the process of weaning herself from him, but he himself had made no overtures. He seemed recently to have retreated into himself, as though there was some private area of thought into which he escaped. It had always been like that, she told herself, but lately it had been more intensely so. She took the bottle out of the microwave and shook it, then put it into Oliver's greedy little fingers. If it were not for the fact that he was at home every evening, she would have assumed that he had another lover.

She went back into the living room with the baby and sat down on the sofa, a little way away from her husband. 'What are you watching? I thought you always watched the news at nine o'clock.'

'Oh, it's just some documentary series that I started to watch last week. About the Crusades. It's rather interesting.'

On the screen a lanky, blond-haired man was pacing about a barren unrecognisable landscape, with buildings in the far distance, and talking.

' . . . and it was here, in May, 1097, that the Crusaders attacked their first major target, the Anatolian Turkish capital at Nicea, now known as Iznik. In June the city surrendered to the Byzantines. Anything, it seemed, was preferable to capitulating to the Crusaders.' [The camera closed in on Charles Beecham's musing features.] 'It was rapidly becoming clear that Alexius was intent on using the Crusaders as pawns in order to achieve his own ends . . .'

Leo enjoyed watching the object of his own private desires. It amused him to reflect that to the outside world he appeared a brilliant, well-respected QC, married, with a young family, the last person in the world who would be engaged in the protracted seduction of another man, the eminent and celebrated historian, Charles Beecham. He absorbed Charles's attractive, lean features as the camera pulled away again. It was more than a mere physical attraction, Leo told himself. Charles was his own age, someone on his own intellectual level, with compatible tastes and interests. The ideal partner. Not that he wanted a long-term partner. Marriage was bad enough. But how enjoyable it would be to be in love again.

'He makes it sound interesting,' murmured Rachel, breaking his train of thought. 'But I doubt if it is.'

'No, you're probably right,' said Leo, reflecting that this was true. He was hardly interested in the Crusades, merely in being able to watch at his leisure as Charles smiled, moved and talked his way through the programme. It was becoming the most perfect kind of infatuation.

Rachel looked down as Oliver sucked the dregs of his bottle. He had fallen asleep again and she could tell from the limp heaviness of his body that she could put him in his cot without disturbing him. The ache of depression which had begun earlier was still with her. She stared unseeingly at the screen and wished that she could turn to Leo and hold him, be held. But he sat as though closed off from the world, and she knew that there was no approach that she could possibly make. It would not help, even if she did. Anything that happened between them now would only be part of the pretence, and she must live with the reality. She stood up, cradling Oliver, looking down at Leo. He did not look up, and after a moment Rachel left the room.

'Don't you ever do any work?' asked Anthony, after he had finished listening to Sarah's account of her day, which seemed to

98

have been largely spent shopping, lunching, and skipping lectures.

She leaned away from him and picked up her glass of wine from the coffee table. They were sitting together on the sofa in Anthony's flat, idly watching television and talking. 'Of course I do. Well, occasionally. I prefer to leave it to the last minute. Get the fear up. Anyway, that's what I did at LMH and I managed to get a two-one.' Anthony remembered his own Bar School year, the standing room only at popular criminal procedure lectures, the poring over notes, essays finished in the small hours, the practicals, the tutorials – his recollection of endless study, coupled with a chronic lack of money, seemed to bear no resemblance to Sarah's carefree existence. 'Don't worry,' added Sarah, running her fingers through her blonde hair, 'there's five months till the Bar exams. Loads of time.' She sipped her wine.

'I'm glad you're so confident,' murmured Anthony, flipping through the television channels.

'Well, it's different for me,' said Sarah. 'I've got connections. I don't need to do particularly brilliantly. Just well enough.'

Arrogant as this sounded, Anthony had to acknowledge that it was probably true. As the daughter of the Recorder of London, she would probably find a tenancy effortlessly. She'd be a good barrister, too. She was sharp, eloquent and fearless. Ruthless, too, he imagined. Reflecting on this, he said, 'You shouldn't be specialising in commercial work, you know. You'd be far better off at the criminal Bar.'

'No, thanks!' said Sarah. 'I certainly don't intend to hack around for the first few years. I want to be where the money is. Anyway,' she added sweetly, nestling against Anthony and sliding her hand up his thigh, 'I thought you were going to take me on as your pupil?'

'Ha. Somehow I don't think that would go down very well in chambers.' He turned and regarded her, then kissed her briefly. He imagined – no, he knew – that this relationship would be over well before Sarah even sat her Bar exams. He was bored already. Bored? Well, disappointed. Disappointed as he always was, when he found that the object of early infatuation did not turn out to be the woman of his dreams, the sympathetic, totally compatible, amusing, kind creature for whom he seemed to be constantly searching. What would they do at the end of this evening? Go to bed, make love – even the thought of that held only minimal interest. When he found himself thinking in this way, Anthony felt a certain self-disgust. He did not like to be the kind of man who discarded girlfriends when things became familiar and stale. How on earth did he imagine he would ever stand being married? Yet he had the notion that one day he would marry. He liked the idea, the theory. But he knew that any wife would have to match up to his ideal, and that ideal apparently didn't exist.

'Stop,' said Sarah suddenly, taking the remote control from his hand. She flipped back a channel. Charles Beecham was now in some sort of echoing, domed interior of oriental design, and saying, ' . . . with the aid of reinforcements from Genoa and newly constructed and quite formidable siege machines, they took Jerusalem by storm on July the fifteenth, and massacred virtually every inhabitant. In the eyes of the Crusaders, the city was purified in the blood of the defeated infidels.'

'I love watching this,' said Sarah. 'Well, not it. Him.'

'I know him. He's one of the Names on the Capstall syndicate,' said Anthony in surprise. He had never watched the documentary series, and knew Charles's face only from the Lloyd's litigation. He watched for a few moments with interest. 'Leo brought him along for a drink after the hearing last Tuesday,' he added musingly.

Sarah reflected on this. She could well imagine Leo and this man sharing a drink. He was just Leo's type. She knew Leo so well, knew all his weaknesses, the kind of thing he liked. She smiled to herself, wondering if the renowned Mr Beecham was gay. Possibly. Hard to tell. Suddenly she turned to Anthony. 'Let's switch this off and take the wine to bed.'

'In a minute.' Anthony was still watching the documentary. It was a habit with him, ingrained since university, to attend when being given information, even if it was irrelevant. At last he dragged his attention from the screen. Sarah had unbuttoned her shirt, and was pulling it slowly from her shoulders. She was wearing nothing underneath, and she took his hand and ran his fingers lightly over her nipples. He felt instantly aroused and kissed her, closing his eyes as she flickered her tongue inside his mouth. Sex, he thought. Even if she wasn't the love of his life, there was always sex. And that, he reflected, was certainly better than nothing at all.

*

'Hold still!' said Felicity, as Camilla wriggled impatiently in front of the mirror. 'I can't do the thing up unless you hold still. There.'

Camilla ran her hands over the soft velvet of the bodice and looked at herself. She would never have dared to buy anything as wonderful as this if she'd been on her own. And she couldn't have done her hair like that. Felicity had twisted it up, securing it at the back of her head in a way that looked expertly careless, leaving a few reddish wisps which curled at the nape of her neck and brushed against her cheeks.

'Are you sure it's going to stay up?' she asked, putting up a nervous hand to the back of her head.

'It won't if you keep on doing that,' said Felicity, standing back and admiring her handiwork. It was six thirty on Thursday evening, and they had come back to the flat in Clapham, which Felicity shared with Vince, to prepare Camilla for her great night. Felicity folded her arms and stared at Camilla. Not bad. Bloody brilliant, considering the way the girl usually looked. Felicity still thought it would have been better if Camilla had let her go the whole hog, though. But she'd refused to have her nails painted, and had drawn the line at too much makeup. 'I want to look a bit like me,' she had protested.

'What do you think?' asked Camilla. Anxiety and the little bit of eyeshadow and mascara which she had permitted Felicity to apply made her eyes large and luminous, and it seemed to her as she observed herself in the mirror that the mouth through which she spoke was someone else's. She still had her doubts about the lip-liner, though Felicity had assured her it was necessary. 'I don't look – well . . . over the top?'

Felicity shook her head. 'You look knockout. I still think you could have done with more makeup, mind. But I reckon our Anthony's in for a bit of a surprise.' Felicity grinned with satisfaction.

Camilla bit her lip and felt a dissolving sensation inside. It hadn't started out like this. She had only wanted his company. But now that Felicity had done what she had done, things felt different. The reflection that gazed back at her from Felicity's wardrobe mirror was lovely, and she actually felt an absurd shred of hope. But it was ridiculous. He had Sarah, and, anyway, she was still only a pupil in chambers, lowest of the low. It wasn't as though he could ever regard her in any other light, no matter how she looked.

'Right. Come on. Taxi time,' said Felicity. 'You want a quick drink to steady you up?' she asked Camilla, glancing at her.

'No, thanks,' replied Camilla quickly. The last thing she wanted was to turn up at Middle Temple with a red face.

They had agreed to meet on the steps outside Middle Temple Hall, to avoid the crush inside. Anthony lounged against the stone pillar in his dinner suit, glancing around. A stream of guests were making their way into the cloakrooms to divest themselves of wraps, shawls and coats, and the air was filled with wafts of perfume and the sound of well-bred voices raised in laughter and conversation. Anthony greeted a few people he knew as they drifted past, and glanced at his watch. In the hall, people were taking their seats. This kind of thing always started promptly, and Camilla had only five minutes if she was to make it for grace.

A young woman with red hair was coming up the steps towards him, a coat over her shoulders, lifting her dress from the stone steps, and Anthony looked past her across the gloom of Fountain Court to see if he could glimpse any sign of Camilla.

'Anthony.' He turned at the sound of his name and stared at the girl standing there. It was Camilla, and he hadn't recognised her. Well, he'd never seen her with her hair up like that, and it altered her appearance quite radically. It made her look poised, feminine.

'God, sorry!' he exclaimed. He was about to say that he hadn't recognised her, then realised that this would sound rather tactless. 'How nice you look,' he added. Camilla smiled.

'Thanks,' she said.

'Shall we go in? They'll be starting grace in a few minutes.'

He followed her through into the vestibule and waited while she took her coat to the cloakroom. In the cloakroom Camilla took a deep breath and stared at herself in the age-spotted mirror. She gave her reflection a quick, unsuppressible smile, then went back out. Anthony glanced round when she appeared, and was quite astonished. Whatever transformation Camilla had undergone since he had last seen her at tea that afternoon, spilling coffee down the front of her black skirt, it was quite remarkable. The sweeping neckline of her dress showed off her pretty shoulders and neck, and she really looked very lovely indeed. One might almost say, sexy. How was it, he wondered, that she managed to conceal her very good figure beneath those awful suits of hers? He smiled in amusement, taking pleasure in the self-conscious smile which she gave in return, and they went into the hall together.

It was part of the Inn's masculine tradition to divide those dining in hall into messes of four, ranged along long wooden tables. Camilla and Anthony found themselves seated quite near the high table, where the more eminent and aged members of the Inn were seated, with a tax barrister whom Anthony knew vaguely from the squash courts, and his girlfriend. There were four young men in the mess next to theirs, two Bar School students and a couple of contemporaries of Camilla's, and they were already beginning to flick bread pellets at each other and indulge in loud hilarity. It was generally accepted that unseemly behaviour would occur on occasions such as this, and even those younger members of the Bar who had not received a formal public school or Oxbridge training in the art of rowdy conduct always seemed to manage to pick it up quite quickly.

The head porter stood at the entrance to the hall and, with an expression of ineffable pomposity, banged his staff twice on the wooden floor. An instant hush fell, and in trooped a self-conscious procession of benchers, some erect and dignified, some slow and stooped, others even more ancient, in wheelchairs or walking with the aid of sticks, who gave the impression of being mothballed and brought out especially on grand occasions such as this, looking baffled and tired, worn out before the festivities had even begun.

Anthony watched them make their way down the hall between the long tables, some nodding and raising eyebrows to acquaintances as they passed by, like ancient figures out of *Gormenghast*. The impression of cobwebby antiquity was heightened by the vast, vaulted roof of the hall, the panelled walls emblazoned with coats of arms, and the dim lustre of the silver chalices and candlesticks on the high table.

When the benchers and their guests were assembled at the high table, the senior porter banged his staff on the floor once again and the senior bencher, with an expression of grave dignity, intoned in a sepulchral voice, 'The eyes of all things look up and put their trust in thee, O Lord. Thou givest them their meat in due season, thou openest thine hand and fillest with thy blessing every living thing. Lord, bless us and these thy good gifts of thy bounteous liberality through Jesus Christ our Lord, Amen.' In a rumbling murmur, all joined in the 'Amen', everyone sat down, and a tide of voices rose to fill the air with conversation.

Anthony was not surprised to find that the food was no better than it normally was at dinner in hall, which was to say, fairly average.

'What do you suppose this is?' asked Anthony, gazing down at the glutinous sauce which cloaked the portions of chicken. 'I mean, does it taste of anything to you?'

'Mushrooms?' said Camilla tentatively. 'Tarragon?'

'Definitely not tarragon,' said Anthony. He filled Camilla's glass with white wine. 'Oh, well, drink some of this and it won't matter.' He raised his own glass. 'To you,' he said. 'And to that extremely lovely dress you're wearing.'

To her surprise, Camilla found that she was not blushing. She had not, since she had taken that last long look at herself before leaving Felicity's flat, felt at all like the kind of person who blushed. In this dress, and with the unfamiliar coolness of the air around her neck and shoulders, she felt quite composed, not at all gauche. 'Thank you,' she said, and smiled at him. She had never properly realised how much difference one's appearance could make to the way one felt. At university and Bar School she had gone about her studies in whatever clothes came to hand, never paying much attention to the way she looked, unless going to a party. She never classed herself with those girls who spent an inordinate amount of time on their appearance. They belonged to another breed, like female students who had affairs with their tutors. The boyfriends she had had weren't the kind who seemed to care much about whether she dressed up or not. When she had started her pupillage, it had seemed to her, as the first female barrister ever to work within the hallowed walls of 5 Caper Court, that she hardly had to make a point of her femininity. Quite the opposite. She wanted to be judged on her intellectual merits, to be accepted as an equal, and it had made sense to her to draw as little attention as possible to the fact that she was female, by dressing in the most functional clothes she could find. She had assumed that wearing makeup, or paying special attention to one's hair, might be viewed in that all-male bastion with suspicion, evidence of a mind which concerned itself with frivolities. The faintly exasperated, patronising manner with which her pupilmaster, Jeremy Vine, treated

Felicity and the other female employees certainly seemed to bear this out.

Now, as she ate and talked, drank her wine and shared the conversation with the other couple in their mess, Camilla realised that the self-confidence which she derived from her appearance was of positive assistance in a social context. It certainly seemed to have an effect upon Anthony, who normally treated her in chambers with big-brotherly forbearance and kindly tolerance. She could not put her finger on the difference in his manner this evening, but there was a certain new regard in it, an interest which she had not detected before. Was this the horrible truth, then – that one won greater respect from men by accentuating one's femininity, instead of playing it down? The mild feminist in her revolted at the idea, but she began to see that there was something to be said for the notion of making the best of one's assets, both physical and intellectual. She realised that it was certainly a philosophy to which Felicity would subscribe.

'What are you dreaming about?' asked Anthony, breaking her train of thought.

Camilla laughed. 'Nothing.' She hesitated. 'Well . . . actually, I was thinking about Felicity, and how she gave me a talking-to the other day.'

'She's rather good at that. I've been on the receiving end of one or two of those myself. What was it about?'

Now Camilla did blush, just the faintest suffusion of her neck and face. 'Oh, I couldn't possibly tell you,' she murmured, and looked away.

She looked so pretty, smiling in that way, her head tilted, that Anthony surprised himself by lifting his hand, placing his finger on her chin and turning her face back to his. 'Go on. Tell me.'

His dark, expressive eyes held hers, and she found herself saying, 'She told me that I don't make the most of myself. That I'm not – well – especially feminine. You know, at work.' She could hardly believe that she had confessed this. Too much wine, she told herself.

Anthony took his finger away, but his gaze remained fixed on hers. He smiled and replied, 'Well, I can only say that if you went around chambers looking the way you do this evening, there wouldn't be a man there who'd be able to get any work done.'

Camilla looked away, conscious of the almost physical pleasure which this remark, and his look, produced in her. At that moment there was a ragged burst of laughter from the back of the hall, followed by a small hail of champagne corks in the direction of the high table. Heads turned, people half rose in their seats to see what was going on, and a subdued scuffling and more laughter indicated that the perpetrators of the champagne cork volley were being escorted from the hall by the porters. The ejection of a group of over-excited students or junior members of the Bar was a regular event in hall, almost as much a part of tradition as everything else.

A tall, blond man on Camilla's left was standing up, craning to watch the rumpus at the back of the hall. He resumed his seat, laughing. 'Bloody brilliant! Did you see that? That was Ferguson, absolutely pissed. What a laugh!'

'Who's Ferguson?' asked Anthony mildly.

Camilla made a face. 'Rollo Ferguson. He was at Bar School with me. He's very bright – or he's supposed to be – but he just goes around doing idiotic things. He got barred from the Devereux for taking all the pictures off the walls and hiding them in the gents in the Edgar Wallace.'

'I'm surprised they let him in here tonight,' said the blond man. 'He's been chucked out of all the garden parties. Bloody funny.'

'Remember that time he rode his bicycle into the fountain?' said another of the young men. 'He was absolutely paralytic!'

'I don't know which he's better at – drinking or pulling women,' said someone else.

'Who's he shagging now?' asked the blond man loudly, and knocked back another glass of wine.

Anthony gave them a mildly disdainful glance, but no one took any notice.

'That blonde who's at Bar School with us,' replied one of the young men. 'Sarah something. She's knocking off some barrister as well, but that doesn't bother Ferguson.'

'Hasn't anyone told him he might catch something?' laughed his friend. 'I know her – she's old Colman's daughter. She doesn't half put it about. Here – watch it!' He broke off as a wine cork caught him above his ear. The conversation now disintegrated into general hilarity. Camilla had remained frozen throughout it, not daring to look at Anthony. Now she took a large sip of her wine and glanced cautiously at him. His face was completely inscrutable, almost as though he hadn't heard. But of course he must have.

Anthony felt Camilla's eyes on his face and was relieved when she looked away again. Why was he surprised? What did he expect from someone like Sarah, whose personality he had only recently begun to understand? God knows how many men she slept with at once. He drained his wine glass and then poured himself another. He knew he had probably had more than enough, but what he had just heard made him feel like getting properly drunk. Why, he wondered, did he care? He had been toying with the idea of breaking it off, anyway. So why did he feel this searing, burning sense of humiliation and hurt? The fact that he was public property, he supposed. The fact that she had talked about him. He was lucky, he supposed, that this lot on his left didn't know his name. She had talked about him openly, people knew that she had more than one lover, and that she was sleeping with him as well as this drunken oaf, Ferguson. That was part of it. The other part was that Camilla had heard. And Camilla knew. Camilla, right at this moment, was feeling sorry for him, and he hated that.

A few seconds passed and then, to his relief, someone at the high table stood up and banged for silence, then began to make a speech. At least there was an excuse not to talk, not to do anything, just to let his furious thoughts roam freely. He could not meet Camilla's eyes, but when he half-glanced in her direction, she was gazing fixedly at the speaker, thank God.

By the time the speech finished, and someone rose to make one in reply, the effect of the young men's conversation regarding Sarah was beginning to evaporate. Anthony turned to Camilla and forced a smile. 'Do you know what?' he said suddenly. 'I feel like getting drunk. Care to join me?'

She managed to laugh. 'Not really. But you go ahead.'

The toasts had begun, and Anthony knocked back a glass of wine for each one. By the time the decanters of port arrived at each mess, he was feeling supremely good. So much so that, in spite of the fact that he knew the effect port had on him, he drank several glasses.

'Don't you think you'd better steady on?' murmured Camilla at a pause in Anthony's drunken conversation with the tax barrister, who was keeping pace with him pretty well.

107

Anthony leaned back, then remembered just in time that the bench on which he was sitting didn't have a back on it. A crash and laughter from further along told him that some other poor sod had forgotten. He smiled at Camilla and nodded. 'You're right. You're absolutely right.' He gazed around. The festivities were breaking up, people were leaving their messes and joining others, the more decrepit members of the bench were making their way out, the more sprightly still passing the port, and a haze of cigar and cigarette smoke floated up into the high, vaulted roof of the hall.

He surveyed Camilla's face tipsily, resisting an impulse to stroke a finger down the creamy skin of her neck, and said, 'In fact, I think we ought to go.'

Camilla felt relieved. She didn't particularly want to be responsible for a drunk and incapable Anthony. She rose and said goodnight to her friends and Anthony, a little unsteadily, rose, too, and made his farewells.

He waited outside on the steps as she fetched her coat, watching his breath plume out into the cold air as other guests trickled past him, voices fading on the night air. Camilla joined him and they made their way across Fountain Court in silence, largely since Anthony was trying to concentrate on walking straight. They reached the gate leading out into Devereux Court and realised that it was locked.

'Bugger,' murmured Anthony. 'I do this every time. It's a sure sign that I've had too much to drink.'

Camilla had half-turned to walk back in the other direction, but Anthony reached out and pulled her gently back into the shadow of the gateway. He leaned against the metal gate, looking at her, then slowly reached up and loosened the hair at the back of her head. It fell down partly, tumbling in waves over her left cheek.

He laughed. 'I've been wanting to do that all evening.'

Camilla put a hand up uncertainly to her hair, conscious of the change in Anthony's manner. His voice was lazy, faintly mocking.

'Come here,' he murmured. She did not move, so he leaned forward and kissed her. There was nothing tentative or kind about it. He just kissed her because he wanted to, and because the idea that she was a very desirable creature had been growing on him over the last hour or so. He had entirely put from his mind the fact that this was Camilla, Jeremy's pupil, whom he saw in chambers every day, and with whom he was meant to be having a pleasant, platonic evening. At that moment she was a pretty girl whom he felt like kissing.

At the touch of his mouth, Camilla felt a warm longing growing within her. This kiss was something she had dreamed about in her idle fantasies in chambers, in all her happy daydreams about Anthony. But even as she enjoyed the feeling of his arms about her, the pressure of his body against hers, she knew that he was kissing her only because he was drunk, that it was something he would not have dreamed of doing if he had been sober. She pulled away.

'Don't,' she muttered. 'You're only doing it because of Sarah – because of what they said about her.'

He breathed heavily and leaned back. He felt drunk, angry and aggressively lustful. Then he laughed briefly. 'Oh, fuck Sarah,' he said. 'After all, everybody else does.' Then he pulled her towards him again, sliding his hand into the bodice of her dress and grabbing clumsily at her breast as he tried to bring his mouth to hers.

Appalled, Camilla twisted away and backed off. 'Stop it!' she said. God, he was horrible when he was drunk! This was not the way she had imagined things. She gazed at him in misery and fury as he swayed and leaned back against the gate, lifting his head up and closing his eyes. Without saying anything more, she turned around and hurried back across Fountain Court, her footsteps slowing as she joined the straggling group of people leaving Middle Temple Hall in search of taxis. Finally aware that he had done something he would regret, Anthony pushed himself drunkenly off the gate, shook his head, and made his way towards the steps leading down to the Embankment and Temple tube station.

Chapter Ten

The worst of it was that Anthony had to pass through the gateway the next morning on his way to chambers, through a dull, cold drizzle. The black iron gates, now open, seemed to stare at him in reproach, and the waters of the fountain danced and splashed mockingly. He groaned inwardly as he passed the blank, closed portals of Middle Temple Hall. The recollection of the previous evening, which had rushed upon him in a nauseating wave as he woke that morning, then ebbed away as he made his way into work, now swept over him afresh. But what had he done, after all, that he should feel so remorseful, so wretched? He had merely kissed Camilla, which was hardly in itself a crime. As far as he could recall, she had kissed him back, too. But he knew that he had been extremely drunk, and he winced at the vague recollection of having put his hand down the front of her dress. He remembered her recoiling from him, and presumed that he had just behaved like a drunken boor. Still, worse things had happened in life. He sighed as he went into chambers. It would just have been better if it hadn't happened with Camilla. There was something annoyingly wet about Camilla which told him that it wouldn't be possible for them both to laugh it off. He gave a furtive glance into the clerks' room, but saw only Felicity busy on the telephone and Henry sorting through the mail. He sped quickly upstairs and into the safety of his room.

A few moments later, Camilla came into chambers, shaking the rain from her umbrella. She had seen Anthony walking across Caper Court as she came through the cloisters and had realised that they were bound to meet at the entrance to Number 5. So she had hung back among the pillars, watching as his long-legged figure strode up the stairs and into chambers. She had a pretty good idea of how he must feel this morning, and, feeling a vague pity for him, didn't want to encounter him quite yet.

Felicity glanced up as Camilla went past the open door of the clerks' room. 'How did it go?' she hissed.

Camilla took off her coat and hesitated. She was clad once again in her dusty black suit and white blouse. 'I'm not sure, really . . .' Her expression was tired, blank.

Felicity glanced round at Henry slitting envelopes with a paper-knife. 'Come on,' she said to Camilla, 'we'll go and get a coffee and you can tell me all about it.'

They stood together in the confines of the narrow chambers kitchen and Camilla stirred her coffee. 'He just got drunk, basically,' she said, and shrugged her shoulders.

Felicity folded her arms and leaned back against the tiny sink. 'What – is that it? He got pissed?'

'Well, no, obviously not *just* that. I mean, we had quite a good time at first. He told me how nice I looked . . . ' A sad, faraway look crossed her face as she recollected Anthony turning her face to his, the way he had said what he said. Then she sighed and looked down at her coffee again. 'It was all fine. Then someone in the next mess unintentionally said something about Anthony's girlfriend – about how she was sleeping around. They didn't know who Anthony was, or anything. It was just – it just upset him, I suppose. And in the end he just had too much to drink.'

'So that was it?' Felicity couldn't hide her disappointment. She had had high hopes of her matchmaking, turning Camilla into a Cinderella. And Cinderella was about right, she reflected, glancing at Camilla now, her hair untidy about her face, bare of any makeup and shiny about the nose and chin, back in those baggy clothes.

'Oh, he kissed me after we had left,' said Camilla, her tone dismissive. 'But that was just because he was drunk. And then he just started groping me, so I walked off.' She drank her coffee and met Felicity's direct gaze a touch defiantly.

'Well, at least he went for you,' said Felicity doubtfully.

'You could put it like that,' said Camilla, and brushed past Felicity to throw the dregs of her coffee into the sink. 'But it was pretty awful, frankly. And if he hadn't been drunk it would never have happened. He would just have said goodnight politely and put me in a taxi.' Felicity was about to disagree, and Camilla stopped her. 'No, don't look like that, Felicity. I happen to know it.

111

Anyway, it was clear from the way he reacted to those remarks about his girlfriend how he feels about her. I suppose I feel a bit sorry for him, and I just want to forget the whole thing.' She glanced at her watch. Jeremy would be in by now, fretting over something she hadn't done, no doubt. 'Anyway,' she added, 'it's rather put me off him, as it happens.' She gave a faint smile. 'I'd better go and get some work done. See you later.' She turned to go, then stopped, and added, 'But thanks very much. I mean, thanks, anyway.'

Felicity still stood at the sink, lips pursed. What a mess. Bloody Anthony, never could hold his drink. But she couldn't believe that Camilla didn't still feel something for him. Felicity decided that there must be some way of retrieving the situation.

Fifteen minutes later Anthony was coming down from his room in his shirtsleeves, some papers in his hand, just as Camilla emerged from Jeremy's room. His heart sank, and his footsteps slowed as he came down the last few stairs. There was no way of avoiding this. He would have had to apologise to her sooner or later, anyway. He just couldn't face that forlorn, devoted look of hers, not when it was tinged with disappointment and reproach as well, as he assumed it would be. But she merely glanced casually at him, and then turned to go down the stairs without saying anything.

'Camilla,' he said. She stopped and he crossed the landing, looking down at her as she hesitated on the staircase.

'Yes?' Her face did not wear its usual enthusiastic, open expression. Her look was polite, almost uninterested.

'I – ah – I just want to apologise for last night. I think I got rather out of hand.' The door opposite Jeremy's room opened and Leo came out, smoking one of his small cigars, his jacket in his hand. He glanced quizzically at Camilla and Anthony.

'Morning, troops,' he said cheerfully, then he added to Anthony, 'You haven't forgotten we're getting judgment in the Court of Appeal today, have you?'

'Blast!' said Anthony, and glanced at his watch. 'I'll be right down,' he said to Leo, who nodded and went downstairs, pulling his jacket on. There was a pause as his footsteps died away, his cigar smoke still hanging faintly in the air.

'It really doesn't matter,' replied Camilla, and shrugged.

'No – well, I just had a bit too much to drink, and I'm – that is, anyway, I'm sorry. I should have got you a taxi.'

'You weren't really in much of a condition to do that,' said Camilla. 'Anyway, why don't you just forget it? Let's both just – forget it.' She gave a faint smile, raised her eyebrows, and went downstairs. Anthony stood uncertainly on the landing, kicking his foot against the banister. Oh, well, not quite as he had expected her to be. Her face hadn't worn that soulful, gormless look he was accustomed to seeing when she looked at him. Disillusioned, no doubt. He couldn't blame her. He went back into his room, picked up his robes, and slipped on his jacket, feeling vaguely and unaccountably annoyed.

Leo had gone straight over to the Law Courts without waiting for Anthony, and when Anthony slid into the seat next to him in Court Number 5, adjusting his wig and slightly out of breath, Leo turned to glance at him.

'You look a little the worse for wear,' he remarked. 'Sorry I couldn't wait, but I wanted to have a word with Dunstable before we started. Here, I got a copy of the judgment from Maurice yesterday evening. You'd already left.' He handed Anthony a thin sheaf of papers stapled together.

Anthony still had no idea of the contents of the judgment, and before he had a chance to ask Leo, everybody was rising to their feet and Sir Neville Graham, together with Lord Justices Manfred and Howell, trooped into court. Lord Justice Howell seated himself very gently, anxious to inflict as little sudden movement as possible on his throbbing head. He, too, had attended Grand Night the previous evening, and had enjoyed himself a little too well. Whereas he had originally been a little irked at having had to write this judgment without the concomitant pleasure of delivering it – for one naturally enjoyed the sound of one's own voice – he was now extremely glad that Sir Neville had taken that task upon himself. He leaned back against the leather padding of his chair and resisted the temptation to close his eyes. Instead he poured a large glass of water for himself from the jug which stood before him on the bench, and sipped at it gratefully.

The Master of the Rolls adjusted his spectacles and cleared his throat, then spoke in the grave, mellifluous tones which he himself very much liked. 'This is the judgment of the court in an appeal from an order of Mr Justice Fry which declared, pursuant to Order 14A of the Rules of the Supreme Court, that certain claims in tort by Lloyd's Names as members of Syndicate 1766 were statute-barred.

The losses occurred because the syndicate became liable to meet very large claims arising principally out of industrial pollution and the use of asbestos in the United States . . . ' There was, thought Sir Neville as he read, something decidedly inelegant about Bertrand Howell's way of expressing himself. Not that it was in any way ungrammatical, but the language was rather stark and unimaginative. It read baldly, like a schoolboy essay. Suppressing a sigh, he continued.

In his seat Anthony, his heart beating quickly, flicked discreetly through to the very last page of the judgment which Sir Neville was presently reading aloud, and fixed his eyes on the final sentence. *'We therefore allow the appeal, discharge the declarations made by the judge and make no orders on the defendants' summonses save as to costs.'* Anthony let out a breath of relief, and looked up. They had won. Thank God, he thought. Leo had been quite sanguine but he, Anthony, had had his doubts. The Names had taken another successful step along their long, litigious road. He could imagine the inexpressible relief this would bring to the likes of Freddie Hendry and Carstairs. To all of them. He glanced at Leo, whose expression was inscrutable, and then at the defendants' counsel sitting on the other side of the court. Their expressions, too, were entirely serene. No annoyance, disap- pointment, surprise or dismay at this judgment. Just another decision. It meant, for them and for the opposing solicitors, that the litigation continued, that the gravy train would still be running for some foreseeable time. No one, thought Anthony, gains anything from all of this except the lawyers. This is bonanza time for us. It's like belonging to some sort of satanic sect, where darkness and tragedy are causes for rejoicing. An oil tanker runs aground, a hurricane devastates coastal towns, a pharmaceutical company makes a disastrous mistake, the high and mighty of Lloyd's of London make gross errors of judgement and fail to ignore alarm bells, and we all swarm down, issuing our writs, settling our pleadings, setting our meters running and watching the pennies and pounds pile up. He sighed. He was only thinking in this way, he told himself, because he was hungover and fed up. If the sun were shining, if he hadn't got drunk last night, if he didn't feel ashamed and irritated with himself this morning, then he would be taking a less jaundiced view of himself and his profession. Like Lord Justice Howell, he resisted the urge to close his eyes and tried to concentrate on the words of Sir Neville.

The Master of the Rolls was himself having difficulty in concentrating on what he was saying, or in making sense of it. 'Likewise,' he read out with disbelief, 'Mr Justice Fry held that the Names had knowledge that they had suffered losses in consequence of the liabilities incurred on the reinsurances to close being substantially greater than the premiums fixed . . . ' Howell's way of putting things was so clumsy that he could scarcely understand half of what he was reading. He supposed he was fortunate that a lifetime of advocacy had given him the ability to say all kinds of things without knowing what he was talking about. It was certainly standing him in good stead at the moment, for he was aware from the sound of his own voice that he was speaking with confidence and authority. But 'likewise'! 'Likewise'? He himself would never have used so infelicitous an expression. But then Bertrand Howell was a grammar school product. Probably used to hang around coffee bars in his youth, where they said that sort of thing. The Master of the Rolls glanced up quickly at the clock as he read. Ten twenty. He promised himself that if the last page of this judgment finished on an even number, he would award himself one of those chocolate doughnuts with his coffee.

After judgment had been delivered, Anthony and Leo conferred cheerfully with Murray Campbell and Fred Fenton outside the courtroom.

'Well, onwards and upwards,' said Murray, hitching his trousers around his portly waist. 'That's the last hurdle before the big final stretch. I rang Basher Snodgrass last night and gave him the good news, so all the Names will know by now. I rather think that we'll have to arrange some kind of celebration. Just something low-key. Drinks and so forth, get them all around to the office one evening. Then we'll have to arrange a long session with the committee and discuss our long-term tactics.'

Two more opportunities to see Charles Beecham, thought Leo. He smiled to himself. Everybody present was focused on the litigation, keen to advance the interests of the Names, while he viewed the whole thing principally as the backdrop to a delightfully protracted seduction. There was no possibility of concluding anything with Charles Beecham while the litigation was still in progress. That would have to wait until the case was over. It gave the weeks ahead a certain drawn-out, tantalising charm. Not that he didn't regard the case itself as enormously important, both for himself and the Names. But work was now second nature with him. This merely added a little spice to the weeks of toil which lay ahead.

Afterwards, as he and Anthony had crossed the Strand together, Leo said, 'Drop your things off and come up to my room. We'll have to sort a few things out, lining up our expert witnesses, and so forth. Then I think we can treat ourselves to lunch at Luigi's, by way of celebration.' Anthony smiled and nodded. Any other day this would have been a delightful prospect. Still, perhaps by lunchtime he would be feeling a little better.

Certainly, after his first glass of wine he was. 'There's much truth in that "hair of the dog" thing,' he remarked to Leo, as they sat at a snug table in the rear of the little Italian restaurant.

'You mean you're using this quite excellent Chambertin merely as a means of topping up your alcohol level? I wouldn't have ordered it, if I'd known.'

'Oh, it's by no means unappreciated, I assure you,' replied Anthony. 'I don't think I'd better have too much more, though. I think I'll order some fizzy water as well. You want some?'

'No, thanks,' said Leo. He had finished his *osso bucco* and now leaned back, looking at Anthony. 'So, what were you up to last night?'

'Don't ask,' sighed Anthony. 'I went to Grand Night at Middle and, for some reason which I can't now fathom, got completely slaughtered.' This wasn't true, he reflected. He could fathom the reason only too well. He just hadn't had the time or the inclination since last night to address the matter of Sarah. She was a pretty poor reason to get drunk, he decided. That was all over now, in any event. He certainly wouldn't be seeing her again. He glanced up and met Leo's eye. Leo was looking at him speculatively, half-smiling.

'Was that why you were looking so sheep-faced when you were talking to Camilla this morning?' he hazarded.

'God, you don't miss a trick, do you?' said Anthony. He put his knife and fork together. The food here was excellent, and had cheered him up considerably, but he couldn't finish it. He signalled to the waiter and asked for some mineral water.

'I have known you for some years,' Leo reminded him. 'And that charming face of yours still gives a lot away.' There was a pause as Leo lit one of his cigars. His words brought back to Anthony the extraordinary intimacy of the first few months of their relationship. It seemed long ago and far away now, but little remarks like that still reverberated. Leo looked up from his cigar. 'So, may one know what indiscretion you perpetrated with Miss Lawrence while in your cups?'

Anthony groaned. 'No. It was all a horrible mistake. I can't bear to talk about it.'

Leo nodded. 'I wouldn't have thought she was quite your style,' he remarked, then added, 'Do you want anything else, or just coffee?'

'Just coffee, thanks,' said Anthony. He stared blankly at the tablecloth. 'No, she's not, as a matter of fact. Well . . . she's a very pleasant girl. I mean, she's quite good fun to be with, and so forth.' He suddenly thought of Sarah, and decided it might do him good to confide in Leo. He poured himself a glass of water, sipped it, and sighed. Leo sat regarding him, smoking, waiting. He could always tell when Anthony was about to tell him something. 'There's this girl I've been seeing,' said Anthony. 'Sarah. She's a student at Bar School. I've been going out with her for a few weeks now.' Leo suddenly remembered the blonde girl whom he had seen that night with Anthony, how she had seemed familiar, and a little chilly shaft of fear struck him.

'Sarah?' he said, his expression entirely unconcerned.

Anthony glanced up. 'Yes. Sarah Colman. Do you know her?'

Leo blew out some smoke, tapped the ash from the edge of his cigar. 'Now that you mention her surname – yes, I do. Vivian Colman's daughter, isn't she? I met her at some party of Sir Basil's last Christmas. Remember her quite well. Very pretty.' He hoped that his voice sounded as nonchalant as he endeavoured to make it. He had no intention of revealing to Anthony that Sarah had once shared his house and his bed for a whole summer, along with a most attractive, but – as it had turned out – dangerous young male friend of hers. That had been quite a summer. But, he thought regretfully, all that kind of thing was well in the past. The fact of Rachel had seen to that. He was not happy to hear that Anthony had fallen into the company of that particular young woman, however. He had a protective instinct where Anthony was concerned, and knew exactly what Sarah was capable of. Anthony might think himself grown up, worldly, but where the likes of Sarah were concerned, he was a mere babe.

'Anyway,' went on Anthony, 'I found out last night that she's been seeing someone else as well. Not a big deal, you might suppose – '

'You mean, she's been sleeping with someone else, as well?' interrupted Leo.

Anthony shrugged, vaguely embarrassed. 'That's what it amounts to. And letting all her friends know that she's been two-timing me.' How absurd that expression sounded, he thought, as he said it. It had an awkward, adolescent quality, but there was no other way of putting it. 'Some of them were in the mess next to ours at Middle last night – I'd taken up a spare ticket that Camilla had, you see – and they began to talk about it.' Anthony paused and had another drink of water.

'Rather poor taste,' remarked Leo. The waiter set their coffee in front of them.

'Oh, they had no idea who I was,' said Anthony. 'Camilla knew them, though. She and Sarah seem to be part of the same crowd. Apparently they were at Oxford together.'

Leo considered this, faintly surprised. From the little he had had to do with Camilla in chambers, she seemed to be a pleasant, frumpy girl, very sharp but rather eager to please, and certainly not Sarah's type at all. He drank a little of his wine and idly stirred sugar into his coffee. 'What happened after that?'

'Oh, I was . . . I was pretty hacked off, frankly. I mean, it doesn't do one's ego a lot of good . . . Anyway, I suppose I drank a bit too much, as one does.'

'As one does,' agreed Leo.

'And afterwards I recall behaving rather badly with our Miss Lawrence.' He sighed and raised his eyebrows, staring at his untouched coffee. 'Actually,' he added, 'she looked extremely nice last night. She'd made quite an effort.' Leo smiled faintly at the unconscious condescension of the younger man's remark. 'I think it was just my baser instincts coming to the surface.' He gave a brief, rueful laugh. 'But she's not the type to take it too well. You know.'

'Hmm. Given that she is wildly infatuated with you – or so chambers' gossip goes – it probably wasn't a very good move on your part.'

'God knows, it wasn't exactly calculated!' Anthony drank some of his coffee. It was hot and pleasantly bitter, and he immediately

118

felt better for it. 'So, naturally, I feel a bit of a fool this morning, and I also have to face the unpleasant fact that Sarah is not what I thought she was.'

'And what did you think she was?' asked Leo musingly, intrigued to know just which one of her many guises she had assumed in the seduction of poor Anthony.

'Well, I was beginning to wonder, actually. It was never going to go the distance, I knew that. We're too different.'

Leo saw his opportunity and seized it. There was potential danger to himself in Anthony's relationship with Sarah. She knew far too much about him for comfort, and if he could help to put any distance between Anthony and that young woman, he meant to do it. 'I'd get rid of her,' he said decisively, stubbing out the remains of his cigar, and lifting his gaze to meet Anthony's.

Anthony nodded. 'Oh, you're right. I've no intention of seeing her again.' Leo felt an instant relief. It was bad enough that Sarah was now part of their world, that next year she would become a barrister, and a constant, living threat to his peace of mind. On the other hand, he knew quite a few things about her, too, which she might not wish to be made public. 'I just sometimes wish,' Anthony went on, 'that I could see things coming. That I didn't keep on doing these appallingly stupid things. Like last night.'

'Oh, put it out of your mind,' said Leo easily, signalling to the waiter for the bill. 'It's probably all for the good. If it's put Miss Lawrence off you, that is. Your pride may suffer, but these chambers infatuations aren't good for the atmosphere, you know.' He suddenly recalled his own infatuation with Anthony years before, and smiled. What he had just said was perfectly true. 'Come on,' he added, 'finish that coffee and we'll get back to chambers. Time to start settling a few pleadings, I think.'

When the phone rang in his flat that evening and Anthony picked it up, his heart sank at the sound of Sarah's voice. He had not yet worked out quite how he was going to end things between them – he had half-hoped she might simply not call him again, and the whole thing would fade away, though he knew that was unrealistic – and had no idea what to say to her now.

'Hi,' she said, her voice cheerful, languid. 'I wondered what you were up to this evening. Whether you wanted some company.'

'Ah – no, I don't think so, thanks.' He hesitated. 'Actually, we won our time-bar point, so we've got the full hearing coming up in a couple of months' time. There's quite a lot of work we have to do before then.' It sounded lame, he knew.

'Hmm. You and your precious Leo.' When she said this, Anthony immediately remembered what Leo had said at lunchtime, that he knew Sarah, had met her at Sir Basil's.

'By the way,' he said suddenly, 'why didn't you tell me that you knew Leo?'

There was a pause, and then Sarah, her voice sharpening slightly, replied, 'I didn't know I did.' She rose from the armchair in which she'd been sitting and paced across the room, holding the telephone, waiting. What the hell had Leo told Anthony? She felt her heartbeat quicken.

'Apparently you met him at a party given by our head of chambers last Christmas.' Anthony wondered why he was bothering with this. It was quite irrelevant to what he really had to say.

Sarah gave an artificial yawn. 'Oh, did I? I went to so many parties and met so many people, I honestly don't remember.' She wondered whether Anthony believed this, or whether he appreciated how unlikely it was that any woman should forget meeting the charismatic and attractive Leo Davies.

But Anthony was too concerned with other matters to give it much thought. 'Anyway, as I say, I'm probably going to be busy with this case most evenings – '

She switched her attention to the evasive, faintly pompous tone in Anthony's voice. 'What on earth's up?' she demanded. 'You don't exactly sound very friendly. What have I done?' Had Leo told Anthony more than he was letting on?

'Look – ' Anthony paused, trying to think how to put it. Sarah waited, tense. At last he said, 'I found out – and you needn't ask how – that you're seeing someone else. Someone called Ferguson. And, frankly, I don't like being messed about with. Or talked about. So I think we'd better call it a day.'

She felt a lurch of fear and anger. She had never intended to let him find out. Who on earth had told him? No matter – he knew now, and he was giving her the push. The realisation appalled her. No – if a relationship was to end, she was the one who ended it. Nobody dumped her. Not Sarah Colman. Her mind veered quickly between the various tactics which she could adopt, and she opted for dismissive nonchalance. She laughed. 'Oh, come on! Who's been spinning you lines? I haven't been seeing anyone else. Rollo Ferguson is just a chum, there's nothing going on.'

Anthony sighed. He had learned enough about her to guess when and why she might be lying, and although he knew she might be telling the truth, he chose not to believe her. It was simpler, in the long run. This thing was going nowhere, anyway, and this was as good an excuse to end it as any. And when he cast his mind back to what those people had said last night, there was little doubt that it was true.

'I'm sorry,' he said. 'Whatever you say makes no difference. I think it's about time we called it a day.'

His tone was so colourless, so final, that Sarah knew better than to put up any more resistance. The last thing she was going to do was abase herself. But she was as human as anyone else, for all her petty deceits and hard little ways, and she felt a pang at the thought of losing Anthony, whom she genuinely liked. He was amusing, good-looking, and he spent more money on her than Rollo Ferguson ever did. But this brief sense of loss was swiftly eclipsed by the anger she felt at his rejection of her.

'Fine,' she said simply, coldly. 'I'll see you around.'

Anthony heard the click as the line went dead, and stood holding the receiver for a few seconds before replacing it. He recalled with regret the pleasant, languorous hours of their lovemaking. That was at an end, now. But it was probably all he would ever remember about the relationship. He was, he realised, relieved at the thought that he wouldn't have to have any more to do with her.

But for Sarah, as she sat staring fixedly at the blackness of the night beyond the window, it was not so simple. He had made her feel humiliated, had done something no one else had ever done, not even Leo, and she certainly had no intention of letting it pass, just like that. Not until she had exacted a little revenge.

Chapter Eleven

'Congratulations.'

Fred Fenton looked up and saw Rachel standing smiling in the doorway of his room. The frown of concentration on his face cleared and he sat back, pushing away the papers in front of him.

'Thanks.' He grinned at her, thinking how immaculate she looked in her grey suit and pink silk blouse. Always beautiful, always unruffled. 'Actually, your husband did most of the work.'

She raised her eyebrows, coming into the room and sitting down in the chair opposite Fred's desk. 'He certainly spends enough time working late in chambers, or locked away in his study.' There was a pause, in which she looked away awkwardly. The things one said ... She supposed everyone thought that her home life must be bliss, the happy couple in their first year of marriage, with their baby son, their carefree existence. She smiled at Fred. 'Anyway, why don't you let me take you out for a drink and a sandwich at lunchtime to celebrate? I feel like a break from these boring Japanese.'

'Great,' said Fred. 'Actually, I've got more than just one thing to celebrate.' He hesitated momentarily. 'I might as well tell you ... everyone will know sooner or later, when it's official.'

'What – you're not getting engaged at long last, are you?'

Fred laughed and shook his head. 'No, though this might help in that direction. Actually, they've made me a partner.'

'Fred, that's great! Well done!' Rachel was genuinely pleased for Fred. He was not a spectacular lawyer, but he was a grafter, and clients liked his unassuming manner, his quiet efficiency.

'Not equity, mind – just salaried.'

'Same as me,' said Rachel. 'Hmm. Maybe they'll give us a slice of their profits one day, if they think we deserve it.'

'One can dream. But I'm happy enough with this. I was beginning to wonder, slogging away for this lot, whether it was ever going to happen. Frankly – ' Fred glanced in the direction of the open door and lowered his voice slightly. ' – the difference between the forty-five thousand I was earning, and the sixty-five I'll be getting at the end of the month is pretty crucial. Linda wants us to sell the flat and put down a mortgage on a house.'

Rachel tried not to show her surprise. 'Sixty-five – that's what they're paying you?'

'Yup.' From the look on Rachel's face, Fred knew instantly that he had made a mistake in mentioning the money, that they had strayed into that landmine territory of salaries. The way she'd asked the question meant that Rachel must be earning less than they were offering him. Yet she'd been made a partner when she joined the firm, a whole year ago. Still, he told himself, watching her with faint embarrassment as she digested this information, what did Rachel have to worry about? Leo must be making a complete fortune. Fred knew only too well how much he was getting for the Capstall case, with his daily refresher on top. Nichols & Co probably realised that blokes needed to be paid more. And Rachel would no doubt be swanning off in another few months to have another baby. Still, it might be better if he didn't mention that he was getting a car as well. After a pause of several seconds he said, 'Anyway, since I've got two causes for celebration, I'll be buying at lunchtime. Do you want to make it just us two, or shall I see if Murray's free?'

Rachel had originally intended that she and Fred would lunch alone – Fred was easygoing, amusing, and she needed the lift to her spirits which he always gave her – but in the light of what he'd just told her, it might be awkward. 'No – ask Murray, by all means.' She glanced down at her hands, then looked up again and smiled. 'I'd better let you get on.'

'Sure. See you about one.'

She closed Fred's door behind her and walked slowly back to her own room. She knew that if it hadn't been for the fact that she and Fred were good friends, she'd never have found out. Naturally Rothwell and the rest of them never intended that she should know – know that they put her value below Fred's, and probably any other male partner. What was eight thousand, anyway? She'd been happy to earn fifty-seven thousand a year. It was a good salary, and since she had married Leo she hardly thought about money, anyway. Until recently.

She sat down at her desk, clasping her hands together and resting her chin on them. That had been the whole point of coming back to work. To regain her independence. After all, the day might come when she and Oliver were on their own. The very acknowledgement of such a possibility caused her to bury her face in her hands. Just a year ago, such a notion had been the furthest thing from her mind, and now the pain that it evinced was almost physical. When she had married Leo, she had been very happy. She had meant it all. She loved him, they were going to be together for the rest of their lives. But their lives, in just a few short months, were already far apart. Reality – both present and possible – had to be faced. The day might come when maximising her earnings was crucial to herself and Oliver. Learning that Fred was to be paid more than her had momentarily shaken her confidence, but she had to be hard-headed about this. She had returned to work to regain a life of her own and she wasn't bloody well going to be sidelined by Rothwell and the rest of those chauvinists. In fact, while she was thinking about it, what was the point in merely demanding to be put on a par with Fred? She had been made a partner a year ahead of him. She was worth a few thousand extra on that basis alone. Rachel lifted the phone and made the brief internal call, asking Mr Rothwell if he could find fifteen minutes for her at the end of the afternoon, as there was a personal matter which she wished to discuss with him.

'No,' said Leo. 'Let's do this with a bit of style. Take a set of private rooms in Upper Brook Street. Much better than your offices. After all, it is Christmas in a couple of weeks. I know an excellent firm of private caterers who can lay on something simple, guarantee us some decent wine.'

Murray raised his eyebrows. Did Leo think Nichols & Co were made of money? Oh, well, in the interests of servicing the clients, he supposed they might as well do it properly. The idea of a drinks party here in the office was a bit basic. He sighed. 'I suppose you're right. There'll be more than just the committee coming, anyway, so we'll need some space.'

'Good. I don't know about your diary, but Friday looks good for Anthony and myself. Have a word with Basher and see what he and the rest of them think.'

When he had put down the phone, Leo swivelled in his chair and gazed out of the window. It was late afternoon and already growing dark. Lamps glimmered throughout the Temple and a chilly winter haze had descended over the river and the Embankment. He gazed at the shirtsleeved figures moving about in the brightly lit rooms of the chambers opposite and deliberated whether or not to seek out Michael and go for a drink. No, he should really go home. He had spent too many evenings working late, using this case as an excuse. It wasn't fair to Rachel. But then, nothing was fair to Rachel. He had very little idea, these days, of what she felt about anything. After he had told her about Francis, he had expected – had half-hoped for – some confrontation, some decisive change in their ill-matched lives. But none had come. Perhaps, when he had told her that the affair with Francis was over, she had assumed that things would get better. No – she couldn't possibly believe that. The manner in which they behaved to one another, the uneasy small-talk and the refuge they sought in domestic trivia, was such a sham. The deadness of their condition together was constant, unacknowledged. But there was Oliver, too. Sometimes the thought of Oliver – Oliver damp and clover-smelling from sleep, small and aggressively alive, darting his looks and smiles at the world – touched him more deeply than anything else he had ever known. But he was baffled by the fact of his son, uncertain what to do for him, about him. He could not see a future in which he and Rachel brought the boy up together, but he could not imagine being without him. Did the way he felt have something to do with the absence of his own father throughout his life? He supposed it must, inevitably.

Leo sighed and turned back round to his desk. Whatever might happen to the three of them was, he felt, beyond his control. They would just have to see how matters developed. Much depended on Rachel, he realised, and on what she decided to do. He himself felt inert. It was just a question of waiting for Rachel to do something.

James Rothwell sat behind the safety of his large desk and eyed Rachel uneasily. He was a tall, well-built man in his late fifties, one of those lawyers who owed more to circumstance and a run of successful cases early in his career than to any special talent. He had become senior partner of Nichols & Co by default rather than particular ability, and had been careful, over the last ten years, to surround himself with a group of young, aggressive partners, members of the new breed of solicitor, more ruthless and greedy than he himself had ever been. They were the strength of Nichols & Co. Not that he was lazy or cowardly, but he preferred to leave the hard-nosed business to them. He had become a solicitor in those not-so-distant days when women were a rarity in the City and, despite the fact that women presently accounted for more than half of the new recruits in the ranks of solicitors, he still tended to regard them as lightweight, unlikely to go the distance. He had been happy, when Rachel Dean had joined the firm over a year ago, to make her a salaried partner. All the other firms in the City had plenty of them. She was extremely good at her job, too. But he had no long-term expectations of her. She was far too beautiful, if rather reserved, to stay single for long, and he hadn't been in the least surprised when she had married and left to have a baby. What *had* surprised him was the fact that she had come back. Why any woman with a husband who earned as much as Leo Davies did should want to graft away from nine to five when she could be at home lunching and playing tennis with other well-heeled wives was quite beyond him. Still, there she was, sitting on the edge of her chair with a set, formal look on her face which told him that some sort of confrontation was coming. He felt unhappy at the prospect. James Rothwell wanted nothing more than an easy life, really.

'So, here we are, then. Now, what was it you wanted to talk about?' he asked, smiling and settling back in his seat, trying to look avuncular.

Rachel did not smile back, but merely glanced down at her hands, which were folded in her lap, and then looked up at him again. 'I wanted to know why there is apparently a disparity between my salary and that of someone like Fred Fenton,' she said. 'I want to know why, as a partner, he is to be paid more than I am.' Then she did smile, briefly, enquiringly.

Mr Rothwell took a slow breath and swivelled his chair rapidly from side to side. 'I – ah – I thought you understood, Rachel, that it is not the firm's policy for members of staff to discuss salaries.' He knew this was a poor stalling tactic, but could think of nothing else to say immediately.

Rachel gave another small, dismissive smile. 'That's really

neither here nor there. The point is, why should I be paid less than Fred?'

Mr Rothwell took another breath and was about to speak when the door opened and John Parr looked in. Mr Rothwell glanced up at him with relief. If there was anyone who could handle this kind of thing, it was John.

Mr Rothwell smiled and motioned him in. 'John, do come in. I think perhaps you can help here.'

Rachel glanced up at John Parr. He was a thin, humourless man in his mid-forties, the least liked of the partners, with a tenacious, unbending character which gave him a reputation amongst other solicitors as a formidable negotiator. Rachel didn't welcome his involvement in the discussion.

As John Parr paced slowly across the room, glancing enquiringly at Rachel and then at his senior partner, Mr Rothwell went on, 'Rachel has come to me with a query regarding the disparity in her salary with that of Fred Fenton's.' He clearly expected John Parr to take over, and was not disappointed. Parr rested himself easily against the window-sill and folded his arms.

'I don't quite see what the issue is,' he lied, frowning in mild puzzlement.

'The issue is,' said Rachel, feeling her heartbeat quicken at the new, antagonistic element which Parr's presence brought to the discussion, 'why you should imagine I am worth less than Fred. I have been a partner for a year now, and yet I understand that you propose to pay him eight thousand a year more than myself.' No matter how she put it, Rachel realised, she sounded like a child complaining that she had been given fewer sweets than another. That was what John Parr's faintly patronising look made her feel, at any rate.

'Well, that's quite simply explained,' replied John Parr easily, as though he couldn't see what the fuss was about. 'We naturally expect more of Fred in terms of commitment and responsibility. I would have thought that was obvious.'

James Rothwell nodded at this, as though he himself would have said exactly the same thing.

Rachel glanced from one man's face to the other. 'Commitment and responsibility? I don't think I quite understand. Are you suggesting that Fred somehow works harder than I do, that he gives more to the clients than I do?' She tried hard to keep the anger from her voice.

Parr laughed and eased himself from the window-sill, pacing slowly round the room. Rachel felt at a disadvantage having to look up at him from where she sat.

'No, of course not. We all regard your work very highly.'

'But you don't seem to value it in the same way,' retorted Rachel quickly.

John Parr sighed. 'The fact is, we expect someone like Fred to give much more than you – we expect him to make himself available in a way that we wouldn't necessarily expect of you. To work late, to take calls in the middle of the night, to be prepared to go abroad at short notice for varying spells of time. You know the kind of thing.'

'But I'm just as prepared as he is to do any of those things,' protested Rachel.

'Well, come now. We appreciate that you have certain domestic ties, we hardly expect you to do any of those things any more.' The tone of his voice was now so overtly patronising that Rachel could hardly control her temper. She allowed it to cool for a few seconds before replying.

'You're actually saying that, because I am married with a child, that I am worth less to you?'

'I'd hardly put it that way. But some people would accuse us of having no sympathy with the problems which working women with families face, if we failed to take regard of your domestic position.'

'But I work just as hard as Fred, I shoulder just as much responsibility as Fred!' She turned to James Rothwell. 'What about those new Japanese clients that I've just taken on? They must be worth quite a bit to the firm.'

There was a pause, and then Mr Rothwell said quietly, 'You may have forgotten, Rachel, but you yourself pointed out, only two weeks ago, that you couldn't be expected to have evening meetings with those very clients. You have to leave at five thirty to get home to your baby. That's what you said.'

Rachel was at a loss to reply.

'My very point, you see,' said John Parr easily. 'Fred wouldn't have got his partnership if he insisted on leaving on the dot every evening.'

There was a silence, then Rachel took a deep breath and glanced at each man in turn. 'I can promise you that I don't intend to let this

128

rest,' she said, rising from her chair. 'You may feel that you have arguments justifying your inequitable treatment of me, but I regard it as sheer sexism.'

John Parr sighed the smug sigh of one who has had the best of an argument. 'You can call it that if you like, but we have to take due account of the amount of time and commitment which staff are prepared to give us.'

Mr Rothwell tried to smooth out matters by interjecting quickly, 'Your salary is due for review in the new year, in any event. I'm sure we can sort something out.'

Rachel looked at the two men, acutely conscious of her own femininity, their masculinity, the vague sense of threat which, despite the moderate, civilised tone of the discussion, seemed to fill the air. Was she, because of her past, sensitised to it in a way which other women were not? She felt a return of the feeling of powerlessness which so often used to strike her in the company of men, the feeling of which Leo had cured her. But there was no Leo now. She could think of nothing to say. She turned and left the room, closing the door quietly behind her.

James Rothwell sat back in his chair and let out a deep breath. 'Just as well she doesn't seem to know about Fenton's car, as well,' he murmured.

That evening Freddie put down the telephone and rubbed his hands, smiling. He rubbed them at the happy thought of the little celebration which was being arranged by Nichols & Co for next Tuesday, and also because it was damned cold in the flat. He didn't like to run the heating too much, what with the cost and so on. Had to watch the pennies these days. That TV licence had been a bit of a shocker. They should let old people off that kind of thing. He must look into the business of paying by stamps that the girl in the post office had mentioned. No matter how carefully he budgeted for his rent and food, the money never seemed to stretch. Somehow that extra bottle of Scotch always crept into the equation. He tried to make a whole one last a week, but it never did. One had to have one's little comforts. He blew on the shiny, purplish skin of his long fingers and went through to the kitchen to boil the kettle. Bit of that instant mashed potato stuff that he'd recently discovered. That would go nicely with one of those little tins of ravioli. Freddie tried not to think of the meals which he and Dorothy used to enjoy in the evenings as a matter of course. She'd been a damned good cook, always proud of her when they gave dinner parties. That game casserole of hers, the pork thing with apples and cream, steak Diane. His favourite had been that one with chicken breasts and asparagus sauce. No one could cook like Dorothy. And they'd had all those fresh vegetables from the garden. New potatoes sweet as nuts, all glistening with melted butter . . .

Freddie slopped the boiling water carefully into the dried heap of instant potato and stirred it with a fork, marvelling at the way in which the granules metamorphosed into a sludgy consistency in an instant. As he stirred he kept a careful eye on the pan containing the ravioli which was heating on the gas stove, bubbling lightly at the edges. He fetched a plate and emptied the ravioli on to it, and spooned the watery potato mess out next to it. Then he uncapped the bottle of White Horse – only a few inches left, must remember to pick up some more tomorrow – and poured a careful double measure into a glass, then added a little cold water. He took his plate, knife and fork, and watered whisky through to the living room and set them on the little table next to his armchair, near to the fax machine. The news of the little celebratory party in Upper Brook Street had quite set him up. There would be decent food, no doubt, plenty to drink, and the added pleasure of talking for as long as he liked about his pet subject, Lloyd's. It was something they all talked about, incessantly, never tiring of it. And it would be so civilised, counsel and solicitors being polite and attentive, nodding and agreeing, listening, allowing one the illusion that one was still well-heeled, that things were still sound and investments profitable. An evening like that was something to look forward to, Freddie told himself, as he dug into his ravioli and instant potato. In fact, it had so cheered him up that he decided he wouldn't watch television tonight. That little bit of reminiscing in the kitchen had been pleasant. It wasn't often that he felt robust enough to think for long about Dorothy, but this evening he would. When he finished his meal, he would have just another little tot of whisky and sit and think about her.

In the cramped dining room of their semi, Alison Carstairs was clearing away the plates from the evening meal. She clattered the unused cutlery from one place-setting back into the drawer and turned to gaze stupidly out at the dark blankness of the window, wondering where Paul was. Half the time now he came in from school, changed, and then went out again, never bothering to return for dinner. She didn't know who he hung around with, but she had a good idea. Last week, when she had challenged him about the amount of time he spent with those louts from the estate, he had simply looked at her sullenly and said, 'First of all you get worried that I'm not making friends at school, and then when I do you don't like them. I can't win, can I?' And he had banged out of the house. Of course she wanted him to have friends, but not those friends. She thought with a wrenching despair of those nice boys at Paul's old private school, and that special friend of his, Wright, with whom he'd gone skiing the winter before last. Skiing holidays were a thing of the past. So were the holidays which they spent each summer at the villa in Tuscany. Paul used to enjoy practising his Italian on the locals. He didn't take Italian now; they didn't do it at the comprehensive. She had a sudden vivid, flashing recollection of Paul and Sophie and Anna, sun-tanned, laughing, splashing about in the pool at the villa. Who splashed there each summer now? she wondered. She sighed again. She and Lucy Wright had been quite good friends, too. They had just been getting to know each other, playing the odd game of tennis at the club, in the months before Lloyd's had taken its devastating toll.

She turned on the tap at the sink in the kitchen, watching the water creep up the sides of the metal basin as she squirted the Co-op economy washing-up liquid into it, and remembered herself. It was not so very long ago, just over a year, and yet it was like looking at a picture of a different woman. She saw herself playing tennis with Lucy Wright, confident, poised, her skin lightly tanned from idle hours on the sunbed, her body elastic and shapely from sessions in the private gym. They had lunched together afterwards on the club veranda, Alison with her white sweater flung carelessly over her shoulders, sitting at a little round table under a green canvas umbrella drinking white wine spritzers, eating avocado and Parma ham salads which had cost twice what she spent in two days on food for the whole family now. They had thought nothing of the cost, just handed over the gold credit cards, laughed in the sunshine. Alison picked up the plates and dipped them into the sudsy water. She supposed Lucy Wright still laughed in the sunshine. The sunshine of a full bank balance, of children happy at their private schools, of a husband who still brought in substantial sums of money to support their easy lifestyle, to buy the holidays in the Caribbean, the cases of wine, the foccacia bread, the tiramisu, the riding lessons, the tennis club subscriptions. Yes, Lucy could still laugh. Alison had seen her in the village last week, as immaculately dressed as ever, the way Alison had once dressed, those stylish, expensive clothes from the chic, overpriced boutiques that she never went into now. But Lucy had been wearing her sunglasses – she still belonged to that breed of women who wore their sunglasses on a winter's day – and had not seen Alison. Or had seemed not to.

Brian Carstairs came into the kitchen and switched on the kettle. He said nothing. He rarely said anything these days, and when he did it was to do with Lloyd's. Alison could not stand to hear the name any more. She could barely look at her husband when he started to talk about this action, the possibility that they would win, that they would deal Lloyd's a telling blow and maybe recover something. As though anything he did or said would change things back to the way they had been. But it seemed to give him a reason for existing. He was obsessed with the litigation. She glanced sideways as he took a teabag from the box, thinking how thin his hands looked. Thin and nervous, red and sore at the ends from where he picked the skin. She hated the sight of them. Shall I mention Paul to him? she wondered, and then felt a heavy lump of despair settle in her stomach. There was no point. He could do nothing, he didn't even care. He had retreated. They had all retreated from one another, they had let this wretched little house, the loss of all their money and precious possessions divide them, wreck their happy little family. It need not be like this, Alison thought. Other families lived on less and were happy. But then, those families knew nothing else. She watched her husband make his tea and leave the kitchen without saying a word. Then she pulled the plug from the sink, watched the scummy water run away, and fetched a cloth to dry the dishes.

When Rachel got home, Jennifer was wiping down Oliver's high chair. The two women smiled and murmured 'Hello' to one another, and Jennifer told Rachel that Oliver had fallen asleep straight after his bath. Not even the solace of a cuddle with my baby, thought Rachel, as she opened the fridge and stared at the contents, trying to think of something to make for supper for herself and Leo. She took out some chicken which had reached its sell-by date and tried to think what to do with it. Her brain felt dead, her soul shrivelled up by this afternoon's humiliating confrontation with Rothwell and Parr. She looked up from the chicken and watched as Jennifer rinsed Oliver's bowl and spoon and placed them in the dishwasher, then bundled up the clothes which he had worn during the day and put them into the washing machine. All her movements were brisk and efficient, springy with youth. A nice job, being a nanny, thought Rachel. The kind of job which would make you feel competent, needed, not reduce you to a quivering mass of insecurity and anxiety. Maybe that was what she should do. Stay at home and look after Oliver. And what then? More insecurity, more anxiety – the kind that led to a nervous breakdown. She'd had one of those before. No thanks. She picked up the chicken and put it back into the fridge. If Leo wanted supper, he could make it himself. She wasn't hungry.

'Right,' said Jennifer brightly. 'I've left a bottle in the fridge for his ten o'clock feed. Oh, and I'll need a couple of quid to pay for the playgroup tomorrow. The kitty's run out.'

'I'll leave some money out, don't worry,' said Rachel.

'Thanks. And is it all right if I take your car tonight? Only I was going to go out with some friends after I've been to the gym.'

Rachel nodded. 'Keys are on the hall table. Have a nice time,' she added. She stood perfectly still in the kitchen, listened to Jennifer going up to her room to get her gym kit, heard her feet coming back down, the gentle slamming of the front door, the sound of the car engine. The house was utterly silent. Rachel left the kitchen and went upstairs to Oliver's room, which was on the landing opposite the bathroom. He had a nightlight, a sort of globe which revolved slowly and threw dim patterns of stars and crescents on to the wall of his room. The air smelt of Johnson's powder. Rachel went over to his cot and looked down at him as he slept, his small chest rising and falling rhythmically, his lips parted. He was wearing a white sleepsuit with blue and green rabbits on it, and as she gazed at him Rachel traced in her mind all the steps which she had not taken, the bath which she had not run, the laughing and splashing she had not heard, the soft skin she had not washed and patted dry. Jennifer had put his sleepsuit on him, had blown into his blond curls as she fastened the poppers, had felt his fat hands on her neck as she lifted him up and put him into his cot. She had said 'night

133

night' to him. Rachel's hands slid down the bars of his cot as she knelt down on the floor, pressing her head against the white painted wood. She closed her eyes. She had no idea what she was to make of her life. What was she, after all? She was not Leo's wife – that was a sham, a joke. Rothwell and Parr had made it clear that she was very much in the second division when it came to being a solicitor. What hope was there of advancement, of making progress in her job, when faced with men like that? And as for being a mother – she wasn't that, either. She didn't know what Oliver did during his day, she didn't watch him play, she didn't bath him or shop with him, or feed the ducks with him. She paid someone else to do that. Overcome by weariness and loneliness, she leaned against Oliver's cot and wept and wept, softly so as not to wake him, feeling as though her body and mind were being drained by unhappiness.

She did not hear the front door close downstairs, nor Leo's feet on the stairs. He paused outside Oliver's room and heard the faint sounds of Rachel's sobs. Hesitating, he pushed the door slightly further open with the tip of one finger and stood there, the dim glow from Oliver's nightlight silvering his hair. He saw Rachel crumpled up beside the cot, her dark head bent, saw her body shaking with crying. He watched her for a few seconds and wished he could find within himself the approximation of love which he had once felt for her, wished he could go and hold her, make it better. Then he turned away, retraced his steps and went back downstairs. Rachel heard his footsteps as he went into the kitchen and lifted her head, knowing immediately that he had been there, that he had seen her crying and had gone away. Downstairs Leo opened the fridge and stared at its contents for a moment, then took out the pieces of chicken and put them on the table.

Chapter Twelve

'I know it's unorthodox,' said Jeremy, 'but the fact is, I'm going to be in Indonesia for two months. I've already spoken to Cameron about it, and, frankly, it seems like you're the only person available to take her on. Besides, you could probably do with another pair of hands on this Capstall thing.'

Anthony stared at Jeremy Vine in dismay. 'But I don't want a pupil. Anyway, she's *your* pupil.'

'Well, I'm not much good to her when I'm on the other side of the world, am I?' rejoined Jeremy irritably.

'Can't Julian have her? Or David?'

'Julian's too junior and David is far too busy. I'm afraid you'll just have to lump it.'

'But there's hardly room in here for another person!' The idea of Camilla sitting opposite him all day while he worked was pretty appalling. No doubt she didn't fancy it much, either.

'Bags of space,' said Jeremy, glancing around. 'Henry says he'll have it sorted out by tomorrow.'

'But what does Camilla think about it?' Anthony couldn't believe she had simply accepted the idea of being moved from Jeremy to Anthony, just like that.

'Not exactly ecstatic, but then she doesn't have much choice. Nor do you. Anyway, my flight's at nine this evening, so she'll be all yours as from tomorrow morning.' Anthony sighed and slumped back in his chair as Jeremy breezed self-importantly from the room. What a way to start Monday. He was still staring with vacant gloom at his desk when Leo came in.

'Right,' he said, slapping a piece of paper down in front of Anthony. 'Actuarial experts, auditors' experts, US law experts, claims experts, marketing claims experts, and underwriting experts. We need to find one of each and get statements from them.' He sat down opposite Anthony and smiled at him. Anthony was grateful for the smile, grateful for the charming familiarity of Leo's face and the pleasure it always gave him.

'Guess what?'

'What?' Leo slid the little mat which Anthony used for his coffee to the edge of the table and flipped it into the air with his fingers, then caught it deftly.

'I've got a pupil. Starting tomorrow.'

'What? Don't be absurd! You can't take on a pupil right in the middle of a case like this – '

'It's Camilla,' interrupted Anthony. 'Jeremy's Indonesian case is so mightily important that it appears he has to move his practice to Indonesia, more or less, and he and Cameron have decided that I should take over Camilla.'

'Well, she could be useful, I suppose,' said Leo, and got to his feet. He chucked the mat on to Anthony's desk. 'I think that's very funny, actually,' he said. Anthony stared at him morosely. 'Very funny indeed.' And Leo left the room, chuckling.

Felicity was quite pleased with herself. It was she who, when Cameron Renshaw had stood grumbling in reception at the prospect of having to find a billet for Jeremy's orphan pupil, had suggested Anthony. He had been going to pass her on to David Liphook until she had told Cameron that David had too much work, and had pointed out that Anthony could do with an extra pair of hands in the Names case. So now Camilla and Anthony would be constantly in one another's company, and if that didn't do the trick, she didn't know what would. Camilla had already taken a few tips from her and had managed to sort herself out some decent work clothes, things that at least made her look female. And Felicity had made an appointment for her the previous week at her hairdresser's near Ludgate Circus, so that now her hair had been cut into a pretty, manageable shape, and didn't look as though rats had nested in it. Altogether a change for the better, thought Felicity, glancing with satisfaction at Camilla as she came into the clerks' room.

'You look nice,' she remarked.

Camilla didn't smile. She felt that she could murder the person whose idea this was. If they had made her anybody's pupil except

Anthony's, she wouldn't have minded. It would be a relief not to have to work for Jeremy any more. But of all the people in chambers . . . 'I suppose you've heard?' she muttered.

'Mmm?' Felicity widened her eyes enquiringly and glanced back at the morning's mail.

'I'm working for Anthony now. They've made me his pupil, because Jeremy's going off to Indonesia for a few months.'

'Well, then, that's nice, isn't it? You'll be able to sort out your differences.'

Camilla sighed and turned away, and bumped straight into Anthony as he came into the room. She backed off and they both looked embarrassed. They had scarcely spoken since the morning after their disastrous evening together.

'Camilla – just the person,' said Anthony quickly. 'I've got someone from Cray Leveson coming round any minute now, but I've just got to dash over to Dunstable's chambers. Can you take this chap upstairs and give him a cup of coffee, that kind of thing? His name's Evans. I won't be five minutes.' And Anthony strode out of chambers and hurried across Caper Court.

Camilla sat listening as Anthony and Mr Evans, an actuarial expert, talked for two hours. She took the occasional note, but had ample leisure to sit pondering the erstwhile object of her affections and considering her own feelings about him. She still regarded him as a most attractive man, she liked his smile and the deceptive innocence of his glance, but she no longer felt that heart-stopping sense of embarrassed inferiority in his presence. She had seen Anthony at his worst – well, in a pretty bad way – and that experience had dispelled her illusions, killed her infatuation. A pity, really. Crushes of one sort or another had always been her emotional mainstay, and she felt a bit lost without one. Still, if she was to be his pupil until summer, it was probably just as well. A schoolgirl crush was not much of a basis for a working relationship, and since she badly wanted to do well at 5 Caper Court, she was probably better off without any distractions.

Anthony regarded the thing in a slightly different light. When Jeremy had dropped his bombshell the previous evening, Anthony had consoled himself with the thought that at least Camilla seemed to have cured herself of her dogged devotion to him, and so working with her wouldn't be too tiresome or embarrassing. On the other hand, after Mr Evans had left and they sat working

137

together in silence, he was aware of feeling peeved by her new, slightly offhand manner. How could any girl be totally infatuated with him one day, and then behave as though he was hardly there the next? Well, he supposed he knew the answer to that, given the dimly recollected events of two weeks ago, but he felt it showed that she was rather unnaturally erratic in her affections. Then he became annoyed by this train of thought and told himself that it shouldn't matter to him one way or the other how she regarded him. She was only a pupil, after all. He should merely be glad that she'd started to dress a bit better, and had had her hair cut decently. She really looked quite pretty today, he thought, as he watched her writing, leaning her head on one hand. She looked up from her work, and he expected her to glance in his direction. But her gaze strayed no further than the law report a little further up her desk. It suddenly occurred to him that he wanted her attention, and so he said, 'By the way, are you busy this evening?'

She glanced up warily, and he realised, to his chagrin, that she assumed he was going to ask her out. Evidently this was not an idea she welcomed. Annoyed, he went on, 'The only reason I ask is because the committee and some of the Names are having a bit of a party – well, no, party's not quite the word – a sort of private celebration over winning the time-bar point. It's this evening at some place in Upper Brook Street. Might be an idea if you came along.'

She glanced away from him and tapped her lips with her pencil, then shrugged. 'Maybe.'

Her casual manner irritated him even more, and he found himself adding pompously, 'You might show a little more enthusiasm. If you're going to become seriously involved in this case, you should want to make a point of meeting some of the people, I would have thought.'

She did not blush or look distraught, as she would have a few weeks ago. Her gaze shifted casually from the window back to him. 'Sorry. I didn't realise it mattered if I went or not. But I'll have to see, anyway. I'll try to be there if I can. Give me the address at the end of the day.' She closed her books and glanced at her watch. 'Mind if I go to lunch now?'

'No, off you go,' said Anthony. He bent his head over his work again, then lifted it as soon as she was gone. God, how arrogant that had sounded. 'Off you go'. Like dismissing a class. She must think him a complete berk. Maybe it was something infectious which he'd caught off Jeremy.

Rachel sat at her desk at the end of the afternoon, signing letters for the evening post, feeling better than she had done the day before. She thought of how she had wept helplessly by Oliver's cot for twenty minutes last night. Maybe there was something cathartic about crying. It seemed to cleanse the spirit. She felt less bowed down by depression and uncertainty. She had even managed, after splashing her face and eyes with cold water, to go downstairs and have a fairly civilised conversation with Leo afterwards. That she had been weeping, that he had witnessed her unhappiness and had failed even to speak to her, was not touched upon. But then, so much between them was never touched upon. No, that hadn't mattered. She had grown used to dissembling, to adopting a pretence of normality. Leo had turned the chicken and some vegetables into a rather appetising stir-fry and they had eaten it together with a glass of wine. She had not told him about her conversation with James Rothwell and John Parr. She had decided to put the matter of her salary in abeyance for the moment, until she could find out what kind of formal steps she could take. Instead they had talked about Fred's partnership, and from there the conversation had led to the Capstall case, and to the party that was being thrown this evening for the Names. Leo had suggested that she should come along. She had said then that she probably wouldn't, that she would rather go home and see Oliver, but now, as she signed the last letter and capped her pen, she decided that she would look in for half an hour or so. A few drinks, some conversation with new faces, might help to sustain her in her attempt to behave like a normal, sane person with an ordinary life.

The party in Upper Brook Street was being held in a suite of rooms regularly hired out for private functions. The furniture and decor were over-opulent and anonymous, the carpets thick and the curtains elaborately patterned and swagged. By the time Anthony and Leo arrived the air was already filled with the hum of voices, as little knots of Names and members of the committee stood around with glasses of champagne, discussing their misfortunes and the future of their litigation. Leo had made a point of arriving late, telling Anthony that it befitted their status as legal stars to make something of an entrance. Being there early to meet and greet was strictly the kind of menial work for which solicitors were cut out, he said.

Anthony was still grinning at this as they handed their overcoats to the young man at the door. They went into the reception room and were given glasses of champagne, and it was only a matter of seconds before heads turned, and several people made their way across to greet Leo and Anthony, intent on annexing and button-holing them before anyone else did. Counsel were regarded by the Names as kinds of guru, omniscient, holding all the clues to the success or failure of the action, and conversational opportunities were at a premium.

Freddie, being slightly deaf and slower than the others, didn't notice Leo make his entrance until it was too late. Blast, he thought, eyeing him greedily from the other side of the room, he had particularly wanted to talk to him about the new Chatset estimate for the run-off on all open years. Freddie took another swallow of his champagne and turned to give another tortoise-like glance in the direction of the kitchen. He had been a bit disap-pointed to discover that this was to be a stand-up affair, but he hoped the buffet was going to be on the generous side. He took it as a good sign that the food wasn't already laid out on the side tables when they arrived – presumably the rations, whatever they turned out to be, would at least be hot. He wagged his head, muttering under his breath the figures which he wanted to put to Leo, and went off in search of the girl with the champagne.

Anthony was standing making conversation of a polite, commis-erating kind with an American woman and her English husband, who, like all Names, allowed the cataloguing of their misfortunes at Lloyd's to dominate all social encounters. And when it came to talking to their lawyers, they were even more vociferous, regard-ing them as people whose job it was to listen to their grievances. Anthony found it all horribly boring. It was bad enough having to work on the case every day of the week without having to talk about it in the evenings. But he recognised, he supposed, that there was some therapeutic value for these people in talking endlessly about it. As though it would make any difference. He glanced at Leo and caught his eye for a fraction of a second, long enough to see that they were both thinking exactly the same thing. He wondered, scanning the roomful of people as he nodded at something the American woman was saying, whether Camilla was going to come. She'd gone off to the library at the end of the afternoon, so he'd just left the address of the place scribbled on a scrap of paper on her desk. Not that he cared. It was just that he'd meant what he'd said about getting to know some of these people. He found himself glancing at the doorway each time someone came in.

Leo, too, was watching the doorway, and when he saw Charles Beecham step into the room, he felt that unmistakable sense of heart-stopping pleasure. It was the feeling for which he lived, he told himself, glancing at Charles just long enough to take in his tall figure, clad in a casually untidy but very expensive set of light tweeds, a pale blue cravat above his white shirt. Charles, as he stood in the doorway and glanced round the room, caught Leo's eye and raised his eyebrows, giving him a smile and nod of recognition. Leo turned back to Basher Snodgrass, who was holding forth on the subject of late joiners to the action with the perfect contentment of knowing that Charles was there, and that he could talk to him and enjoy him at his leisure later in the evening.

Anthony had managed to make his escape from the American woman and her husband and was just about to join Murray and some of the more sensible and agreeable Names, who were laughing and talking in a corner, when he saw Rachel. He had not seen her for almost nine months, and the sight of her gave him something of a shock. But as this ebbed away, he realised, with relief, that the jolt he had felt was nothing to do with the way he had once been in love with her. He scanned her face as she glanced round the room, thinking that she looked as lovely as ever, with her dark, shining hair and pale face, wide mouth and eyes, and faintly hesitant manner. But nothing about her touched and pained him as it had once done. Leo had been right. He did fall easily in and out of love. He realised that he should speak to her and went over, collecting a fresh glass of champagne from a tray for her on the way. She glanced round in surprise as he touched her arm, and then this look was replaced by one of faint relief. She coloured slightly at the sight of him.

'Oh, Anthony! How nice to see you again. It's been – it's been quite some time, hasn't it?' Her voice was bright, but still edged with hesitancy.

'Nine months,' he said, and gave her a smile. 'Here.' He handed her the glass of champagne and she took it, then looked around the room.

'Leo seems pretty well taken up,' she remarked.

Anthony, following her glance, saw Leo surrounded by a little group of Names, mainly women, so far as he could see, and all over fifty.

'Lloyd's groupies. Leo's sort of the Bruce Springsteen of the legal world at the moment.'

Rachel laughed and sipped her champagne. 'And what about you?' she asked. 'Why aren't you surrounded by Lloyd's Names, all hanging on your every pronouncement.'

'I'm just the roadie,' replied Anthony. 'You know, tuning the guitars, humping the equipment. No one wants to talk to a junior, when they can have the real thing. Anyway, Leo loves it. I don't.' He turned and gave her an intent gaze. 'You're looking very well,' he said. She wasn't, he thought. She still had that calm beauty about her, but there was definitely a change, something nervy and tense about her, despite the smile.

'Thank you,' she said automatically. There was a pause, in which the sight of Anthony after so many months made her wish, suddenly and desperately, that it had been Anthony and not Leo with whom she had fallen in love, that it had been Anthony who had held the key, who had been able to lay to rest all the fears and dark shadows of her past. She did not think life with Anthony would be a complicated, unreal matter. But that was all dead and gone. Here she was, talking to him as to an old friend. Only he was not enough of a friend for her to tell him everything. How she wished there was someone to whom she could tell everything. 'So you're both on this Capstall case?' she said. 'It must be rather fun to be working with Leo,' she said. 'He's so amusing – people like being with him . . .' she added faintly. She glanced round again, and Anthony thought he saw a look of panic in her eyes.

Anthony cast around for something to say. 'Are you – are you doing anything special over Christmas?' he asked. Rachel was about to reply, but at that moment Charles Beecham joined them, and in the same instant Freddie came up beside Anthony and gripped his elbow in an unpleasantly tight, shaky grasp. He had been unable to get anywhere near Leo, so had decided he would make do with this fella Cross instead.

Ignoring Freddie for just a moment, Anthony shook Charles by the hand. 'Charles. Good to see you. Rachel, may I introduce Charles Beecham? Charles, this is Rachel Dean.' Then he added, 'Excuse me, won't you?' before turning patiently to Freddie.

Anthony, without realising it, had introduced Rachel by her maiden name. But then, that was the way he had always known her. Rachel decided to let it go, and smiled at the man standing before her. 'Charles Beecham? Why do I know that name?' she asked, and sipped her champagne. She had drunk most of it out of nervousness while talking to Anthony, and it gave her a pleasantly mellow feeling.

'Hah.' Charles gave a laugh of embarrassment and looked away. 'Now, either you're teasing me, which I probably deserve, or else you mean it and I'm going to be horribly humiliated. Either way, I come out of this looking fatuously arrogant.'

'Ah.' Rachel smiled. 'That means you're famous.' She hesitated and then laughed, raising a hand to push her dark hair gently back from her shoulder. 'In which case, I'm the one who's going to be humiliated.'

Oh, do that again, thought Charles, watching the way her shining hair slid from her fingers, his gaze travelling to her face, resting on the almond-shaped dark eyes. He had seen Rachel from the other side of the room ten minutes ago, had been completely transfixed by the sight of her, and had spent eight of those ten wretched minutes trying to talk his way free from Mrs Honoria Hunter so that he could get near to her while she was still talking to Anthony, and be introduced. She was absolute perfection, he thought, shining like a lovely light amongst this roomful of drones, bores and cranks. Charles was disposed to a fairly jaundiced view of his fellow Names this evening on account of yesterday's late night at a restaurant with friends, and several bottles of wine too many. He almost hadn't come this evening, but he'd been in town, anyway, going over the scripts for his new series, and thought he might as well kill an hour or so and imbibe some free champagne before catching the train back. If he hadn't come, he now told himself, he would not have met this paragon. The idea was agonising. Was she as good as she was beautiful, he wondered? Then he realised that he was staring at her, that it was his turn to say something, and summoned back the words Rachel had uttered a few seconds ago.

'Actually,' he said, 'unless you're interested in the Crusades, or the Mogul Empire or esoteric nonsense of that kind, there's no reason why you should have the faintest idea who I am.'

She frowned, and he loved that, too. Then her eyes widened. 'Oh – how stupid of me! You do those documentaries on Channel Four, don't you?'

'I'm afraid so,' he said.

Rachel was about to say that Leo watched the programmes, but something – the champagne, the pleasure of talking and joking with this suddenly familiar stranger – made her decide not to. She would not couple herself with Leo. Just as she had gone back to work to regain her independence, so she was going to have to assert it in other ways, too. She was herself, nothing to do with Leo. So instead she said, 'It must be rather irritating, being recognised by people – or half-recognised,' she added with a laugh.

'No, I'm still vain and immature enough to enjoy it,' replied Charles. 'Or maybe that's just because I'm just not famous enough. I suppose that it would become a bit irksome if one were, say, Michael Fish.'

Charles, panicked by the idea that if he didn't hold her interest this divine creature would depart from him for ever, continued to talk in a random fashion about the nature of celebrity, recounting a number of amusing anecdotes which had the virtue of being told against himself. Rachel listened, glad to be able to laugh and mean it, feeling more at her ease than she had done for a long time. She had been right to come, she thought, to get out and talk to other people. It helped one's mood. She watched Charles as he talked, taking in the faintly creased, suntanned face, the aquiline nose and grey-blond curls. He was even more attractive than he looked on television, she thought, somehow more alive and arresting. She supposed that television diluted images, adumbrated personalities. There was something vivid and fresh about this man, and he was very funny, in a hapless, self-deprecating way which she liked.

Leo, by now rigid with the boredom of discussing the iniquities of Alan Capstall, glanced across and saw Rachel laughing and talking to Charles. He was surprised by the feeling of slight annoyance this gave him, and wondered whether he should go over. No, he decided, he wanted to keep Charles entirely apart from any other personal areas in his life. He wanted the complete, unadulterated pleasure of talking to Charles on his own. He turned back and tried to concentrate on what Basher Snodgrass was saying about the American Superfund legislation.

'Now, look, you've run out of champagne,' said Charles, taking Rachel's glass from her. 'Let me get you a refill.' He looked round for the waitress, anxious to keep Rachel to himself for a while longer. He had noticed the wedding ring on her left hand, but that didn't perturb him. It never had in the past. When love struck, nothing else mattered. He was thoroughly enjoying the giddiness of this thrilling encounter.

'Oh, no – really,' said Rachel. 'I have to be going. I only looked in for a few moments.'

God, she was going. What to talk about, how to detain her? 'So, tell me, are you one of us? I mean, are you a Name?' he asked, opening up a new vein of conversation.

'No!' Rachel laughed. 'Do I look like one?'

'No,' sighed Charles. 'You're far too young and beautiful. And you haven't mentioned Lloyd's once in the last ten minutes.'

Rachel laughed again and blushed. 'Actually, I work for Nichols and Co.' She gestured towards Fred and Murray. 'They're colleagues of mine.'

'Oh. Ah.'

'But I'm afraid I really have to be going now . . . '

'Listen, listen . . . ' Charles laid a hand on her arm. How cool and smooth her skin was. 'Why don't we have lunch together some time?'

She was momentarily startled. She looked at him, at the droll, faintly pleading expression in his eyes. She imagined that few women could resist that particular look. For a moment she hesitated. Why not? She liked him. He was charming, amusing – and if Leo could lead his own life, surely she could. But she was too afraid, too unready.

'No – no, I'm sorry. That's not possible. I'm very flattered, Mr Beecham, but I don't really think my husband would be . . . ' Her voice trailed away. What would Leo be? Nothing. It was probably what he wanted – that she should start seeing someone else, so that he could be relieved of guilt, and do exactly as he pleased himself. 'Anyway, I really must be going. I did enjoy meeting you.' The smile she gave him was divine, that of a fleeing goddess.

Charles watched her go with regret. Oh, well, he'd been wrong about the wedding ring. Sometimes it meant something, sometimes it didn't. She was an utter peach, though. Pity. Like all romantics, Charles possessed the ability to convince himself instantly that he had met the love of his life, the woman of his dreams. But if it should turn out that the woman of his dreams was not available or open to persuasion, he rarely wasted time moping over it. That was the beauty of possessing a shallow nature. One's caprices could be switched on and off at a moment's notice.

Rachel went over to Leo and told him that she was going home, and he nodded. Not even for the sake of public appearances did they kiss on parting. It did not occur to either of them to do so.

When she was gone, Leo saw that Charles was standing by himself in the middle of the room, one hand in his pocket, sipping his champagne with an air of boredom. He excused himself from Basher and went over.

'Charles,' he said, 'good to see you.' He shook Charles's hand, delighting in the fact that no one in the room could possibly be aware of the significance to him of this small physical contact. And for Charles? He still could not tell. Charles had dropped no hint during their encounters so far. But then, he was a man of discretion, and must realise the circumstances of this case were not appropriate to an acknowledgement of mutual attraction.

'Leo,' said Charles with a smile of genuine pleasure. 'How are you?'

Leo lowered his voice. 'Bored rigid, if you want the truth. I was hoping you'd show up, so that I could at least have a bit of sensible conversation.'

'I nearly didn't come, actually,' said Charles, swirling the champagne in his glass, wondering if it would be wise to drink any more. Rachel had slipped from his mind already. 'But I happened to be in town this afternoon, so it seemed the polite thing to do – pop along, you know.'

Leo's heart fell slightly at this. Clearly Charles had not regarded the possibility of seeing Leo as of any special significance. Or perhaps he was being deliberately casual as a way of masking his feelings. Leo so much wanted Charles to reciprocate what he felt that he made himself believe this. 'Tell you what,' said Leo, glancing round, conscious that his mouth was dry. He took a quick drink from his glass. 'After another twenty minutes or so I rather think I'll have done my duty by this lot.' He glanced in the direction of the buffet tables, where food was now laid out, and where Freddie Hendry was making heavy play among the chicken legs and vol-au-vents. 'And I'm not keen on this particular kind of food. What say we escape for dinner? There's a rather good restaurant round the corner which I've been meaning to try.'

Leo felt his pulse quicken with anxiety as he watched Charles make a face and glance at his watch. He had not felt this way about anyone for a long time. The balance was cruelly out, and he was glad that Charles had no idea of how abject Leo felt his position to be. That balance, Leo told himself, must be perfectly redressed in the months before he made his move. They must come to one another on equal terms. In the meantime, the best he could do was to hope that he might at least secure Charles's company over dinner for an hour or so here and there.

'I'm afraid I have to get the eight o'clock train back down,' said Charles, genuinely sorry at having to turn Leo down. He could have done with a decent dinner – that awful sushi stuff the television people had insisted on having for lunch hadn't gone far, and the thought of Leo's conversation and a couple of bottles of good wine was appealing. For a moment he was sorely tempted. But he knew himself too well, knew his own weaknesses. He'd only finish up drinking too much and regretting it in the morning. And with the punishing work schedule of the next few weeks, Charles knew he couldn't afford to do that.

'Maybe some other time,' said Leo, masking his own acute disappointment with an easy smile.

'Yes. Yes, definitely. Anyway, I just have to have a few words with Basher before I go for my train. Good to see you, Leo . . .' Charles lifted his hand in farewell, and Leo raised his glass in return. He watched Charles's tall figure weaving through the little groups of people, and sighed inwardly, letting his idle hopes and fantasies for the evening subside. Well, he'd better just get on with this PR exercise. He'd talked to just about all of the Names already, except for Freddie, so he might as well get that over with. In a resigned fashion, Leo went over to where Freddie was ham-fistedly trying to roll up a few chicken legs in a napkin, just managing to cram them into his pocket before Leo arrived.

On her way out, Rachel passed Anthony standing near the doorway. He smiled at her and murmured goodbye, and she noticed his gaze stray to the stairs, where a red-headed girl had just arrived. The girl passed her, and she heard Anthony say, 'So you decided to honour us with your presence, after all?' Despite his faintly caustic tone, Rachel could tell that he was pleased about something.

Rachel went downstairs, buttoning her coat. As she paced slowly down the dark street towards the gleam of lights and traffic of Park Lane, she decided that she would watch Charles Beecham's documentaries from now on. At least it would give her something pleasant to think about. She wished she was the kind of woman who could have said yes to him. Sighing, she turned up her coat collar against the cold.

Chapter Thirteen

The City ushered in Christmas with its customary spirit of commercial bonhomie. Everywhere – on office walls, on the sides of filing cabinets, pasted on windows – hung the masses of Christmas cards sent out by firms to choke the postal service, depicting the Thames in winter, snow on St Paul's, and containing seasonal greetings in any number of languages, designed to cover the global market. The window-sill and mantelpiece of every executive, broker, lawyer and accountant boasted an array of invitations from other executives, brokers, lawyers and accountants to an endless round of drinks parties and festive get-togethers. Cases of wine, bottles of Scotch, parcels of smoked salmon and hampers from Fortnum's and Harrods were delivered daily in the offices of chairmen and managing directors, and secretaries everywhere, in time-honoured ritual, bestowed upon their bosses a variety of tasteless mugs and ties in exchange for Belgian chocolates and bottles of Cacharel.

At 5 Caper Court there was a distinct atmosphere of frivolity and cheerfulness, rather like that at the end of a school term. People took long lunches, or came in late after cocktail parties and drinks parties in the various Inns, and the steady stream of work slowed perceptibly. Christmas fell on a Sunday that year, and the annual chambers party was to be held on Friday evening. Thursday saw Felicity in a state of high elation, organising the arrival of the champagne and food and wearing a large, dangling pair of Christmas-tree earrings with tiny flashing lights. The sight of her so depressed Leo as he came into the clerks' room to drop off some post before leaving to go home that he almost resolved not to attend the party. Normally Leo enjoyed Christmas, but this year a mood of anxiety and gloom had settled on him. Twelve months ago he would not have believed that his life could have drifted into its present unhappy confusion. There were days when he felt that he had lost sight of his own identity. Once it had been simple – he had a public face, that of a high-flying, handsomely paid barrister with all the material and social trappings of a successful and happy bachelor, and in private he conducted himself as he pleased, taking his pleasures with men or women, according to his fancy of the moment, enjoying the fact that his secret world was entirely his own, shared with no one. Now – now he was married, for the sake of his career, to someone whom he could never love as she wished to be loved, caught in a relationship in which the carefully contrived domestic conversations which had held it shakily together had recently descended into constant bickering, the father of an infant son whose very existence both puzzled and profoundly moved him, and there seemed to be nothing private or personal left. He still had his work, was still known and admired as a QC, but the magnitude of the Capstall case demanded all of his time and attention, so that he no longer enjoyed the stimulus of a varied range of work, regular court appearances and the customary string of successes which inflated the ego and the bank balance. He lived and breathed Lloyd's, the audit evidence, run-off contracts, open years, RITCs, time and distance policies, asbestos and pollution liabilities, and seemed destined to remain so immersed for the next year. There was Charles, there was the pleasure of being in love, but somehow his married state and claustrophobic domestic life rendered it faintly absurd and pathetic. He had nothing he could call his own.

Now the sight of Felicity in her jaunty earrings, with a sprig of mistletoe tucked in the bodice of her low-cut jumper, made him wish time could suddenly leap ahead by two weeks, obliterating the prospect of the holiday that was to be got through. He and Rachel had not discussed how they were to spend the time. They discussed nothing now. It had occurred to Leo that he could just take off to Wales, spend Christmas with his mother, leave Rachel to her own devices, but this seemed callous. Besides, he would have to endure his mother's questioning. And it would take matters no further. No, he decided, as he dropped his letters in the tray, tonight he would talk to her. They must resolve certain things, find a modus operandi. Otherwise life would be insupportable. Revolving this in his mind, he didn't hear Felicity as she called out goodnight, but merely turned and walked out of the clerks' room, grim-faced.

'Bloody hell,' remarked Felicity to Henry. 'Look at the face on him. Like a smacked arse. Doesn't believe in the festive spirit, obviously.'

When he got in, Rachel was still not home. The sight of Oliver's expensive pushchair in the hallway lowered Leo's spirits even further. In the living room toys and bricks lay scattered across the carpet, and from upstairs he could hear the sound of Jennifer talking to Oliver as he splashed in his bath. That was another thing, thought Leo, kicking a stuffed rabbit aside as he crossed the room to the cupboard where the drinks were kept. The nanny. He and Rachel might be virtual strangers to one another, but somehow the presence of an outsider, even if unseen and unheard most of the time, heightened the tension. Why couldn't Rachel stay home and look after Oliver herself? God knows, she didn't need the money.

Jennifer came down with Oliver, clean and powdered and in his pyjamas, the tendrils of his hair still damp and fragrant with baby shampoo, and murmured hello to Leo. She did not look at him. When Leo was around she behaved as though somehow faintly embarrassed, and this irritated Leo even more.

He did not respond to her greeting, but merely snapped at her, 'I wish you could make sure his toys and things were cleared up before we came home, Jennifer. It's rather annoying to find the place cluttered up with them.'

'Sorry,' she said. 'Rachel usually asks me to leave them out so that she can play with him.' She moved around the room, quickly picking things up and putting them in the toy box. Then she bent and kissed Oliver, and left the room without another word. Leo stood nursing his Scotch and staring down at Oliver, who sat slapping his rattle with a fat fist. Then Oliver looked up at Leo and smiled, and Leo sighed and smiled back, realising that this was probably the first time today that he had done so. He set down his drink, and was about to squat down and pick Oliver up when he heard Rachel come in.

She appeared in the doorway, her face drawn and tired. 'You're late,' he observed. 'I thought you were making a point of leaving the office on time these days.'

She was instantly stung by this remark. Because of the discussion she had had last week with Rothwell and Parr, she had been trying since then to convince herself, and them, of her equal worth to male partners in the firm. This evening she had stayed behind an extra forty minutes trying to sort out a tanker problem in Sri Lanka, anxious not to be open to accusations of putting her domestic life ahead of her clients.

'Has it not occurred to you, Leo, that Oliver is as much your responsibility as mine?' Rachel ran tired fingers through her hair. 'Why can't *you* get home by six thirty every night? Why should *I* be the one who always has to rush back?'

Leo picked up Oliver and cradled him against his shoulder, feeling a warm patch of dribble soak through his shirt. 'Because you're not the one pulling in half a million a year. That's why.'

I can't get away from it, thought Rachel. Not at the office, not here. You are what you earn. And you earn what you earn because of what you are, apparently, not what you do. 'Thank you,' she said coldly, 'for putting it in such clear terms.'

They said nothing for a moment, then Leo turned and sat down in an armchair, stroking Oliver's head. Rachel watched him, oddly aware that Leo was holding the baby tenderly, yet like a weapon. Then he said, 'Sit down. You look very tired. I want us to have a talk.'

The words filled her with a slow, dissolving panic. What was he going to say? That it was all at an end, that she must leave, that he would keep Oliver? In her tired and abject emotional state, each one of these seemed neither unlikely nor unreasonable. Another, stronger part of her knew that that was nonsense. But she wished, as she went to pour herself a drink to fill in the interminable seconds until he spoke again, that it was she who was holding Oliver, and not Leo. It was as though that made her vulnerable, and him dangerous.

She poured herself a glass of sherry and sat down on the sofa opposite him, sipping at her drink, her other hand toying idly with a *Winnie-the-Pooh* cloth book. She waited, not meeting his eyes.

'I want to make a suggestion,' said Leo. 'I want us to try and reach an understanding. The way we are – the way we behave to one another – is not a good thing. For us or for Oliver. I think we should try to clarify the situation.'

'Is this your way of saying that you want a divorce?' asked Rachel. Her heart was hammering, and she fought to keep her voice and expression neutral. It was what she had feared for weeks. She had been schooling herself in the ways of not loving Leo, but at a moment such as this one the strength of her feeling for him rushed to the surface. She did not want to lose him, awful as things were between them. She had told herself that it was hopeless, yet she still hoped.

There was a pause, which seemed to Rachel interminable. 'No,' said Leo. He had thought long about this. In many ways it was the obvious solution to their predicament, but something held him back from such a step. Each time he thought of the house without Rachel and Oliver, he felt something approximate to fear. It was hardly that, but it was enough not to want to push them away altogether. He still felt affection for Rachel, was aware that, when things had been less complicated between them, he had enjoyed her company more than that of most people. If they could reach an understanding about their lives, maybe they could recover something of that. Above all, there was Oliver. Leo did not perfectly comprehend his feelings for his son, but he knew that he did not want Oliver to grow up without a father, as he himself had. And he had seen enough of divorce and its sad trappings to know that his relationship with Oliver would be irrevocably damaged if he and Rachel were to divorce now.

Rachel said nothing for a moment. 'I don't understand you, then. How do you intend that we should – clarify the situation?'

Leo sat Oliver on the end of his knee, jogging him idly. 'You must have known ever since you married me that our relationship wasn't going to subsist on a conventional level.' He spoke so calmly, not even looking at her, that Rachel was filled with a sudden anger.

'Must I?' she retorted. 'Don't you realise that, right from the very beginning, I have known nothing, Leo, absolutely nothing?' She heard him sigh slightly, but for the moment she cared nothing for his distaste for rows, for scenes. 'You seem to have forgotten, but when you asked me to marry you, you said that you loved me, that you were finished with – with ... boys, young men – whatever ... ' Her angry outburst faltered as she groped for words, and Leo cut in.

'What's the label you're trying to find for it? Homosexuality, bisexuality, asexuality? So that you can compartmentalise it, treat it as something separate from me? Well, I'm afraid that it *is* me, it's part of my personality, and I can do no more about it than I can about the shape of my nose.'

Rachel sat back in despair, trying to fight back the tears she could feel rising up. Was it worse trying not to love someone than loving them? she wondered. She drew a deep breath and tried to keep her voice steady. 'Then why – why did you ever tell me that you would change? Why have we been going through this whole charade?'

Leo was silent for a moment. He couldn't tell her the truth, couldn't admit to her that it had all been a convenient device. He spoke slowly, carefully. 'Perhaps ... perhaps then I thought that being married, leading a different life, would bring about some kind of change in me.' He bobbed Oliver on his knee, and Oliver gurgled with delight. Leo waited for her to say something, but she said nothing, and he could sense her anger fading away into weariness and incomprehension. 'Look,' he said, turning to her, 'I told you once that I don't go the distance. I thought I could be the kind of person that you want, but it's obvious to both of us that I can't. I can only be myself, and all that is very complicated.'

'By which you mean that you don't want me any more. Not physically. But why am I stating the obvious? That all finished months ago.' She took a sip of her drink and looked away from him.

'That's part of it. I don't know what I want. But that could change. I can't say. But what I want is for us to try to lead independent lives for the time being, not to maintain a pretence. To understand one another. I want us both to bring up Oliver. But we can't do that if we're both pretending that there is a – a certain kind of relationship between us, when there isn't.'

Rachel laughed. 'What? Let's just be good friends?'

'If you like. Yes.'

Rachel contemplated her sherry glass. As usual, Leo, she thought, you want it all ways. You want Oliver, so you must keep me. But you don't want me. You want other people, the kind of life you used to lead. Yet if you have to try to live up to expectations as a husband, you can't do that. You still believe that I love you so much that I'll stay with you whatever – but you'd like the atmosphere at home to improve. So you're cutting a deal.

And what's in it for me? I still have you – but only on certain terms . . . She felt suddenly weary and confused, and very close to tears.

'Do you mean – ' She could hear her own voice shaking. ' – do you mean that if I need you, if I need comfort, as I needed it that night last week, that I can come to you? That you will be kind to me, without my expecting anything more?'

God, I am a shit, thought Leo suddenly. How lonely she must be. He set Oliver on the floor, where he began to whimper, and went over to her. She had begun to weep, and he raised her to her feet and, for the first time in weeks, put his arms around her. He remembered the last time he had made love to her, after their conversation in the restaurant about Francis. He had wanted to know then whether he still commanded her unconditional love, and his curiosity had been satisfied. It would be the simplest of things now to take her to bed, to use sex as a means of helping this along. God knows, ever since he had first met her he had slept with her as a means to an end, in one way or another. Why not now? But he knew at this moment that he could not even manufacture the desire, not while he felt as he did about Charles, who seemed to consume all his waking fantasies. To make love to her now would only create new hopes in her, hopes which he had no wish or intention to fulfil. So, in answer to her question, he merely replied gently, 'Yes, that is what I mean. I don't want there to be any unkindness, but – '

Her tears subsided, and she wiped her eyes with the back of her hand. 'But you want to lead your own life without being accountable to anyone.'

'I'm afraid so. Yes.'

There was a long pause, and then she nodded. 'It's what you'll do, anyway,' she murmured. She was filled with a sudden disgust and anger with herself for being so weak as to cry. What was the point of all this, anyway? It was just Leo salving his wretched conscience. She pushed herself away from him. 'Then you might as well go and get on with it.' And she stooped and picked up Oliver from the floor, then went to the kitchen to make supper. Life had to go on.

Domestic trauma of another variety was erupting in Felicity's flat in Clapham. She had arrived home from the office, earrings still flashing, to find Vince in drunken ill-humour, pacing round the kitchen with a glass in his hand, still in his working overalls.

'Bloody fucking bastards!' he said, by way of greeting. Felicity pondered this for a moment.

'Who is?'

'Those bloody bastards I work for! Worked for, I should say. They've only fucking gone and made me fucking redundant, haven't they?'

Felicity sat down. 'Oh, Vince. Oh, God, I'm sorry.'

'Fucking British Telecom. What a fucking Christmas present.'

Felicity glanced at the table and saw that Vince had drunk the best part of a bottle of vodka. 'That's not the answer, you know. Getting pissed.'

'Oh, and you know the answer do you? Get out of here.' He gave her an angry shove and she backed off.

'Don't you bloody well take it out on me!' shouted Felicity, eyes blazing as she pushed him back. 'Just 'cos you lost your sodding job, don't go getting at me!'

He raised an unsteady warning finger. 'Don't you fucking start, Fliss! I'm warning you! I'm not in the mood!'

'You don't raise your finger to me, mate! This is *my* flat, and you don't warn me about nothing, see?' She gave him another push. Generally when they argued, much pushing and shoving went on, but it never came to anything more. Usually Vince became sullen, and eventually apologetic. But this evening he was too drunk for any of that. He suddenly raised his fist and clipped Felicity neatly on the side of the jaw, and she fell backwards against a chair, slipping to the floor.

'Just get off my case, Fliss!' He stood over her, and she sat dazed, realising that he was quite prepared to hit her again.

'Get out!' she yelled, rage and tears quivering in her voice. 'You bastard! Get out!'

He made another threatening move, then turned, grabbed his jacket, and went out, slamming the door violently. Felicity sat nursing her jaw, feeling the bone tenderly, listening to his footsteps thumping down the stairs. Shaking, she got to her feet, crying and still holding her jaw.

When she awoke the next morning, Felicity realised that Vince was not there, that he hadn't come back all night. She examined the reddish patch on her jaw in the bathroom mirror. She could easily cover that with makeup. It would be at its worst in a couple of days, just in time for Christmas. She thought of the brief argument with Vince and felt unbearably miserable. She had just decided to ring chambers and say that she was sick and wouldn't be coming in, when she remembered the party. She was largely responsible for organising it. Cameron and Henry weren't capable of getting it together without her. She would have to go in. The last thing she felt like, she reflected moodily, as she searched through her wardrobe for something suitable to wear, was a party. Still, maybe Vince would be back when she got home, and they could make up. She should probably have been more sympathetic. But he still shouldn't have hit her.

By the end of the afternoon Felicity had recovered her spirits. No one had noticed the mark on her jaw beneath a good dollop of No. 7 panstick, and she had convinced herself that Vince would be there, full of contrition, when she got home. He was always ready to make up. His temper was like that. Up one minute, and gone the next. At six o'clock she was just about to close the switchboard and get things ready for the party, when the phone rang. Her hand hovered in indecision. She could easily just flick on the answering machine. Instead, she picked it up. 'Five Caper Court,' she sang in her phone-answering voice.

'Fliss? It's me, Vince.'

Her heart rose. 'Oh, hello,' she replied, trying to keep her voice stiff and unfriendly.

'Listen, I'm sorry for all that stuff last night. I was well out of order.'

'Too right you were,' agreed Felicity, but ready to forgive and forget.

'I just wanted to tell you, though, that I'll be stopping by to pick up my gear tomorrow. I'm moving out.'

'You what?'

'Well, like you said, it's your flat. And I've just had enough, Fliss. I mean, it's been getting to me for months that you earn more than I do, and now I'm earning nothing. I'm sorry I hit you, and all, but I've made my mind up. I just want us to cool it.'

'What do you mean?'

'I dunno. I just want to give it a rest for a while. You and me. Stuff like last night, it's doing my head in.' She said nothing, could

157

think of nothing. 'I'll be round tomorrow evening, anyway.' And he hung up.

She had sunk on to her chair as they talked. Now she replaced the receiver slowly, and sat looking stupefied. Vince, her Vince, had dumped her. She was filled with a cold, dead emptiness such as she had never known. They'd been together over a year now, they'd had such a laugh together, really good times. They had ups and downs like everyone, but nothing serious. And now he was telling her it was finished.

'Coming upstairs for an early snifter?' Cameron Renshaw, the tall and portly head of chambers, had rolled into the clerks' room and stood twanging his braces jovially. She stared at him for a second or two, then forced a smile.

'Yeah – yeah, I'll be up in a minute. Just got to fix my face.'

He went out, and Felicity sat perfectly still for a moment, listening to the voices and laughter as people made their way to the party upstairs. She would think about it later. What she needed right now was a drink. More than one.

An hour later, as Felicity was downing her ninth glass of champagne, Rachel was busy sorting through Oliver's clothing drawers and flinging items into an overnight bag. Her own suitcase was already packed and standing in the hallway downstairs. She had decided earlier today that she could not spend Christmas with Leo. The more she thought about what he had said the night before, the angrier she became, and she realised that she badly needed to get away from him, to try to think clearly and objectively about it all. She glanced at her watch, anxious to get away before he came back. She didn't want to have to talk to him, or to tell him where they were going. She wanted, for a few days, to be as free from him as possible. Only that way could she face things, make decisions.

She closed Oliver's bag, picked him up from where he sat chewing a brick on his playmat, and took him downstairs. She zipped him into his snowsuit, buckled him into his seat and carried him to the car. It was bitterly cold, and she huddled her coat around her as she hurried round to the driver's door and got in. She had tried to ring her mother to tell her she was coming, but there had been no answer. Still, it would be after nine by the time they reached Bath, and she was bound to be in by then. Rachel turned the key in the ignition and pushed the heater switch, shivering slightly. The dashboard glowed as she turned on the headlights, and she drove away from the house with a sharp sense of release.

Henry stood with Anthony, watching Felicity's behaviour growing louder and sillier. Several members of chambers were becoming rather embarrassed, not good at handling this kind of thing. She was their clerk, after all.

'Henry,' said Anthony, 'hadn't you better do something?'

'Me? Why me?' Henry watched Felicity uncomfortably as she poured herself another glass of champagne with a whooping noise, splashing the carpet. A sprig of holly stuck askew from her curly hair.

'Oh, you know, because . . . Well, you live near her, don't you?' said Anthony with sudden inspiration. 'Look, the best thing is if I ring for a cab, and you see her home.'

Henry nodded moodily, and Anthony went to the telephone.

Ten minutes later, Henry was helping a giggling Felicity into the back of a taxi, trying to stop her coat from falling off. He gave the driver Felicity's address, and as they drove off down Middle Temple Lane she lurched against him, which made her giggle more. The sprig of holly jabbed painfully into Henry's face, and he turned, frowning, to try to disentangle it from her hair. As he did so, Felicity laid her head upon his shoulder and sighed.

'Henry, I do love you,' she murmured, snuggling up against him. Startled, Henry inched away, but she moved even closer, and he realised that he very much enjoyed the feeling of Felicity's warm body nestling cosily against his. He glanced down at her face, half in shadow, half bathed in a glow from the street lights. She looked very pretty, her eyes closed, her mouth curved in a smile. He drew in a deep breath and, on a nervous impulse, bent his head and kissed her. She did not, as he had half expected, pull away. She returned his kiss, and then she put her arms around his neck and drew him down so that they were both almost lying in the back of the taxi seat, and kissed him passionately and drunkenly for several minutes. Henry was astonished, delirious. He came up for breath and then kissed her again. She seemed to be enjoying it all very much, so he slid a tentative hand inside her coat, and then dipped his hand into the low-cut neck of her jumper and stroked her breast, filled simultaneously with wild desire and panic at his daring. But Felicity only arched her back towards him and let him caress her as much as he wanted. By the time the taxi reached Clapham, Henry was in a state of ecstatic longing.

The jerk of the taxi pulling up brought him to his senses. He untangled himself from Felicity and sat up, smoothing down his thin hair and adjusting his tie, while Felicity hauled herself upright in an ungainly fashion, tucking in her bra strap and beginning to giggle again. The taxi driver glanced caustically at them in his mirror. 'That'll be five eighty, mate.'

Henry hesitated for a long and difficult moment. This could be his big chance, his great moment. She was so drunk that she would probably let him do anything. But the stern morality which guided Henry in all matters came to the fore.

'I'm going on actually. To Dulwich. I'll just see my friend upstairs, then I'll be back down.'

The driver held out his hand. 'Fiver on account. Not that I don't trust you, or anything.' His voice was laconic. He'd had too many runners. Henry rummaged in his pocket and produced a five pound note. Then he helped Felicity out of the cab and took her upstairs to her flat on the second floor. Felicity, swaying unsteadily, found her key in her handbag and unlocked the door. She turned to Henry and put one sleepy arm around his neck. 'Don't you want to come in?' she murmured, smiling.

Henry struggled with himself. Why not? After ten minutes the taxi driver would just go off, content with his fiver. And he would have Felicity all to himself . . . But he knew, sadly, that he could not possibly take advantage of her. No, if this evening meant anything, then it could wait until she was sober. Oh God, he hoped that it did mean something, that it wasn't just the effects of a bottle and a half of Moët & Chandon. Hadn't she told him that she loved him?

'You get yourself some coffee and a good night's sleep,' said Henry gently, disengaging her arm. Then he leaned towards her and gave her mouth a brief, regretful kiss, before going back down to the waiting taxi.

The dregs of the party were drifting into the night. Leo had left long ago, and Anthony was no longer quite sure why he was still there. He had spoken to Camilla a couple of times that evening, and had found himself glancing across occasionally to check that she hadn't left. There she still was, helping one of the more public-spirited secretaries to pile plates and glasses together. He went across to her.

'I'm off in a moment. I could walk with you to Embankment, if you like,' he said diffidently.

She glanced at him. 'Yes, all right. I'll get my coat.'

They left chambers together and walked in silence down Middle Temple Lane. A drunken knot of students was roaring and laughing outside the gates, and one of them whistled and yelled at Camilla as she and Anthony passed. Anthony glanced at her, but she was gazing thoughtfully straight ahead at the river. He could think of nothing in particular to say to her, and then suddenly realised that it didn't matter, that walking in silence with her was really quite peaceable. There was no sense of strain.

After a few moments he stopped in his tracks, and said, 'Do you know, I'm really rather hungry. I never eat the kind of junk they put out at office parties.' She turned and looked at him.

'I know what you mean. I could do with something to eat.'

'There's a place I know in the lane leading up to Charing Cross,' said Anthony. 'Why don't we go and have something there?'

'All right,' said Camilla.

They carried on in silence to Embankment station, and then walked up to a little Italian restaurant. It was only after they had ordered some pasta and the first glasses of wine had been poured, that they began to talk. They began with the party, and then work, the Capstall case, and then mutual acquaintances, their families, and at the end of the evening, when Anthony eventually asked for the bill and glanced at his watch, he realised that they had been talking for three hours. And he felt neither tired nor bored. In fact, he would happily have carried on talking to Camilla for another three hours. Camilla, as she watched Anthony sign the bill, felt exactly the same thing.

It was ten o'clock when Rachel pulled up outside her mother's little terraced house in Bath, and saw with relief the glow of light behind the drawn curtains. She unbuckled Oliver's seat and lifted it from the car, then fetched their bags from the boot. She struggled up the little flight of steps with her burdens and rang the bell. After a few moments her mother opened it and looked at Rachel in astonishment. She was slender and dark, like Rachel, but she wore much more makeup, that of an earlier era, red lipstick and pencilled brows. Her hair was fastidiously set, and she was dressed with the careful attention of a woman who wanted to give the appearance of being a youthful fifty, even though she was older.

'Good grief! Rachel! Why on earth didn't you ring?'

'I did, but you weren't in,' said Rachel. The cold had woken Oliver up and he began to squall. Mrs Dean glanced down at him and backed into the hallway, opening the door to let them both in.

It was warm in the hallway, too warm, and the air was filled with the smell of whatever Mrs Dean had had for supper.

'Well, this is a surprise.' There was no particular warmth or cheerfulness in Mrs Dean's voice. 'You'd better come through.' Rachel dumped the bags and followed her mother down to the little living room, Oliver now wailing lustily. 'Not,' added her mother over her shoulder to her daughter, 'that it's terribly convenient. It is Christmas, you know.'

Rachel sighed, and began to wonder whether she shouldn't just have stayed in London.

Anthony and Camilla walked from the station down to the tube. They parted at the ticket barrier, Anthony to take his Westbound train to Kensington, Camilla the Northern line to Kentish Town. There was nothing in this, Anthony told himself. He had no intention of kissing her goodnight, or anything like that. This was purely platonic. Besides, Camilla didn't look as though she expected anything like that. Still, just after he had said goodnight to her, he found himself adding, 'Are you especially busy over Christmas?'

'No,' she replied, tucking a strand of hair behind her ear. 'Not especially.'

'I thought we might go out some time. See a film, have dinner.'

She nodded, then glanced away. 'Yes. Yes, that would be great.' She turned and went down the steps, and Anthony found himself standing and watching her until she was completely out of sight.

Chapter Fourteen

When Leo got home on Friday evening, he noticed immediately that Rachel's car was gone. As he came in through the front door, Jennifer was coming downstairs with a zipped-up holdall and her coat, ready to go off home for the holiday.

'Did – ah – did Rachel say where she was going when she went out?' he asked the girl. That was another thing – he would have preferred Jennifer to address them as Mr and Mrs Davies, but Rachel had insisted from the beginning that she and Jennifer should call one another by their Christian names and there was no going back now. Jennifer, however, never addressed Leo by his Christian name – she never addressed him as anything at all.

'No. No, she didn't,' replied Jennifer. 'She must have gone out when I was having a shower.' Jennifer's eyes met Leo's, and their expression was blank. Leo was very conscious, suddenly, of Jennifer's complete understanding of the tensions in the household, and of how her knowledge gave her a curious kind of power. 'She took Oliver with her,' the girl added.

Leo nodded, standing there in his overcoat, tossing his keys lightly in his hand. He glanced away, then back at Jennifer. She looked very pretty, he noticed, made up in a way that was not usual with her when going about her domestic chores, her hair fluffed up and gleaming. She was wearing Doc Martens, black tights and a very short skirt, and a baggy denim jacket. There was something almost insolent about her careless, youthful vitality, and the entire situation made Leo feel somehow middle-aged and impotent. The girl knew so much, said so little. She was watching him now with a bland, incurious expression approximating pity. There was an awkward pause and then, suddenly wishing to elicit from her some response that would give a clue as to what she thought about them, Leo remarked, 'You must think us an odd household.'

She gave a vague smile and bent to pick up her holdall. 'Every household's odd,' she said. 'You just get used to it.' Her words were those of the dispassionate observer. Of course, thought Leo, she doesn't care what we do, so long as we pay her wages. 'I have to get to Euston for my train,' she added, almost apologetically, in case Leo was thinking of detaining her further in conversation.

'Right, right,' said Leo, turning away and dropping his keys on the table. 'You get off. We'll see you ... after the holidays, I suppose.'

'Yes.' She hesitated, then added, 'Merry Christmas.'

He glanced at her, wondering if he detected any irony. But her face betrayed nothing. She's just a child, after all, he thought. Why should he misjudge her, invest her with non-existent malign feelings? It was paranoia. He sighed. 'Yes. Merry Christms, Jennifer.'

When she had gone he wandered into the kitchen, aware of the utter silence in the house. There was no note. He went upstairs, and looked in Rachel's wardrobe. Most of her clothes were still there. In Oliver's room his toys still lay in their box beneath the window and, as far as Leo could see, the drawers were still full of his clothes. But she was gone, and Leo could tell from the silence that she would not be back soon. He went back downstairs and fixed himself a drink. Obviously the idea of spending Christmas together had been too painful. Where would she go? There were not many options. He didn't think she would descend on her friend Marsha at such short notice. She'd probably gone to her mother's in Bath. Leo rubbed his hands over his face and wondered whether he should ring her there. For some reason he felt an urge to speak to her. That was absurd, he told himself. He should be glad of her absence, for God's sake, glad of the freedom from guilt and hostility. He should, at this moment, be hoping that it might become permanent. Then he could be himself again. But he realised, as he finished his Scotch and stared into the empty glass, that all he felt was a slight, childish anger that she should leave him all on his own at Christmas.

The smell of cigarettes and hot tea was one which Rachel always associated with her mother. It filled the kitchen as they sat there the following morning, Mrs Dean reading her *Daily Mail* and sipping tea as she smoked, while Rachel spooned baby rice into Oliver's mouth and took the occasional bite of toast. Eventually her mother put down the paper and sighed.

'Well, I don't know what to suggest.' She paused, glancing reflectively from her daughter to her grandson. Her face, naked of its makeup, had a raw, pale look. Her eyebrows, plucked to the finest line, to be pencilled in later, gave her an expression of surprised vacancy. 'I mean, we've already booked the restaurant for tomorrow, and I don't know if they could squeeze another one in. And there's Oliver – I don't think the girls want their Christmas lunch spoiled by a crying baby, frankly.' Mrs Dean was referring to her cronies, five other women in their fifties who, for various reasons, were husbandless and therefore spent their time together in a variety of social pursuits.

'Oh, it doesn't matter,' said Rachel. The thought of having Christmas lunch with her mother and five cackling friends in a third-rate restaurant was not her idea of fun, anyway. She supposed she'd imagined that she and Oliver and her mother would just spend a quiet Christmas Day together. It was her own fault, she knew. During long spells of absence from her mother, she always managed to create an image of her that was not quite real, investing her with non-existent warmth and sympathy. Those qualities had been there once, Rachel thought, long ago, before the business with her father. Rachel knew her mother had never quite forgiven her for that, had always believed that for Rachel's father to have done those things to her – the things the police said he had done – she must have somehow encouraged him. Relations between them had been difficult ever since. Yet something still brought her back to her mother. She gazed into Oliver's wide, blue eyes as she gently scraped the remains of baby rice from around his mouth with the spoon. Maybe all children were like that. Oliver banged the table of his high chair with his hands and Mrs Dean looked at him dispassionately.

'You brought all his things, I see,' she remarked. 'This wasn't just intended to be an overnight visit, was it? You still haven't told me what's happened between you and Leo.'

Rachel shrugged. 'Just something. You know the way things can get between people. I had to get away for a while. I'm sorry if it's messing up your plans . . .'

Mrs Dean planted the flats of her hands on the table and rose to her feet. She was still dressed in her candlewick robe, fluffy mules on her feet. 'Oh, have no fear, Rachel, my life is going to carry on as normal. Though I don't see why you come all this way to stay, if you can't even tell your own mother what's been going on.' Her tone was childish and resentful.

'Oh, Mum, it wouldn't help if I told you. I came because I wanted to see you, I needed somewhere to go over Christmas. I don't want to talk about it. I don't need to be asked.'

Mrs Dean folded her arms and regarded her daughter. 'Your trouble is, Rachel, you don't like men. You've got a coldness about you. I can imagine what it is between you and Leo. That kind of man –'

Rachel gave a bitter laugh. 'Mum! You don't know anything! You don't know anything about him or about me. Just leave it.' She wiped Oliver's face with his bib and then plucked him from his high chair. Why had she come? This resentful bickering would just go on and on throughout the visit. 'Look, when I've got Oliver dressed I'm going to take him out. Then maybe when we come back we can all go out to lunch – '

'Oh, I've already made arrangements with Connie, I'm afraid. You seem to have come here expecting me to be sitting at home, idle and friendless. I can assure you my life is quite busy enough. I really do think it is thoughtless of you just to arrive on my doorstep like this, and expect me just to drop everything, especially at Christmas.'

Rachel sighed in exasperation. 'Right. You get on with your own plans, and we won't interfere with them, I promise you.' She knew that if she were to sit down and tell her all about Leo and his bisexuality and the kind of marriage they had, and explain to her why she needed to get away and think about it all, that her mother would be appalled, but mollified by the fact that Rachel had confided in her. But Rachel shrank from the idea of such intimacy. She wished there were someone she *could* tell, someone disinterested, but sympathetic and trustworthy. Whoever that person was, it certainly wasn't her mother.

A bitter wind had sprung up as Rachel wheeled Oliver in his pushchair down the suburban streets, heading for the centre of town and the shops. The sky was white, oppressive, with grey scudding clouds, and the sight of the shop windows filled with Christmas displays and tinsel depressed her spirits even further.

Tannoys had been set up above the shops to relay seasonal music to the shoppers, and a Salvation Army band at the end of the street was chiming out 'Silent Night' in competition with tinny drifts of 'Frosty the Snowman'. She and Oliver watched the band for a few moments, and then, tugging Oliver's woollen hat further down on his ears, Rachel realised that she should probably buy her mother a Christmas present. The presents which she and Leo had, separately, bought for Oliver, were already wrapped and in the boot of Rachel's car. She turned Oliver's buggy around and pushed it in the direction of the antique shops in the back streets, hoping for inspiration there.

Charles Beecham cackled demonically under his breath as he slid into the last vacant parking place, deliberately avoiding the indignant eye of the old woman in the Nissan who'd been waiting to get in ahead of him. Well, it helped to be on the right side of the road, he thought to himself, as he got out, preparing to set his features into an expression of astonished innocence in case the woman confronted him. But she had driven off angrily, and Charles, smiling, got his ticket from the pay-and-display machine and locked his car. He liked last-minute Christmas shopping. He wasn't one of those people who bought things well in advance and had them all wrapped up two weeks before Christmas. That took all the fun out of it. Anyway, he found that his most successful gifts were always purchased in an inspired last-minute panic, generally around five twenty-five on Christmas Eve. He'd already got his son, Nicholas, some books which he knew he wanted, and now it was just a matter of finding something for Chloe, his daughter, who would be coming down on Boxing Day. Chloe was usually easy – she liked oddities, knick-knacks, Victoriana. He should find something outrageously overpriced in one of the antique shops.

It was just as he was coming out of the shop with the art deco silver photo frame which he had bought for Chloe that he saw Rachel. She was standing on the other side of the street, her hands thrust into the pockets of a dark blue woollen coat, and he wouldn't have recognised her if she hadn't, at that moment, turned to glance momentarily to her left. He remembered that clear, sad profile instantly. Even with her long, dark hair turned into her upturned collar he recognised her. He was filled once again with that delightful, poignant shock which he had experienced on first seeing her at the Names' party. Then he remembered that she hadn't exactly reciprocated his feelings of instant love, and had in fact turned him down when he'd invited her to lunch. He hesitated on the pavement, wondering whether he should speak to her. No, there was no point – she'd used the fact that she was married as an excuse not to go out with him. The chap was probably somewhere around, and he didn't feel like standing in this bitter wind making small-talk to the husband of someone he fancied and could not have. Besides, he couldn't remember her name. That was always embarrassing. But then she turned and, before he could make his escape, she saw him, and smiled in recognition. Meeting her again was inevitable, he realised, and he raised his hand in greeting and stepped across the street. She looked very pretty, and he felt a heart-warming surge of rekindled lust as they shook hands, and a sense of relief when her name came back to him.

'Hello! This is quite a surprise!' he said. 'Ruth, isn't it? Sorry, I've forgotten your last name.'

She smiled. 'It's Rachel, actually. And I remember you perfectly. I even watched your last programme. I enjoyed it very much. What are you doing in Bath?'

'Oh, spot of shopping. You, too?'

She nodded. 'I'm trying to find something for my mother. I'm hampered by a distinct lack of enthusiasm, however.'

'Oh dear,' he murmured. God, he did like that smile of hers. How could he have forgotten her? How could he even have been casting an eye at that Boxer woman when there was someone like this in the world? He suddenly had the feeling that she was on her own. There didn't seem to be a hubby hovering around. 'Why don't we go and have a coffee? Maybe the warmth will inspire you. I'm getting frozen standing here, to be honest.'

'That's a good idea.' She turned away, and he saw her reach out to the pushchair standing by the shop window. All he could see of Oliver were two fat red cheeks and staring blue eyes. The rest of him was covered in hat, mitten and blanket. Oh God, she had a baby. Well, what did he expect? Anyway, it wasn't as though he was going to seduce her in a coffee shop. Still, it did hamper things, somehow.

'And who's this handsome young man?' he hazarded, hoping that it wasn't a girl. Didn't look like a girl, but one never knew.

'This is Oliver,' said Rachel, smiling, and bending down to stroke his face. The baby smiled back at Rachel, then the smile faded to inscrutable blankness as he turned his gaze on Charles. Boy doesn't like me, thought Charles. He knows I have designs on his mother.

'Come on. There's a place I know round the corner.'

In the café the windows were misted with steam, and the ubiquitous faint jingle of Christmas music filled the air.

'Right,' said Charles, setting down two cups of coffee on the Formica-topped table. 'Tell me the story of your life.' He spooned sugar into his coffee and stirred it.

'Hmm. That wouldn't make for very festive conversation, I can assure you. Who were you buying presents for?'

'My daughter Chloe. She's coming down on Boxing Day with her brother. I've already bought Nicholas his presents. A life of Samuel Taylor Coleridge and a book about the Rossettis. Keen on that kind of thing, you know.'

'You and your wife must be looking forward to seeing them both. How old are they?' She was watching him musingly. He looked older than she remembered, more weather-beaten than he appeared on television, but still as attractive. She liked the way he smiled, the way it creased his face, lit up his eyes.

'Twenty-four and twenty-two respectively. But I haven't got a wife. Well, I had, in the dim and distant past, but she's married to some stockbroker and living in Tonbridge. Serve her right, I say.' Rachel laughed. 'What about you?' he asked after a few seconds. She glanced up at him quickly. 'I mean,' he added hastily, 'have you bought your husband his Christmas present? You look like the organised type.'

Rachel looked down at her coffee. She could smile and say glibly, oh, yes, make something up, then change the subject. But somehow, with this man's kind, curious eyes fixed intently on her, she could not lie. In the moment before she had turned and seen Charles Beecham outside the shop, she had been thinking about Leo, thinking of how barren their relationship had become when they could not make even the smallest token gesture of buying one another a gift. Last year she had bought him a book which she knew he wanted. It hadn't been easy to find, but she had enjoyed seeking it out, enjoyed anticipating the pleasure it would give him. He had bought her a silver necklace. Only a year ago, and yet it seemed an interminable space of time. She looked up, essaying a smile. 'Not exactly,' she replied. 'We're not spending Christmas together, you see.' The note of calm sadness in her voice touched him instantly. He paused tactfully, stirred his coffee, trying to think of something to say apart from 'Oh?' When he looked up again, however, he saw with a pang that her eyes were brimming with tears.

'Oh God, look . . . ' He wondered what to do, how to console her, but could think of nothing.

'I'm sorry,' muttered Rachel, shaking her head and drawing a hand over her eyes. She sat very still for a few seconds and then took her hand away, blinking back the tears. She smiled shakily. 'I'm sorry. Christmas can be such a bloody miserable time of year, can't it?'

'God, how true,' said Charles earnestly. 'I'm just going to pretend tomorrow's an ordinary day, till the kids come down on Boxing Day.' He spoke merely to fill in time, as his eyes searched her face. Then he said tentatively, 'Do you want to tell me about it, whatever it is?'

Rachel drew in a deep breath and gazed at Charles. She badly wanted to talk to someone, and he looked so sympathetic and reassuring. 'My husband and I haven't been getting on too well recently . . . ' she began, and her voice trailed off. Then she suddenly laughed and shook her head. 'God, that's pathetic.' She glanced down sadly at Oliver, sitting in his pushchair next to the table with a bottle of juice in his fists. When she spoke again her voice was flat, matter-of-fact. 'My husband, you see, is bisexual. And promiscuous. Our lives have become somewhat fractured as a result. Well, you can imagine . . . But he doesn't want to lose Oliver and he seems to think that we can live our lives together, but separately, under the same roof. That's what he has suggested, at any rate. I've come down here to my mother's to get away from him for a while. To try to look at it all dispassionately. Make some decisions.'

'And?'

To his horror, her eyes began to fill with tears again. It wasn't that he didn't like women to cry – it just panicked him, he never knew what to do, whether to hit them, or hug them, or what. Charles sat there helplessly, watching as she cried quietly, her hands over her face. Two old women at the table opposite looked at

Rachel and shot him accusing glances. It's not me! he wanted to tell them. It's nothing to do with me! He patted her uselessly on the shoulder and murmured, 'There, there . . . '

Then her tears subsided, and she produced a tissue and wiped her eyes. Charles marvelled that there was no streaked mascara, no blurred lipstick. She even cries beautifully, he thought. And this husband of hers was clearly off the rails, and off the scene – for the moment, at any rate. He watched her, aware that she was about to impart her next confidence, and composed his features into sympathetic concern. All this must be a promising basis for something, he told himself. Shoulders that women cried on generally turned out to be good for other things.

Rachel sighed and went on. 'I don't think I should have come down here. My mother and I aren't the best of friends, exactly, and she resents Oliver and me landing ourselves on her doorstep. I suppose I expected a bit more of a welcome. Anyway, she's going out with friends tomorrow, and I just feel that maybe I should swallow my pride and go back to London . . . '

'Do you want to do that?' He rested his chin on his hands and sat contemplating her.

'No. No, I don't. It's the last thing I want. So I think we'll just have to sit it out in Bath for a few days.'

'You can't do that,' said Charles, and sat back in his chair. 'In fact, I have the solution. There am I, all alone in my house for the holidays, with no one to cook for or to talk to. Why don't you come and spend Christmas with me? Go back to your mother's, tell her you're going, then just pack everything up and come home with me.'

She shook her head and laughed, sniffing back the last of her tears. 'No, I couldn't possibly . . . Thank you, but I – '

'Why not?' expostulated Charles. 'Why sit all alone in Bath when we could be keeping one another company?' She glanced up at him hesitantly, and he realised that she was probably remembering how he had asked her out the last time they had met. Hastily he added, 'A purely platonic invitation, I can assure you. No hidden agendas. Just two people spending Christmas together. Well, three, actually.' He turned and grinned down at Oliver, who immediately screwed up his face and began to cry. 'I've got some people coming round for drinks this evening, just a mild pre-Christmas booze-up, but tomorrow will be restful and enjoyable, I promise you.'

171

Rachel smiled shakily. Why not? She liked this man, she much preferred the idea of spending the day with him than alone in her mother's house. 'All right,' she said suddenly. 'We'd love to come, thank you.' And she reached down to unstrap Oliver and lift him on to her knees.

Charles was both surprised and pleased. He hadn't thought she was the kind of person to do something on impulse. Too staid, too well brought up to agree to come and stay for a few days in the house of a man she hardly knew. But that was the good thing about television, you see. It was a kind of ready-made reference. They saw you on the box a few times and people felt they knew and trusted you.

'Excellent!' he said. He enjoyed taking charge. 'After this we'll go and find your dear mother a Christmas present. Then we'll go and have a really good lunch somewhere. Then we go back to your mother's, you give her her present and tell her you're not staying. You pack up while I wait in the car, then you follow me back to my place.'

Rachel looked at him with hesitant doubt. It all seemed so simple and sudden. 'Are you really sure you want us?' she asked.

You, he thought. You, any time. But there was to be nothing like that. Charles was a romantic realist. If this was to be his next love, if this damaged, fragile, beautiful creature was to be enticed into his bed, then the next few days could be only the groundwork. This must all be taken slowly and surely, Charles told himself. This was someone worth waiting for. He looked from her to Oliver, and decided against smiling at him again. It didn't seem to go down too well. 'Absolutely,' he replied. 'I cannot think of two people whose company I would like more.'

'Well, I don't know,' said Mrs Dean, as Rachel brought her things downstairs. 'Here one minute, off the next.' She jiggled Oliver and kissed him behind his ear, and Rachel reflected that this was the first time she had held him or been affectionate to him since they had arrived. 'Who is this friend, anyway?' She peered through the open front door to where Charles sat sprawled at the wheel of his BMW, lying back with his eyes closed, listening to the nine lessons and carols from King's College on the radio and hoping that the police weren't going to be out in force that afternoon, nabbing people over the limit, since he'd actually drunk the better part of the bottle of wine which he and Rachel had shared at lunch.

'Charles Beecham,' said Rachel, knowing that there was no possibility that her mother ever watched Channel Four, unless it was to watch the racing.

'Shall I tell Leo where you are, if he rings?'

When her mother said this, Rachel suddenly realised that Leo and Charles must know one another – he'd been at the party, he was one of the Names. He was one of Leo's clients! How could she have been so stupid as not to think of this before? Thank God, thank God, she hadn't mentioned his name when they'd been talking. She hadn't, had she? She was sure she hadn't. And he didn't know her married surname. Having told Charles that her husband was a promiscuous bisexual, it wouldn't exactly do for him to discover that this same husband was the Names' QC. Whatever she felt about Leo, she didn't want to sully his career. 'No,' she said to her mother. 'I'd rather you didn't tell him anything. He won't ring, anyway. I can promise you that.'

She kissed her mother, took Oliver, and strapped him into the car, then loaded the luggage. Charles's car pulled away from the kerb, and then Rachel followed, while her mother stood on the doorstep, watching until they were out of sight.

An hour and a half later, Rachel was sitting on the cushioned window seat in Charles's sparsely furnished drawing room, trying to make out the walled garden through the darkness, sipping a mug of tea while Oliver slept in his travel cot upstairs.

'This is the most beautiful house,' she said, and turned to smile at Charles, who was drinking his own tea in an armchair near the fireplace.

'It was my brother's, before he died. I thought I was going to have to sell up recently – nearly did, actually – because of this Lloyd's business, but fortunately my series has been sold overseas, so I'm not entirely broke. Not yet. The trouble is, it's a bit large for one bloke knocking about on his own, and I haven't really got round to furnishing it properly. A lot of the rooms upstairs are still empty, and a couple downstairs. Even this could do with a few more bits and pieces.'

Rachel glanced around. She would love to furnish a room like this all on her own. The whole house. Leo had decided how the house in Hampstead should be – he had such exact taste, such firm ideas, that she had never really had much of a say. Maybe that was what she needed. Somewhere of her own. But she didn't want to think about all of that right now.

Seeing the far away expression on her face, Charles asked, 'What are you brooding so mournfully about?' then immediately added, 'Sorry. Tactless question.' He got to his feet. 'Come and help me in the kitchen. Most of my friends are only interested in seeing how much of my alcohol they can consume, but I have to put out some food, just for the look of the thing.'

Later in the evening the house began to fill with Charles's friends, drinking, smoking and talking, drifting from room to room. As he moved amongst his guests with champagne bottles and jovial remarks, Charles took a peculiar delight in glancing occasionally at Rachel, who was sitting once more in the window seat, talking to people, apparently enjoying herself. She was an enigma to his friends, inspiring speculation, and he feasted privately on the fact of having her here, of knowing that she would still be there tomorrow after they had all gone.

That night when she went to bed, Rachel felt as though some weight had been lifted from her. She was free for the moment from all the burdens of familiar things. Charles's house was a haven, a nowhere place, and she was unutterably thankful that for the next day or two she could escape from the realities of her existence, and not think further ahead than the next few hours.

For Felicity, it was one of the worst Christmas Eves she had ever known. She had woken late that morning with a sickening hangover, scarcely able to remember any of the events of the night before, beyond drinking far too much champagne, trying to persuade Roderick Hayter to dance with her, and then being put in a taxi. She had woken beneath the duvet to find herself still fully dressed, her makeup smeared and smudged on her face, her hair bedraggled, her head aching foully. And then she had remembered Vince. Everything had come rushing back to her with depressing force. She had cried for half an hour until she felt worn out and worse than before. Then she had got up, showered, drunk a few cups of black coffee, and had a cleaning blitz around the flat. That had been therapeutic. In the afternoon she had gone to do some last-minute shopping with her friend, Lorraine. It had helped, being able to talk to Lorraine about her break-up with

174

Vince, but by five thirty she was back alone in the flat, her headache worse than ever, facing the prospect of Vince coming round to take his belongings and leave her life for ever.

She changed out of her jeans into a skirt and a tight black sweater which Vince liked, having bought it for her birthday, and put on a careful amount of makeup. She wondered whether to pack his things up, as a gesture to show she didn't care. But she did care. She cared very much. Each time she thought about what was happening, she started to feel tearful, but had to make the effort not to cry because it would make her face look awful. By the time seven o'clock came she began to feel jumpy. Every time a car pulled up in the street outside she went to the window and looked down. Not that Vince had a car, but if he was coming to pick his stuff up he would get one of his mates to bring him. She had left all his things in the wardrobe and drawers, hadn't touched anything. Why should she go to the trouble of putting his stuff together for him?

At eight o'clock she sat down and switched the television on, but the banal and cheerful Christmas programmes only made her feel more wretched and lonely. She began to wish she'd taken Lorraine up on her offer of coming round to keep her company. She'd refused because she knew this was something she and Vince had to sort out alone, and because Lorraine was a bit nosy and morbid that way. She'd have enjoyed it too much.

By the time nine o'clock came, Felicity was miserable and furious. Why couldn't he just come and get it over with? He must know what he was putting her through, on Christmas Eve too. She made herself another cup of tea and ate three Tesco's mince pies.

At ten o'clock, with a feeling of sick despair, she realised that he wasn't coming. She had a vision of him in a pub somewhere, with his mates, or chatting up some other girl. He would have forgotten all about her. Vince was like that. In his mind he'd already ditched her, so she didn't matter, her feelings didn't matter. In a fury, Felicity went through to the bedroom and wrenched Vince's pathetically few belongings out of the wardrobe and drawers and flung them in a heap on the bed. Then she went through to the kitchen and fetched a black bin liner, and stuffed everything into it – shoes, jackets, T-shirts, paperbacks from the living room, CDs, even his marijuana plant, which he'd been cultivating lovingly on the kitchen window sill. She dragged the bag to the front door of the flat and dumped it outside on the landing. She couldn't stay here tonight, she decided. She would ring her mum and tell her she was coming early. She and Vince had been invited round to her mum's place in Camberwell for Christmas lunch, only now there would be no Vince.

She had just picked up the phone when she heard footsteps on the stairs outside. Her throat constricting, she waited for the footsteps to continue up to the next floor, but instead they turned along the corridor and stopped outside the flat. Felicity replaced the receiver and sat down on the sofa and waited, wondering whether Vince had seen the bin bag, investigated it. He might just pick it up and go. But she hadn't heard the sound of a car or taxi pulling up. The next few seconds seemed very long, and at last she heard the scrape of his key in the door, then it opened. When Vince appeared in the doorway of the living room, she could tell he'd been drinking. He had that maudlin, bleary look. She sat with her arms folded, conscious of how quickly her heart was beating.

'Hello,' he said, and glanced round the room in a useless way.

'Your stuff's on the landing,' she said. 'I've been waiting in all bleeding evening. Some Christmas Eve. You could have come by earlier.'

He looked at her for a long moment and then shook his head. His dark hair was uncombed, and fell around his handsome, unshaven face. 'No, I couldn't,' he said.

'What – too busy putting beer down your face? Or lining up your next bit of stuff?' She had told herself she was going to stay cool, unconcerned, but the words gave her away. All the bitter unhappiness which she had felt since his phone call yesterday came rising to the surface.

He gave a sigh and sat down on a chair next to the dining table. 'No. No, I just couldn't. I mean, I just couldn't face it.'

'Well, face it now. I told you, your gear's outside.' And she got up and went over to the mantelpiece, where she had suddenly noticed his cigarette lighter lying. She turned and gave it to him, and he stretched his hand out listlessly. 'You might as well go,' she added. 'I'm going round my mum's in a minute. That's another thing – you can leave your key.' She watched as he leaned both his elbows on the table and buried his face in his hands. Then he said something, but she couldn't hear what it was, the words were indistinct. 'What?' she asked.

He took his hands away, looked up at her and said in a slow, blurred voice, 'I'm a bloody, useless failure, Fliss. That's why I'm getting out. I'm no bleeding use.'

Repressing the desire to agree with him, she said, 'Oh? I thought it was because you were fed up with me. Fancied a change. That's the way it came across yesterday.' Her heart beat hard and hopefully.

'It's not you. It's me. The fact that I've got nothing to offer. I can't take it, day in, day out. You with your good job, you paying the rent on this place, you buying the food, paying the telly, and everything. You can afford to go out for meals, have holidays abroad, and that, but what about me?'

'What about you? I told you I could pay for both of us to go to Spain at Easter. Anyway, you could pay for yourself if you didn't piss it all away down the pub or in the bookie's.'

'Yeah, well, there's nothing to piss away now, is there? Got no job, got nothing. That's why I can't stay.'

'It's up to you,' Felicity replied shortly, her voice concealing what she felt. She gazed down at him. Suddenly, to her horror, his shoulders began to shake, and he was crying. Vince, the hard man, actually crying. 'Oh, come on,' she said in a gentler voice. 'How come you got yourself into this state?' She knelt down next to him and put her hands on his knees. 'Anyway, d'you think I'm going to let you move out? How you gonna look for another job dossing at a different mate's every other night? You have to look the part, you know.'

His tears were short-lived, and he wiped his hand quickly across his eyes. 'You don't want me, Fliss. I'm fucking useless, man.'

'Not to me you're not. Just 'cos you lost your job, chucking in everything else isn't the answer.' She reached up and stroked his head. 'Say you'll stay.' From her position of sound, maternal strength she knew she could afford a little gentle pleading to bolster his ego. It was going to need a good deal of bolstering over the next few weeks. He wasn't likely to find another job in a hurry, not unless it was something menial. And how was he going to take that humiliation, while she carried on earning as much as she did? Barrister's clerks did all right. How times had changed from the days when she was just a secretary earning peanuts, while Vince always seemed to be flashing dough around, coining it on the horses, raking it in from overtime with BT. It wasn't fair. 'Go on,' she murmured, stroking her hand over his stubbly cheek.

He shrugged, then leaned down and embraced her, and she knew that he would not be leaving. 'You chucked my gear out,' he said reproachfully.

'Well, you can bring it back in again.' She kissed him on the mouth. There was one way she could think of immediately to restore a bit of his masculine confidence. 'And then you can get us a bottle of wine out the fridge and come to bed.'

Chapter Fifteen

On Christmas morning Charles slept until after ten. When he woke, he lifted his head slowly from the pillow and was agreeably surprised to find that he had only the mildest of hangovers. Turning over and propping himself against the pillows, he suddenly recalled Rachel's presence in the house, and realised that it had been the prospect of spending today with her which had stopped him from going over the edge last night, as he normally would have done. He ran his fingers through his hair and yawned hugely, contemplating the day ahead. At that moment there was a knock on his door, and then Rachel put her head round, her manner hesitant and a little awkward.

'I wasn't sure if you were awake,' she said, and smiled. 'I looked in earlier, but you were still asleep.'

The thought of Rachel coming into his room and observing him while he slept both embarrassed and touched Charles. With natural vanity, he wished that she did not have to see him like this, yawning and stubbly and bleary-eyed, and without his pyjama jacket. Charles did not like pyjama jackets. 'How long have you been up?' he asked, smiling back at her, folding his arms behind his head and trying to look nonchalant.

'Oh, since eight. Oliver, for once, let me sleep in. Would you like a cup of tea? I've made some.' Charles knew instantly, with gratitude but also mild irritation, that she had cleared up from the night before, that he would find everything neat and pristine when he got up.

She came a little further into the room, still holding the door, and Charles could see that she was dressed in a loose-fitting white shirt and jeans. Her feet were bare, her hair washed and shining. He had a sudden fantasy, one in which she came over to his bed, and let him slowly unbutton her shirt, unzip her jeans, and draw her into his bed and his arms. It was insupportably erotic, and, he knew, highly unlikely. He sighed.

'Tea would be marvellous.' She turned to go, and he added, 'Merry Christmas, by the way.' This is the moment, he thought – come on, turn around again, smile that smile, come to my bed, be my Christmas present. Oh, to unwrap you . . .

'Merry Christmas,' she replied, then disappeared.

'What shall we do today?' Rachel sat on the rug in front of the fire with Oliver, who was playing with a big red plastic bus, complete with passengers and luggage, which Leo had bought him. She glanced up at Charles. He was sitting in an armchair nearby with his second mug of tea. He had showered and shaved, and was wearing a comfortable pair of old, dark blue corduroys and a faded grey sweatshirt which, she noticed, matched his eyes. She felt very easy with him, she realised, and rather happy. He sipped his tea and let his glance wander from the fire to Rachel's slender, naked feet. He had never found any woman's feet so provocative. Was there any part of her which was not simply beautiful? he wondered. Then he heard her question.

'Sorry. Miles away . . . What shall we do?' He glanced at his watch. 'Tell you what. The Boxers always have a get-together after church on Christmas morning. It's a standing annual invitation. Why don't we slouch along to that, do our convivial bit, and then come back here and I'll cook lunch? The fridge is pretty well stocked up. I get a siege mentality at Christmas. Batten down the hatches, you know.'

'Are you a good cook?' asked Rachel, stretching her feet out to the warmth of the fire, and bending to kiss Oliver's soft head.

'Brilliant,' replied Charles nonchalantly.

Rachel laughed and rose to her feet, padding across to the window seat. There she sat, looking out at the frost which still covered the grass and branches of the trees, untouched by the wintry sun. There was a comfortable silence, during which Oliver sucked each of the passengers of his bus in turn, and Charles gazed at Rachel, thinking that he would never look at that window seat without wishing to see her there. What a fool I am, he thought. She is someone else's wife, going through a bit of a crisis, and I am nothing to her, nor ever likely to be. I'm twenty years older than she is, too. Probably just sees me as a father figure.

Rachel turned round. 'Should I change?' she asked doubtfully.

Charles thought of Lucy Boxer, who was always so chic and overdressed, and who had in recent weeks been making distinct overtures to him. He had a malicious notion that he would like to dent her ego by turning up with someone who, in a shirt and jeans, could look as effortlessly lovely as Rachel. 'No,' he replied. 'You look perfect as you are.'

Three hours later, while Charles was standing in his kitchen in a Wallace and Gromit PVC apron putting the final touches to his pheasant with cream and calvados, Leo stood moodily by the sink in the house in Hampstead, eating half an avocado with a teaspoon and drinking the remains of a Bloody Mary. He had spent the morning trying to work, but was restless and dispirited and had made little headway. He dropped the avocado skin into the bin and stared out at the garden, in which a lone blackbird hopped and pecked. The sudden sound of the telephone startled him, and as he went to pick it up, he knew immediately that it would be his mother, ringing from her sister Clare's house in Ruthin, where she was spending Christmas. He made an effort to sound cheerful as he wished her a merry Christmas, and listened for a few moments as she told him how his aunt was, and how many of his cousins she had seen so far. Leo tried, in that brief space of time, to think of some way of warding off the inevitable enquiry after Rachel and Oliver, but when it came, he found he could not.

He hesitated for a moment, then said, 'They're not here, actually.' There was a certain inevitability about telling his mother the truth. It was almost as though he had need of her concern, or pity, or even condemnation. All of those things.

'What's happened?' asked his mother, after the briefest of silences. Leo could hear the note of fear in her voice, and thought suddenly of how it must have been for her when his father had left her.

He drew in a deep breath. 'Oh, we've had a couple of problems lately. Nothing serious. Just ... Anyway, she's gone to spend Christmas at her mother's.' I think, he added mentally.

'Oh, Leo ... ' His mother's voice was slow and heavy with shock and disappointment. Well, he could understand that. She had been so disproportionately happy when he had got married, so pleased about Oliver. And she liked Rachel. She liked and trusted Rachel, and Leo knew, from the tone of her voice, that at this moment she unmistakably, and quite rightly, blamed him for whatever had gone wrong. The depth of her reproach was there in the very way she spoke his name.

He replied with defensive briskness, 'Yes, well, she'll be back in a couple of days. It's nothing to worry about.' God, now he had guilt to add to everything else. Why? Why should problems between himself and Rachel cause him to feel guilt where his mother was concerned? No use wondering, he supposed.

Maeve Davies instinctively moved to close the door separating her from the roomful of Clare's noisy family talking and laughing over the remnants of Christmas lunch, then tugged her cardigan around her as though chilled, the receiver close to her ear. She fought for something to say, something that would not be intrusive or too demonstrative of the panic she felt. They hadn't been married a year, and now this. She read so much about how easily people divorced these days, how families broke up. And Oliver – she'd seen him only twice since he was born. What if this meant that she would hardly ever see him from now on? As the fears began to pile up rapidly in her mind, the only thing she could think to say was, 'I don't like to think of you all alone at Christmas.'

Leo let slip a small sigh, half relief, half resignation. At least she wasn't going to launch into an anxious, in-depth enquiry into the state of his marriage. Not that that was her style, anyway. With Maeve, it was the things left unsaid which possessed the greatest force. 'I'm all right,' he said. 'It's not as bad as it sounds.'

'Really?' It was a naked plea for reassurance, not about him, but about Rachel and Oliver, the whole thing.

'I promise.' There was an uneasy silence, in which he could think of no way of prolonging this miserable conversation. 'Now go and wish that lot a happy Christmas from me. I'll speak to you in the New Year.'

When he put the phone down, it was as though the air about him was filled with unspoken questions, reproaches, demands for information. All the things she had not said. It had never occurred to Leo to wonder what kind of expectations and hopes his mother might have about him as a husband and father. Now, although she had said nothing, he knew exactly. And he was well on his way to disappointing her. No wonder he felt guilty. He must get out of the house, he realised. Its silence and emptiness oppressed him. He had tried to pretend that this was just another Sunday, but the knowledge that it was Christmas, that everywhere else people were with other people, bore in upon him. He wanted to see Oliver. He wanted to see Oliver with his red bus. God, it was pathetic. The truth was pathetic.

He put on his overcoat, locked up, and drove into town, through ghostly suburban streets where no one walked, past shuttered shops, and along main roads which on an ordinary day would have been crowded with traffic. He drove slowly along Embankment, deserted except for a few lonely cars swishing past him, and turned in through the gates to Middle Temple Lane. He parked his car and got out. The Inns, Inner and Middle, were totally silent, the windows of the elegant grey buildings gazing blankly down on the cobblestones, not even a breath of wind to tip the branches of the tall plane trees etched against the winter sky. It was bleak, lonely, but Leo found something uplifting in the utter silence and grandeur of the place. It was peculiarly pleasant to have it all to himself, to be the solitary figure walking through the cloisters and past the hushed stairwells, his footsteps ringing on the deserted flagstones.

Leo walked up past the church, where lights still shone from the service earlier that morning, and across the Strand into Lincoln's Inn. He had no idea of where he was going, simply intended to walk and think, try to open up and examine his life. His life. He remembered a time when that life, his own, private hours away from the places in which he now walked, had been one of excitement and gratification – the clubs, the boys, the early hours of the morning, the tantalising knowledge that anything and anyone could happen next. And above all, love. Love of a peculiar, fleeting kind. Where had all that gone? Perhaps, thought Leo, it was just as well it had gone. I am middle-aged, he told himself. I am forty-five. What business have I to be yearning after that kind of thing? His footsteps slowed, and he gazed around, his breath foggy in the cold, quiet air. It was wrong to think that anyone ever became too old for love. The body might slow, the joints might stiffen, the faculties weaken, but the heart remained capable of passions as painful and transporting as any experienced at seventeen. In many ways those feelings were more poignant in middle age than in youth. Too often unspoken or unrequited, too often perceived for the follies which they were. He stared around at the trees, soaking in the unaccustomed Christmas Day silence of the City. The very sky seemed like the vaulted roof of a great, hushed cathedral. He thought of Charles. There had been a time, once, when he would have basked in his growing affection and passion for another man without any sense of shame or foolishness, but something was creeping upon him of late, some sense of opprobrious self-evaluation. Or maybe he was falling into the trap of perceiving things through the eyes of the world. He suddenly wished fervently that he and Charles were twenty-one, and that he could indulge his feelings, his passions, as heedlessly as once he had. It could not be wrong to want to feel, for as long as one could, the helpless, dangerous delight of love.

Leo turned and glanced towards the buildings in New Square, and suddenly thought of Frank Chamberlin. Frank was a High Court judge, now in his late sixties, and one of Leo's oldest friends and confidants. There was much about Leo which only Frank knew and understood. He lived in residential chambers in New Square, a set of rooms at the top of Number 55. Leo wondered if he was there now. Little chance, he supposed. Although Frank was a bachelor and had lived in those rooms since Leo had first known him, he supposed that there must be family, relatives somewhere, with whom he had gone to spend Christmas. Still, since he was here, it was worth calling on him to find out.

Leo walked back down along the pavement to Number 55 and went in and up the four flights of stairs to Frank's chambers. The stairwell was musty, the silence in the building deep and old. Leo rang the bell and a few seconds later, to his surprise, he heard slow footsteps, and then Frank, tall and stooping, and wearing carpet slippers and a baggy cardigan, opened the door. A smell like the smell of school dinners wafted down the dim hallway, and from a room somewhere came the sound of a television.

'Good God!' said Frank. 'Leo!'

'I was taking a stroll through the Inn, so I thought I'd stop by on the off-chance,' said Leo, smiling at Frank's astonishment.

'Come in, come in . . . ' Frank shuffled back and ushered Leo in. 'Go on down to the sitting room,' he said, adding as he followed Leo down the hallway, 'I had Tom Lyle and his wife over for lunch, you know. They left just half an hour ago, had to go over to her sister's in Putney. Extraordinary, you dropping by like this. But very welcome. Always welcome. Go right in. Here, give me your coat. Whisky?'

'Whisky, please,' said Leo, handing Frank his overcoat. He sank into one of Frank's battered leather armchairs with a sense of utter gratefulness. Here, for an hour or two at least, he could enjoy some whisky and some safe, masculine conversation, escape from the realities and problems of his own life.

'So . . . ' Frank handed Leo a crystal tumbler filled with two generous measures of Scotch, then went over to switch off the television, on which he had apparently been watching the Christmas omnibus edition of *Coronation Street*. 'What brings you round here on such a day, eh?' He settled himself into another armchair and rested his own glass of Scotch precariously on the broad leather arm as he adjusted the cushions behind him. Then he sipped his drink and eyed Leo with clever, watery old eyes.

'I needed company,' replied Leo. 'Rachel's gone to her mother's with the baby.'

'Ah.' Frank nodded and drank again, smacking his thin, dry lips. 'Tom gave me this,' he remarked. 'Jura Malt. Very good, I think. Mince pie? Mince pie to go with it?'

Leo could not help smiling. 'Yes. Yes, that would be very nice.'

'Shan't be a tick.' Frank went out, presumably to the kitchen. Leo sat nursing his Scotch and looking around him. The furniture was solid and unremarkable, like that of a headmaster's study, the carpets faded, the bookcases dusty. The sweetish pungency of nicotine hung over everything, even though it was three years since Frank had managed to give up his thirty a day habit. Leo listened to the heavy tick of the clock on the mantel and knew suddenly that Frank was not going to ask him about Rachel, or probe him further about his unexpected presence here. The subject would only be broached again if Leo himself initiated it. Did he want to talk about it? Leo wondered. Frank might understand. Frank, after all, had been the person who had once suggested to Leo that he should marry, that a wife might be a useful means of scotching dangerous rumours. But Frank would have no answers, Leo knew. No, he decided, as Frank reappeared with a plate of mince pies, he would not touch upon his own life. They would talk of other things and people. Otherwise, thought Leo, as he glanced out of the windows at the darkening afternoon sky, he might be tempted to weep over the awfulness of it all.

*

The call came from the police station at four o'clock. In a way, as she stood in the living room doorway listening to Brian take the call, Alison Carstairs was not in the least surprised. Paul had gone out straight after breakfast, too wrapped up in some surly, awful world of his own to pay any attention to stupid things like Christmas presents or his family. The hours had passed – not too badly, the girls had liked their presents even though she and Brian hadn't been able to afford much – and everyone had eaten the Christmas lunch which Alison had cooked. Everyone except Paul. They would all have been quite cheerful – well, better than usual – if it hadn't been for the fact of Paul's absence. Alison had kept everything waiting for an extra half-hour in the hope that he might come, but she knew in her heart of hearts that he would be out all day. Doing what, she could only conjecture. He told her nothing these days. When she had found out towards the end of term that he had been truanting from school, she and Brian had tried to talk to him about it, but had met with only a dogged refusal to discuss anything.

Now, as she watched her husband's anxious, weary face, Alison told herself that it had been only a matter of time. She felt oddly calm, resigned to whatever awful thing he had done. She had gathered from the nature of Brian's terse remarks into the telephone that the police were involved, but that there had been no accident, that Paul was perfectly well. After a fashion.

'Well?' she asked, as Brian put the phone down.

'Joyriding,' replied Brian tonelessly. 'He and two other lads from school stole a car. The police caught them just outside Foxedge. I have to go down to the police station.'

The girls had come up behind Alison, listening, their faces childishly aghast at the realisation that their brother was in trouble. And on Christmas Day.

'What's Paul done?' asked Sophie, staring from her father to her mother.

'Nothing,' said Alison, turning and herding them back into the living room to their half-finished game of Monopoly. 'It's just something Daddy has to go and sort out.'

She watched from behind the net curtains as Brian walked down the short pathway through the shabby little front garden to where the car stood by the pavement. She had a sudden memory of the courtyard behind the old house, the space between the house and the converted stable block where the cars were always parked. His sleek, yellow E-Type, her gleaming Land Rover, the pretence of practicality over sheer ostentation. Look at us, we have money. She thought of Paul sitting in the police station. Was this how it was to be from now on? Was this really what a sudden fall from wealth and comfort did to a family? She would never have thought that material things could matter so much. All she could hope was that this incident, the shock of getting into such trouble, would have reduced Paul to a condition where she and Brian could reach him, so that at least they might talk and try to mend things. They had to hold on to each other now, since there was nothing else to put their faith in.

Charles and Rachel had sat for a long time over lunch, finishing their wine, Charles talking reflectively about his past marriage in the hope of eliciting more from Rachel regarding her own.

'Of course, Hetty and I were just children when we got married. You think you're grown up at twenty-two, but you don't realise how much there is still to learn. You only discover that later.'

Rachel leaned back in her chair, running her hands through her hair. Outside the dusk was gathering, and the shapes of bushes and trees in Charles's garden were blurring into darkness. Charles had switched on two lamps, one on the dresser, the other near the window, and the kitchen where they had eaten was filled with a low, warm light. 'I'm only twenty-eight,' she said, 'yet sometimes I feel that I've learned everything there is to learn. Except how to make life work.'

'How old is your husband?' asked Charles, chin on hand.

'Forty-four – no, five,' replied Rachel. She tilted her chair forward again and stared into the remains of her wine, wondering what Leo was doing right now.

Charles was faintly surprised at this. He had imagined her husband as being roughly her own age, the kind of person who was young and confused enough to be bisexual. Not that he had much idea what that entailed. He simply marvelled that anyone married to someone as lovely and desirable as Rachel should want to go around – well, the thought of doing that with other men was pretty disgusting. Charles had always played the strictly liberal line, all in favour of equal rights for homosexuals, lovely chaps – and girls, of course; lesbians, too, absolutely – but when it came to the nitty-gritty, what actually went on . . . He decided not to think about this, but to concentrate on the practicalities of Rachel's dilemma.

'If it's not an impertinent question,' hazarded Charles, 'how do the two of you come to be married? I mean, if he's . . . '

Rachel smiled sadly. 'I'm not entirely sure any more. I was in love with him, of course. He must have loved me, needed me, something like that. And I suppose I had the idea – well, it's that old cliché, women thinking they can change men. I thought that if –' She almost said Leo's name, but checked herself in time.' – that if he had me, he might not need anyone else. He had already told me that there would be no more affairs with other men. I believed him. I wanted to, God knows. And,' she sighed, 'there was Oliver. All in all, given the combination of ingredients, I suppose I shouldn't be surprised that it's all gone wrong.'

Charles rose and went over to a cupboard, from which he took a bottle of Chartreuse and two small glasses. 'Come on,' he said, 'let's have a glass of this and enjoy the fire in the drawing room. If it hasn't gone out.'

They left the kitchen and went back to the drawing room, where the fire was low but still flickering, casting shadows against the walls. Charles switched on a small lamp and chucked two more logs on the fire, while Rachel sat down on the hearthrug, slipping off her shoes and drawing her knees up as she leaned back against the log basket. Charles poured her a glass of the liqueur and handed it to her, then sat down in the armchair opposite her. The light from the fire cast a sheen on her black hair as she stared at the tongues of flame around the logs, which had begun to crack and sputter.

'So,' said Charles, resuming the conversation where they had left off, 'what about his suggestion – what your husband said about leading separate lives but staying together?'

Rachel did not look at him. She continued to stare at the fire, and was silent for a long moment. Then she said softly, 'I don't know. I suppose it's a possibility, but I don't think I could stand it for long.' She grimaced and sipped her liqueur, found herself about to say 'Leo's different', and paused. 'My husband is different. He's really a very detached person. I'm not. I couldn't live like that. God knows, we have, effectively, for the past two months, and it hasn't exactly been pleasant. I think he's met someone, you see – some man – and he wants to start an affair with him. That's my guess. He just wants – well, sort of permission, I suppose. To do as he pleases. But still have us. Me and Oliver.' She sipped again. 'Oliver, mostly. If I go, Oliver goes. He doesn't want that.'

Charles ran his fingers through his hair. 'Then why doesn't he just accept the way things are? Get on with life, give up having other men, women, whatever. If he wants to preserve the status quo that badly, I would have thought he could.'

'Ah, but you don't know my husband. He's a most persuasive negotiator, and totally self-interested. If there's a way of having it all without losing anything, then he'll find it. Anyway, he's already acknowledged to me that the sex thing is a weakness, something he either can't or doesn't intend to control. So.' She shrugged.

He gazed at her as she brooded by the firelight. So beautiful. A perfect Madonna. One was simply grateful that the divine infant was sleeping upstairs. He voiced his thoughts. 'I don't understand how he can be such a fool, married to someone as truly lovely as you are.' His voice was soft, reflective. Rachel glanced up at him, and Charles held her gaze for a long moment. He wondered vaguely, mellowed by the wine and the general ambience, whether now would be a good moment, whether he should just join her on the hearthrug, take her in his arms, hope for the best.

Rachel, her dark eyes fastened on his, divined something of this, and realised that she had been attracted to Charles ever since she had first met him. A faint thrill of nervousness passed through her. Until she had met Leo, she could not bear to be touched by any man, had been unable to allow anyone close enough to make love to her. The psychological scars left by her father and by later traumas had been too deep. It was partly why she felt so utterly emotionally dependent upon Leo. She wondered now if perhaps Leo had in some way healed her, had helped her to trust... That seemed absurd, given the way he had betrayed her. But she was able, she realised, to look at Charles now, to know his thoughts, and feel entirely unafraid. Perhaps it was not so much to do with Leo, as with Charles himself, his kindness, his easy good humour which made the mildly sensual gleam in his eye quite unthreatening. Even so ... even so, she hoped he would not do anything to spoil the perfect peace of the moment. At this point in her life, with all its confusions and uncertainties, she had no wish for anything beyond this pleasant, platonic friendship.

It's all too ungainly, thought Charles. I'll just creak when I get up, and crack when I bend down. Or in my state I might fall over altogether. Then I'd have to lie there on the carpet pretending I'd fainted, or had a seizure, or something. Anyway, the setting might be perfect, but the timing's not.

Charles let his lustful thoughts subside, took another sip of his drink and added, 'Actually, your gorgeous young presence in the house is going to earn me a lot of kudos in the eyes of my children tomorrow. I do hope you're going to let them labour under salacious misapprehensions.'

Rachel laughed. 'If you like. But I think the sight of Oliver is going to alarm them, unless you explain things.'

Charles rubbed his chin. 'True. They'll start to worry about their inheritance. Not that they've got one, given the rate that Lloyd's is swallowing up my money.'

The thinnest of wails sounded from upstairs. 'Oliver,' said Rachel, putting down her glass and getting to her feet. Graceful as a gazelle, thought Charles, suddenly realising that Rachel's very youthfulness made him feel incipiently aged. Was this a good thing? He liked to think of himself as still possessing a certain youthful charm. 'Bring him down here,' he said, 'and we'll teach him how to play backgammon and gin rummy.'

In London, Leo was watching a film which he had videoed months ago but had never had time to watch before, and wishing that he could expect at any moment to hear the sound of Oliver crying upstairs, so that he could go up to him. He was horribly conscious of the silence, and wondering when on earth Rachel was coming back. He had drunk too much Scotch at Frank's, and after the initial spurious warmth and sense of well-being, it had merely left him with a headache and an even deeper sense of depression. For the first time that he could remember in years, he realised that he felt lonely.

Chapter Sixteen

Late in the afternoon on Boxing Day, Rachel decided that she had to go back to London. Not that she particularly wished to. Every single moment of time spent in Charles's house had been a pleasant release from tensions in her own. Even his children, of whom she'd been faintly apprehensive, were as easy and pleasant as he was. Nicholas was a younger version of his father, but with darker hair, and Chloe was pretty and intense, faintly suspicious of Rachel at first, until she perceived that there was no romantic relationship between Rachel and Charles.

She had sat with them all at lunch, listening to their conversation, their jokes, and realising wistfully that this was something that she and Leo would probably never create. There was a closeness, a genuine affection, which had taken years to achieve. At least it was pleasant to be a part of it. It lifted her spirits, made her feel human, included, and she saw that the past few months of her life had been cold and devoid of real happiness. How strange it was, she thought, watching Chloe playing on the carpet with a chortling Oliver, that one's mind and life could gradually become numbed by a flat sense of unhappiness, so that one was left feeling that this was the only way to be. It was not the only way to be. But, for the moment, that was the way her real life was, and she had to go back to it and sort it out as best she could.

'Stay another day,' said Charles. But even as he said it, he was aware that it might spoil the stolen pleasure of these last two days to try to prolong it. Charles, with all the experience of middle age and countless love affairs, knew, too, that there was a certain progression in matters of the heart, and with a sensitive creature like Rachel, things must be managed carefully. Stage one had been very nicely accomplished. The marvel of it was that he had

191

established an affectionate intimacy without so much as laying a finger on her. Yes, the groundwork had been nicely laid. She could not now refuse to see him in London. They were friends, after all.

'I can't,' said Rachel, but smiling, pleased that he had asked. 'I get the feeling I haven't been very fair. I didn't even leave my husband a note. I assumed that he would know where I'd gone, but if he rings my mother and finds I'm not there ... ' Then it occurred to Rachel, if he had rung her mother's and found she wasn't there, where would she tell him she had spent Christmas? Well, she would simply have to worry about that when the time came. A dragging reluctance to go filled her, but she fought it. 'Anyway, we have had the most wonderful time. I'm very glad I bumped into you in Bath.'

'So am I,' said Charles. 'Otherwise you might still be at your mother's having a nervous breakdown.'

An hour later Nicholas brought Rachel's bags and Oliver's travel cot downstairs and loaded them into the boot. He and Chloe said goodbye to Rachel and kissed Oliver, and then went back into the house, leaving Charles and Rachel together by the car. Charles watched as Rachel strapped Oliver into his seat, Oliver sucking one of the passengers from his bus.

'God!' said Charles. 'The bus!' He ran back into the house and reappeared a few moments later with the red bus. Rachel put it on the back seat with the rest of his things.

'Thanks,' she said, and thought fleetingly of Leo. It would not have gone down well if his present to Oliver had been left behind.

Maybe, thought Charles, it would have been cleverer to let her forget Oliver's bus. It would have afforded an excuse to see her. But he had the feeling, as he opened the car door for her, that he wouldn't need an excuse.

'Well, thanks again for – for everything. I think it's done me a lot of good,' said Rachel. She felt a little awkward, not quite sure how to say goodbye. Charles solved the problem by taking her hand lightly and leaning forward to kiss her swiftly on the cheek. It was a comradely kiss, and the squeeze he gave her hand was the 'be brave' kind, nothing more.

'It's done me good, too,' replied Charles. 'I feel years younger.' At least he'd drunk less than he normally would have. He leaned down to the window to wave to Oliver. 'Be good to your mother, young man,' he said.

Rachel laughed. Much of what Charles did and said made her laugh. Not because he was particularly funny, but because he seemed to enjoy life, would rather be cheerful than not. She was going to miss his good humour. She got into the car and started the engine, then drove slowly down to where the gravel driveway met the road. She turned to wave to Charles before setting off, and felt a pang at the sight of his tall figure waving back. She thought fondly about him, and about the past two days spent with him, for most of the journey home, and it was only when she reached the outskirts of London that she turned her mind to Leo, and what they would say to one another.

Anthony and Camilla wandered through Kensington Gardens after lunch that day, talking idly, watching the ducks on the cold water of the Round Pond, and a handful of children playing with new bikes or boats. A biting wind whipped grimy leaves along the pathways. Anthony turned up the collar of his coat.

'Give me your hand,' he said to Camilla, stretching out his own. She laid her hand in his, and he rubbed her chilly fingers, then bent his head to kiss them. She felt her heart dip as he did this. Then he put her hand into his overcoat pocket with his and pulled her close to him as they walked. She smiled, and he glanced at her and caught this.

'What?' he asked. Over lunch they had talked of things remote from themselves, and there had been nothing to presage Anthony's sudden demonstration of affection. Yet they both knew that they had slipped into the warmth of intimacy perfectly naturally. The night of the chambers Christmas party had been a fresh beginning, erasing all memory of Camilla's infatuation, of the unhappy events of Grand Night. It had established a new friendship, entirely replacing the former imbalance, when each had been closely conscious of their disparate status in chambers. Now they regarded one another entirely as equals.

'Nothing,' replied Camilla. 'Just smiling.'

He stopped suddenly, put his arms around her and held her against him for a long moment. He could feel his own heart beating quite violently, and was not sure why. He had a sense of rightness, of completeness with her, that he could neither understand nor explain. He stroked her hair lightly with his hand. Then she lifted her head and he kissed her for a long time, without thinking about anything at all.

'The trouble is,' he said at last, leaning back a little to look at her and brush some strands of hair from her eyes, 'you are so impossibly nice. I can't think of another word for you.'

'I had a teacher at school,' murmured Camilla, 'who was always telling me off for using that word in my essays. "Use a descriptive word instead, Camilla!" she would say. And I would think, well, nice is a descriptive word. The trouble is, it applies to everything.'

'No,' said Anthony. 'Just to you. You are the nicest thing I know.' And he kissed her again.

After a while they resumed their walk, Camilla leaning against Anthony, her head dipped against his sleeve, feeling extraordinarily, wonderfully happy.

'You know,' said Anthony, 'that no one in chambers must know about this. Not that the situation has ever arisen before, but I have a feeling that certain kinds of relationships between barristers and their pupils might be frowned upon. So I shall have to treat you with my customary stern indifference. Will you mind that?'

She looked at him and laughed. 'I won't care.'

'Hmm. Actually, it will be quite good fun. Pathetically childish, but amusing, pretending something isn't what it is.'

'And what is it?' she asked softly.

'I don't know,' said Anthony. He looked at her, touched her mouth with his finger, tracing her lips. 'I honestly don't know.' But he had his hopes.

Freddie fumbled for the light switch as he set his suitcase down, then closed the door of his flat behind him. It had a musty, abandoned smell about it, even though he had been away for only a week. Bit much being sent packing on Boxing Day, he thought. But his son's wife, Gemma – dreadful, silly name for a dreadful, silly woman – had booked up some skiing holiday for the family over the New Year, so he'd had no choice. When Alec, his son, had been driving him to the station he'd managed to have a bit of a moan at him, but Alec had merely said that he'd told Freddie about it well in advance.

'You knew before you came that we were going away on the twenty-seventh,' he had said in mild exasperation.

Freddie had replied that he'd known nothing of the sort, but the fact was, he couldn't remember whether he'd been told or not. Didn't matter now. Here he was, shops all shut, nothing to eat, no milk except for that longlife stuff, abandoned by his own son's family as soon as Christmas was over. He muttered to himself and stepped forward into a little heap of newspapers. He'd forgotten to cancel them. Remembered the milk, but forgotten the papers. Oh, well. He stooped slowly to pick them up. At least he would have today's paper. Could see what was on television. Though he'd watched a damn sight too much of the thing over the last few days. No conversation to speak of, that family, except when he and Alec had escaped down to the pub. That had been more like it. Father and son. He'd been able to tell Alec about the Lloyd's litigation, fill him in on some of the City gossip. It was good to be able to show Alec that his father was still keeping abreast of things, pitching in, even though he was on the far side of seventy.

Freddie took off his coat and wandered into the kitchen, filled the kettle and switched on the radio, listening to a bit of Radio Four while he pottered about. He glanced in the cupboards and saw that he had some corned beef and half a packet of Smash. That would do for supper. And he had in his suitcase the bottle of Famous Grouse which Alec had given him after a trip to the off-licence.

Freddie made a mug of tea and went through to the living room, conscious of how cold it was. He turned on the gas fire, blowing gently at it to ignite it, then glanced at his watch. Five to seven. Might as well switch on his electric blanket now. When he had done that, he settled down in an armchair with his tea, unaware that he had been talking to himself below his breath for the past fifteen minutes, as he had gone about his little tasks. It was something he did much of the time now. He took a sip of his tea, then, muttering, glanced across to the window, where the curtains were as yet undrawn. Snow. The first thick flakes drifted in ghostly silence past the window pane, dimming to invisibility in the darkness. Snow. Hadn't seen snow in London since he and Dorothy came to live here two years ago. He settled back in his armchair, recollecting how the garden of the house in Hampshire had looked after a fall of snow, the little statues by the herb garden softly shrouded, the walk past the yews down to the wood an avenue of mysterious, wonderful white. The little lone birds that hopped about near the fountain in the deep, wintry silence. He remembered once taking a walk down to the pond to see if it had iced over, then trudging back up to the house, glancing up and seeing Dorothy waiting, looking out from the french windows, the room behind her warm and welcoming, tea by the fire. That picture had remained imprinted on his memory ever since. He closed his eyes and wondered whether it was snowing in Hampshire now, and who was looking from those windows at the hushed splendour of the garden that had once been his.

Alison closed her son's bedroom door. The sigh which she let out made her body shudder perceptibly. After a second she heard him turn his music on. His refusal to talk to her about anything was pure defiance, as was the music, but the fact that he kept the volume at a reasonable level indicated a certain contrition, she thought. God, having to read signs, instead of being able to speak to him. She went slowly downstairs. Well, she supposed it happened to plenty of boys, getting into trouble with the police. Only not her son, not her Paul. It was never meant to happen to him. When they had had money, she had seen it as a sort of protection, private schools to keep her children away from malign influences. Had she been right? Did this prove anything? Paul might have got into trouble regardless. Children did, wealthy or poor. Look at all the problems they had with drugs at those public schools. She thought of the court hearing that would take place in the near future, and her stomach tightened with fear. It would be in the local paper. Lucy Wright would read about it. God, why did she always think of Lucy Wright as a metaphor for the censorious wide world? She was only Lucy Wright, after all.

Alison paused at the foot of the stairs. It wasn't the court appearance she was worried about, or the aftermath. They probably wouldn't do much to a sixteen-year-old committing his first offence. No, it was Paul himself. Paul and the long term. God, the worry . . . It was as she stood there that she heard the sound, and thought at first that it was muffled laughter, that it was the girls playing some game somewhere. And then she realised it was not that. She took a step towards the door of the little workroom in which Brian kept all his Lloyd's papers and correspondence, then stopped, listening to the appalling sound of her husband sobbing uncontrollably. A sudden anguish made her put her hand out to the doorknob. Then she drew it back. There was nothing she could do or say. She couldn't comfort him, tell him that this was just a little thing, that Paul would straighten out in the long run, as teenagers did. Because it was not really to do with Paul – only partly. It was all bound up in the great parcel of guilt which Brian had put together, and which began and ended with Lloyd's and the money, the world, which they had lost there and would never recover. She stood for a few seconds and then, because she could not help and could not bear to listen, stole quietly away.

Leo was standing in the kitchen with his hands in his pockets, watching the beginning of the nine o'clock news, when he heard Rachel come in. He turned his head and regarded her through the open doorway as she took off her coat, unbuckled Oliver from his baby seat and took off his snowsuit. He turned his attention back to the television as she came down the hallway with Oliver in her arms.

'Hello,' she said.

He had not thought about what he would say when he saw her. He had not known what he would feel. But now he knew. He felt relieved. Annoyed, but relieved.

'Merry Christmas,' he said.

She sighed. 'I'm sorry. I couldn't bear to be here. Here, you take him.' She passed Oliver to Leo, who snuggled the baby against his shoulder, enjoying the small, compact feel of him.

'Did you go to your mother's?'

'Yes,' replied Rachel. Clearly he had not spoken to her mother. Anyway, it was true. She had gone to her mother's, initially.

'How was she?'

'Not exactly ecstatic to see us. Is there any wine in the fridge? I need something.'

'I think so.' He put Oliver into his high chair and gave him a spoon to bang with. Then he switched the portable television off and paced round the kitchen slowly. Rachel poured them both a glass of wine, realising that she felt oddly nervous. 'What did you do?' she asked.

He smiled. 'You can imagine.' There was a silence, punctuated only by Oliver smacking the tabletop with his spoon. 'So – ' Leo stopped pacing and looked directly at her. ' – have you done any thinking?'

'About what you said?'

'Yes.'

Rachel sat down at the table. 'Yes. Yes, I have. That was partly why I wanted to get away.'

'And?'

'Leo, isn't it a bit soon for this? I've only just got back.'

'I want to know how things are going to be resolved.'

'*You* want to know how things are going to be resolved?' She gave an ironic laugh, shook her head. 'Leo,' she said after a moment or two, 'do you think there is any future for us?' She could not help suddenly thinking of Charles and Nicholas and Chloe, how close they were. Close even in the absence of their mother. Maybe it would be better if she and Leo just cut their losses and parted. The effect on Oliver might not be as dreadful as Leo supposed. But nothing was that easy. She was still in love with Leo, still ready to take any chance that might bring him back to her. And that was why she asked this question, with hope.

He looked steadily at her. 'I don't know,' he said at last. Then he turned and glanced at Oliver, smiled at him and stroked a chubby hand. 'I told you, life is very confused for me at present. Call it some kind of mid-life crisis, the male menopause, whatever.'

'Do you want there to be? Do you want there to be a future?'

Oh God, thought Leo, she wants me to say that there is a chance in the future that I will love her again as she loves me, which is impossible. All I can do is lie, say yes, and gain some time. Then at least Oliver will be there each evening.

'Yes,' he said slowly. 'That's why I suggested we stay together – nominally, at least. Because I like to think things may change.' He felt no compunction as he told this lie.

Relief and hope touched her heart. 'In that case, we can try it for a few months. It seems an impossible way to conduct a marriage. But then this marriage isn't . . . ' She was lost for the appropriate word.

'Conventional?'

'I always intended it to be perfectly conventional,' replied Rachel. 'It's you who is unconventional.' He was standing just a foot away from her, and the sight of his familiar, handsome face after an absence of two days still had its old effect on her. She almost willed him to take her in his arms, kiss her, make love to her as he used to. But she could read in his eyes only neutrality, and a complete lack of desire. All she could do was to hope that this arrangement might, in time, return him to her.

'Good,' said Leo, as though some delicate negotiation had been satisfactorily concluded. 'Now, are you hungry?'

She was not surprised by this sudden switch of tack. 'Yes, yes, I am, as a matter of fact.'

'Why don't we have a takeaway? A curry, or something.'

'If you like. You order. I'm too tired.'

She watched him as he picked up the kitchen phone, realising that the past two days had helped her. She had been able to conduct that brief conversation, which Leo appeared to regard as having settled matters, in a clear and balanced way, without any of her former sense of desperate apprehension. Something of Charles Beecham's relaxed approach to life must have rubbed off on her. Whatever it was, she felt less pessimistic. She could only wait and see what the next months were to bring, after all.

'It's snowing,' she remarked, as Leo put the phone down. 'Quite heavily.'

Leo walked over to the window and looked out. 'I hadn't realised. If it goes on like this all night it'll be quite deep by the morning.' He thought about the con he had with Murray Cameron at nine thirty the next day, wondered how the trains would be. No point in driving. His heart lifted at the thought of being back in chambers, and he turned and plucked a surprised Oliver from his high chair, lifted him against his shoulder and carried him to the window. 'Look,' he said, pointing to the white flurry of flakes ebbing into the dark night. 'Snow.' Oliver goggled at nothing in particular, while Rachel sat at the kitchen table and watched them both, her chin on her hand.

Chapter Seventeen

'Two things,' said Felicity.

Leo looked up from the notes he was reading. He could tell from her face that Felicity was on an organising blitz. She had them every month or so, and he assumed that it was something menstrual, or to do with phases of the moon. There would be a sudden flurry of snappily arranged conferences and hearings, fees would be raked in, people's affairs sorted out, and Felicity would generally behave with uncharacteristic briskness. He supposed that, on this occasion, it could have something to do with the New Year. Like many people with gossamer willpower, Felicity was given to making resolutions. Leo knew this because they had both tried to give up smoking five months ago, he his cigars, she her fags. Each had taken comfort in the failure of the other. 'What?'

'One, you've got a date for the Capstall hearing.'

Leo sat back in his chair and stared at her. 'Already? When?'

'Last week in February.' Felicity thought he looked tired. Pinched, her mother would have said, or peaky, the shadows beneath his eyes and high cheekbones giving him a gaunt, exhausted look. Even the divine Leo had to age, she reflected. This case probably wasn't doing him much good. He worked all hours. So did Anthony, but Anthony was only young, he could push himself to the limit, and still have time for other things. Thinking of which, she'd have to have a chat with Camilla, who'd been going around since the beginning of the New Year looking quietly happy in a closed-up way.

Leo groaned. 'I don't believe it. Christ, two months to prepare. I may be dead by mid-February, at this rate. Go on, what's the other thing.'

'The other thing is that Sir Basil is doing the hearing.'

'Sir *Basil*?'

'So I've been told. Anyway, must get on. Ta ta.'

When she had gone, Leo swivelled round in his chair and stared out of the window at the few scraps of greyish snow that still clung to the slate roof of the chambers opposite. Sir Basil Bunting had been, before his elevation to the High Court bench a year ago, the head of chambers at 5 Caper Court, a magisterial, old-fashioned figure who had prided himself more on the calibre of his clients than on his grasp of the law. He had become head of chambers in days when nepotism was more widely practised than today, and although he had been a competent advocate, his skills had been those of diplomacy and courtly cunning, rather than legal acuity. Leo wondered whether the old boy was really up to the task of absorbing and understanding the vast wealth of statistical evidence with which he would be bombarded when the Capstall hearing got under way. Feeling like stretching his legs in any event, he decided to go and mull matters over with Anthony.

When Leo went into Anthony's room, Anthony was staring in a trancelike fashion at the bookcase, his face wearing an expression of vacancy which Leo knew, from experience, masked deep thought. Anthony roused himself from his meditation and glanced at Leo, sighing.

'I'm trying to work out how to draft this bit about the Lloyd's solvency return.'

'Well, if it helps to concentrate your mind, Felicity's just told me that they've set the date for the full hearing in six weeks' time.'

'Oh, wonderful. How are we going to get our act together by then?'

'If we have to, we will, I suppose.' Leo strolled over to the window, hands in pockets. Anthony, looking up at him from where he sat at his desk, noticed the slack lines on the skin of Leo's neck where the collar of his blue shirt touched it, the slight thinning of his hair, and reflected, as Felicity had, on Leo's ageing. He must be heading towards forty-five, thought Anthony, making a rapid calculation. Or was it forty-six? 'The thing is,' said Leo suddenly, 'I think I'll have to bring in another junior. We can't carry this workload between us.'

'There's always Camilla,' said Anthony. He felt an unreasonable sense of intrusion at the idea of another barrister muscling in on the territory which was his and Leo's. He liked the exclusivity of working with Leo, of maintaining the intimacy of the relationship which had been – still was – so important to him.

'She's very able,' said Leo. 'She's a great help. Very bright. But there's a natural limit to what she can do, as a pupil. Where is she, by the way?' he added, glancing at the empty desk.

'I've sent her off to dig up everything she can on asbestos. The Johns–Manville business, the US court decisions, medical research, market reports, that sort of thing.' He was quite glad that this work kept her out of chambers for stretches of time. He was too professional, and she too meticulous, to allow the fact that they shared a room to rob him of his powers of concentration, but there was no denying that her presence four feet away from him charged the atmosphere and inevitably distracted him. He had seen her every other evening since just after Christmas, ten days ago, and had got no further than prolonged and delightful spells of kissing her. There was, for someone of Anthony's age and temperament, a natural physical tension when she was around. Although there was nothing calculating or predatory in his attitude, it was difficult not to succumb to the temptation of devising ways and means of taking her to bed. She was an entirely different proposition from Sarah, and he was not entirely sure how things were to develop.

Leo nodded, then said, 'I think another junior is inevitable. Someone to devote their time exclusively to the asbestosis and pollution points and work up Camilla's research. You can't possibly do that as well as all the accounting stuff, and I've got to start drafting my opening speech.'

Anthony could see his point. 'I suppose you're right,' he murmured.

'Anyway, I'll attend to that. The other piece of news is that Sir Basil is going to be doing the full hearing.'

'Sir Basil? That bodes well,' replied Anthony.

'What makes you say that?'

'Well, leaving aside the point that no High Court judge who is also a Name would be allowed to hear our case, I can't think of anyone more likely to be biased in favour of the Names. His brother-in-law, Frederick Choke, has lost an absolute bomb on Lloyd's. He's on every duff syndicate you can name – Feltrim, Gooda Walker and, of course, Capstall. He's had to sell up his farmland, get rid of his vintage car collection, flog off the French château . . . '

'My heart fairly bleeds,' murmured Leo.

'You remember Edward Choke, chap who used to be a pupil here?'

'Vaguely.'

'He's Frederick Choke's son, Sir Basil's nephew, and he told me all this when I met him last week. Apparently his mother has been in an awful state about it all. So Sir Basil's heart has doubtless been moved by the iniquities suffered by his sister at the hands of Capstall et al. Can only be good for us.'

'If you say so,' said Leo. 'But I think you misjudge the righteous Sir Basil. I certainly wouldn't bank on anything. He's the kind of man who might deliberately lean the other way, if he thinks anyone might accuse him of bias.'

At that moment Camilla came in, bringing an aura of cold from the freezing day outside. Anthony felt an expansive internal pleasure at the sight of her, and she gave him a warm, fleeting smile as though she knew this. 'Hello,' she murmured to Leo.

As Camilla took off her coat, Leo glanced briefly from her to Anthony, and was aware of an imperceptible shift in the atmosphere, the unmistakable tension that bound two people together and excluded the other. There's something going on between them, he suddenly thought. He knew this instinctively and certainly, even though Anthony did no more than glance at Camilla as she sat down at her desk, setting down the bundle of notes she had brought in. His mind flitted over the times he had been with them recently, remembered the studied, offhand manner with one another at tea in the common room. A deliberate smokescreen. Well, put two attractive young people in close working proximity for long enough, and a certain chemistry was bound to evolve, he supposed. But he could not help feeling a certain pang at the thought that Anthony's heart and mind should be devoted to another person, as they had once been to him. Leo knew that even after he left the room Anthony and Camilla would continue to behave with exactly the same circumspection as they did now, but even so, his perception of how matters stood made him feel that he should leave. 'Don't forget Murray Campbell is coming over with Snodgrass and Carstairs at four,' he said. And he left, aware that he was childishly and irrationally irritated by the idea of Camilla and Anthony together. So far as life in chambers went, he was too accustomed to regarding Anthony as his own special property.

Henry felt that suffering in silence for a week was long enough. Since work in chambers had resumed after the Christmas holiday last Tuesday, Felicity had behaved as though nothing had happened that night after the chambers party. Henry could hardly believe it. He had spent all Christmas in agonies of longing and doubt, and when he had come into chambers on the morning after Boxing Day, he had expected to know the best – or the worst – from Felicity. Now he could stand it no longer. It was nearly lunchtime, people were drifting out of chambers towards sandwich bars, and Felicity was sitting in front of the computer, chewing on her thumbnail and swearing horribly under her breath.

Henry came up behind her and said tentatively, 'Felicity?'

'Bloody hell! "To copy edit. com files from the DOS directory to the FRUIT directory . . ." What's a frigging fruit directory when it's at home?' she demanded, turning and looking up at Henry. Henry sighed and leaned over to press a couple of keys on the keyboard, and the files that Felicity wanted sprang up on the screen. He could smell the faint fragrance of that perfume she wore – some cheap thing, but he didn't care, it was hers, Felicity's.

She grinned in delight. 'You are brilliant. Thanks.' She pattered at the keyboard for a few seconds, and then leaned back. 'Sorted. Yeah, what was it?' she asked, swivelling round in her chair.

Henry paused as Roderick passed by, pulling on his jacket and dropping a brief in the basket on his way out. He waited until Roderick had left, and then said, 'I've been meaning to talk to you.' After a moment's hesitation, he added, 'I mean, in case you'd been wondering . . . ' He faltered again. This was not easy.

Felicity folded her arms, which elevated her generous bust slightly, and frowned at Henry. 'Wondering what?' Her glance slid briefly to the clock. She hoped this wasn't going to take long. It was ten to one, and she was meeting Vince for lunch. He'd had an interview that morning with a security firm and she was impatient to learn if he had got the job.

'Well, wondering why I hadn't said anything. Since that night.'

'What night?'

'The night of the chambers party. When we – when I took you home in the taxi, and – and – '

He seemed terribly embarrassed, almost unable to get his words out. Felicity had forgotten all about that evening. The bits which she had ever been able to remember in the first place. What on earth was Henry driving at? Then a cold, awful fear crept upon her. He couldn't mean . . . They hadn't . . . had they? Oh God, no! No, she would remember . . . wouldn't she? She'd been drunk all right, but what if . . .? She couldn't remember anything between getting tight on champagne and waking up on her bed the next day.

She leaned forward, her manner suddenly sharp, startling Henry from his confusion. 'What? You took me home and what?'

'Well . . . you know . . . in the taxi.' Henry looked down at his hands, plaiting his fingers together.

In the taxi? No – that wasn't possible. In the *taxi*? 'Henry, I'm not sure what you're talking about.' He raised his eyes to hers, and she waited with faint dread.

'Well, you kissed me – I mean, I kissed you, and – well, a bit more than that. Nothing much, really.' He was finding this painfully difficult. 'And you just seemed to like it. We both did. Then I dropped you at your flat. And it was – the thing is, afterwards, it sort of made me think . . . ' He stopped, stared at her. All he wanted to do was say, 'I love you, Felicity,' but the words would not come out.

And then she did that awful thing. She giggled. She put her hand up to her mouth and laughed, mainly from relief, and partly because it struck her as funny. The sound made Henry feel as though he had been slapped. He blinked. She sat back in her chair and laughed again. Then she said, 'Oh God, Henry, I didn't mean – look, I didn't think what you said was funny, or anything. It's just that I thought, when you were going on about what happened in the taxi and everything, that we'd – well, you know. Done it.'

He gazed at her, realising that it had been no more than a light-hearted piece of drunken fun for her, what she could recall of it. She was even suggesting that it was not beyond the bounds of possibility for her to have had sex with him in the back of a taxi, just because she had been tight. He felt faintly appalled. Did she really think he would have, could have done such a thing? He looked down, untwining his hands and rubbing his palms against his trouser legs. 'No,' he murmured. 'Don't worry. It was nothing like that.' He remembered the softness of her flesh as he had touched her, caressed her, and could almost have cried.

She was silent for a moment, puzzled. Why was he bringing this up? Then she realised that whatever had happened in the taxi – and it clearly hadn't been much – he had misinterpreted it, had been hoping that it meant something. She had always known intuitively that Henry had a bit of a thing for her, but now she saw that matters had got out of proportion, thanks to the aftermath of the chambers party. She broke the embarrassed silence. 'Well, then,' she said gently, leaning forward as if to reassure him, 'that's all right, then. No harm done.' There was a pause. Still Henry did not look at her. What a fool he felt. 'Listen, Henry,' she added, 'I really like you. We're good mates. But whatever went on, it didn't mean anything. I was just drunk, that's all. I'm sorry.'

He sighed. 'No. No, I know.' He rose. 'Anyway, look . . . just forget I mentioned it. Just forget it altogether. Please.'

She nodded slowly and watched him walk out of the clerks' room, then sat for a while, thinking how sad things were for some people, how they always picked the wrong people to fall in love with.

Rachel was lunching with a friend from the firm of solicitors where she had worked before joining Nichols & Co, a woman in her early forties called Anthea Cole. She was small, spare and energetic, expensively dressed in a businesslike fashion, with a face which was still gamine and pretty, but with the faint aridity of early middle age. Anthea had been Rachel's mentor at her old firm, had seen her through her articles, and had encouraged her to develop an assertive manner, aware that beneath Rachel's hesitant manner there lay genuine talent and ambition. She had been pleased when Rachel had been offered a partnership at Nichols & Co, and at Rachel's and Leo's wedding she had watched and wondered, hopeful that her protégée would not be consigned ultimately to a life of domesticity and child-rearing, yet half-envious, too. She, Anthea, had no children. Now she sat listening to Rachel's tale of discrimination at the hands of her fellow partners.

'Of course, Rothwell fobbed me off with some stuff about a salary review in the new year, but so far as I can see everyone's pay, including Fred's, has gone up by a couple of thousand. Which leaves me in exactly the same position. And yesterday I discovered, quite by accident, that they've given him a car as well.' Rachel shook her head. 'I honestly can't believe it.'

Anthea sipped her coffee and gave Rachel an expressive look. 'You're only a woman, my dear. What do you expect? No doubt they imagine that, being married to Leo, the salary issue is neither here nor there. That's the way their minds work.'

'But they shouldn't care who I'm married to! I'm me! What if – what if I was on my own, and had to rely on my money to bring up Oliver? Why shouldn't I be treated exactly as Fred is treated? They made some noises about "commitment" and how they wouldn't expect the same dedication from someone with a young family, but that's rubbish. I know it is. I should be paid for the job I do. Everything else is irrelevant.'

'You're right, of course. But it doesn't always pay to be right. When I was your age – well, a few years younger, just starting out – I saw the way the cards were stacked. I decided that I simply had to outperform any man around me.'

Rachel smiled. 'Which you did.'

'Which I did,' agreed Anthea briskly. 'But one discovers, eventually, that women can't have it all. The great Shirley Conran myth is a lie. You can't work from nine till five, and be a wonderful mother, an amazing cook and hostess – not without an army of help. I thought I could make a career for myself, a really good one, and still have time for all the rest. A family, the lot. Then I began to look at the other women around me and saw that the deal wasn't cutting that way.'

'It's true,' murmured Rachel. 'My nanny, Jennifer, clocks off just when I get in, and there's still washing to do, ironing to attend to, meals to cook, shopping at the weekends . . . ' At least, thought Rachel, as she catalogued the domestic chores which crammed her hours outside work, it keeps me from dwelling too much on where we're all going, how we're going to be in five years' time.

Anthea nodded slowly. 'I realised it was a question of priorities, and so I decided to put my work first. Max and I agreed that we wouldn't start a family until I'd got a really secure footing in the hierarchy at work. It seemed to me that lots of women put off having children until they were in their late thirties, and it didn't seem to matter. If anything, you had more money to spend on bringing them up. That was what I thought.' She broke off, staring at her coffee. 'And then we discovered it wasn't as simple as all that. Babies don't just come to order. God, when I think of all the time and money we spent, the tests, the endless visits and consultations . . . The worst of it was being told that if I'd decided to get pregnant in my twenties, I probably wouldn't have had any problems.' She glanced up at Rachel. 'But that's the breaks. No children, but a powerful, lucrative job and no domestic ties.' Rachel noticed that Anthea's knuckles as she crumpled her napkin in her fist were white. Even in her moments of vulnerability, Rachel realised, Anthea was terse, unemotional. 'What a choice. I think, now, that I would sacrifice every paltry thing I've gained over the last twenty years, if we could only have a family. What is it, after all?' She looked up at Rachel and shrugged. 'It's just a job, when all's said and done. Just a job.'

Rachel thought of Oliver and nodded. 'At least you still have Max,' she said.

'You say that as though the having of Leo might be in some doubt,' said Anthea in arch surprise, her moment of semi-confession past.

Rachel smiled ruefully. No, she would not tell Anthea. She couldn't bear to explain to anyone how things were. She had been able to tell Charles, though. Why was that? She sighed, and looked away. 'You never know. I mean, with Leo. That's partly why I'm so anxious to make a success of my job. To be taken seriously. Not to be palmed off with second best just because everyone thinks that Leo is the answer to everything. I want to feel that if ever it's just Oliver and me, I can still hack it. Make a decent life for both of us. I live in fear, I suppose.'

'I don't know what to tell you about the set-up at work. Go to see your employment partner, I suppose. I'm sure you could get a sex discrimination case off the ground, if that's what you want.'

Rachel shook her head. 'That's not what I want. It seems too petty. It's like whining about the unfairness of everything. And what chance would I stand of an equity partnership if I stirred things up like that? No, what I want to do is to prove myself. There's a Pacific Rim conference coming up in Australia in a month's time, and I'm thinking of telling the partners that I'll present a paper. The Japanese clients I've been telling you about give me a sort of edge. The thing is, if I go, it means leaving Oliver.'

'Go. You've got a nanny. That's what nannies are for.'

'But it means asking Leo to be home early each evening to

take over, and he's got this Lloyd's hearing coming up sooner than he expected. I think he's got too much to do for me even to ask him.'

'Rachel! Stop putting Leo ahead of yourself, just because he's a man! Pay the nanny overtime, for God's sake! Double time, if needs be. Make some use of Leo's money while you've got it. If you can show that lot at Nichols and Co that you're prepared to go abroad on business, and do a damn good job into the bargain, then things will change. You'll be able to make threatening noises, say that unless you receive equal treatment, you'll sue them. The way things are these days, that will have them quaking. Very bad publicity.' Anthea's eyes shone, and everything she said filled Rachel with a sense of resolve.

She nodded. 'You're right. I'll do that. If I can prove to them that I'm as good as any man around the place, including Fred Fenton, then they haven't got a leg to stand on.'

When she got back from lunch, Cora called out to her from reception.

'Two messages while you were out,' Cora said, handing Rachel the telephone notes. 'One from Mr Nikolaos. Could you ring him back urgently at his Piraeus office. He sounded in a bit of a tizz.' Rachel groaned, wondering what fantastically complex mess her pet Greek shipowner had managed to get himself into this time. 'And the other was from a Mr Beecham. Didn't leave a number, didn't say if he'd ring back.'

'Thanks,' said Rachel, and turned towards the lifts. She realised that she was smiling. It pleased her to know that Charles had called. She had few male friends outside work, and she liked the idea that he had been thinking about her. Of course, it could never be more than a friendship – she had too much hope invested in Leo and their future together. Still, it would be nice to see him. Perhaps he would call later. But the afternoon passed, and by the time Rachel left the office at half past five, there had been no word from Charles.

Camilla sighed deeply and leaned back, weary of the documents she had been reading for most of the afternoon, and glanced at her watch. Nearly six o'clock. Anthony came into the room, his session with Leo and Murray Campbell over.

'How's it going?' he asked.

'I don't think I ever want to read another word about asbestos. I've just finished a light-hearted little report entitled "Asbestos: A Social Problem", plus medical reports from the *Lancet*, the *British Medical Journal* and the *British Journal of Industrial Medicine*. They've taken me the better part of three hours.'

'Cheerful stuff, I imagine.' Anthony dropped his papers on his desk and sat down.

Camilla grimaced. 'None of it exactly reflects well on Lloyd's. It's pretty obvious that the warning signs were there as far back as the early seventies. All those decisions of the US courts, construing insurance policies in strict favour of plaintiffs, circulars sent round the market by the Asbestos Working Party. Listen to this. This is an American attorney specialising in defending insurance companies addressing a meeting of the Lloyd's Underwriters' Non-Marine Association in 1981.' Camilla leaned forward, and the earnest expression on her face as she tucked her hair behind one ear and bent over her notes made Anthony smile slightly. '"There will be many more claims than we can possibly anticipate from toxic substances . . . such claims will often take many years to manifest themselves, and the pounds and dollars involved will be far greater than we can possibly imagine."'

'That's why Alan Capstall and others began to write those run-off contracts,' said Anthony, and yawned. 'To satisfy their auditors that they had made adequate provision for latent disease claims. I suppose it looked like good business – high premiums, good potential profits when margins on conventional policies were falling. But very, very rash, as it turned out. And, of course, all the outside Names knew nothing about what was going on. The run-off premiums were totally inadequate for the risks being carried. Asbestos claims began to mount, the US courts went for the deep-pocket approach, and bang – disaster for Freddie, Charles, Basher and all the rest of them.'

'What I don't understand is why Capstall and the others didn't see what was coming. There was all the medical literature available, and our research into asbestosis seems to have been ahead of the American stuff, if anything. You would have thought that someone like Capstall would pay attention to that kind of thing, since he was in the business of assessing risks. What made him write all those run-offs?'

'A mixture of arrogance and stupidity, I'd say. Which is why Leo should have a field day with Mr Capstall when he gets him in the witness box,' said Anthony, laying down his pen. 'Though no doubt Capstall will be busily blaming the reinsuring under-writers. It'll be interesting to watch.' Anthony glanced at his watch and looked speculatively at Camilla. 'Now, it's six o'clock and I don't have to talk to you about run-off contracts or long-tail syndicates any more. What are you doing this evening?'

Camilla smiled. 'Nothing.'

'In that case, I suggest we go back to my flat and I'll cook us a meal. Adam's going to the theatre.'

Camilla hesitated. She'd been back to Anthony's flat before, but Adam had always been there. She was aware, from the way in which things were going, that going to bed with Anthony was inevitable, and the idea, though desirable in itself, filled her with apprehension. When it came to sex, Camilla knew she was somewhat naive, but she couldn't pretend to sophistications which she didn't possess. She had had no more than five boy-friends since the age of sixteen, and apart from occasional ses-sions of what women's magazines used to call 'heavy petting', her sexual experience consisted of a series of unsatisfactory and guilty couplings with a university boyfriend in his room at the hall of residence two years ago. At that time it had seemed like something she should do, part of becoming grown up, and she'd felt that once she'd started it, once it had become part of the relationship, she had to go on with it. Lust or enthusiasm hadn't played much of a part. Her feelings about Anthony were entirely different. When he kissed or touched her she was conscious of acute desire, and she knew, as she gazed at him across the space between their two desks, that she couldn't spend the evening alone with him without something happening. Anthony, she assumed, possessed a wealth of sexual experience. She imagined that his past must contain a string of lovers – Sarah, for instance, was only one of them. She dreaded the idea of her own gauche-ness, of her inability to compare with someone as knowing and lovely as Sarah. She had no idea, really, of what Anthony would expect, but when she thought back to the sweaty embraces with Derek in the Clem Attlee hall of residence two summers ago, she did not feel particularly confident. She had always been shy about her body, and even the knowledge that Anthony cared about her, wanted her, did not convince her of her own desirability.

'Why don't we just go out?' she said diffidently. 'I mean, you needn't go to the trouble of cooking.'

She met his eye, and he knew immediately what she was thinking, what she was afraid of. This was something they couldn't skirt around any longer. He shook his head. 'No. I like cooking. And I feel like staying in, for a change.'

'All right,' she said, wondering if it would be.

Camilla sat self-consciously on Anthony's sofa, trying to read the paper and failing. She could hear Anthony clattering around in the kitchen, ostensibly putting some food together for them both. Since they had come back to the flat she had grown aware of a distinct atmosphere, an unmistakable sexual tension which made her nervous. She wished, really wished that they had gone out, instead of coming here. Then it could just have been as it usually was, and the most she would have had to anticipate would be a kiss at the end of the evening. What on earth was she worried about? she asked herself. It was absurd – after all, she wanted it to become a proper love affair. It was the kind of thing she had desired very much in the days when she had hero-worshipped Anthony. But that had been different. That had been fantasy, and this was very much real. Camilla sighed and tried to focus once more on the paper. But her thoughts wandered back remorselessly to sex and Anthony. She had to face it – however easy and affectionate she might feel nowadays in his company, the thought of going to bed with him terrified her. What if he didn't like her with her clothes off? What if she didn't know what to do, was too inexperienced for him? The whole prospect was depressing, and she knew that that was the last thing it should be.

Anthony turned down the heat beneath the pasta which he was cooking and glanced at his watch. Then he picked up the bottle of wine which he had opened, plus a couple of glasses, and wandered through to the living room. Camilla was sitting sideways on the sofa, her knees drawn slightly up, almost defensively, staring at the paper, unaware that her skirt had slid back to reveal the tops of her black stockings. That, together with the slightly troubled, childish look on her pretty face made her look extremely – if unintentionally – erotic. Anthony handed her a glass of wine and sat down next to her on the sofa. Camilla sat up awkwardly, pulling down her skirt, the newspaper sliding to the floor.

'Cheer up,' he said, taking a sip of his wine and stroking her cheek. He leaned over and kissed her softly on the mouth, then drew back, contemplating her. 'You are,' he said thoughtfully, 'incredibly sexy. Did you know that?' They looked at one another for a few seconds, and then Anthony took the wine glass from Camilla's hand and set it down on the floor next to the sofa. 'Come here,' he said, drawing her towards him and kissing her with greater intensity.

Oh God, thought Camilla, this was too nice, far too nice. And clearly Anthony thought so, too. He unfastened the top two buttons of her blouse and kissed her skin just above her breasts, his breathing growing harder, and Camilla, in spite of herself, arched her body slightly towards him at the pleasurable sensation. Why was it, she wondered, that her body seemed to respond so effortlessly, so easily to everything he did, when her mind was doing frantic, unconnected things somewhere else? She could feel his hands sliding inside her clothing, over her breasts, and with a little moan she lay back on the sofa beneath him, let him kiss and touch her. Then she heard herself say, for some reason, 'What about the pasta?'

'Oh, sod the pasta,' muttered Anthony, and began feverishly to try to unfasten her clothing.

Camilla struggled into something of an upright position. 'No, really,' she murmured, 'won't it burn? I mean – shouldn't you . . .'

Anthony stopped what he was doing and looked at her. She could feel his chest rising and falling beneath his half-unbuttoned shirt as his breathing slowed. 'What *are* you going on about?' he asked. Camilla said nothing, tried to straighten her hair, and Anthony pushed her gently back on the sofa, resuming his kissing and exploration of her underwear. But again she pushed him off. 'Don't,' she muttered.

'Don't?' Anthony propped his head on one elbow and looked at her in astonishment. 'It's not the pasta that's bothering you, is it? Come on, what's up?'

'It's just . . .' Camilla let out a sigh and met Anthony's gaze. How absolutely lovely he looked, she thought, with his hair all

213

rumpled, that little pulse beating his neck. What on earth was wrong with her? Maybe she should just tell him, get it out of the way. She drew in her breath and said, 'If you want to know, I really don't think this is such a good idea. I mean, it's just . . . I'm not, you know, very experienced.' He said nothing. Oh, God, thought Camilla, this was coming out all wrong. What did she sound like? She put her hands over her eyes so that she would not have to look at him and said quickly, 'Actually, I'm quite scared of this. Of you. I'm frightened that I won't be any good. And everything has been so nice between us up till now, that I just think it would be awful if we made a mess of things.'

There was a silence, and then Camilla could feel his body shaking against hers. She realised he was laughing. He pulled her hands away from her eyes. 'I'm sorry,' he said, still laughing. 'But you are so sweet. You really are.' She watched him uncertainly as his laughter died away, leaving only a smile so thoroughly filled with affection that she began to feel distinctly better about everything even before he spoke. 'I don't want you to worry about anything at all. There is absolutely nothing *to* worry about. Don't think about it. Do what comes naturally. I have to say that, until you started going on about the pasta, you were doing it very well indeed.' He kissed her lightly. 'Would it help,' asked Anthony gently, 'if I were to tell you that you are the most desirable, the most fantastic turn-on anyone could imagine? And that I want you very, very much?' She nodded, and he kissed her again, drawing her against him so that she began once more to feel that familiar, dizzying heat spreading through her body. Only this time her anxiety had subsided, and she returned his kiss hungrily. Anthony drew his mouth away from hers. 'In that case,' he said, 'I shall go on telling you all night, because it's true.'

Half an hour later she was lying face down on the rumpled sheets of Anthony's bed, inert, drowsily happy. She smiled and shivered as Anthony drew his fingers lightly across her shoulders, then dipped his head to kiss the curve of her back. He lay down, his head next to hers on the pillow, lightly lifting strands of hair from the side of her face so that he could look at her properly. She was wonderful. Soft and voluptuous, eager and wonderfully unspoilt. He lay looking at her, and thought how completely he loved her. Nothing could be more worthwhile than the amount of time he had spent getting to know her, learning gradually that he wanted her in a way which he had never wanted anyone else before.

She looked back at him, trying to fathom the faraway look in his eyes. 'What are you thinking?' she murmured.

'I'm thinking,' said Anthony, shifting slightly and turning his head to stare at the ceiling, 'how stupid I have been up till now. How I have always got things the wrong way round.' He looked back at her. 'But now they are just as they should be.'

She smiled. He had been absolutely right. She had worried about nothing. Clearly sex with someone you really loved was very different from any other kind. Anyway, she had taken him at his word and had done what came naturally, and it had been wonderful. And in spite of her own sense of awkwardness, Anthony seemed to like her very much without her clothes on, so that was all right. In fact, it was more than all right. She felt prized, desired, perfect . . . and then suddenly remembered what Anthony had been doing in the kitchen before all this.

'I'm still a bit worried about that pasta,' she remarked.

'Oh, bugger,' said Anthony, and leapt out of bed.

Chapter Eighteen

Rachel went to Mr Rothwell next morning with her proposal for attending the conference in Sydney. She had discussed it with Leo the previous evening and he had seemed perfectly happy for her to go, so long as Jennifer was able to work during the evenings. In fact, he had been enthusiastic and supportive in a way which quite cheered her up. Now, as she sat before Mr Rothwell in his office, she felt confident, buoyant.

'... so I thought I could present a paper on mycotoxins in cargoes. I've noticed that it's something which exercises our Japanese clients when it comes to food cargoes, and there doesn't seem to have been much coverage of it so far. I've been studying the Working Party's latest report, and I think it would make an original topic.'

James Rothwell swivelled his chair from side to side and regarded Rachel thoughtfully. Ever since that confrontation with her at the end of last year he had felt rather wary of her. That cool, beautiful composure of hers had always daunted him, and the business of salary differentials had added a certain guilty unease. Still, she hadn't mentioned it again. No doubt she realised that it was only a point of principle, and that she and her husband earned enough money between them to make it not worthwhile fussing over. He was somewhat surprised, however, that she was so keen to travel to this conference, and leave her baby for a week. Perhaps there was some hidden agenda. He mulled over her suggestion for a few seconds.

'All very complex and scientific, though, isn't it?'

'Exactly,' said Rachel. Her manner was not exactly eager, since she was too contained to manifest that kind of emotion, but her voice took on a certain intensity. 'There's an enormous amount of scientific literature on the subject, and the governments in different countries all seem to issue different guidelines. I think it would be useful to provide simplified background information and some advice on what shipowners should do if they run into problems over mould growth in cargoes.'

James Rothwell nodded. It would be quite impressive to have someone from the firm covering this kind of area, and Rachel was sufficiently meticulous to ensure that any paper she presented would be of the highest standard. Those looks of hers would go down well, too. Her Japanese clients had brought in a great deal of useful extra business, and this could be a way of courting some more. The firm could do with some Pacific Rim expansion. 'Very well,' he said. 'If you think you can get it together in two weeks' time. I understand you've got quite a heavy caseload at the moment?'

'Don't worry. I'm sure I can handle it.' She would just have to find time after Oliver was asleep.

Rachel left Mr Rothwell's office, mentally calculating the amount of office time she could set aside for working on the paper, and found the phone ringing in her room when she returned. 'Hello?'

'Rachel? This is Charles. Charles Beecham.' At the sound of his voice she smiled with pleasure and sat back in her chair. 'Sorry I couldn't call back the other day. I had to spend all afternoon doing a voice-over for this series. Anyway, how are you?'

'I'm fine. And you?'

'I'm being run completely ragged at the moment, if you want to know the honest truth. I've been banging backwards and forwards between the studio and the British Library for the past two weeks. I'm trying to research my next series on the history of China. I thought I knew quite a lot about it, but in fact I know practically next to nothing. Which is not good news for someone who's meant to be presenting an authoritative historical perspective.' He wondered if he was babbling. 'Anyway, it would do me a large amount of good to see you. How's your work going?'

'Very well, actually. I'm about to start putting together a paper on mycotoxins in food cargoes,' replied Rachel. It struck her for the first time how much she liked Charles's voice, which seemed to be racy yet relaxed at the same time.

'Now that,' said Charles, 'sounds fantastically boring. Just the

217

thing to take my mind off the Shang dynasties in 12BC. I feel I need to go into a catatonic state just to wind down. Why don't we have lunch together, and while you talk to me about those thingies in cargoes I can drink too much wine and let my eyes glaze over.' And feast themselves upon you, he thought. He had had several vivid and erotic fantasies about Rachel since she had stayed at his house over Christmas, and on the more metaphysical side had felt distinct pangs each time he passed the window seat in his drawing room. With any luck, he told himself, relations between her and her husband might have deteriorated even further. Not a charitable thought, he knew, but sometimes one had to press the worst kind of hopes into service in the cause of a successful seduction.

Rachel laughed. It was wonderful, talking to a man who amused you. Leo had once, when he had cared to. Thinking of this, she remembered the deal which they had struck about leading separate lives. There could be no harm in having lunch with Charles, could there? Yet she knew that even having to ask herself that question was an indication that she did not entirely trust her own feelings where Charles was concerned. And she was well aware that Charles's intentions regarding their relationship were not of an entirely platonic nature. Still, it would simply be a question of making sure the thing stayed purely friendly. 'Yes,' she replied. 'I'd like that.' She flipped through the pages of her desk diary. 'Next week doesn't look too busy.'

'No,' replied Charles firmly. 'Now that you've said yes, I want to see you as soon as possible. Waiting till next week would be pure torment.' No harm in a little positive flirtation, thought Charles. Can't pretend to be too platonic and matey, or the signals get distorted. She's got to fancy me a bit, after all, even if she thinks we're just good friends. 'In fact, today – no, can't do today. Tomorrow. How about tomorrow?'

Rachel laughed, a little taken aback. 'Well, it's a little sudden, but I suppose . . . '

'Excellent,' said Charles briskly. 'Caprice. You know Le Caprice? Let's say twelve thirty. How's that?' They might not have a table at such short notice, but he'd just have to pull rank, play the Channel Four celebrity card. In fact, he'd pop into the restaurant personally on his way back from the studio later today. A smile known to work miracles should be put to good use.

'Fine,' said Rachel. 'I'll see you then.' And Charles, in his mercurial fashion, hung up and was gone.

That evening, Sarah was sitting in her favourite wine bar with a handful of friends. It was eight thirty, she knew she should be preparing for that tutorial on letters of credit and documentary transfers tomorrow morning, but she couldn't be bothered. If she smiled seductively at Benjamin, that swot with the over-active sebaceous glands in her tutorial group, he would let her copy out his work and, with a few subtle amendments, she could pass it off as her own. He had been getting a bit iffy about that lately, and she might have to resort to something a little more tantalising than smiling to keep him sweet. Not an appetising thought, but anything was better than staying home working every night. Not that she had any intention of failing her Bar finals. She would wait until the exams were four weeks away, and then get her head down. As these thoughts passed through her mind, she turned and glanced with mild interest at the newcomer to the group whom someone was introducing, casually appraising him with her habitual half-smile. He was tall, with a lazy, sardonic face, and dark hair which fell over his eyes, which he pushed back every so often with his hand. He sat down next to Sarah with his drink. He put out his hand and she shook it.

'You're a solicitor? Which firm do you work for?' asked Sarah.

'More Church,' replied the man. 'Know it?'

'Vaguely,' replied Sarah, raising her glass to drink, aware that she was being subjected to an appraisal every bit as arrogant as her own. She noticed that the man had a pleasantly drawling voice of the public school variety, which she always found something of a turn-on. To her it betokened a superb indifference, which she preferred to everyday demonstrations of polite interest. Those bored her. She added, 'I'm sorry. I didn't catch your name.'

'Richard Crouch,' he replied.

'What kind of work do you do?'

'Oh, shipping, commercial stuff . . . Actually, I'm involved in the Lloyd's litigation at the moment. Acting for a firm of auditors, Marples and Clark.'

Sarah's glance narrowed imperceptibly. 'You mean this Capstall thing – where the Names on his syndicate are suing the managing agents, and everyone else in sight?'

Richard glanced at her in slight surprise, but without adjusting his pose of casual unconcern. 'Are you familiar with the case?'

'Hmm.' Sarah smiled and let her glance slide away. 'You might say that.' And as she thought of Anthony, not without a tiny pang of bitterness, one of those coincidences of thought and event occurred, and she looked towards the doorway and saw Anthony himself coming into the wine bar with Camilla. They went to sit at a table near the window, while Sarah and her friends were tucked further back in the smoky recesses, but still she could see him quite clearly. Her pulse quickened slightly at the surprise of encountering him. She had imagined they might bump into each other before now in the confines of the Temple, but this was, in fact, the first time she had seen him since they had spoken on the phone. Her attention distracted from the man at her side, she watched as Anthony said something to Camilla, then reached out and put his hand over hers before getting up and going over to the bar. Sarah turned away quickly, anxious for some reason she could not presently fathom, not to be seen by either Anthony or Camilla.

She turned back to Richard Crouch. 'I'm sorry – what were you saying?'

'It was what you were saying, actually – about the Capstall case.'

'Oh – ' Sarah hesitated, glanced briefly again at Anthony as he walked back to his table with a bottle of wine and two glasses. 'Oh, yes . . . I . . . ' She was about to say that she knew someone who was involved in it, and then she was fleetingly touched by malicious inspiration. 'Actually,' she said slowly, mischievously, catching Richard's eye, 'I heard something rather interesting the other day about a couple of the barristers who are working on that case.'

Richard's lazy expression brightened. Like all City solicitors, he relished good gossip. He raised his glass and drank, his eyes on Sarah's face, and murmured, 'Do tell me.'

'Well,' Sarah leaned forward and lowered her voice slightly, 'apparently the two counsel who are acting for the Names have been having a bit of a fling together.'

He stared at her in mild but genuine astonishment. 'The two instructed by Nichols and Co? But that's Leo Davies and – and – what's the other chap's name?'

'Oh, I forget,' murmured Sarah. 'They're in the same chambers. Anthony something.'

'Cross. Anthony Cross,' recalled Richard. 'Good grief. You mean they're actually . . .?'

Sarah shrugged. 'Apparently. It's what I've heard. Quite a passionate affair, by all accounts.'

At that moment another man appeared and tapped Richard on the shoulder. 'Come on. I booked that table for half eight.'

Richard glanced up at him and drained his glass. Then he said to Sarah, 'Sorry, have to go. Meeting some friends for dinner. Anyway . . . ' He paused, looking at her thoughtfully, '. . . it was interesting talking to you. See you again, perhaps.'

'Bye,' murmured Sarah, half-smiling. She watched him leave. Then she sat back in her chair, musing, wondering how long it would take that little breath of scandal to seep through the ranks of barristers and solicitors working on the Capstall case. If her judgement of Mr Crouch was correct, she imagined it would not be very long.

The next day Charles sat waiting for Rachel in the restaurant, trying to concentrate on the newspaper which he had brought with him, glancing up each time someone came through the door, his heart taking a little dive of disappointment when it wasn't her. A number of women diners glanced across occasionally at the lanky, good-looking man in the corner with the greying blond hair, vaguely recognising his features and trying to place him, but he was oblivious of their attention. He felt exactly as he had done when he was sixteen, and had waited forty-five minutes outside the fish and chip shop in Richmond High Street for the girl he had thought would be the love of his life. Valerie. He would never forget her. She hadn't showed up. Maybe Rachel wouldn't show up either. He sighed, returned to his paper, and was just becoming interested in an item about genetic engineering in tomatoes when she appeared. He hadn't even seen her come in. Suddenly she was just there, smiling down at him, and he scrambled away his paper and stood up, leaning across to kiss her. Heads in the restaurant turned again.

As she sat down, he marvelled at how vivid and compelling the reality of her was. His imperfect recollections of her were insipid by comparison. She was wearing her hair tied back, revealing her long, slender neck, and was wearing some woollen, clinging dress of greyish blue. She looked older, more sophisticated than she had done in shirt and jeans, and Charles felt faintly intimidated by her composure. He had no idea that Rachel had spent twenty minutes that morning deciding what to wear, or that her apparently serene manner now was due to nervous restraint. She had told herself that she had no business worrying about what to wear. It was only lunch with a friend, after all. Why, then, had she felt a faint tremor of guilt as she fastened on the silver filigree necklace which Leo had given her the Christmas before last, when she had supposed him still in love with her?

But any faint troublings of her conscience were eclipsed now by the sight of Charles. He smiled his broad, captivating smile, but without his usual self-conscious intent.

'You look – ' The appropriate superlative eluded him. ' – very well,' said Charles, gazing at her, then glancing away as if in search of a waiter, in case his admiration was too obvious.

'Thank you,' replied Rachel. 'I think I'm a great deal better than when I last saw you.'

Again his heart took a little tumble off the springboard. Oh God, she and her husband were back together again, everything was sorted out, and he was going to have to sit through an agonising lunch listening to a rhapsodic account of how perfect her marriage was. He needed a drink. Forcing a smile, he asked, 'You mean everything's all right now? With your husband, I mean?' It really was ridiculous the effect that she had on him. Charles Beecham, the suave media personality, the handsome lothario, reduced to a mass of nervous longing by this cool creature.

Rachel glanced away dismissively. That was one subject she definitely wanted to steer clear of. 'No, nothing's changed there. Apart from the fact that we've agreed to the truce I told you about. He leads his life and I lead mine. Now – ' She smiled, picked up the menu and scanned it, ' – let's forget all that and talk about something pleasant.'

Over lunch they talked easily, animatedly. Rachel asked about his children and his work, and Charles, especially after his second glass of wine, basked in the knowledge that he was being amusing and scintillating, and that she was enjoying herself. He loved the way her blue eyes seemed to grow even more incandescent when he made her laugh, so he tried to do it as often as possible. And when Rachel was explaining to him the mysteries of toxic mould growth in food cargoes, he was able to sit and take pleasure in simply watching her, without listening to a word she said. At one point she broke off, smiling, and shook her head.

'You're not remotely interested in any of this, are you?'

He sat back, arms folded. 'Not in the least. But I could spend all day listening to you. So long as I'm not expected to take notes and answer questions afterwards, that is.' He paused, then said softly, musingly, 'Do you know how incredibly beautiful you are?'

Rachel ducked her head slightly, looking away. She was not accustomed to being talked to in such a way, and had none of the usual skills of female repartee with which to respond. 'No,' she murmured. 'At least, I don't think I am.' She looked round quickly for the waiter. 'I really think I could do with more coffee,' she added.

Charles, watching her, suddenly realised that lunch was nearly over, and that, apart from being amusing and companionable, he had not advanced his cause one whit. Instinct took over, and he surprised even himself by using a tactic which he had not employed for years. He leaned forward, caught her gaze, and said in no more than a murmur, 'Don't laugh at this, but I have fallen terribly in love with you.' He did not smile, and the words, the earnestness of his voice, astonished Rachel. For several long seconds neither said anything, but as they looked at one another, each was conscious of an honesty of exchanged emotion. Good God, thought Charles, maybe it's true. Maybe I actually am in love with her. Not just fancying her, or lusting after her, but completely and helplessly nuts about her.

Rachel managed to glance away. 'No, you're not,' she said faintly. That he had spoken as he had, that they had looked at one another so candidly, had made her realise just how dishonest she had been about her possible feelings for this man. All it had taken were those few words, and she felt intensely vulnerable. Oh, just to be loved by someone as kind and easy as he was ... But she pushed the thought aside. There was still Leo. There would always be Leo. Charles was the kind of man who probably made love to as many women as took his fancy. It was nothing more than that.

His voice went on, earnest and gentle. She had never heard him speak like this before, and was surprised at how easily it moved her. 'I'm going away on Saturday. To China. For this series. Can I see you again before then?' he asked. The atmosphere between them was suddenly charged, and he decided to see how much emotional capital there was to be made out of keeping it at this pitch. No frivolity.

She looked at him. 'No,' she said, and knew instantly that she spoke against her will. But what else could she do? While there was Leo, still the possibility of a future with him, there could be no question of letting anyone else into her life. And Charles, she sensed, was dangerous.

'When I get back, then? I'm only going for three weeks.'

She hesitated. 'I'll be away. At this conference. But I couldn't, anyway. Look, Charles – '

'Don't. Don't try to tell me that this is nonsense. You have no idea – ' He broke off, his gaze still fastened on her face, then suddenly smiled ruefully. 'I shouldn't have opened my mouth. I can't bear to see you looking at me in that guarded, unhappy way. Look, forget what I said and just – just behave as though I had never said anything. Please. Too much wine, got carried away by your intoxicating presence. Now, smile at me. Please?' He looked so droll and pleading that she could not help but smile. A tension within her relaxed. 'Good,' he said, deciding to steer the atmosphere back to sunnier waters, pleased with the way in which matters had significantly intensified. 'But no matter what you say, I have to see you again. If only to continue the seminar on mould growth, or whatever it was.' He motioned to the waiter for the bill. 'I'll call you.' She opened her mouth to speak again, possibly in protest, and before she could say anything he added, 'I don't care how often you say no, I'll keep calling.' He gave a carefree smile. 'Now that I've found you, I have absolutely no intention of letting you go.' When he said this, Rachel was conscious of feeling a mixture of helplessness and anxiety. If only everything could be entirely beyond her control, in the way that he suggested. But life wasn't like that, she knew.

Lunch finished in the same companionable way in which it had begun, but there was no escaping the new emotional element which Charles had introduced. He kissed her goodbye in the same brotherly fashion as before, and the hand which he raised as her taxi drove away was no more than the casual salutation of one friend to another. But as she tried to marshal her concentration at work that afternoon, Rachel's mind kept slipping back to the things he had said in those few profound moments, and the expression in his eyes, and each time she felt a delicious and irrepressible thrill at the recollection. As for Charles, as he ambled back into the restaurant for another glass of wine and a quick chat with some friends he had caught sight of in a corner, he felt well pleased with the day's doings.

That evening Leo came home tired and dispirited. He felt as though he had been wading through run-off contracts for half a lifetime, and the Capstall case, which had seemed so attractive in its significance at the outset, was beginning to oppress him. It consumed every waking moment, and, although the spirit of determination with which he fought every case was in no way dimmed, he longed for some variety in his working day, some change of pace. The total absorption which the case demanded gave him an odd sense of isolation, which was heightened by the fact that he now felt oddly cut off from Anthony, who spent most of his free time with Camilla. As he parked the car and locked it, Leo reflected on this, ruefully acknowledging to himself that he found it difficult, as he had always done, to accept that anyone should displace him in Anthony's life.

He paused by the car, staring up at the blank windows of his big house. God, he thought. Only four years ago he had been in love with Anthony, and even though it had never amounted to anything in the long run, he had always supposed himself to be paramount in the younger man's affections. Not even Rachel had stood between them, ever. Oh, Anthony had thought she had, but Leo had known otherwise. And now there was this girl. Leo tossed the car keys lightly in the palm of his hand, staring down at them, thinking coldly of Camilla. He would be a fool to let Anthony make the same mistake that he had made. He knew Anthony, knew his susceptibility. The best thing for Anthony would be to remain single, uncommitted, leading his own life, instead of getting caught up in the tangle of other people's. He glanced up again and saw the light come on in Oliver's room, then Jennifer drawing the curtains. He sighed and let himself into the house.

Rachel was in the kitchen, putting dishes into the dishwasher.

'I ate with Oliver and Jennifer,' she said, glancing over her shoulder at him. 'I want to spend the evening working on my paper. I hope you don't mind making yourself some pasta. I took a sauce out of the freezer, but you'll probably have to warm it in the microwave.'

'No, that's fine,' he said. Her voice was bright and rapid, he noticed, as though she was especially cheerful about something. For some reason this irritated him.

Rachel detected the weary note in his voice. 'Are you all right?' she asked.

'So so.' Despite the inevitable distance which existed between them, he felt like sitting down, having a drink with her, telling her about the pressures of the case, but just as he was about to suggest it, she closed the dishwasher and said, 'Right. I'm going to lock myself away now.' Then as she reached the door she turned and added, 'Oh, that documentary thing you've been watching – the one about the Crusades. It's the last programme tonight. Tell me when it comes on. I'd like to watch it, too.'

She went out, and Leo stood thinking about Charles Beecham. He hadn't seen him since before Christmas. It did infatuation no good to be starved of sight and sound of its object. Even that pleasant little piece of speculative fantasy was not sustaining him at present. And he could think of no pretext for getting in toucch with Charles. There was always the settlement offer which it was rumoured Lloyd's might soon be making, and which he would then have to discuss with the Committee. He might see him then. But for the moment he would have to nourish himself with Charles's last programme, enjoy him at one remove. It was better than nothing.

He went into the living room and poured himself a large drink. The idea of cooking supper bored him, and, although he had brought home some papers to look at, he couldn't face them. He had had enough of Alan Capstall for one day. He picked up the newspaper from a chair and glanced through it, unconsciously registering the sounds of Rachel switching off Oliver's light after saying goodnight to him, her feet on the stairs, the sound of the study door closing. Leo chucked the paper aside and remembered the novel which he had been reading before Christmas. It had been rather enjoyable, easy. He hadn't had a moment to look at it since. That would fill in the time between now and nine o'clock, something to help him unwind.

He went upstairs, his drink in one hand, loosening his tie with the other. Jennifer, crossing from the bathroom to her bedroom on the floor above, caught sight of him and stood looking down at him, tightening the belt of her towelling robe as she did so. She felt, as she always did, a little rush of excitement at the sight of him, his silver hair, his handsome, tired features. He was easily the most attractive man she knew, much better than the boys of her own age that she met in pubs and clubs. Leo possessed sophistication, and there was something aloof in his manner towards her which Jennifer found particularly challenging. Over Christmas she had discussed him at length with her best friend, speculating on the possibilities of going to bed with him. She had never done such a thing in any household she had worked in before – none of the husbands so far had been remotely fanciable – but she knew plenty of nannies to whom it had happened. From the currents of tension between Leo and Rachel, Jennifer guessed that they no longer slept together. Someone like Leo, mused Jennifer, as she watched him unbutton his collar and slip off his jacket before going into his room, must need someone, something. She could think of one way of arousing his interest. Slowly, thoughtfully, she padded downstairs, until she was only a few steps away from Leo's bedroom door, which stood ajar. She waited, sponge bag still in hand, the tendrils of her curling hair damp from the shower. Either he had gone in there to change, or to fetch something. After a few seconds she heard his feet approaching the door, and she quickened her pace to hurry down the last few steps, so that she and Leo collided as he came out of his room. She dropped her sponge bag, and as they murmured apologies to each other and she bent to retrieve it, she contrived to let her robe slip open slightly. Leo's gaze could not help but be arrested by the sight of Jennifer's soft round shoulders and childish breasts before she quickly pulled the edges of her robe together again and tightened the belt, apparently in clumsy embarrassment. He was aware, as he caught the faint fragrance of her clean, soaped body, of his own instant arousal.

'Sorry,' she murmured, 'I was just going down to the kitchen to fetch a drink.' She gave him a quick, uncertain smile and went downstairs. He stood watching her, his eyes fixed on her legs, the peach-like curve of flesh where her thighs disappeared beneath the hem of her short bathrobe. He came slowly downstairs a moment later and went into the kitchen, where she was standing with her back to him, pouring herself a glass of juice from the fridge. He put his book on the table and began to prepare supper for himself. Neither spoke to the other, but there was a heightened awareness, an almost palpable sexual tension, which secretly delighted Jennifer. She smiled to herself as she left the kitchen, dipping her head to drink from her glass. He could have made a move there and then – she could tell he had wanted to – but he probably didn't think it was a good idea with Rachel only a few rooms away. Well, she could wait.

Later that evening, Leo and Rachel sat together and watched Charles Beecham, Rachel curled up in an armchair, Leo stretched out on the sofa, each containing their own private thoughts and fantasies, while an unknowing and pre-recorded Charles lectured them on Pope Innocent III and the Albigenses. Upstairs in her room, Jennifer watched for a few moments and grew bored. She switched off the television and lay back on her bed, thinking about Leo.

Chapter Nineteen

The following week, on a raw, blustery Thursday afternoon, Leo left his room in chambers and went slowly downstairs, yawning and stretching, with the idea of going over to Inner Temple for afternoon tea. He was conscious of a stiffness in his legs and neck from sitting for so long at his desk, and it occurred to him that he should take some time off from the rigours of this case and have a game of squash. He hadn't played in ages, simply hadn't had the time. For a moment he toyed with the idea of ringing up Charles Beecham and inviting him over to his club for a game. But he didn't even know if Charles played. If he had wanted to capitalise on that budding friendship, he should have done it earlier. To get in touch with the man now might seem somewhat contrived. Besides, there was still too much preparation for the case to allow for romantic distractions. No time or energy even for love, thought Leo ruefully. He went out, taking a deep breath of the chilly January air to shake off his feeling of lassitude, and as he passed through Caper Court and into the cloisters, he saw Anthony striding towards the common room from the direction of the library. There was someone who had plenty of time for everything. Law and love. He quickened his pace and came up beside Anthony, falling into step with him. Anthony glanced up and smiled.

'I was just thinking about you,' said Anthony. The words touched Leo instantly with pleasure. There were few people in the world, he thought, who could affect him as Anthony did. But then, there were scarcely any others for whom he cared as much.

'Oh?'

'Wondering if we shouldn't try to fix up a game of squash. I'm rather conscious of being out of condition these days.'

Leo laughed at the coincidence of thought. 'Yes, I know what you mean,' he murmured, and pushed through the swing doors into the warmth of the common room, and the murmur of conversation and tinkle of teacups. 'But we'll have to make it some time before next Thursday. Rachel's going off to a conference in Sydney for a couple of weeks, and I won't have any free evenings. Domestic duties, and so forth.'

Anthony glanced fleetingly at Leo as he paid for his tea. He had never seen Rachel and Leo's baby, found it peculiarly difficult to imagine Leo as anyone's father, let alone a dutiful and doting one. He was too accustomed to perceiving Leo as an independent, emotionally unfettered being. He thought suddenly of Leo as he had been when he had first met him – a debonair bachelor, charismatic and witty, intellectually brilliant, but above all, a loner. There were certain activities in which one could not envisage Leo engaging, and those included changing nappies and cuddling infants. He tried to repress a smile at the thought, but Leo caught it. 'What?' he asked, as they sat down together.

'Oh, nothing. Just finding it hard to imagine you looking after a baby.'

'It is no joke,' remarked Leo grimly. 'In fact, you may come over one evening while Rachel's away and see what it's like.' He sipped his tea and then leaned back, smoothing a hand over his silver hair. 'Actually, Oliver is a very good child. Well, he is so far. Quite what he'll be like when his mother is away, I can't say. Anyway – ' Leo took a small cigar from his case and lit it, abruptly changing the subject. ' – I meant to tell you that I asked Fred Fenton the other day to instruct Walter Lumley as second junior.'

'God, no,' groaned Anthony.

Leo glanced up in surprise and faint annoyance. 'What have you got against Lumley? He's extremely able. Roderick said he was invaluable on that joint venture case last autumn. Or are you just jealous of another rising young star? Don't like the firmament too crowded?'

'Leo, I couldn't care less if he was the next Lord Denning. He's just such a – a weasel.' Anthony thought of Walter Lumley, his small, pointed face and bright, penetrating eyes behind his glasses, and could think of no other word.

'You don't hold the poor fellow's looks against him, do you?' Leo's voice was faintly cold. He blew out a little cloud of cigar smoke.

'It's nothing to do with the way he looks. If you'd been in his tutorial group at Bar School, you'd know what I mean. He was always so watchful, so smug, ready to pounce with the right answer. And I don't think he washed his hair more than once a month.' Anthony shifted restlessly in his chair, aware that he was sounding a trifle childish. 'He's just not – well, he's not your average, decent chap. There's something off-putting about him.'

'But you'll admit that he's bright?' enquired Leo, setting down his empty teacup.

'Oh, yes. Yes, I'll give you that. Supernaturally so. It might help him if he was a bit less brilliant.'

'Then that's all I'm interested in,' said Leo. 'I don't care if he never takes a bath, so long as he can help us win this case. And by all accounts, I rather think he can.' Leo rose. 'Find out if there's a court free after five tomorrow night, and we'll have a game and a couple of drinks afterwards.' He gave a quick smile, then left the common room. Anthony felt faintly uncomfortable, and wished that he had said nothing against Lumley. Leo had a way of making one feel small, sometimes. He sighed, and drank his tea, glanced at his watch. He thought he had detected a change in Leo's manner towards him of late, something slightly off-hand, as though Anthony had in some way offended him. At that moment Camilla came into the common room, and Anthony felt his heart expand with pleasure at the sight of her. As she came towards him, it suddenly occurred to him that Leo's behaviour towards Camilla had altered, too. Formerly casual and aloof with her, Leo had recently become critical, picky about her work and occasionally subjected her to cutting little remarks of reproof. Perhaps it was the strain of the case, thought Anthony. It must affect them all. But he knew in his heart that Leo must have perceived the relationship between himself and Camilla, and that it had fanned a little flickering flame of jealousy in Leo. Certain things never change, thought Anthony, remembering his own impotent sense of humiliation and loss when Leo had married Rachel. He could not fathom the bond between himself and Leo, had no idea of what it consisted, and what might affect it. Camilla sat down in the chair which Leo had recently vacated, and smiled at him.

'You look miles away,' she remarked.

'I was. I was thinking about Leo.'

She set down her cup of tea and made a face. 'I said hello to him on my way in, and he just looked straight through me. Why were you thinking about him?'

Anthony gazed reflectively at the table between them, and suddenly wondered what he would do, if he was asked to choose between Camilla and Leo. It was an absurd thought, and he had no idea why it had come into his head. He tried to push it away and looked up, switching his attention to her features. 'Oh, no reason really. I just worry about him sometimes, that's all,' he replied.

He had never done anything so petty in his life. Why had he just cut the girl dead? wondered Leo, as he made his way back to chambers. He could think of absolutely no reason, except a sheer fit of ill-temper brought on by the sight of her – young and attractive, carefree, happy. And part of Anthony's life. The conversation with Anthony, too – he shouldn't have ended it so abruptly. True, Anthony's occasionally immature opinions might make him impatient, but it was no reason to cut things short. Half the reason for going across to tea had been to relax, have some conversation, get away from chambers for a while, and here he was on his way back ten minutes later, in a bad mood. Oh God, thought Leo, this was probably what happened as one got older. Irascibility, a brooding sense of envy at the sight of youth taking its easy pleasures, making its casual judgements . . . He glanced up and saw Cameron Renshaw coming through the archway from Middle Temple Lane, his portly frame clad in a fine new blue cashmere coat. Cameron was putting on weight. He moved less briskly than he once had, nimble as a cat in the way of so many big men. How old? Leo wondered. Sixty? Sixty-one? In fifteen years' time, he thought, I shall be that age. It was not a new thought, but in his present mood of mortal awareness it caught him like a sly blow beneath the ribs. He watched as Cameron paused at the entrance to Number 5, catching his breath before mounting the stone steps. He glanced across and saw Leo approaching, and nodded in greeting.

'Been to tea? I thought of popping over, but I've got a con in fifteen minutes. Rush, rush, rush . . . ' They went in through the door together, Cameron unbuttoning his new coat with a touch of pride. 'Like m'coat?' he asked Leo ingenuously. 'Savoy Taylors. In the sale. No other bastard big enough for it to fit, I suppose.' From behind the clerks' desk Felicity began to remind Cameron about his conference, and he flapped at her dismissively with the papers which he held in his hand. 'I know, girl, I know! Not bloody senile yet. Rustle me up a cup of tea, would you, there's a sweetheart, and bring it upstairs. Parched.' He turned back to Leo. 'Now.' He jabbed a gentle finger at Leo's waistcoat. 'Been wanting to have a little word with you about new tenants.' They began to mount the wooden stairs, Leo keeping pace with Cameron's slow tread. 'What do you make of this new girl of Jeremy's? Camilla Thing.'

'Lawrence. She's Anthony's pupil now, actually.'

'Whatever. Is she any good? I understand she's been helping you with the Lloyd's business.'

They reached the landing, and Leo hesitated. 'She's – she's very good. First-class mind, very quick . . .'

'But?'

Leo shrugged. 'No "but". There have been times when I've thought she lacked the aggressive touch, I suppose.'

'Got no balls, you mean?'

'Something like that,' replied Leo, giving Cameron a caustic glance. 'But of late she seems to have been gaining confidence. And, of course, she needs experience.'

'Hmm. She'll get plenty of that soon enough.' Cameron resumed his progress up the stairs, Leo at his side. 'Well, I must say she strikes me as being of the right calibre. And – I never thought I'd say this – we need a woman in chambers. Got to keep up with the times. I propose that we offer her a tenancy at the end of her pupillage.'

'Already?'

'Strike while the iron's hot. I've heard very good reports about her from others in chambers, and with a starred first from LMH, she'll get other offers. I don't want this set getting a reputation for being chauvinistic or stick-in-the-mud. Seven KBW have got two women already, and I gather they pile in the work.'

'Fine. I'm all for it.' Leo's bland expression betrayed nothing.

Cameron paused outside his room, puffing slightly, his new coat slung over his arm. 'Good. I'll put it forward at the next chambers meeting. Oh, and there's the question of new premises to be discussed as well –'

At that moment, Leo could hear the phone ringing behind the closed door of his own room. He nodded. 'Fine. We'll discuss it. I can hear my phone.'

Cameron nodded in dismissal and Leo went into his room, wishing that Cameron had not further depressed his spirits by mentioning the matter of new premises. He had enough upheaval in his life at the moment, and had no real wish to leave the familiarity of 5 Caper Court. He sighed as he picked up the phone.

'Murray Campbell for you,' said Felicity's voice.

'Fine. Put him on.' Leo sat down behind his desk, unbuttoning his jacket with his free hand and slinging it over the back of his chair.

'Leo? Got some news that should make you sit up. Chris Upjohn from Fairchilds has just been on. Lloyd's want to settle. They're prepared to make the Names an offer.'

Leo sat forward, his face alight with interest. He picked up a pen and opened a notebook.

'How much?'

'Forty-nine point four million. That's without including the auditors, and no cap on liability.'

'Hmm.' Leo pondered this. 'It's not ideal. What the Names want is to know that the claims won't keep on rolling ceaselessly in. Money in hand will mean something to the likes of Freddie Hendry and Brian Carstairs, but we have to look ahead. Honoria Hunter and old Snodgrass wouldn't sniff at it either, but what they're interested in is having the lid put on their claims.' He paused, doodling a series of lines beneath the figure of £49.4 million which he had jotted down. 'And I'm not at all keen on the idea of assigning the auditors' claim . . . What do you and Fred think?'

At the other end, Murray sighed. 'It's an offer. If we accept it, at least the Names don't run the risk of going to court and losing. If that happens, they end up with nothing, except a packet in costs. This way, they get a hundred per cent of line. You're never going to do better than that.'

'Oh, I don't know,' mused Leo. He paused in thought once more, then said, 'It's something to put to the Names, in any event. We'd better call a meeting and thrash it out. I'd like to have a word with Anthony and get back to you, if I may.'

'Fine. I'll wait to hear from you.'

Leo hung up and sat back in his chair. Apart from the faint sense of relief at the fact that Lloyd's were nervous enough to want to settle the claim, the fact that the offer fell short of the ideal only galvanised him into wanting to push on with the litigation. He relished the prospect of a day – or more – in court with Capstall, and had confidence in his own ability to win. There was something lukewarm about settling, particularly on these terms. But then, one never knew how far the thing might be open to negotiation. It was improbable that the high and mighty of Lloyd's would agree to capping the liability of the Names, absolving them of any future indebtedness. And what if Murray was right? What if they were never going to do any better? His mind ran quickly over the scenario of the next few days. Murray would inform the committee, a general meeting of the Names action group would be called to discuss the proposal, and he, Leo, would have to address them on the advisability, or otherwise, of accepting. He had enough arrogant belief in his own powers of persuasion to know that most of the Names would be guided by what he said. In the end, much would depend upon which way Leo pushed them. He rubbed his hands over his face for a brief moment, as if to smooth away the stress and anxiety which this case had brought, then stood up. He would go and talk to Anthony.

Freddie sat in the silence of his flat, gazing at the letter in his faintly trembling grasp, then at the leafless branches and grey sky beyond his window, then at the letter once more. A little drift of steam wafted from the mug of Lemsip at his side. He'd had the gas fire full on all day – God alone knew what the bill was going to be like – but still he was cold. The last time he had placed a hopeful hand on the radiator on the other side of the room, it had been no more than warm. He had two pairs of socks on, a jumper, his jacket on top of that, and a muffler round his neck. It was all this sitting around that made a man cold. Could feel his toes like ice, and the ends of his fingers had gone mauve. If it weren't for this blasted chest of his, he'd go out for a good, brisk constitutional. Trouble was, he'd be wheezing like a walrus by the time he reached Museum Street, and this cold of his was bad enough without getting soaked in the icy drizzle which looked as though it might start at any moment.

Maud's letter was welcome, and yet he could have done without it. An invitation to spend a month or so in the warm Madeira sunshine was tantalising – agonisingly so. In the face of this filthy January weather, it was almost too good to contemplate. Trouble with his sister was, she'd completely lost touch with reality. Well, his reality. She didn't seem to understand the extent of his Lloyd's losses, seemed to think that he was living in some kind of palatial mansion flat, no worries . . . All very well for her and Jack to invite him out there, but how was he supposed to manage the damned fare? Now, if they'd offer to buy his plane ticket, that would have been another matter. The warmth of Madeira would be excellent for his health, clear up this touch of bronchitis in no time. But then, Maud and Jack weren't exactly wealthy, either. It was good of them to invite him, really.

Feeling depressed and lethargic, Freddie put down the letter and drank off some of his Lemsip. Disgusting stuff, did no good, but he'd been told to take it. He sighed and got up from his armchair to look at the television page of the paper. Racing from Newmarket on Channel Four. Might as well. He was just about to switch the television on, when the phone rang. Eagerly Freddie crossed the room, picking up the whole telephone and placing it on the table next to his armchair before settling down to answer it. In his isolation, a phone call was a luxury to be enjoyed. At the sound of Basher Snodgrass's voice, Freddie's former lassitude left him, and when the words 'settlement offer' came down the line, he felt a prickle of hope and excitement. This was what they had waited for. This could be the change of all their fortunes.

Twenty minutes later, Freddie put the phone down and sat in thought, the dry ends of his fingertips stroking the salt-and-pepper bristles of his moustache. He could feel his heart still beating rapidly from the electrifying discussion he had had with Basher. This was the kind of thing he needed, something to jolt him out of his invalid state, give vigour to the days. So Lloyd's wanted to settle, eh? Basher had mentioned something about 100 per cent of line. He did a rough mental calculation. Good God, thought Freddie, if this settlement came off, that would mean a payment of £80,000. The difference it would make to his life was too stupendous to contemplate. He could get out of this dingy flat, for a start, salvage something of the dignity which he struggled so hard to maintain these days. It was damned hard, when you had to pinch and scrape all the time. This would put an end to all that. He would get out of London, move somewhere quiet, somewhere he could make a few friends with people of his own class and outlook. Haywards Heath, or Woking. Games of bridge in the evenings, golf, a car to get about in, decent meals . . . What did he care if there was no cap on future liabilities? He was eighty-two, not likely to enjoy more than another few years, with his heart. Not even Lloyd's of London could pursue him beyond his grave. His eye strayed to the letter which lay on the carpet where it had fallen, and he felt another little jolt of excitement. He stooped to pick it up, unfolded it slowly. The possibility of a settlement with Lloyd's changed this, too. Madeira, a long holiday in the sun with his sister and brother-in-law. He could give up this flat and stay out there for a few months, possibly, before deciding where to settle. This time, when Freddie stared out at the bleak rooftops of Bloomsbury, he saw only the golden possibility of his changed fortunes. Then the fax began to chatter, and Freddie sat collecting the pages as they curled out, reading Murray Campbell's missive to the committee members avidly, as though to make his dreams a reality.

'How much would we get?' asked Alison, leaning her head on her elbow, gazing across at her husband. Since his telephone conversation earlier that afternoon with the solicitors, Brian had sat in his cubby-hole for three hours, going over figures, scribbling calculations, sifting pieces of paper. Then he had emerged, and had told her that Lloyd's had offered to settle. She had felt her heart lift – not so much at the news, as at the unaccustomed excitement which Brian clearly felt. Still she did not allow her hopes to rise much. She was too used to disappointment, to the settled sense of financial hopelessness which this Lloyd's business had fixed in her.

'A hundred per cent of line,' said Brian, scanning the figures before him and then jotting something further down. Alison noticed that the plastic end of the biro he used was ragged, bitten and split. There was always something feverish about him these days, whether in hope or despair. But she was past worrying. This was how he was.

The words meant nothing to her. 'I don't understand,' she replied, trying to keep the irritation from her voice. They were sitting together at the kitchen table, and behind them supper was overcooking on the stove. From the room above she could hear the children arguing, a door slamming, Paul's stereo turned up, then more shouting. 'What's a line?'

'It's the amount of insurance which the underwriter can write on your behalf.' He looked up at her, pushing his glasses back on his thin nose, his voice taking on the quiet, patient tone he adopted when helping the children with their homework. Not that Paul did much homework these days. 'Let's say your deposit with Lloyd's is ten thousand. That means your line will be double that, twenty thousand.'

'Our deposit was fifty thousand,' said Alison, slowly working out the calculation. 'That means – '

'It means that if this settlement came off, we would get something in the region of a hundred thousand.'

There was a silence. Alison rose and went to the cooker, turning off the gas beneath the pan of rice. She turned, leaning against the edge of the work surface. She could feel the increased beat of her heart. 'That's what we would get? That much?'

'Well, there would be tax . . . ' Brian stared vaguely at the figures before him. 'It would depend how the payment is treated. But, yes, that's the offer. There's no cap on future liabilities. We would still remain exposed. But it would mean – ' Brian hesitated, then looked up at her. 'It would mean that we wouldn't have to declare ourselves bankrupt.'

'Bankrupt?' She stared at him in astonishment. 'You never told me it was that bad!'

'We're heading that way, certainly,' said Brian, automatically beginning to pick at a little shred of skin on his index finger. Alison closed her eyes momentarily. It seemed to her that the future was a dark, dangerous tide which rose and fell, threatening to engulf them all one moment, and then ebbing away the next, only to roll remorselessly in again.

'This settlement offer – will the Names accept it?'

Brian nibbled anxiously at his finger. 'I don't know. Murray Campbell says that there will be those who'll want to hold out in the hope of getting more if they go on with the litigation.' He shrugged. 'Then there's people like us. We're not like half of those fat cat Names, people who've only lost their second home and have had to sell the Rolls and make do with a Jag. We need this settlement. We can't afford to wait. We'll go under long before the litigation ends. If we can get a hundred thousand out of the bastards who got us into this in the first place, it means I might be able to start something up again. I've got contacts. I'm not exactly a spent force.' His smile was no more than a bitter spasm. 'I started the last business with only a small amount of capital. I don't see why I couldn't get something going. I've done it once before.'

Alison stood gazing down at him, at his thinning hair, his dark, anxious eyes. He looked much older than forty-seven. But she was aware of his reserves of energy, knew that if his hope and ambition could be rekindled, then he might be capable of anything. For a moment she allowed her hopes to rise impractically. If Brian had enough to start a new business and make a success of it, as he had in the past, then they might be able to get their heads above water. Brian had explained to her that, even if they accepted this offer, they would still have to face unforeseen future liabilities, but by then they might be able to pay those. It was just a question of building something. He was right. They had done it before. Why should they not do it again? All they needed was a fresh start. This offer could change their lives, turn Brian back into something of the person he had once been . . . But what if it fell through? What if the rest of the Names decided to go on with the litigation? God, what a monster hope was, the way it generated fresh fears to gnaw at one. 'So what happens next?' she asked. 'Is there some sort of vote?'

'There's to be an Extraordinary General Meeting some time next week, I'm not sure yet which day. The Names will meet then and decide.' He suddenly sounded tired, as though the excitement of kindling new possibilities had worn him out with its futility.

She knew she had asked the question before, but could not help repeating it. 'Do you think they'll accept?'

Brian shook his head. 'I don't know. I don't know . . . ' He sighed. 'I just hope to God, for our sakes, that they do.'

Chapter Twenty

The Extraordinary General Meeting of the Names was called for Friday of the following week. Rachel had left for Sydney the day before, and as Leo sat at the kitchen table that morning, drinking his coffee and scanning the notes spread out before him, Jennifer came in with Oliver balanced on her hip. She glanced at Leo and murmured good morning, conscious of a small, inner excitement as she spoke. Every utterance, now that she and Leo were to be alone together for two weeks, seemed charged with extra significance.

Leo sighed as he gathered his papers together. 'Morning,' he murmured absently. He rose and glanced briefly at Jennifer. He was perfectly well aware of the finely tuned atmosphere that the girl had created recently, was only too familiar with the modulations of voice and body language which signified availability. He had not lived and loved so long without learning those lessons. As he put on his jacket, slipping his spectacles into his pocket, she turned away, splashing some water into a glass at the sink and murmuring to Oliver. He smiled to himself. She was perfectly aware that he was watching her. It was spoken in the very curve of her hip, the movement of her head as she tossed her hair from her face. Games. Adorable, tantalising little games. Leo did not think he would ever grow tired of them. How he loved the cunning innocence of the young.

He put his papers into his briefcase and closed it. 'Right. I'll be off,' he said. For all his sense of control over the situation, he realised that whatever he said to her must sound stuffy, middle-aged, betraying nothing of his own delicate perception of matters. What else did one say to the nanny on leaving the house? Whatever currents might run beneath it, the situation demanded platitudes, polite smiles and enquiries. 'Got anything special planned for the day?'

Jennifer slipped Oliver into his high chair. Leo noticed that all her movements were slow and studied, as though part of a performance. Part of the game. She looked up and smiled. She wished that she could prevent herself from smiling so much when she looked at Leo, but the sense of pleasurable excitement that bubbled within her was irresistible. 'Oh, I'll take him to Tumbletots, maybe to the park,' she replied idly. 'The usual. You know.'

Leo nodded, and then there was a momentary silence. 'Right. Well, I'll see you this evening, I suppose. Shouldn't be too late.'

Jennifer nodded in reply, relishing the domestic intimacy of the situation. 'Have a good day,' she called as he left the house.

Anthony stood on the steps of Church House in Westminster, where the meeting of the Names had been convened, amusing himself by studying the individuals as they passed through the doorway, listening to the odd snatches of conversation which he caught. Everyone attending the meeting seemed well-dressed, regardless of the impecuniosity of which they constantly complained, with only the occasional touch of flamboyance or eccentricity, and all the voices were middle-aged or elderly, silvered with gentility, fractious with grievance. Every eye gleamed with a certain determination, an eagerness to get down to the matter of this offer. If there was one thing the Lloyd's Names never tired of, thought Anthony, it was the business of talking about their money, past or present, existent or non-existent. Thinking ahead to the proceedings which would unfold that morning, he felt a slight nervousness in the pit of his stomach. He had not yet decided, despite long confabulations with Leo and Murray and Fred Fenton, whether this offer from Lloyd's was a good thing or not. Listening to the shreds of discussion from the Names as they made their slow way into the building, he could glean no hint of the general mood. Well, they would all know by the end of the day.

He and Leo caught sight of one another at the same instant, just as Leo was crossing the square, and each felt the same pleasurable rise of the heart at the sight of the other. They went into Church House together, past the table where Camilla and some assistant solicitors from Nichols & Co were handing out name tags and agendas to the arriving Names, and mounted the broad stone steps. The discreet rumble of voices from those already seated greeted them as they entered the hall.

'That's us,' murmured Leo, nodding towards the platform which faced the audience at the far end of the circular hall, and on which stood a long table, with a microphone and lectern in the centre, and chairs ranged on either side. Anthony glanced round at the sea of faces and hoped that neither Murray nor Fred would palm off any questions from the audience on him. He might feel perfectly at ease speaking in the intimate, civilised surroundings of a courtroom, but the idea of having to address this belligerent lot was not one which he relished. He had no doubt that, when their mood got ugly, these well-dressed, respectable members of the middle classes might be a force to be reckoned with. He was thankful that it was Leo, and not he, who had the task of advising the Names that day, especially since a proportion were bound to disagree with whatever he said.

Basher Snodgrass came forward to greet them, but his manner was somewhat distracted. 'This overhead projector that they've given us,' he muttered, indicating a small table where the apparatus stood. 'I don't think it's working properly. The arm keeps swinging down.' In his capacity as chairman, Basher clearly felt some trepidation. 'Anyway,' he sighed, 'let me show you both where you're sitting. Anthony, you're next to some chap from the *Guardian* – can't remember his name – and Leo, you're here next to me.' Basher glanced up and saw Freddie Hendry making slow but firm progress towards the platform, and hurried away. Freddie approached Leo and Anthony and began to talk to them, leaning on the table with tremulous, bony hands. He appeared prepared to stand there talking all day, until Brian Carstairs arrived, sheaves of paper under his arm, and hustled Freddie into a seat further along the table.

A sense of anticipation seemed to run through the hall as Basher mounted the platform and tapped the microphone, blowing into it experimentally. Anthony averted his head to hide a smile, and caught sight of Brian further along the table. His face was drawn and pinched, and he kept blinking agitatedly, glancing nervously out at the audience and then up at Basher as he prepared to speak. There might be a lot riding on this for someone like Brian, thought Anthony. He noticed that Freddie, having divested himself of his overcoat, had forgotten to take his woollen gloves and scarf off.

Still, he looked happy enough, in a self-important way. Anthony leaned out slightly to get a view past Basher, and saw that Leo was seated next to Charles Beecham. They were chatting together with an easy familiarity and, as Charles laughed at something which Leo had just said, it occurred to Anthony that Charles was an exceptionally attractive man for his age. Then he wondered, with a faintly cold shock, whether Leo thought so, too. But at that moment the journalist from the *Guardian* slid into the seat next to Anthony, out of breath, just as Basher began to speak, and Anthony put the thought from his mind, and turned his attention to the meeting.

'Ladies and gentlemen,' said Basher, 'we are here today to consider the matter of the offer which, as you all know, has recently been put forward by Lloyd's in settlement of our claims. I propose to run this meeting in the following way: Mr Henshaw, of the council of Lloyd's, is going to speak to you in favour of the settlement – ' Basher turned with a courteous smile towards the narrow-shouldered man in glasses, who was sitting with his arms folded in a somewhat defensive posture near one end of the table. There was a brief pause, during which all eyes in the hall swivelled towards this quisling in hostile appraisal. ' – and then James Cochrane, who is known to you all already as a member of the committee, will speak against the offer. After we have heard from these two gentlemen, I shall ask our leading counsel, Leo Davies, to address us with his views on the matter. But first of all, to supply some background as to the precise nature of the offer which has been put forward, I will ask the committee secretary, Brian Carstairs, whose work on behalf of us all has been so invaluable over the past few months, to speak a few words.'

Basher sat down, and Brian, gathering up some papers, moved to the middle of the table, where the overhead projector stood. He glanced nervously at the screen behind him, and then began to address the meeting on the matter of specific figures, using slides to give breakdowns and show how money would be apportioned.

After a few minutes, Anthony found his attention wandering. He glanced round the hall, admiring the light panelling, wondering if it was made of ash or some other wood, then up at the brass rails of the gallery. He found himself craning his neck to decipher the gilt lettering which ran round the base of the circular window crowning the roof of the hall. 'Holy is the true light and passing wonderful, lending radiance to them that endured in the heat of the conflict; from Christ they inherit a home of unfading splendour, wherein they rejoice with gladness evermore,' he read slowly. He wondered how much comfort any of those present today might derive from that. Not that the attention of any one of them was likely to stray as far as the ceiling; they were too busy concentrating on the vital matter of their money, and what Brian Carstairs was telling them about it. If they were ever to get it.

Then suddenly there was a small clatter, and Brian stopped speaking. Anthony glanced across and saw that the arm of the projector had dropped down, halting Brian's slide presentation. There was a moment's confusion while Brian tried to prop it up, and Basher rose from his seat and left the platform. A faint murmur rose from the audience. Brian, who was clearly upset by the interruption, tried to carry on speaking, but the projector arm swung wildly down again and this time there was laughter. Brian turned away from the projector and announced that he would carry on without benefit of the charts. He looked nervous and flustered as he tried to find the place in his notes where he had broken off, and Anthony was just beginning to feel sorry for the man when he became aware of a movement behind his chair. Glancing down, he was astonished to see Basher crawling along behind the chairs on his hands and knees, a screwdriver in his hand. While Brian was still speaking, he rose up slowly from behind and tried unobtrusively to mend the projector, which merely succeeded in distracting Brian even more. When the entire arm of the projector fell on the floor, convulsing Anthony and the man from the *Guardian*, and most of the audience, Brian sat down in mute fury. Basher murmured to him for a few seconds, and Brian eventually rose and resumed his talk. But the whole incident had thrown him, and whatever points he tried to make seemed to have lost their force. As he sat down at the end, he felt that he had been made to look ridiculous.

Then Freddie rose and began to make an entirely irrelevant point about Names' subscriptions coming out of the litigation fund, and had to be told firmly by Basher that the time for questions would come after the speakers for and against the motion. Freddie raised his eyebrows and resumed his seat, mumbling, and then Henshaw, the representative from Lloyd's council, got to his feet.

His speech urging the Names to accept the offer was quietly impressive. He did not cajole them, did not belittle the litigation which they had undertaken, but merely recited the facts coldly and baldly, reminding them that only a limited amount of money was available, and that this, too, might be lost to them all if they continued with litigation which might ultimately prove fruitless. When he sat down, he had done his job by reminding them all of the awful possibility – or was it a probability? – that if they did not accept what Lloyd's had offered, they might end up with nothing more than a bill of costs. The mood in the hall was quiet and sober at that moment, the amusing distraction of the projector forgotten. Basher glanced and nodded at James Cochrane, who rose from his chair, a tall, craggy figure, and moved across to the microphone.

Cochrane's mode of address was entirely different from Henshaw's impersonal approach. This was a man accustomed to addressing businessmen and captains of industry in robust tones, and he wasn't going to pussyfoot about.

'Ladies and gentlemen,' he began, 'what we've got here is an offer from Lloyd's for forty-nine point four million pounds, and Mr Henshaw here has just told us that that's pretty good. Well, not from where I'm standing. From where I'm standing, I can see collective losses – all yours and all mine – estimated at a hundred and fifty-four million at least.' He paused, then repeated the figure slowly. 'A hundred and fifty-four million. In the face of that, I say this offer is chickenfeed. It's ludicrous . . . ' He had his audience. Anthony listened in admiration as he swept them along with him, enumerating all the reasons for rejecting the offer, talking about protecting the hardest hit, seeking a greater contribution from Lloyd's to the litigation fund. By the time he had got on to the failure of the DTI and the government to regulate Lloyd's, and dragging in the Inland Revenue for good measure, even Freddie was nodding reluctantly. Cochrane ended on a high note, quoted briefly from Shakespeare, and sat down. The murmur which rose from the audience was clearly sympathetic. Anthony looked along the table and saw that Brian Carstairs was looking pale as he raised his water glass to drink. He tried to catch Leo's eye to gauge his expression, but Leo seemed to be gazing distractedly at the table.

Leo was, in fact, staring at Charles Beecham's hand. It was

resting on the table, and Leo watched with fascination as the slender, expressive fingers toyed with a pencil, then drummed abstractedly on the table. He studied the clean, curved lines of the broad nails, the light hairs on the back of his hand, and felt himself totally consumed by that dizzying sense of infatuation which he had experienced in Charles's company before, and which he had almost forgotten until now. It was adolescent, he told himself, to be so moved and touched by the mere sight of his hand. It was some months since he had last seen Charles, and he had been totally unprepared for the emotion which surged up in him at the sight of the man. For an instant he felt a touch of sympathy for Jennifer. He knew exactly how she felt. Then he lifted his gaze, trying to concentrate on what Basher was saying in response to some question from the audience. The questions went on for several minutes, the different voices, the sleek, the plummy, the fine and reedy, all the clear, assured tones of the middle and upper-middle classes, drifting across the hall. Leo scarcely listened. He already knew what he had to say to these people. He had little interest in them, in their perceived injuries, and felt no pity for them as they aired their petty grievances. His attitude was entirely professional. This was just a case, one which he felt was good in law, and which he knew in his heart he could win. How much the Names might get out of it in the end, he hardly cared. He half-listened as Freddie Hendry made a surprisingly good point about reconstruction and renewal, and then as another Name, presumably a broker himself, provoked the derision of the rest of the Names by enjoining them not to push the brokers too far, Leo's eyes strayed once more to the strong, clean lines of Charles's hand, and then to his thigh stretched out beneath the tabletop.

'...We really must call a halt to the questions now,' Basher was saying, 'or we'll never get on.' He turned to Leo. 'I think that we should all be grateful to hear the views of our leading counsel, Leo Davies.'

A familiar sensation, like a small electric current, passed through Leo as he rose to speak to them. He had notes jotted down on a slip of paper, but did not glance down at them.

'Ladies and gentlemen...' Anthony smiled slightly at the sound of that silken, easy voice, with its slight Welsh lilt, '...what I have to say is brief and, I hope, to the point. Lloyd's have made you an offer of forty-nine point four million. You have heard Mr Henshaw say that it is the best you will get. It is true to say that no one can stand here and guarantee you a better offer or a greater recovery. If you press ahead with the litigation, there is no certainty of ever recovering anything. That is a risk which all litigation carries.' Leo paused and looked steadily round his audience. 'But it is my considered view, looking at the merits of this case, that most of the Names here today should ultimately succeed. To what extent is, of course, another matter. I cannot guarantee how much money is available under the errors and omissions policies, but I would remind you that the offer under consideration, excluding the auditors from the settlement as it does, will severely restrict recovery from them. You are already aware that, under the terms of the offer before you, there is no cap on your future liabilities, and these may be substantial. If you continue the action against the auditors and win, then it is they who will bear those future losses. To many of you, that may seem too much to give up. It seems so to me...' Anthony listened attentively, glancing occasionally at the audience. There was no question that every carefully weighed word which Leo uttered was having its effect. He managed to neutralise all Mr Henshaw's sombre warnings regarding the penalty of the action's failure, and, in the most cautious and circumspect fashion, stirred in the Names a sense that to accept the Lloyd's offer would rob them of a potential victory. At last he concluded, '...I cannot advise you whether to reject or accept the offer today. That is a matter for each individual. But I can recommend that you should weigh matters very carefully before abandoning a claim which offers your only real prospect of a full recovery, and an end to future liabilities. Thank you.'

As he sat down, Leo knew that he had reminded them with his closing words of the one factor which should sway the majority against accepting. The probability, should they ultimately win, that any future liabilities – and it was those dreaded demands for money which overshadowed the lives of each and every one in that hall – would be paid by the auditors. It was all that really needed to be said.

Leo felt Charles's hand on his arm as he leaned towards him to murmur something. Leo did not catch his words, merely nodded in reply, but it was enough just to feel the faint pressure of his hand upon his sleeve. Then it was gone, and Basher was standing up to suggest taking a vote. 'So – all those in favour of accepting the offer, raise your hands.' Basher glanced round the hall, and there was a susurration as of birds' wings as arms went up. Anthony looked out at the audience, then along the row on the platform. Brian's hand had gone up instantly, Freddie Hendry raised his shakily, still in its woollen glove. To his surprise, Anthony saw that Basher had his hand up, Cochrane throwing him a scowling glance. Charles Beecham's arms remained folded, and both Honoria Hunter's heavily-ringed hands rested in her lap. It was not easy to see how many in the audience had voted for accepting. A fair proportion, it seemed to Anthony. 'And all those against?' Basher gazed out, and this time it was clear which way the vote had swung. Many, many more hands were raised now. There was an angry murmur from some parts of the hall, and someone began to protest angrily at the manner in which the meeting had been conducted. Other voices joined his, and a small, elderly woman in the front row stood up and began to mouth furiously, her voice completely drowned in the hubbub around her. Anthony sighed and stretched his legs. This, he knew from past meetings, was par for the course. He glanced at his watch. Nearly two. Camilla would be busy lugging papers back to chambers when this was over. He wondered whether he and Leo might go for a quick sandwich and a chat.

Basher Snodgrass eventually managed to bring the meeting to order, and informed everyone that it was perfectly clear that a majority had voted against acceptance of the offer, and that the matter would go back to their solicitors for further discussion. Even the angriest among those present realised that there was nothing more to be done that day, and people began to disperse. Anthony managed to palm an irate and garrulous Freddie off on Fred Fenton, who cast Anthony a reproachful look as he made his escape. Anthony merely grinned, and turned in search of Leo. But Leo was already at the door of the hall, deep in conversation with Charles Beecham. Again there was the bright sound of Charles's laughter in response to something Leo had said, and at the sight of the two older men together Anthony felt a faint pang. There seemed to exist between them a camaraderie which he did not recognise in his own relationship with Leo. As he made his way out of the hall alone, he noticed Brian Carstairs sitting on a bench just outside the doorway, a bundle of papers on his knees, staring at all the people as they descended the stairs. He hesitated, then went up to him.

'Unpredictable things, these meetings, aren't they?' said Anthony. 'That was a nuisance about the projector.'

Brian looked up at him, and it struck Anthony that Brian's face had an exhausted look, as though he had just run an enormous distance. 'It doesn't really matter now,' said Brian.

'No . . . well . . .' Anthony paused. 'Are you heading back into town? We could share a cab.' He had no real wish to share a taxi with Brian Carstairs, but he was conscious that the man was depressed, and needed to be rallied in some way. Only he couldn't think how.

'No.' Brian shook his head. 'I'm just going to sit here for a while. Then I'll be off home.'

Once more Anthony hesitated. Something told him he couldn't just leave him here like this. But the man had said he was going home, after all. 'Right,' he said after a moment. 'I'll see you soon, then.'

'Yes,' said Brian, and he watched Anthony as he sauntered downstairs and out into the cold January air.

When Leo got home that evening, Jennifer was in the kitchen, finishing her supper and flicking through a magazine. When he said good evening, she merely smiled at him.

'Oliver asleep?' he asked.

'I don't know,' she replied. 'I left him ten minutes ago and he seemed quite sleepy. I haven't heard a sound from him since.'

'I'll just go up and look,' said Leo, slipping off his jacket and slinging it over his shoulder.

Oliver's bedroom was bathed in a muted glow from his nightlight, and there was no movement from his cot. Leo stepped quietly across the room and looked down. Oliver was fast asleep, his blanket kicked off, his chubby arms outstretched and his bottom in the air. He looked like someone in free fall, thought Leo, gazing at the small, totally inert little body, dense with sleep, lips parted, lashes grazing his cheeks. He looked down at him for a long time, thinking about Charles, then about Rachel, and wondering how life was to resolve itself, and how things would be between Oliver and himself in fifteen years' time. Then he sighed, stroked Oliver's cheek with his finger, pulled his blanket up around him and left the room.

Downstairs, Leo went into the living room and poured himself a drink. He could hear the sounds of Jennifer clearing up in the kitchen. She had created such a charged atmosphere in the house that, even a room apart, he was strongly conscious of her. He stood in the middle of the room, sipping his drink, waiting for her to come through from the kitchen, as he knew she would. Sure enough, after a few minutes she appeared in the doorway. She said nothing, merely leaned against the doorframe. She was wearing some sort of cropped top and jeans, her everyday wear, but Leo realised that her very stance, her expression, even the casual way in which she folded her slim arms, exuded such sexuality that she might as well be stark naked. Leo wondered if she had rehearsed this, so studied and perfect was the moment, or whether she'd picked it up from some film or other. He was amused almost to the point of smiling broadly, but he sipped his drink instead, wondering what she would do next. In fact, after spending two hours with Charles – and he wondered what young Jennifer would say if she knew of the true object of his desire – it occurred to Leo that he was feeling quite horny, to borrow one of Felicity's cruder expressions. His gaze shifted from her face, with its clear eyes and childishly provocative mouth, and travelled down over her body. She watched him as he did this, and felt a delicious sense of expectancy rise within her. But Leo decided that it was not really an option. With Rachel away for another two weeks, it would only make the rest of the time he had to spend alone with Jennifer tiresome. Possibly demanding. Still, it was something to be borne in mind.

'Going out tonight?' he asked her, thinking that this interlude of pregnant silence had lasted long enough.

'I hadn't any plans,' replied Jennifer.

Leo tossed back the remains of his drink and set the glass down on a table. He moved towards her, and her air of expectancy was almost palpable.

'Well, make sure you lock up when you come in, if you do decide to. I'm going to have some supper and an early night.' He brushed past her in the doorway. 'Goodnight,' he added.

Jennifer said nothing for several seconds. As he went into the kitchen Leo smiled to himself. Nothing like a little sexual tension to alleviate the tedium of domesticity, he thought, opening the fridge.

Then he heard Jennifer say goodnight, her voice brittle with chagrin and assumed carelessness, and she went upstairs. Now, thought Leo, if she had been a little older and more experienced, she would not have let the moment pass so easily. But that was part of the attraction, he supposed. She was so very, very young.

Alison spooned mashed potato from the pan into a Pyrex dish and marvelled at the silence in the house. Even though the children were all in for once, there wasn't the usual thump of music, or the sound of arguments, or television. They must all be busy in their rooms. Odd, she thought, how these spells of peace could occasionally descend. These days she had grown used to the constant racket of five people trying to live together in a house which was too small for them, where tempers were frayed and dissatisfaction soured the air. She put the dish of potato into the oven to keep warm and went to the foot of the stairs and called to the children that dinner was ready. Then she went down the hall to Brian's room. He had been in there since he had come back from town, no doubt busy with his never-ending figures. His news that the settlement offer had been rejected had been a blow, but Alison still felt fairly sanguine. As she'd said to Brian, the very fact that Lloyd's had started trying to settle showed that they didn't want the case to fight. They'd probably come up with an improved offer in another week or so. To this, Brian had said nothing.

She knocked lightly on the door. 'Brian? Dinner's ready.' He did not murmur in reply, so she knocked again, a little louder. Still silence. She could hear the children's feet on the stairs as they came down, then went into the kitchen, talking about something, beginning to bicker. Alison opened the door and saw her husband lying on the floor next to his desk. Several of his best ties were knotted together and fastened at one end to the doorknob, and at the other around his neck. She took a few steps across the room, feeling a slow, dread chill rise up and spread throughout her limbs. She reached out and touched his hand, knowing before she even felt it that it would be quite cold. She had read about people hanging themselves in this way, without jumping off chairs or putting ropes over beams, but she had never been quite sure until this moment how it was done. And she felt a momentary hatred of him for leaving her in this way, knowing that while it ended it for him, everything – the debt, the demands, the ceaseless worry over the children – must go on for her. Now she would have to cope with it all on her own.

Chapter Twenty-one

The news of Brian's suicide reached Fred Fenton and Murray Campbell the following afternoon. Alison had rung Charles Beecham, who was the only member of the committee whom she knew, and told him. Shocked, Charles had called Nichols & Co, and then Basher.

'My God, that's terrible,' said Murray, when Fred came to his office to tell him. 'I know he'd been having a hell of a time of it, losing his business, and so forth, but I'd no idea ... How did he seem to you at the meeting yesterday?'

Fred shrugged. 'The way Brian always did. A bit on edge. He voted to accept the settlement, that much I know.'

Murray sighed. 'It makes you realise just how this Lloyd's business gets to people, how it takes over their lives. Destroys them. If he was really in severe financial difficulties, I suppose this settlement could have looked like something of a lifeline. Still, you'd think he would have realised from the start that there was a good chance people would vote against it.'

'I don't know,' mused Fred, strolling over to the window and gazing out at the Lloyd's building, its chrome and glass structure stark against the City skyline. 'The poor man did his best to set out the proposal in a favourable light when he did the breakdown for the Names. It didn't help that his slide show went off the rails. Projector broke. But that's neither here nor there. Before Leo spoke, I think the vote could have gone either way.'

'You mean our silver-tongued Mr Davies talked them out of accepting?'

Again Fred shrugged. 'He just said what he thought. But, yes – he's got all that charisma, that authority. They listen to him.'

'All the same, it's unnerving to think what must have been

253

passing through Carstairs' mind, to make him take the ultimate step ... Hanged himself, did you say?' Murray glanced up at Fred.

Fred nodded. 'From a doorknob. Just fastened something round the doorknob – a cord or something, I suppose – and put it round his neck. Then – bingo. Mind you, I've never quite understood how people do that.'

'I know,' agreed Murray. 'Doesn't really sound feasible, does it? Still, he managed. Poor Brian. What a way to put an end to your worries.'

With a reluctant sense of duty, Charles felt, having phoned Basher, that he'd better tell Freddie. It would give the poor old geezer a bit of a nasty shock if the first he heard about it was when he got his copy of the *Evening Standard*. Freddie's reaction, when Charles rang him, was sorrowful but stern.

'Can't say I'm surprised,' he said. 'I always thought the man didn't really have it in him to see the thing through.' Charles noted, not for the first time, that Freddie talked about the litigation as though it were some sort of military campaign. 'It's Carstairs' widow and children that I feel sorry for.' He sighed, a deep, rib-shaking sigh. 'No, Beecham, when it comes down to it, I can't help thinking that it's a bit of a coward's way out.'

'Well, I don't know about that,' protested Charles. 'It can't be an easy thing to do, you know – hang yourself. I mean, come on, Freddie ... '

'I'm sorry, I can't take a maudlin view. The man had a duty to his wife and children. Now they're left completely in the lurch.'

'But think of how bad things must have got for him,' said Charles, who could imagine only too easily the overwhelming sense of depression and futility which had forced Brian to his last, desperate act. 'Anyway,' he added, 'there's no sense in discussing it. I just felt I'd better let you know.'

'Quite. I suppose now we'll need to think about appointing a new committee secretary,' observed Freddie.

'Yes, well, I don't think that's something that needs to be rushed into quite yet,' replied Charles, thinking what a ruthless old sod Freddie Hendry could be.

Anthony was quite shaken by the news. When he put down the

phone after talking to Fred, Camilla looked across at him in concern. 'What was that?'

'Brian Carstairs hanged himself yesterday. He went home after the Names' meeting and – just hanged himself.'

'Oh, God . . . '

'I spoke to him just after the meeting. He was sitting outside, and I thought he looked a bit odd. Jesus, I didn't think . . . ' Anthony broke off and looked away from Camilla, staring unseeingly at the papers before him. Why had he not insisted that Brian come with him? Why hadn't he just made more of an effort? Perhaps it wouldn't have made any difference in the long run, but then again . . . 'I have to go and tell Leo,' he said abruptly, getting up from his chair.

As he ran down the short flight of steps to Leo's room, Anthony recalled the brief, but telling speech which Leo had made at the meeting. No one could say whether it had been decisive, but perhaps Leo would see it that way and hold himself partly responsible for the tragedy.

Leo, when Anthony told him, looked at him blankly, and Anthony assumed that he was stunned by the news. 'The thing is, I don't think you should hold yourself in any way responsible,' went on Anthony.

Leo took off his half-moon spectacles and gazed at Anthony. 'I? In what possible way could I regard myself as responsible for Brian Carstairs' imbecile actions?'

'Well, no, of course – I didn't mean that you were, in any sense. I was just – I mean, it's pretty obvious that it was the outcome of the meeting which pushed him over the edge. I didn't want you thinking that the things you said yesterday – '

Leo laughed abruptly, swivelling in his chair. 'Good God, man, you credit me with far more of a conscience than I possess. I'm sorry the man is dead, but the fact that I may have swayed the outcome of the vote is irrelevant. I did what I thought best in the interests of all. The offer was a dud.'

There was a momentary silence as both men regarded one another. Anthony realised he had been wrong. Because Leo had in the past shown himself capable of depths of feeling, of tenderness, that was no reason to suppose that he was, in general, kind. Or possessed of the same sense of conscience as Anthony. If he, Anthony, had made that speech yesterday, if he had twisted fate against Brian Carstairs, he would now be tormented with guilt, or at any rate a kind of anguish that he might have been partly responsible for such an awful result. Then Leo said, 'I know what you're thinking. But everything is very much a game, Anthony. A matter of chance. And – well, Brian was just one of the losers.'

Anthony nodded. 'Yes. Well, anyway, there it is. I thought you should know.'

'Thank you.'

Leo sat staring at the door after Anthony had gone. More and more these days he was aware that he and Anthony no longer seemed to connect. Something was being lost between them. After they had patched things up at the end of last year, when he had managed to re-establish himself in the focus of the younger man's affections, the old harmony between them had sprung up. But now . . . It was due to Camilla, he supposed. She was a poor influence, thought Leo. The last thing Anthony needed was that kind of dampening down, his fires of independence and freedom suffocated by female affection. Christ, give the girl half a chance and she would have him married and burdened with a mortgage and three children in no time. And Leo knew all too well, from his own experience, what a mistake that could be. On the other hand, Camilla was no fool. She'd worked hard to get where she was, and she was on the verge of being offered a tenancy at 5 Caper Court. Suddenly a thought struck Leo. Perhaps, if the girl's sense of ambition were strong enough, there was a way that Leo could save both her and Anthony a lot of trouble.

Leo met Camilla on the stairs quite by chance just after lunch. He noticed that she had a notebook and a couple of books under her arm. 'Not off to the library by any chance, are you?' he asked.

'Yes, I am. I've been turfed out of the room. Walter Lumley and Anthony are going over all the US asbestosis judgments, and they need my desk.'

'Well, while you're there, would you mind picking up a copy of MacGillivray and Parkington? Mine seems to have walked.'

Camilla nodded, and was about to carry on down the stairs when Leo added, 'By the way, I'd like to have a chat with you some time – about your future in chambers. The rest of the members of chambers thought it would be a good idea. Perhaps we could have dinner together?'

Camilla, surprised, said 'Yes – yes, if you like.' She felt herself blushing under Leo's intense blue gaze. She found him somewhat intimidating, and the idea of dining alone with him daunting. Besides, the prospect of whatever it was he had to say to her unnerved her, too.

'How does next Friday sound?' Rachel was due back the following Saturday morning, and it appealed to Leo's sense of order to have this particular manoeuvre accomplished before then.

'Yes, I'm sure that's fine,' said Camilla.

'Good. If you hang on for a bit longer in chambers – say, till seven – we can go somewhere straight from here. Don't forget the book.' He gave her a quick smile and carried on upstairs.

When she got back from the library at the end of the afternoon, Walter Lumley was gathering his papers together in preparation to leave. She had formed no particular view of this young man when he arrived earlier, save that he carried a rather fusty aroma around with him and had the demeanour of a fifty-year-old, despite being in his twenties. Now, however, as he studiedly ignored her and carried on talking to Anthony, she began slowly to dislike him. Clearly Walter belonged to that unattractive breed of barrister which treated pupils as the lowest of the low, and tended to behave as though they did not exist, save to fetch and carry. He did not even perform the simple courtesy of thanking her for letting him use her desk, or in any way acknowledge that he had inconvenienced her. He said goodbye to Anthony without glancing in Camilla's direction and left the room, a slight, stoop-shouldered figure. She made a face at his departing back as Anthony closed the door.

'What a creep,' she murmured. Anthony went over to the window and opened it.

'I told you he was. And he doesn't score very highly on the personal hygiene front. It's not BO exactly – more a sort of studious whiff. I think it gets stronger the harder he thinks. Let's have some fresh air.'

'I'll bet he's a virgin.'

'What – you think little Walter's problems could all be solved by a bit of strenuous sex, do you? Very chauvinistic attitude, I must say.' Anthony came over and kissed her briefly. For a second Camilla thought of telling him about her encounter on the stairs with Leo, but some instinct stopped her. She realised that she was secretly rather flattered that Leo had asked her to dinner. Why had he? He said he wanted to discuss her future in chambers, and that was something he could just as easily have talked to her about in his room. With a faint feeling of guilt, she moved away from Anthony and picked up the copy of the book which he had asked her to bring from the library. The prospect of taking it to him suddenly held a certain charm which it would not formerly have done.

'Leo asked me to get this from the library. I'd better take it to him.'

But when she knocked on Leo's door and went into the room, she found it empty. Conscious of a mild, irrational disappointment, she laid the book on his desk and went back upstairs.

The prospect of going out with Leo began to preoccupy Camilla as the days passed, and by the time Friday came, she had reached a certain pitch of anticipation and apprehension. She dressed carefully that morning, putting on an ivory silk blouse instead of her usual cotton one, and a black crepe wool suit which Anthony liked because it showed off her figure. She managed to convince herself that she was only going to this trouble because she had no idea where they were to dine, and should play it safe, but somewhere at the back of her mind lurked the knowledge that Leo was the kind of man whom every women would instinctively want to please. And so she would take a little more trouble than usual.

Leo had already worked out his strategy in advance. He took her to a small, up-market Italian place tucked away in the back streets of Seven Dials, where he had booked a quiet booth at the end of the restaurant. He studied her as she read the menu, trying to establish what it was that had so captivated Anthony. She was attractive, certainly, with good skin and very pretty eyes, and although Leo personally preferred his women on the gamine side, there was no question that the girl had a good figure. Certainly she looked a lot better these days than she had when she had first joined chambers. In those days she had been a complete bluestocking, but clearly she had learned a thing or two under Anthony's influence. But most of her attractions, Leo decided, lay in the superficiality of youth – the clear eyes, fresh skin and soft hair would fade eventually, and she would become as her mother doubtless was, merely another buxom, comfortable, middle-aged woman.

Leo steered the conversation skilfully along, talking idly at first about the Capstall case, and then bringing up the subject of Brian Carstairs' suicide, knowing that Camilla's views on this, doubtless youthfully earnest, must move their dialogue subtly on to a more personal level. By this time Camilla had drunk a glass of wine, and she felt less inhibited with the thoughtful, charming Leo of this evening than she did with the exacting, acerbic person she knew from work.

'I was wondering, though...' She frowned slightly, clearly nervous about what she was about to say, '... I was wondering how it affected you. Personally, I mean.'

They had talked about it, Leo realised, she and Anthony. His response to her was quite different from the one he had given Anthony a week ago.

'Brian's death?' Leo pursed his lips, stared briefly at his wine glass and then looked up directly at her. He knew only too well the effect his look could have on people, particularly in a moment of faint intimacy, such as this one. He could tell from her eyes that it had worked with her, that she was momentarily captivated. It was an important part of this evening's work, he told himself, to flatter her, to leave her with a pleasant uncertainty as to the exact meaning of his words and looks. 'I suppose,' he went on slowly, 'that I feel sorry that I played any part in it. That sounds worse than it should, I know, but when we are part of people's lives, we affect them in ways too subtle or tremendous to understand. There is, if one chooses to view it in a certain light, a causal connection between the speech I delivered at that meeting and Brian's decision to kill himself – but it is very slight.'

'You persuaded the Names to vote as they did – you acknowledge that?' Camilla's voice was bold, but underscored with a light note of apology.

He favoured her with another candid look, and this time held her eyes slightly longer. 'It's my job,' he said. 'I am an advocate. I enjoy persuading people, on any level. Anyway, what I said was what I believed.'

'But surely you can't tell people what to do, unless they really want to do it.'

'Can't you?' said Leo in vague surprise. Then he smiled and added quietly, 'I think you can, you know.' Camilla was aware that there was something in Leo's voice and eyes which had a disturbing effect upon her. She was still trying to fathom it as he turned the conversation away from Brian and on to the subject which they had purportedly come here to discuss. 'So, tell me how you think you're getting on in chambers. Everyone thinks very highly of you, but I'd like to know how you see things.'

Camilla took a deep breath, grateful for the pause during which the waiter cleared their plates away. 'Well, I'm very happy. I mean,' she added hastily, in case Leo should think she was referring to Anthony, 'in every sense. I like the people. I like the work. I must admit that I was a bit nervous when I started – you know, about whether I could handle the work.' She paused and watched as Leo poured them both some more wine. 'But I think I can. I don't doubt my competence now. I think it's just a question of handling cases, of getting experience.' Then she startled Leo by throwing him a question. 'Do you remember what it was like when you first started? I mean, did you have misgivings?'

Leo sat back, smiling. He remembered only too well his supreme self-confidence, his utter belief in his own brilliance. Oh, to be twenty-two again and know the things one did not know then. He met Camilla's gaze. 'No. Absolutely none. I was convinced that I was the greatest thing ever to hit commercial litigation. Which is the right way to be, I imagine. It's now that I'm older and wiser that I have misgivings.'

She smiled. 'Perhaps you're right. Anyway, I like to think that I could cope.'

'Yes, I'm sure you can. In fact, Cameron wants to offer you a tenancy. We spoke about it a week or so ago.'

She looked astonished, delighted. That was one of the charming things about the young, reflected Leo – their way of evincing emotions with total openness, whatever their pretensions or assumed sophistications. Not that this girl had many.

'Really?' She had flushed slightly with pleasure and surprise. 'God, that's – that's wonderful!'

'Didn't you think it was on the cards?' asked Leo.

'Well – I hoped so, of course, but it's not the same as actually knowing . . . '

'Naturally, the thing has to be properly agreed upon at the next chambers meeting . . . ' Leo hesitated for a moment, then went on, 'There is just one thing, however – it's a little delicate, which is why I thought we should discuss all this over dinner.' He glanced up at her. She was looking at him with faintly anxious expectation. He took a sip of his wine, then said, 'You and Anthony have been seeing quite a bit of each other recently, haven't you? Outside chambers, I mean.'

'Yes,' replied Camilla simply.

'For how long – a few weeks, say?'

'Something like that.'

Leo nodded. 'We don't have any Chinese walls, you know – chambers isn't run along the lines of big City institutions, where relationships between employees are discouraged. But I have to tell you candidly that the thing with Anthony could make difficulties for you.'

'How do you mean?'

Leo laughed and made a wry face, as if truly uncertain how best to express himself. But he knew exactly how he intended to express himself. Had known for a week. 'Let me see . . . Well, one of the key ingredients to running a successful set of chambers is harmony. Total co-operation and good mutual understanding between everybody, tenants and clerks alike. Now, I have absolutely no right to speculate on how serious your relationship with Anthony might be, but it could ultimately have some bearing on whether or not you get your tenancy.'

Camilla felt her heart begin to beat hard. Suddenly the idea of being robbed of the prize of a tenancy at 5 Caper Court seemed impossibly dreadful. She would do anything, she thought, any-thing, to avoid it. She had worked hard for four years to get to this point, and her entire future career at the Bar was now at stake. 'I'm not sure that I follow what you're saying,' she said. 'I don't quite understand why it should matter.'

Leo sighed, as if with regret. 'Let's put it this way. If you and Anthony should ultimately break up, as young people so often do, then that could be potentially bad for the general atmosphere in chambers. To be frank, it is desirable that relationships between people in chambers should be friendly, but neutrally so. Of course, since you are the first woman we've had in chambers, the problem hasn't arisen before now.' Leo had to prevent himself smiling at this point, recalling his own relationship with Anthony just a few years ago and wondering what Camilla would make of that, if she knew. 'Cameron may not be aware that you're seeing Anthony, but most of the rest of us know, and I can't guarantee that it won't go against you at the next chambers meeting.' Nothing like the obfuscation of a good double negative, thought Leo.

Camilla stared at him. 'You're telling me I should stop seeing Anthony,' she said simply.

He paused, then nodded. 'To put it bluntly – yes. Please don't think that I haven't given this a good deal of thought. I like you, and I think you are extremely promising. And I'm telling you this because I don't want your career spoiled for the sake of – ' He paused, letting the silence lend its own significance.

Camilla stared at the table, pondering this, and then she said slowly, 'I'm very fond of Anthony.'

Leo let a few seconds elapse, and then said, 'For someone like you, someone as intelligent and attractive as you are, there will always be plenty of people, you know.' His voice was silken, casual. Camilla looked up and met his gaze, and in a sudden, clear-sighted moment, she realised everything. As though in little shock waves, memories of Leo with Anthony, the way he looked at him, spoke to him, came back to her, and recollections of Leo's attitude to her, his faint irritability and resentment, suddenly crystallised into understanding. Leo was trying to annex Anthony, to ensure that no one else should possess that which he, Leo, wanted for himself. And this was part of it, this intimate dinner, the faint seductiveness of his manner, this whitewash about relationships in chambers. She had learned enough about Leo to know that he, of all the members of chambers, was the least likely to be concerned about such things. If it had come from Jeremy, or Roderick Hayter, she might have accepted it. But not from Leo. This was purely an attempt on Leo's part to distance her from Anthony. Her astonished mind was still trying to cope with this revelation, when it suddenly occurred to her that even if Leo had some hidden agenda, it might be that what he had said was true. Maybe, in the eyes of the other members of chambers, her relationship with Anthony was likely to jeopardise her chances of getting a tenancy. She returned Leo's steady blue gaze, watching his eyes narrow slightly against the smoke of his cigar. Well, there was a way round that one. This tenancy might be the most important thing in the world to her, but there was no real reason why she should forfeit Anthony into the bargain. She felt almost surprised at the cold calculation of her own thoughts, but then again, she told herself, this was the way one grew up. Certain situations taught you more and more about yourself. And she was not the fool Leo took her for.

Leo watched her, waiting for her response. At last Camilla said, 'Yes, I think I understand.'

The waiter brought coffee, and there was a long silence. Leo stubbed out his cigar and sat eyeing her meditatively as she stirred her coffee.

'Don't do anything hasty. Take a few weeks to think about it. Nothing's going to be decided until Easter. For all I know, you may decide that this relationship with Anthony is too important to throw away. Think about it and let me know.'

Camilla looked up at him. 'I don't really need to think,' she replied, with a coolness which faintly surprised Leo. 'I know my priorities. And I want the place in chambers.'

Leo smiled and nodded. 'Good.' He raised his glass. 'Then here's to your prospective tenancy.'

Camilla returned his smile, and said nothing.

An hour later, Leo swung his car into the driveway, reflecting on the evening's work. What he had told Camilla had been roughly true. There might be those in chambers who looked askance on her relationship with Anthony. He had doubtless done everyone an enormous favour. With a pleasant sense of accomplishment, Leo got out of the car and locked it. He glanced up at the house and saw the faint glow of Oliver's nightlight behind the blind, and, on the next floor, Jennifer's light behind her curtains. She was still awake. Over the past two weeks there had been nothing more between them than the usual domestic exchanges, but the atmosphere had remained fraught with sexual tension, although of a more subdued nature than on that first evening. As he let himself into the house and hung up his coat, Leo realised that the effort of the last few hours of contriving the most minor of seductions – one of which Camilla had been largely unaware – had left him with a certain appetite. Was Jennifer worth the bother? he wondered. But before he had time to consider this question properly, he heard a door close at the top of the house, and the sound of Jennifer's feet on the stairs. Bemused, Leo waited.

She appeared eventually on the first floor in her dressing gown, her feet bare, rubbing her eyes. She looked like a child, he thought.

'I hope I didn't wake you,' said Leo, dropping his car keys on to the hall table.

'No,' she said, and came down the rest of the stairs. 'I was just reading.' She spoke in an oddly listless way, and he was instantly aware that she had abandoned her self-regarding, predatory manner. 'There were three phone calls for you, and one of them wanted you to ring back tonight. I took the notepad upstairs without thinking.'

She handed him the pad of paper, on which she had scribbled the names and numbers of the callers. He took it from her, glanced at it, then chucked it on to the hall table. 'They can wait,' he said. Then he looked at her. She had a wonderfully warm, tousled look about her. 'Everything all right? Oliver go down quietly?'

She nodded. 'Yes.' Then she yawned and turned back to the stairs. 'Goodnight.'

It was too much for him, that she should have so easily discarded whatever desire she had had for him. Her very disinterest felt like a challenge. As she reached the foot of the stairs he said softly, 'Jennifer.'

She turned and looked at him. He watched her hesitate, and then the expression on her face underwent a subtle change, a flicker of curiosity in her eyes. That in itself he found instantly arousing. 'What?' she said.

He moved towards her, and she stood perfectly still. 'What?' he repeated, and smiled. Then he leaned forward and kissed her, unfastening the belt of her dressing gown, finding beneath it perplexing folds of winceyette. 'What the hell are you wearing?' he asked between breaths, as she kissed him feverishly back. 'It's my nightie,' she said. 'It gets really cold at the top of the house.'

'Then come upstairs,' said Leo, unwinding her arms from around his neck and turning her in the direction of the stairs and his bedroom, 'and get it off. Right away.'

Chapter Twenty-two

Rachel's trip to Sydney was, in many ways, a therapeutic release for her. Being on the other side of the world from Leo, she began to appreciate the tension and uncertainty that characterised their existence together. She missed him, and yet she felt temporarily relieved, as though from some oppressive weight. But absence, too, lent an illusion of hope, and she found herself, in intervals of time spent alone, constructing new hopes, new possibilities for the relationship, and wondering whether he missed her, deceiving herself with the notion that time spent away from her might make him want her once more.

Her paper, which she delivered at the beginning of the second week, was extremely well received and this had the effect of boosting her self-esteem. The fact that she was being a successful ambassador for the firm made her feel more robust about her position within it, and she developed the conviction that Mr Rothwell would no longer be able to employ arguments about commitment and flexibility to hold her back.

She missed Oliver, too, but guiltily enjoyed being without the ties of motherhood for fourteen days. The conference was as much a social as an academic affair, and Rachel realised that most of the men there, those without wives in tow, seemed to regard it as mandatory to make a pass at any attractive and apparently unattached female, but she managed to handle it all with an aplomb which she had not possessed two years before.

Something which she had not appreciated was the assiduity with which Charles seemed determined to pursue their relationship, even finding out somehow the name of the hotel she was staying at and sending a large bouquet of white roses to her room on the first day, with a card which read, 'Because they remind me of you. All love from your relentless admirer.' He telephoned her, too, and she found their conversations – which Charles was clever enough to keep friendly and neutral – extremely comforting, being so far from home. The fact that he cared enough to call her in what must have been the early hours of the morning in England both touched and amused her. The thought of him kindled in her a warmth which she tried to feel, but could not feel, when she thought of Leo. All she felt then was a dull ache. Unlike Charles, Leo had not troubled to phone her, although she herself had called a couple of times, ostensibly to see how Oliver was. Leo had been friendly, but there seemed to be a kind of blank, unaffectionate space between them, which left her sad but unsurprised.

By the time the two weeks were nearly over, she was more than ready to get home. On the day before she was due to leave, a good number of the delegates had already left, and there was generally a fag-end feeling about the conference, as though the game had been played out. On impulse, and longing to see Oliver again, Rachel changed her plans and booked a seat on a flight which would arrive in London late on Friday, instead of at lunchtime on Saturday.

Which was why, when she had paid off the taxi and let herself into the house, she found Leo in the kitchen in his dressing gown, a bottle of wine in one hand, and two glasses standing on the worktop. She was too tired to notice the two glasses, and only mildly surprised to see that Leo was pouring himself a drink – and wine, at that – at eleven thirty on a Friday night.

From the heart-stopping moment when he heard the key in the front door and realised that it could be no one but Rachel, Leo knew that there was nothing to be done but to play the situation out, step by step. He had left Jennifer in bed upstairs, and now, as he watched Rachel come through the doorway into the kitchen, he could only hope that the girl had heard Rachel come in, that she would have the good sense to slip silently upstairs to her own room. He must, he knew, proceed on that assumption. As he prepared himself for the slight effort of making everyday conversation with his wife, there rose in Leo a sudden feeling of utter distaste for the predicament in which he found himself. Never in his life had he been forced into a position of humiliation and deceit, and he found the experience profoundly unpleasant. Before his marriage, he had been answerable to no one, had led his life without guilt or the need for dissembling, and even after it he had tried to maintain that position, cruel though it might be to Rachel. But to be found frolicking with the nanny was, he realised, perfectly abject.

These thoughts raced through his mind as he watched Rachel slip off her jacket. He carried on pouring the glass of wine and handed it to her. She shook her head, giving him a tired smile as she sat down. He leaned forward instinctively and kissed her in greeting, thankful that Jennifer wore no perfume, yet at the same time detesting the fact that it should even matter to him.

'I hadn't expected you back till tomorrow. You should have rung me and I would have met you at the airport.' He tried to keep his voice light and unconcerned, but was half-listening for sounds from above.

'I changed my flight at the last minute. You know how it is with these things. Everybody started to drift off yesterday – or was it the day before? – and I decided I would, too. I didn't want to drag you out to the airport late at night.' She slipped off her shoes, picked them up and put them in her lap. 'How's Oliver been?' she asked.

Leo sipped some of the wine which he now no longer wanted, his body concealing the presence of the second glass on the worktop behind him. 'He's been excellent. I'm sure he's missed you, but it's not easy to tell . . . ' Leo tried to concentrate, to think of something to say. 'He's trying to pull himself up on things, but he doesn't quite make it. Falls back with a bump on his nappy.'

Rachel smiled and yawned. 'That I must see. But right now I'm going to bed. My body clock is all over the place, so I'll probably wake up in four hours, but at the moment I feel as though I could sleep for ever.' She got up and padded across the kitchen, her shoes in her hand.

He could think of nothing to say to detain her which would not be completely artificial, and realised that he should have found some pretext for going up ahead of her, to make sure that Jennifer wasn't still there, but that it was now too late for that. She was at the foot of the stairs. He wondered suddenly, helplessly, whether Jennifer might not be the kind of little vixen who would deliberately stay where she was just to create some kind of domestic drama. He hoped to God she wasn't.

But Jennifer was quite oblivious of Rachel's arrival. When Leo had gone downstairs to fetch them both a drink, she had rolled happily over on the bed and begun to fiddle with the radio alarm, trying to tune it in to Kiss FM, or Capital. She did not hear the door, was unaware of the brief conversation taking place in the kitchen, and by the time Rachel had reached the landing outside the bedroom, was lying back naked on the sheets, eyes closed, listening to Mick Hucknall.

Rachel had only an instant to wonder why Leo had the radio tuned in to whatever station it was tuned to, before she saw Jennifer. The shock went through her in a swift tide, then evaporated, leaving her feeling stunned and cold. And angry. The room was lit only by the glow of a lamp on the far side of the room – how very like Leo – and Rachel snapped on the overhead light. Jennifer sat up blinking, and gazed at Rachel with an expression of horrified astonishment that in other circumstances would have been almost comic.

'I think you're in the wrong room,' said Rachel, amazed that she managed to keep her voice level and cold, and watched as Jennifer made an undignified scramble for the nightdress and dressing gown which she had so enthusiastically discarded half an hour before. Jennifer was saying something confused and apologetic, but Rachel did not listen. 'Get upstairs to your room,' she cut in. 'Tomorrow morning you will pack and go, and I will sort out the matter of your wages with the agency. Leave your keys on the hall table.'

Jennifer, conscious of the humiliating fact that she was beginning to cry, bundled up her things and ran upstairs to her room. Rachel passed a shaky hand across her face and took several deep breaths to calm herself. She stared at the bed, at the sheets rumpled and spilled across the floor, and then turned to go back downstairs.

Leo was standing at the foot of the stairs, one hand in his dressing-gown pocket, the other holding a small cigar. He had listened to the little scene between Rachel and Jennifer and had groaned inwardly, but he could not help feeling a light underscoring of amusement as he watched Jennifer's pretty bottom in retreat.

'You're not fucking Noël Coward, you know,' said Rachel coldly. This startled Leo slightly, as Rachel was not given to swearing. He glanced at the cigar in his hand.

'No,' he murmured. 'No, indeed I am not.' He tried to put a note of apology into his voce, having already decided that the best way to handle this undignified incident was to treat it with light unconcern.

She went past him and into the kitchen, waited for him to follow her in, and then closed the door.

'Has this been going on all the time I was away?' she demanded.

'No. Actually, it was more a spur of the moment idea when I came in this evening,' replied Leo idly. He was determined that this conversation would be brief, that he would not allow it to develop into a full-scale row. Those were things which he could not abide and which he always did his scrupulous best to avoid. 'I'm sure you're not exactly surprised. I'd already explained to you how things were to be – '

'Yes, but I didn't expect it here, in this house, in our bed!'

'I shouldn't trouble yourself about it,' said Leo calmly. 'She's of no significance, I can assure you.'

Rachel's voice dropped from anger to a level chill. 'She may be of no significance to you, Leo, she may just be another casual screw, but believe it or not, she is quite important to me. Don't flatter yourself that I'm angry because I found you in bed with another woman. I no longer care whom you sleep with. The reason I'm angry is that, because of your laughable sexual incontinence, I have just lost a bloody good nanny. And it's me, not you, who is going to have to waste precious time and energy finding another.' She ran her fingers through her hair, and breathed deeply, glaring at him. 'And now I'm going to bed. Let's just hope you haven't got some young man stashed away in the spare room.'

She left the kitchen, and Leo stood for a moment in the middle of the room, gazing at the glowing tip of his cigar. She had surprised him, certainly. He had never heard her speak in such a way to him before, and he was irritated by the fact that it was she who had had the last – and the best – word. It was not pleasant to be made to feel like a mildly degenerate fool. Still, the thing was over and done with now. Of course, there would be repercussions, but he could not trouble himself to think about those now. Leo sighed, ground the remains of his cigar with a little hiss into a puddle of water in the sink, and went upstairs.

For the rest of the weekend they avoided one another as much as possible. Rachel spent Saturday ringing round nanny agencies and compiling a list of girls to interview over the coming week, desperately hoping that she would find someone suitable quickly. She took Oliver shopping, ate with him in the evening, and left Leo holed up in his study, working. On Sunday, after a dismal morning, during which she and Leo hardly spoke, she took Oliver for a long and lonely walk in the park.

She sat on a bench, Oliver beside her in his buggy, and watched other small children wheeling around among the pigeons, listening to their shouts. She gazed at the families, at the mothers and fathers who chatted idly and smiled and followed their offspring with unconsciously proud eyes, and then thought of the hopes she had built up over the last two weeks. Well, she thought with an inward sigh, there was nothing like distance to lend enchantment. She had to face it. The bargain that she and Leo had struck was purely a licence for him to behave as badly as he wished. She could see now that nothing was likely to change for the better. Leo intended to conduct his life entirely for his own pleasure, without any regard for her or Oliver. That she was theoretically allowed to do the same was neither here nor there. That was just a sop to his conscience. He knew she would just hang around waiting, hoping. Christ, how little he must think of her, she told herself bitterly.

A flock of Canada geese suddenly rose from the boating lake in a flurry of icy water and shrill honking, and Oliver laughed and waved his hands. Rachel smiled involuntarily as she looked at him. God, he was like Leo, even at this age – the same eyes, same shape of face, even beneath the baby chubbiness. She thought of Leo as he was with Oliver, and reflected that it was only in those moments that he showed a true, sincere tenderness towards any other living being. The rest was just ego, ambition and appetite. She wondered why he didn't just divorce her and have done with it. He didn't want her, that was now perfectly obvious. He would make love to the nanny – at least that supplied a certain titillation – but his own wife was simply too humdrum, too easy. She felt tears rising to the surface and blinked them back, rummaging in her coat pocket for a tissue. It was pointless feeling sorry for herself. The question was – what now? She could not, she knew, bear much more from Leo. She must put some distance between them. If anyone was to leave, it should be him. She was the wronged party, after all. But the idea of asking Leo to get out of the house seemed faintly bizarre. She could imagine only too easily how calmly, how obliquely he would decline to entertain the idea. And if he refused, what would she do? Start divorce proceedings, make things acrimonious? Her mind shied away from the very thought. Her instincts were merely those of flight. As at Christmas, she simply wanted to bundle herself, Oliver and their belongings out of the house and get away. Where? There was Leo's country house, but that was impossible. She could not take refuge from him in a place that was so very much his.

Her mind began to busy itself with thoughts of letting agencies, of flats, of the possibility of staying with friends, and then she let the thoughts die blankly away. She was too tired. Anyway, the priority was to find someone to look after Oliver until she could get a new nanny. She thought suddenly of Trudy, a woman who had been in hospital giving birth at the same time. They saw one another occasionally, and Rachel knew that Trudy had a nanny for her little girl. She would probably be happy to help out, if the nanny didn't mind. This piece of inspiration cheered and relieved her. She would ring Trudy when she got back.

Rachel rose and pushed Oliver back through the park and up the street to the house, the house that was so large and beautiful and useless. As she approached it, gazing up at its windows, she realised that she would feel no compunction about leaving it. It was Leo's house far more than hers, and she had never known any special happiness in it. Would Leo be surprised or sorry when she eventually found the time and energy to organise her departure? She imagined not. For a moment she stood outside the front door, staring at it, and wished, with an aching, searing hopelessness, that she could walk in and find him changed, everything changed to the way it had been when she had first known him, when she had believed utterly in his love for her. It was like the game she had played as a child to conjure up a delicious fear, when she imagined to herself, as she approached her childhood home, that she might go into the kitchen through the back door and find strangers there, and the furniture different, and no one would know who she was, gazing blankly at her. And there had been the sweet relief at finding her mother in the kitchen as usual, and everything just the same. She thought briefly of her mother in her little house in Bath, much changed from the person of her childhood, and wondered how it was that affections, people, could be so utterly transformed by time. The house, when she let herself in, was silent, but a glow of light shone from beneath Leo's study door. It made no

271

difference whether he was in or out, Rachel told herself as she pulled off Oliver's mittens and unbuttoned his coat. The gulf between them now was too wide, too deep, ever to be bridged.

Rachel passed James Rothwell in the corridor at work the next morning, and he greeted her with faint surprise. 'Didn't expect to see you in today. Thought you'd take a couple of days off to recover from your trip.'

'I came back a day early, so I thought I might as well come in,' said Rachel.

'How was it? Paper go down all right?'

'Oh, I think so. We made some valuable contacts, too, people who look like putting a bit of business our way.'

Mr Rothwell raised his eyebrows and gave a gratified nod. 'Excellent. Clever girl. Pop up to my office about two and we'll have a bit of a debriefing, eh?'

'Fine.' Rachel carried on down the corridor to her office. Clever girl, indeed. Patronising old git. She was conscious this morning of a new sense of determination running like a steel thread through her unhappiness. Taking charge of her life, the prospect of excising Leo and all that attendant uncertain misery, gave her a strength of purpose. The mere business of organising the details was therapeutic, leaving her little time to brood. Trudy was perfectly happy to let her nanny look after Oliver until Rachel made other arrangements, so that was one small weight off her mind. Now all she had to do, when her caseload allowed enough time, was to sort out somewhere for herself and Oliver to live. This wasn't going to be any temporary departure, and it was important to find the right place. She had no intention of rushing it. The wretched situation between herself and Leo would just have to be endured until she could find something. She knew that the Capstall hearing was coming up in two weeks' time, and with any luck that would keep him so busy that they wouldn't have to see much of one another. Rachel didn't think she could bear it otherwise.

When the phone rang, and the receptionist spoke Charles Beecham's name, Rachel realised with a little stab of guilt that he had been entirely out of her thoughts for the past forty-eight hours. Leo was enough to contend with. She sighed as she asked for him to be put through.

'Hello, Charles.'

'Hi. I wanted to make sure you were back safe and sound.'

'Oh, I'm safe all right,' murmured Rachel, 'but I'm not so sure about sound. In fact, I think I'm falling apart.'

'That's just jet lag. Look, I thought we could have lunch – I'm up in town today. I'd really like to see you.'

Rachel realised, listening to his voice, that she would like very much to see him, too, to talk with some sane, cheerful representative of the opposite sex who was not Leo. 'I can't,' she said reluctantly. 'I've got too much to catch up on, and I have a meeting with the senior partner at two.'

'What about dinner? I'm going to be holed up in the country for the next two weeks, working on this series, so this is my only day.'

'Sorry. We've had something of a domestic crisis, and I haven't got a nanny at the moment, so there's no one to look after Oliver.'

'Bring him along! I haven't seen the little guy since Christmas, anyway. It's time he and I had a man-to-man chat.'

Rachel laughed. She had no real wish to spend any time in the same house as Leo at the moment, and any escape would be a relief. She didn't start interviewing prospective nannies till tomorrow evening, so why not? She hesitated momentarily, then said, 'All right. I can't make any guarantees about Oliver's behaviour, though.'

'Can't make any guarantees about mine,' replied Charles cheerfully, then gave her the name of a restaurant. 'Eight all right?'

'Make it eight thirty,' said Rachel. 'That gives me time to get back and pick him up.'

'Right. See you then.'

In the restaurant that evening Oliver sat in a high chair, looking round with bright, attentive eyes at everything and everyone, banging a steady accompaniment on his high-chair table with a spoon.

Charles's enthusiasm for the company of Oliver was genuine, but moderate. He would have preferred to have Rachel to himself, but if this was the only way that he could see her, so be it. He breathed a deep, inward sigh of pleasure at the sight of her, the poised, vulnerable loveliness that he found so challenging. She was not overtly sensual, but Charles felt that in the depths of those dark blue eyes lay a certain sexual promise, one which, with luck, he would take great delight in exploring and developing.

'So what happened with the nanny?' asked Charles, after they had ordered. He snapped a breadstick and handed half to Oliver.

Rachel did not look at him for a moment, deliberating whether or not to tell him. It would have been easy to say something oblique and casual, and deflect the subject, but somehow the urge to tell someone was overwhelming. She wanted professions of outraged sympathy, someone on her side.

'I came home,' she replied, looking up at Charles with a wry, small smile, 'to find her in bed with my husband.'

Charles paused in the act of eating the other half of the breadstick, and exclaimed with gratifying horror, 'No! My God . . .'

'Well, not exactly in bed with him – he was down in the kitchen, pouring them both a little post-coital glass of wine. But she was upstairs in our bed, so it was all quite obvious.'

'Hell's bells,' murmured Charles. He took a long draught of his wine, thinking that here was a starter for ten. This chap just couldn't keep it still, could he? First he knocked off other blokes, then the nanny . . . Mind you, leaving a fellow alone for two weeks with a nubile young nanny, you could see how it happened. Perfectly understandable, but not excusable. 'So – what happened?' he asked, his instinct for good, confiding gossip and domestic drama nicely aroused.

'I sent her packing – well, she went the next day, and I – well, I don't know if I really said enough to Leo . . . ' Her voice trailed away, and she stared thoughtfully at the food which a waitress had just placed before her. It was the first time, oddly, that she had ever referred to Leo by name but, although the name registered with Charles, he made no connection between the fiend in human form and anyone of his own acquaintance. Then Rachel went on, 'You see, if it had really shocked me, if it had been the first time he had wounded me, or damaged our relationship, I suppose I would have been more – more incensed. Do you know what made me *really* angry? It was the fact that, because of him, I had to get rid of a perfectly good nanny, someone whom I thought I liked and trusted, and whom Oliver liked.'

'Well,' observed Charles, scooping up strands of linguini, 'clearly she wasn't someone to like *or* trust.'

Rachel sighed and shrugged her shoulders. 'Not as far as my husband was concerned. But it didn't stop her being good at her job. Now I have to go through the rigmarole of finding another, and that's something I could have done without, quite frankly. And that's another thing.' Rachel's eyes were bright with anger and she had flushed lightly, making her, Charles thought, look prettier than ever. He wondered if another bottle of this rather good house red might oil the wheels a bit, and glanced round for the waiter. 'I don't see why it should automatically be *me* who has to recruit a new nanny. I wasn't responsible for her leaving! Just because I'm Oliver's mother.'

Charles murmured to the waiter and then turned his attention back to Rachel. 'Why didn't you tell *him* to go and find a new one, then?'

Rachel paused in the middle of cutting up bits of spaghetti for Oliver and gave Charles a look of exasperation. 'Because nothing would happen. Because it all goes over his head. It's something to do with upbringing. He's one of those men who is used to seeing the women around him running households, busying themselves so that he and all the other men he knows can sail serenely on with their lives. We – I need a new nanny, so I'm the one who gets it done.'

Charles refilled her glass surreptitiously, and she drank some more to cool her annoyance. 'So,' said Charles, 'what now?' He held his breath. She couldn't be so daft as to sit there in the same house as this chap, waiting for him to have a go at the next nanny, or find a new boyfriend, could she? She must have had it up to here by now. Unless, of course, she loved him so much that she would put up with anything. There were women like that.

'I'm leaving him,' replied Rachel, meeting Charles's gaze.

He nodded thoughtfully, betraying nothing of the ecstatic delight which filled him. 'Where will you go?' He gave a little frown, having to work to control the muscles of his mouth from spreading into a happy grin.

'I haven't worked that out yet. I'm certainly not going to just start packing bags and flying out of the house. I'll have to see a lawyer about a divorce, I suppose, and think about money . . . '

A divorce, thought Charles. This was the real thing. Open season. 'But you can't go on living with him, can you? I mean – ' He shook his head in disbelief. 'You should be out of there like a shot.'

'Where would I go?' asked Rachel. 'I've got to find somewhere decent, permanent, with enough room for a nanny. And I've got work to think about. This is quite an important time for me. I have to plan things carefully, so it'll just have to take as long as it takes. Not,' she added, 'that I wouldn't leave now, if I could.'

'Come and stay with me,' said Charles simply.

Rachel laughed. 'No, I couldn't. That's kind of you, Charles, but I couldn't. I mean, Christmas was one thing, but – '

'I'm serious,' interrupted Charles. 'It's the perfect solution. You could commute to work from Salisbury, station's a car's throw away, and the village is teeming with apple-cheeked girls who would love to nanny for you for a bit. That would give you a base, a bit of security, and you could take your time about looking for somewhere for you and Oliver. You may think that you could handle living with your husband for a while longer, but I can assure you, now that you've made your mind up to go, the sooner you go, the better.' Her gaze met his, and he gave a warm, reassuring smile and added, 'There is no hidden agenda, I assure you. This is just an offer of help to a friend in need.'

Rachel believed him. She looked at those calm, grey eyes, and that nice, relaxed face and believed him. The idea was very tempting. There was an atmosphere at home so poisoned that even now she shrank from the idea of going back there. Her recollection of Charles's house was that of a haven, a warm and friendly sanctuary. But then she recalled the conversation they had had before she went to Australia. Was it a sensible idea to go and live with a man who had professed to be in love with you? Her mind wrestled with this for a moment. But he had said there was no hidden agenda, and she was fond enough of Charles to believe that, knowing how wretched she was, he wouldn't try to take advantage of the situation. 'All right,' she said, and smiled. 'If you really mean it. I'll trespass on your hospitality a second time. But I promise that it won't be for long. Really. I don't want to interfere with your work.'

An amazing glow of lustful pleasure filled Charles. She had said yes. It had to happen. She couldn't be under his roof for – oh, a fortnight at the outside, without . . . The thought was too much. He struggled for some commonplace expression of satisfaction. 'Excellent. It's by far the best thing to do, to make a break as soon as you can. And you won't interfere with anything, I promise you. I don't work in the evenings, so it will be a pleasant change to have company. The evenings can be a bit lonely, sometimes,' lied Charles, who spent most of them boozing in the village pub, for want of better things to do.

The rest of the meal was spent planning the practicalities of moving Rachel in, and which rooms she and Oliver should occupy, and this naturally made for an intimate atmosphere of collusion. So much so, that when the bill had been paid and they were outside on the cold street searching for a taxi, it was all that Charles could do, when Rachel turned her face up towards him to ask something, to stop himself from making a passionate grab for her there and then. But he restrained himself, only too well aware that a premature move like that could easily ruin everything. Besides, he thought, glancing warily at the baby's unnervingly steady blue gaze, Oliver would have got in the way.

Chapter Twenty-three

On the way home in the taxi after dinner with Charles, Rachel had decided that she might as well tell Leo as soon as possible that she and Oliver were leaving. So she delivered the news the next morning, while she was spooning cereal into Oliver's mouth and Leo, in the now customary silence which characterised breakfast, was drinking coffee and scanning the newspaper. When she had spoken, Leo stared unseeingly at the paper for a few seconds, then looked up at her.

'Where will you be going?'

Rachel had already thought hard about what she would say in reply to this inevitable question. The fact that Charles was a Name on the Capstall syndicate, and one of Leo's clients, put them all in a difficult position. She had been at pains to conceal Leo's identity from Charles, and it seemed to her that it would only further muddy already murky waters to tell Leo that she was going to be staying with Charles Beecham. Beyond the issue of the barrister –client relationship, Rachel knew that Leo would assume that she and Charles were having an affair. And she didn't feel like putting herself in the defensive position of trying to persuade him otherwise. So, instead, she had decided to leave Charles out of it. There was really no need for his name to be mentioned, after all. The arrangement was purely a temporary one, and in two or three weeks she would, with luck, have found somewhere to live.

'To stay with friends. I'll give you the address and phone number, though I can't think of any reason why you should have to get in touch. I'll probably only be there for a few weeks, anyway, while I try to find us somewhere permanent.'

At this, both of them glanced towards Oliver, who had taken the spoon from Rachel and was gnawing at it with such teeth as he had. Leo felt a pang of uncertain emotion as he looked at his son, and thought of how silent and cold the house would feel without him. This was what he had wished to prevent, though he saw now that the departure would have come about eventually. He had married Rachel under false pretences, and events had shown her that. It should not have surprised him that she was leaving – he had already told himself that it was likely – but he had not expected the news to affect him quite as it did. Outwardly, he accepted it calmly enough, but in fact he was shocked, and his mind was racing with a tumult of illusory regrets and wild notions of reparation. But, as he sat looking at Oliver, he let them die away. There was no future for himself and Rachel. The affection which he felt for her was deadened by their life together, though it might return once there was distance between them. It would never amount to more than that. But Oliver ... For a mad, fleeting instant it occurred to him that he might try to gain custody of his son, but even as he thought it, he knew that such an effort would be damaging for everyone, and that, anyway, he would not wish to take Oliver from his mother, even if he could.

There was a long silence between them, as each thought their separate thoughts, Rachel pretending to be absorbed in the business of retrieving the spoon from Oliver and wiping his mouth with his bib. Now that she had told Leo she was leaving him, she suddenly felt horribly vulnerable, as though she might cry. Depending on what Leo said next, there was a real danger that she would. It was the last thing she wanted. She got up and took Oliver's dish and spoon to the sink, intent on getting out of the house as fast as possible. Hoping that by changing the subject, by saying something irrelevant, she might deflect any further exchanges between them, she began to say, 'I have to drop Oliver off at Trudy's, so – '

But Leo cut in. 'I want to see Oliver, you know. I'll want to see him at weekends, and I want to be able to spend time with him in the holidays, when he's older. I want – ' He stopped, not knowing what it was he wanted next. Rachel looked at him, reading in his eyes the boyish anxiety and desperation of someone whose own father had dropped from his life without a word, all those years ago. She had never before seen such vulnerability in his expression, and suddenly felt unbearably sorry for them both, for Leo and for Oliver. But it was not up to her. It was up to Leo, and he had accepted without question the fact of their departure. He had not asked her to stay, so Oliver must go, too. Fighting the urge to allow her tears to rise to the surface, she looked away.

'Of course. I wouldn't deny either of you that, you know that. It's something we'll have to sort out with the divorce.' The word hung in the air, unspoken before now. There was a short silence, and then Rachel sighed, wondering if Leo might, at this, say that he did not want to contemplate anything so final. But he said nothing. 'But not this weekend, I'm afraid. I'll be too busy packing and moving things out.' Again there was another pause. 'Now, I'd better get going.' She moved towards the high chair, but Leo was there first, unstrapping the baby and plucking him from the seat. He held him for a moment, the soft, slight weight, and then handed him to Rachel.

During the two weeks which followed, in the run-up to the hearing, Leo was able to immerse himself in work, staying late in chambers, going back to the house in Hampstead only to sleep and bath and change his clothes. Only once did he go into Oliver's empty bedroom and stare about him; after that he did not open the door again. So far as he was able to give the matter any thought, he decided to put the house on the market as soon as the hearing was over. It had become hateful to him now – too big, and too desolate. He would find somewhere smaller and more central, like his old mews house, but with room enough for Oliver when he came to stay. He would have to provide somewhere for Rachel and Oliver to live, of course, but it was up to her to find the place she wanted. The practicalities would have to be dealt with later, when he had more time to spare.

While Leo prepared himself for the hearing, and tried to put his personal problems to one side, the little whisper of rumour which Sarah had put about that night weeks ago in the wine bar had grown into a low murmur. Richard Crouch's penchant for idle gossip had ensured that it was soon currency amongst certain solicitors that Leo Davies, leading counsel for the Names in the Capstall case, was conducting an affair with Anthony Cross, one of his juniors and a fellow member of chambers. It was just the kind of scandal which delighted a close community such as the Bar, and as the day of the hearing approached, the word was gleefully spread amongst the massed ranks of the barristers who were acting on behalf of the underwriters and the various agents.

The first that Anthony heard of it was when Walter Lumley came to 5 Caper Court to go over some statements with him. When they had finished the morning's work, Walter remarked, as he gathered up his papers, 'I think you and Leo might make an attempt to stop the rumours that are going around, you know. There's a possibility that they could damage our case.'

'What rumours?' asked Anthony in astonishment.

Walter gave a sly smile. 'Oh, I'm sure neither of you thought it would get about. But it has. Everybody knows that Leo's wife has left him, and everyone's pretty sure why.'

Naturally, though without any obvious source, the news had percolated through chambers that Rachel had left Leo. Anthony had been saddened, but not surprised, and had given it little further thought. It was no business of his, until Leo chose to make it so, and so far Leo had said nothing to him. Now Walter's smirking reference to it puzzled and annoyed him.

'I don't know what you're on about,' he said. 'If you're trying to tell me something, for God's sake why can't you just come out with it? What rumours are you talking about?'

Walter stood up, tidying his papers into his briefcase. 'That you and Leo are having a – shall we say, relationship?' He met Anthony's astonished gaze. 'You know – an affair. It's none of my business, of course. What you and Leo do in your private life is up to you, but I do happen to be involved in this case and I don't think that having this kind of scandal going about is very helpful.'

Anthony took a deep breath, and laughed. 'Oh, come on – don't tell me you believe such a load of rubbish!' He was unnerved by what Walter had told him, but determined to treat the matter casually. Yet as he spoke he couldn't help glancing in a guarded fashion at Walter, who responded by pursing his lips and raising his eyebrows. This mildly cynical intimation of disbelief irritated Anthony even more, and he said scathingly, 'For God's sake, you should know better than to go around believing second-hand hearsay. I've got a girlfriend, Walter. I'm not sleeping with Leo.' The very words brought an image to mind which made Anthony's pulse quicken, suddenly reminding him of feelings which he knew – had always known – lay dormant only through his own endeavours. He thrust the thought aside, and added, 'It's just a piece of mischief-making, something to throw us before the hearing. Ignore it. I certainly intend to.'

'As you like,' said Walter, shrugging. 'But I thought it was something of which . . . you and Leo should be made aware.' There was a wealth of implication in the pause which Walter dropped into this remark. 'I'll see you later.' As the door closed, Anthony found himself wanting, as he had so often wanted in the past, to punch Walter Lumley's obnoxious face. He sat down at his desk, sighing, and wondered whether he should bother Leo with the fact of these rumours. Then there floated into his mind a memory of being kissed by Leo, a dim recollection of the all-consuming love he had once felt. Suddenly it did not seem so long ago or far away. It was with an effort of will that he pushed the image from his mind.

That afternoon at tea, he managed to get Leo on his own and tell him what Walter had said. Leo frowned, then gave a shrug. 'Just someone stirring things up. Facile in the extreme. I wouldn't let it worry you.'

Anthony added, on impulse, 'He said that it was why you and Rachel had split up.'

At this Leo gave a sharp laugh. 'Moved you in with me, have they? Well, well.' He sipped his tea thoughtfully, then gave Anthony a long, musing look. 'Those times have long gone, though, haven't they? If they were ever there.'

Anthony felt uncomfortable, conscious that the intimacy of this conversation stirred within him feelings which he had suppressed years ago. He shook his head. 'It doesn't worry me. It's just a pain, at a time like this.'

Leo passed a hand over his silver hair, a faraway look in his blue eyes. 'It doesn't help, certainly. We must just ignore it. What else can we do, after all?' And he turned to look at Anthony, resting his elbow on the arm of his chair, and his chin on his hand. Leo's blue eyes met Anthony's in a gaze of such intensity that after a few seconds Anthony was forced to look away.

Initially, things did not go quite as Charles had planned. During the weekend in which Rachel and Oliver moved in, he received a phone call from his agent telling him that he and a film crew were to fly out on Monday to a remote province in eastern China, somewhere north of the Yellow River, to reshoot some documentary footage which the producer had decided was unsatisfactory. Marvelling at the amount of money people were prepared to spend just to have him standing around in a landscape that might as well be somewhere in Spain, mouthing about Zhang Qian introducing alfalfa to China, Charles also cursed the fate which would prevent him from spending cosy evenings with Rachel and embarking upon his seduction.

Rachel was dismayed by the suddenness of Charles's enforced departure. She had been looking to him for company, for cheerful conversation to distract her from her unhappiness. When he had gone she found the evenings, once Oliver had been fed and put to sleep, long and lonely, with too much time spent in angry and disgusted reflection on Leo's treatment of her. To ward off such thoughts, she took to wandering around the house, first with the natural timidity of a guest, but eventually with greater boldness and curiosity, drawing books from shelves, staring at paintings, fingering the knick-knacks and possessions which Charles had accumulated over the years. One evening she ventured into a room which served partly as a guest bedroom and partly as a depository for the excess of books which Charles had acquired. She pulled a book from one of the upper shelves of the bookcase to examine it, and as she did so, grimy drifts of dust floated down on to her clothing and hair. She stepped back in disgust. She had already noticed downstairs that Charles's cleaning lady, Mrs Dobey, seemed to get away with as little as possible, but here was evidence of wilful neglect. Glancing around, she noticed, too, that an antique mirror on the wall opposite was lightly filmed with grime. Moving from one piece of furniture to another, she could see that only cursory attempts had been made to take proper care of anything. No doubt Charles was too preoccupied to pay much attention to rooms which were rarely used, but to Rachel's fastidious mind such laxity was unbearable. When she had lived alone, she had been meticulous in looking after her flat, polishing and cleaning regularly, taking particular pleasure in seeing that everything was pristine and neat. Disorder and dirt upset her. She couldn't possibly leave the room in this state.

She went downstairs and through to the kitchen to search for dusters and polish, her energies fired by the prospect of attending to chores which gave her so much mindless pleasure, but which had been denied her in the house in Hampstead. That evening, and on most evenings thereafter, she set about making good the deficiencies of Mrs Dobey, partly for the sheer enjoyment of it, and partly in an earnest desire to repay Charles in some small way for his kindness. She found reassurance and comfort in cleaning. For Rachel, keeping things spotless had always been a kind of therapy, a way of imposing order on a chaotic and threatening world. Soon every mirror, bookcase and polishable surface was dust-free and gleaming. It had necessitated a little tidying up in the process, but Rachel liked to see things in order.

The effect of all this domestic activity was to reduce Rachel to a much calmer frame of mind. Thoughts of Leo were pushed aside by the trance-inducing business of seeking out dirt, running dusters over neglected picture rails, hoovering areas beneath pieces of furniture which had not received the attentions of a vacuum cleaner for months, possibly years. So immersed did she become, that traces of disorder round the house became something of a fixation. A couple of evenings before Charles was due to return from China, while she was cooking Oliver's tea, she noticed that Charles had arranged his kitchen utensils in an oddly haphazard manner, putting wooden spoons with tea cloths, and table mats in various different drawers, intermingled with potato peelers, plastic bags, pieces of string and old ballpoint pens. Presumably he was always too busy to keep things neatly arranged, but it must make working in the kitchen just as tiresome for him as it did for her. How did he ever find anything? She pulled a few things out of one drawer with a view to rearranging them, then hesitated. Would he think it presumptuous of her to move things about? No – he couldn't possibly have meant to have things in this chaotic state. It had just come about gradually, and no doubt he would be grateful to find things rather better organised. Thus reassured, she fed Oliver his baby rice and apple, and then began to sort things into more sensible locations.

While he was away, Charles began to worry that Rachel might have found somewhere to live in his absence, thus scuppering all his hopes. But when he got home two weeks later, exhausted, fed up, and popping Immodium to keep a stomach bug at bay, he was relieved to find her still there. That evening she cooked for him, duck with some sort of plum sauce, and dauphinoise potatoes, which were a particular favourite of Charles. His sense of well-being completely restored by the prospect of a decent meal, and his stomach griping only slightly, Charles fetched a bottle of wine from his cellar and rummaged about in the drawer for the corkscrew, enjoying the tantalising proximity of Rachel as she busied herself at the stove. Then he realised suddenly that he was looking in the wrong drawer. This one was full of table mats. He closed it and glanced at the drawer next to it. No, it wasn't the wrong drawer. This was where he kept the corkscrew and the potato masher, all those bits and pieces, surely... Or was he going bonkers? He opened the drawer again, frowning at the contents.

'What are you looking for?' asked Rachel.

'The corkscrew,' replied Charles, closing the drawer again and opening the other one, which turned out to be full of tea cloths, and bibs. Bibs?

'It's here,' replied Rachel cheerfully. She opened the drawer next to the cooker and produced the corkscrew. 'I moved those things over here next to the cutlery. It didn't seem very logical to have them in that drawer. Really the table mats should be there, nearer to the table, you see. And I thought it was handier to have the cloths and things in the drawer nearest the sink. The clingfilm and foil are in here now. I hope you don't mind.'

But dammit, thought Charles, if he'd wanted the corkscrew and things over there, he'd have put them over there. For an instant he hesitated, then smiled and took the corkscrew from her. 'Right.' He nodded. 'Absolutely right. I have no sense of order.' He turned away and began slowly, thoughtfully, to open the bottle. Oh, well, it didn't matter particularly. It was just going to be a pain to keep opening that drawer for the next few months in expectations of finding the corkscrew, and finding table mats instead. Habits were rather hard to change at forty-five.

The evening passed off very pleasantly, and Charles was more than tempted to capitalise on the intimate, cheerful atmosphere, but he decided that it was best to leave it a few days before making his move. The next morning, as he went into his study to start work, he was enjoying a most agreeable little fantasy which involved Rachel undressing him, sinking to her knees... What the hell had happened in here? He stared at his desk, where last week he had left a series of piles of notes all carefully arranged, covering the desk, admittedly, but in an order which only he understood, for the purposes of cross-referencing. What he was looking at now was a bare surface, and a neatly stacked pile of papers in one corner. He turned to the other desk, which was at right angles to this one, and on which stood his computer and a variety of books which he had left open at key pages. To his relief, these remained untouched. With a sigh, Charles sat down, and realised that there was something wrong with his chair, too. The two, thin, well-worn velour cushions which had always rested upon the rather hard padded leather seat of the chair were not there any more. Grinding his teeth, Charles rose and searched the room, but the cushions were nowhere to be seen. The prospect of having to spend the best part of an hour re-assembling his little piles of notes was bad enough, but he couldn't even begin that task until he had retrieved his cushions.

'This is un-fucking-believable!' snarled Charles to himself as he roamed from room to room, seeking his cushions, and alarming the girl from the village whom Rachel had hired to look after Oliver for the next few weeks. 'Have you seen my cushions?' he demanded. The girl, Jeanette, looked at him as though he were mad, and Oliver, sitting transfixed on the floor with a brick in either hand, began to cry. 'No, of course you haven't!' muttered Charles, and left them. He found the cushions eventually in the kitchen, and seized upon them with a glad cry. At least he could sit down now. Returning to his study and replacing the cushions on his chair, Charles sat down and looked about him. This was not the work of Mrs Dobey, his cleaning lady. She knew better than to lay so much as a finger on anything on his desk or tidy away his open books. Besides, he thought gloomily, staring at the space behind his computer where little fluffy whorls of accumulated dust had sat so comfortingly for so long, it was beyond her competence to have dusted everything so thoroughly. This had to be the work of Rachel. He sighed a deep sigh. She probably thought she was being helpful, getting his existence into order. Obviously she was the fastidious type – he should have realised that by the way she dressed, and the fact that Oliver was always neat and clean and shining. Well, he would have to have a word with her about it that evening. She might be beautiful, and he might adore her and want her passionately, but there were limits to what a man could stand.

He decided to broach the subject after dinner that night, which was a curry cooked by Charles, and not very well cooked at that. The irksome beginning to his day had left him feeling broodingly resentful, a mood which wasn't helped by the fact that Oliver seemed to have been crying non-stop all evening. He was teething,

Rachel explained, getting up every now and then from her meal to walk him up and down the kitchen in an attempt to soothe him, stroking his fat, reddened cheek with her hand. After a while he began to grow a little quieter, and Rachel laid him experimentally in his pushchair, lined with a fleece, which was standing in one corner of the kitchen. Damned nuisance, thought Charles, glancing at it. He had already caught his knee on the thing twice, but Rachel said she had to have it there, it was the only way she had been able to get Oliver to sleep over the past two weeks in what was, to him, a strange, new environment. Miraculously, as they both stared suspensefully at him, Oliver, with a faint, sighing whimper, closed his eyes and fell asleep. Thank God, thought Charles, who thought he had the beginnings of a headache and was toying with the idea of taking a Nurofen.

Rachel picked up their plates and tiptoed to the sink with them, glancing briefly at the baby. Charles got up, picking up their wine glasses and the bottle, and took them through to the living room, where the fire had burned low – too low, he thought despondently, to chuck another log on. It would never take. He sighed and refilled their glasses, then stood gazing down at the dying embers of the fire, wondering how he could tactfully suggest to Rachel that she shouldn't interfere with his things, without sounding too critical or ungrateful. He didn't hear Rachel come in and turned to find her standing quite close behind him. He smiled, faintly startled, then said, 'Sorry, dinner wasn't one of my finest culinary efforts.'

She smiled back, picked up her wine and sipped it, then set the glass down again. She folded her arms and stood staring down at the fire. 'It was great, really. I'm just sorry Oliver was so wretched all evening.'

There was a small silence, and then Charles said, 'Listen, there's something I just thought I'd mention . . . ' God, how was he going to say this? He was terribly bad at this kind of thing, and she had just thought she was being helpful, after all. Maybe he should forget it. Then he looked at her, saw the softened, lovely lines of her face in the glow of the firelight, and his heart turned over. She glanced up and caught his look, and in that moment the two of them stood perfectly transfixed, gazing at one another, before Charles leaned down and kissed her, tentatively at first, then urgently drawing her against him. As he did so, Rachel half-expected to feel afraid, as she had always felt with any man before Leo. But there was no fear, just perfect acceptance. She wondered, as she kissed him back, achingly grateful for the feeling of his long, lean body against hers, how long she had wanted this to happen. Probably from the very first time she had seen him. But in all those months she had been too bound up in her own private pain with Leo, still hoping for the best, trying to pretend that Charles was nothing more to her than a friend. He was whispering to her between kisses, his voice feverish and incoherent, and Rachel felt a wonderful happiness expand within her. In her mind's eye, lost in the pleasure of kissing him, it was like one of those time-delay shots of a flower unfolding, over and over, a combination of overwhelming emotional and physical sensation. At last Charles took his mouth from hers, holding her face between his hands and looking at her unbelievingly.

'I meant it when I said I was in love with you. I completely and utterly and absolutely adore you.' His voice was unsteady with emotion, and Rachel felt instantly that this was a man of complete sincerity, whose declared love was as real and honest as Leo's had ever been false and beguiling. There was a boyish earnestness and longing about him which captivated her entirely.

'Do you?' she whispered, unable to think of anything else to say, unable to take her eyes from his.

Charles nodded slowly. 'God, yes. And if you don't let me take you to bed now, I think I will go entirely mad.' He kissed her again, and Rachel felt too dizzy with desire to resist.

After a moment she drew her mouth away from his. 'I have to put Oliver into his cot first,' she said softly, pausing for a moment before she turned and left the room. Charles leaned back against the fireplace, trembling slightly, conscious of a pulse beating hard in his throat. He had not anticipated this, had not even been thinking about laying a finger on her this evening... He marvelled at the perfect timing achieved by a total lack of planning and wondered, waiting for her to return, whether he had not meant what he had just said to her, or whether he was just carried away by the intoxicating prospect of bedding her at long last. Whatever he felt or did not feel, he decided he would leave the matter of his study for another time, and began earnestly to pray that Oliver would not wake up in the next hour or so.

*

Felicity was standing over her desk, a copy of the early edition of the *Evening Standard* spread out in front of her at the jobs vacant section, while members of chambers trickled back in from lunch. 'Fitter/turner wanted'. What was a fitter/turner, then? Whatever it was, Vince was probably not capable of becoming one. She sighed. It must, admittedly, be pretty boring being a security guard for Marks & Spencer, standing watching middle-aged women buying underwear all day and with no mates to have a crack with. But it was the only job Vince had been able to get, and now he was going to jack it in. Given that he'd convinced himself he had to have a job to stop feeling like a kept man, she could just imagine how things were going to deteriorate once he was back on the dole again. She stared at the paper despondently. Panel wirers, paint sprayers, HGV/diesel fitters . . . The problem with Vince was that he had no training for anything. What had he ever done by way of gainful occupation, apart from a paper round at the age of fifteen and helping his dad out in the market? Then she suddenly remembered – he said he had worked on the mini-cabs one Christmas when he'd had no money. He wouldn't want to go back to that, not the hours they worked, but what if he could become a proper taxi driver? He'd probably like that, reflected Felicity. He liked driving, enjoyed criticising other people's road behaviour, and he would doubtless enjoy the kudos of a black cab, sitting outside Charing Cross Station reading *Penthouse*. She could just see it. But black cabs cost money, and you had to train really hard. She wouldn't mind putting up the money for a cab, if he could do the training. She was earning a fair whack here, far more than she had ever imagined.

Her thoughts were interrupted by the sight of Camilla coming in, wearing the same morose, absent-minded expression that Felicity had seen for the last few days.

'What's up with you, then?' she asked. 'Got a mouth on you like a dog's bum. I thought everything was wonderful in the world of young love.'

Camilla came in and sat on the edge of Felicity's desk, taking off her jacket. 'I am caught on the horns of a dilemma,' she replied.

'Oh, yeah?' said Felicity with only vague comprehension.

Camilla ran her fingers through her hair and sighed. 'I can't talk about it here, but I really would like to tell someone.'

'What are you doing after work?'

'Nothing.'

'Let's go and have a drink and a good girlie talk, then,' suggested Felicity cosily.

Six o'clock found them in a wine bar in Chancery Lane, discussing Camilla's fortunes over a glass of chablis.

'So, what's the problem, then?' asked Felicity.

'It's Leo. At least, I think it's Leo,' replied Camilla.

'Oh, yeah? What's he done, then?' Felicity sipped her drink and waited, chin on hand.

'He hasn't done anything. That is – ' Camilla broke off. She looked candidly at Felicity, hoping that it wasn't too indiscreet to talk to one's clerk like this. 'What do you think goes on between Leo and Anthony? Their relationship, I mean.'

Felicity was surprised, not by the question, but that Camilla should ask it. In the months that she had known them, Felicity had become aware of the subtle currents of emotion between Leo and Anthony, seen the way the older man looked at the younger, observed his voice and manner, and come to her own conclusions. Felicity was a girl who had seen and done much, and her experiences had bred in her an awareness which other people in chambers did not possess, protected as they were from the outside world by their upbringings. They, so far as she knew, had perceived nothing out of the ordinary. She took another sip of her drink, glanced warily at Camilla, and decided to hedge the question.

'I don't quite understand what you mean. What are you getting at?'

Camilla sighed. 'I'd better explain. You see, I had a talk with Leo. He says they're going to offer me a tenancy.'

'That's good. About time they had a woman at that place. Sexist sods.'

'The thing is,' continued Camilla, 'Leo made it pretty clear that I wasn't likely to get it unless I stopped seeing Anthony. Went on about the importance of maintaining balanced relationships in chambers, that sort of thing.'

'Bollocks,' said Felicity. 'I don't know all that much about it, but I don't think Mr Renshaw could care less. And he's the head of chambers. They're more interested in getting decent tenants than worrying about who they're knocking off. I'll bet if Mr Renshaw wants you to have this tenancy, you'll get it regardless. You know what's important in the long run to that lot? Work and money, and not necessarily in that order. They wouldn't be offering you a tenancy if they didn't think you were going to bring in the work. And you will.'

'Mmm.' Camilla stared thoughtfully at her drink, then raised her eyes to Felicity's. 'So why did Leo go to so much trouble to warn me off Anthony?'

There was a brief silence, then Felicity said, 'You know the answer to that one, or you wouldn't be asking the question.' She took a sip of her drink and set the glass down. 'He's jealous.'

Camilla nodded. 'That's the conclusion I came to. I know from things Anthony has said that he regards his relationship with Leo as special, important, but I didn't realise quite how much it mattered to Leo.'

'So what are you going to do?'

'Well,' said Camilla, leaning back in her chair, 'it seems to me that I don't have to make any sacrifices at all. I'm going to tell Anthony – '

'I wouldn't tell him about Leo,' interrupted Felicity quickly.

'No, I wasn't going to. I'll just say that I think it might be a good idea for the sake of appearances to cool things between us until I've definitely got the tenancy. Leo says they'll make a firm offer around Easter time. And after that . . . '

'After that you can both do as you please, and no one can touch you for it,' Felicity said, grinning.

'There is one slight problem, however.'

'Leo.'

'Quite. He's going to speak to me again about it, I know, and I'll have to tell him that I'm prepared to stop seeing Anthony for the sake of getting my tenancy. He'll believe me. I can tell by the way he looks at me that he thinks I'm a bit of a dope. Oh, very bright, and all that, but easy to manipulate. And I'm a little apprehensive about how he's going to feel when, in a couple of months' time, he realises that I never meant to give up Anthony at all.'

'Yeah . . . ' Felicity scratched her chin thoughtfully. 'I like Leo, but he can be a right bastard. The kind of bloke you'd rather have on your side than not.'

'Quite. I'm sure, if he wanted to, that he could make my life in chambers fairly difficult, particularly as a new tenant.'

Felicity shrugged. 'I'd say that's a risk you have to take. I wouldn't let him try to run your life for you. Not if you think Anthony's worth it.'

'Oh, he's worth it. He definitely is,' said Camilla with a smile. She finished the remains of her wine. 'It's been useful talking to you. Thanks. I was wondering if I wasn't reading too much into Leo's attitude to Anthony, but I don't think I am.'

'Always happy to help,' said Felicity. 'And remember, if things do get a bit dodgy in a few months' time, you've always got an ally in me.' And that, thought Felicity, as she reflected with some pride on her growing power as 5 Caper Court's clerk, was no small thing.

Chapter Twenty-four

On the first day of the Capstall hearing, Freddie looked out of his bedroom window and saw the early glimmer of sunlight spreading across a clear, cold sky. A good omen, he thought to himself, as he stood lean-shanked and shivering in his little bathroom, engaged in the routine strip wash learned long ago at his Wiltshire preparatory school. At this time in the morning, the water was not yet sufficiently hot for a bath. Like a general readying himself for battle, Freddie had been busy in preparation for this great day. He had spent the day before yesterday in the Laundromat with his stock of shirts and underwear, and yesterday he had stood at the ironing board for the entire afternoon, ensuring that he would have a freshly ironed shirt ready each day. Didn't want to waste time fiddling about in the mornings. He'd have to be in court bright and early, keeping an eye on things, making sure everything went smoothly. Freddie had an idea that his presence in court for this hearing was indispensable, and that somehow his own close attention to the proceedings would facilitate their proper running. He felt that the very fact that he had risen at five thirty this morning to prepare himself had got things off to a good, brisk start.

When he had eaten his Bran Buds and drunk his coffee, it occurred to Freddie that he should remind Charles Beecham that Carstairs' widow might want to attend the hearing. Beecham lived near her, after all, and could bring her up to town. He glanced at his watch. Nearly six. Still, Beecham was probably an early riser, beavering away on those books and documentaries of his. He'd give him a call.

When the phone rang by his bedside, Charles resolved not to answer it. He had a notion that the very fact of making this decision would stop it ringing. But since the thing seemed to be beyond his exercise of will, and just went on trilling, he eventually reached out a groping hand and picked it up.

'Freddie,' he groaned, when he heard the clipped, eager tones. 'Freddie, it's ... it's ... ' Charles focused on the bedside clock. ' ... it's six o'clock, for God's sake. What is it?'

Freddie explained that he thought it might be an act of Christian charity to ask Mrs Carstairs if she'd like to come along to the hearing. 'You know, it might be something of a personal thing for her. In the light of her husband's death.'

'Freddie,' sighed Charles, 'she has children. She has to get them to school and so on. I can't imagine she'd want to attend. And, anyway,' he added, 'I'm not going to be there myself.'

Freddie expressed his astonishment that a member of the committee of the Names' action group should think of being absent from court on the first day of the hearing. But then, he thought to himself, Beecham had always struck him as not really being one of the stalwarts, tended to shirk his responsibilities somewhat.

'I've got rather a lot of work on at the moment, as it happens,' said Charles patiently. 'And I can't imagine a lot's going to happen today. I'll come up when things have got properly under way.'

'I see,' grunted Freddie. 'Well, if you can't be there in person, I'll make sure I report the day's proceedings to you later on.'

'You do that, Freddie. Just make sure,' he couldn't resist adding, 'that they haven't got your phone tapped.' He replaced the receiver and lay back. Rachel turned over sleepily next to him, and he lifted a length of her silken black hair from her shoulder.

'Who was that?' she murmured, her eyes still closed.

'Just an old codger. One of the Names. It's the first day of the Capstall hearing today.'

Rachel, her mind clearing itself of sleep, thought of Leo, wondered if he was feeling his usual assured, buoyant self. Then she opened her eyes and smiled at Charles. She couldn't care less. Leo would win. He always won, and good luck to him. Charles, drawing her towards him, feeling the warm, lazy touch of her body against his, told himself that actually Freddie had done him something of a good turn. They still had half an hour before Rachel had to get up to go to work.

It had taken much labour and a great effort of organisation to accommodate in Court Number 25 the vast array of paperwork which the Capstall case had generated. There were box files everywhere, stacked around the court, ranged before the bench in circular stands, and piled between the solicitors in cardboard filing boxes. Freddie, sitting at the back on the public benches, marvelled at the thought that Leo and his juniors must somehow have made themselves masters of this great wealth of information. He glanced down to where Leo, Anthony, Walter and Camilla sat, thinking that they looked almost a forlorn little foursome in contrast to the massed ranks of lawyers on the right-hand side of the courtroom. The bevy of barristers on the other side, dipping their wigged heads to confabulate, moving around with a rustle and billow of black gown, reminded Freddie of so many sleek crows. There must have been about sixteen or seventeen of them. He wished, just for the sake of the thing, that the lawyers on the Names' side were in greater numbers. Still, he thought, it reminded one of Agincourt, the few against the many. In his excitement, he felt his heart swell at this thought, and he muttered, 'The fewer men, the greater share of honour. God's will! I pray thee, wish not one man more . . . ' He saw Basher Snodgrass give him a curious look from further along the bench, so he coughed and stopped.

Camilla was sitting next to Anthony, attentive, alert, wishing that she had more to do, anxious for things to begin. She glanced round. The murmurings amongst the lawyers were languid, people even looked bored as they adjusted their wigs and fiddled with their lap-tops, waiting for the hearing to commence, but Camilla was conscious of an undercurrent of tension in the atmosphere. She heard Leo laugh, and turned to look at him. Anthony tapped her arm and nodded in the direction of a very tall QC who was pacing round with an abstracted air.

'With the amount he's earning from this case, you'd think he could afford better shoes.'

'Who is he?' asked Camilla.

'David Underwood. He's leading counsel for the underwriters. He earns a fortune, but it's a standing joke that he wears the oldest suits in the Temple. I think he's only got one tie. He's actually very shy when you meet him socially – almost inarticulate, sometimes – but in court he's quite a different creature.'

Leo, who was keyed up to a fairly high pitch, leaned towards Anthony and murmured, 'I've bet Underwood a case of claret that he can't get the word "Lilliputian" into his opening address, by the way.'

Anthony laughed, and at that moment the usher intoned, 'Court rise.' Through a door at the back of the court emerged Sir Basil Bunting, tall, sleek, white-haired, and looking ineffably self-important. This was, after all, something of a landmark case, whose outcome would affect the futures of many. Sir Basil's serene features, as he eased himself into his thronelike chair, betrayed nothing of his anxious and fervent hope that he was going to understand the issues sufficiently to issue that judgment because, from what he had read so far, he wasn't at all sure that he did. Still, this was the easy part. When everyone was seated, he put on his half-moon spectacles, and cleared his throat.

'Mr Davies, before you open this case, there are certain matters which I wish to raise.' He looked around the court with mild gravity. 'This case has already subjected and will continue to subject the parties to strain, but I expect the trial to be conducted in accordance with best Commercial Court practice.' That sounded sufficiently authoritative, he thought, let them know he wasn't going to stand any nonsense. 'Secondly, a great deal of the background to this case should be capable of being reduced to agreed statements and charts. I expect the parties to co-operate in the early stages of the trial so that the common ground material is agreed. It is all too easy in these matters to move into confrontational mode, so I would be grateful if counsel, in their opening statements, would identify materials that are agreed, or are likely to be capable of agreement.' That, at least, would reduce the amount of argument and, accordingly, the risk that he might lose track of what was going on. Having delivered these brief admonitions, Sir Basil glanced at Leo and nodded.

Leo rose, and was conscious for the first time in his life that he did not feel his customary superb confidence. He and Anthony might have shrugged off those juicy rumours about their supposed relationship, but here, today, beneath the casually suggestive glances and sly smiles of his fellow barristers, he felt a distinct unease. He cursed inwardly the destructive miscreant who had spread those idle little lies, so clearly designed to distract and upset himself and Anthony at the outset of this important hearing. It had occurred to him often enough over the past few days that, had things been otherwise, they might not have been lies at all. That fact alone disturbed his equilibrium, and made it harder for him to brush the whispers aside. Nevertheless, at this moment he did his best to thrust such thoughts to the back of his mind, and his voice, as he began to speak, was as assured and coolly persuasive as ever. No one, glancing up at the silver-haired, handsome figure, would have guessed how many cares and distractions pressed in on him from all sides.

'My Lord, the plaintiff Names in this case claim damages from the defendant members' agents, the defendant managing agents, Mr Alan Capstall, the active underwriter of syndicate 1766, and Marples and Clark, the auditors, for negligence. It is as a result of that negligence that the Names have been drawn into the nightmare world of the US tort system, and have been – and will continue to be for the foreseeable future – on the receiving end of insurance and reinsurance claims generated by that system, a system where the primary aim of jurisprudence developed by the courts, and of the legislation enacted by Congress, appears to be to ensure that he with the deepest pocket pays, irrespective of all other considerations. My Lord, insurers are deemed for this purpose to have deep pockets, and so are reinsurers. In particular, Lloyd's Names are deemed to have deep pockets but, although their liabilities are unlimited, their funds, as is by now well known, are not. It is important to remember throughout this case that we are dealing here not with giant corporate entities, but with ordinary people who, having put their affairs into the hands of supposed experts, as the system at Lloyd's requires, now have no control over what is happening to them. Some of the plaintiffs are persons of wealth. To them, their Lloyd's losses may be no more than an inconvenience, albeit a serious one. Others, however – and certainly the majority – have been hard hit, as have their families. Homes, farms, treasured possessions have been sold to pay losses to which Names should never have been exposed. Death is no escape. Very often estates cannot be wound up because of continued exposure to Lloyd's losses. My Lord, the amounts involved are frightening. The declared loss in the 1992 syndicate accounts for the 1984 open year are £163,989,000. Chatset currently estimates a further deterioration of 400 per cent of stamp . . . ' His voice had taken on a steady momentum, and with an imperceptible rustling sigh, the court settled down to listen to Leo expound the grievances of the Names and the faults of the several defendants.

*

297

It was three days before Leo finished his exposition of the case, during which time his discourse was frequently interrupted to enable a variety of points regarding confidentiality, chronology and cross-referencing to be dealt with. No amount of oratorical skill could make the material which Leo had to present anything but tedious in the extreme, and he was grateful for those little intervals during which he could resume his seat while counsel for the parties on the other side rose and fell, their voices with them, points of relevance and irrelevance drifting through the courtroom as the hours ticked by, while Sir Basil struggled to make sense of it all. At the back of the courtroom Freddie dozed, waking occasionally to gaze bemusedly at the little games of patience which many of the solicitors, yawning and restless, were playing on their laptop computers. A handful of Names dropped by occasionally to see how their case was progressing, but after a baffling half-hour or so they would drift off again, disappointed by the unelectrifying atmosphere pervading the proceedings.

At the end of the third day, as the hands of the clock crept towards four twenty and dusk gathered outside, Leo, to his relief, was close to completing his reiteration of the basic points.

' . . . And that, my Lord, is the case reduced to its core elements. Unless I can assist your Lordship further – ' At that moment Leo bent to listen as Walter whispered a few words to him, then straightened up. 'I am told that some significant discovery has come forward very recently from Marples and Clark, which I have not seen, but which my juniors say I must reserve the right to come back to tomorrow morning. I am told it will take only a few minutes, but I understand that it is crucial.'

'Subject to that, you have finished?' enquired Sir Basil.

'Unless I can assist your Lordship further.'

Sir Basil shook his head. 'No, I congratulate you on covering so much ground with so much thoroughness in three days. Thank you, Mr Davies.' He glanced round at the other lawyers. 'Ten thirty tomorrow morning, then.'

Leo breathed a heavy sigh of relief on the way out of court. 'Now we'll see what Sir Basil manages to make of the evidence,' he murmured to Anthony. 'Gurney tells me that he's been ringing up everyone he can find each evening to try and help him understand the points.'

'What happens tomorrow?' asked Camilla.

'God knows,' said Leo. 'I've bored everyone for long enough, so the other side will just want to pitch straight in and bring on their witnesses of fact, the underwriting witnesses and so forth. Then we'll have the expert witnesses, then Capstall, and I suppose Underwood and the rest of them will manage to get their three ha'penceworth in along the way. This isn't a model case in terms of procedure, you know. Everything's bound to be – '

'Shambolic,' said Anthony with a grin.

'Flexible, I was going to say, with a modicum of tact,' replied Leo in dry tones. He glanced round in search of Murray Campbell and caught sight of his portly figure as he leaned against the wall, papers beneath his arm, deep in conversation with Freddie. 'I'm just off to have a word with Murray. See you all tomorrow.'

Anthony glanced at his watch and leaned towards Camilla, murmuring to her, 'Now that we're off the hook, I propose that you and I go and have a drink and then something to eat.'

Camilla nodded. 'Yes. All right.'

'Good,' said Anthony. 'I'll see you back in chambers in fifteen minutes.'

Rachel drove down the road from Charles's house towards the station, still smiling at the thought of Charles at the kitchen window, raising one of Oliver's fat hands to wave at her, and tried to fathom the situation in which she now found herself. Two weeks ago they had been no more than friends, and now she was sharing his home and his bed, and a domestic arrangement which Oliver seemed to find highly satisfactory. But there had to be a next step, a moving on, and it was up to her to make it. The trouble was, she had no idea of how their relationship was to continue if she and Oliver moved back to London to a house of their own. She supposed she and Charles could see one another when he came up to town, possibly at weekends, but it would be odd, sort of upside-down, for things to be reduced to that sporadic level after the unbroken serenity of the present. She sighed as she thought of the house in Kew whose details she had received at the office yesterday. It seemed entirely right – it had three bedrooms, a large garden, and was tucked away in a pretty backwater. Commuting wouldn't be a problem, and there were good local nursery schools. She had arranged to see it later that afternoon. So why did she sigh as she thought of it? she wondered. Anyway, she had more mundane things to do before that, such as going to see John Rothwell and asking for an increase in salary that would put her on a par with Fred Fenton. And a car, which would enable her to sell her present one. It might be months before she and Leo sorted out a divorce, and she and Oliver had to live until then. She would need the extra money. Not that she thought it would be a problem, after her paper at the conference, and the fact that she had brought in two new valuable clients as a result.

When Rachel's car had disappeared from sight, Charles carried Oliver through to the living room and let him crawl around there with his toys. Jeanette was due to arrive in a few minutes. He idled through to his study, where his papers and books had been rearranged into a pleasing state of disorder, and stared out of the window at the leafless mulberry tree, contemplating the day. He was having lunch in Salisbury with an old university friend, Timothy, who was staying there for a few days, and he was looking forward to a boozy reunion. The prospect was sufficiently festive to make it seem hardly worthwhile starting any serious work, he thought. Anyway, a pleasant kind of lassitude seemed to have overtaken him recently. Was that a result of regular sex or decent meals? he wondered. He heard the back door open and close, and then Jeanette called through to him, announcing her arrival.

'Right-ho,' called back Charles. 'I'm just in my study, sorting a few things out.' He was struck by the ease with which a domestic routine had recently been established in the house. It was pleasant to have people around, to have coffee brought to one, and to work away in the knowledge that, when evening fell, someone would come home, and there would be food and conversation. On the other hand ... On the other hand, there were those horrible moments in the night when Oliver would wake crying and, even though it was Rachel who went to him, Charles would find sleep slipping irretrievably away. And he missed those long, deep silences when he and he alone occupied the house, those evenings when he could stay in alone if he wished to, or amble down to the pub and spend the evening in drinking and idle banter. He missed being himself, in some ways. But when he thought of Rachel, when he thought of that delightful, slender body, and the hours spent in bed together – hours which, together with Oliver's nocturnal squalls, rendered him hollow-eyed the next day – he almost groaned aloud at the idea that that should be taken from him. Did he want her to stay indefinitely? he wondered. In some ways the thought was appealing, in others . . . Was he in love with her? Or was he already missing that heart-slipping sensation of longing for the unobtainable which gave life so much of its relish? Maybe it would be better if she was in London, so that he could only see her now and again, and could keep that tantalising little flame of uncertainty alive. 'As usual, Beecham,' he sighed, 'you haven't the foggiest idea what you really want.'

Rachel sat listening to John Rothwell, hardly able to believe it. 'You mean that you're simply not prepared to review my position?' she asked. She had been so full of confidence when she had come into his office five minutes before, certain that all her hard work and determination over the past month would be rewarded by a change in attitude towards her.

'It has already been reviewed,' said Mr Rothwell, glad of the sense of security which his large, semicircular desk afforded him. 'But only in the normal way, under the annual review at the beginning of each year. We cannot go beyond that.'

Rachel took a deep breath. 'Mr Rothwell, when we last spoke on this subject, you said that you had reservations about my – my commitment to the firm. You said you felt that, because I am married with a child, that I couldn't be relied upon in the same way as someone like Fred Fenton. I feel that I have demonstrated over the past few weeks that I'm every bit as flexible as any man in this firm, that I don't necessarily put my family first, and I'm asking you now for a good reason why I shouldn't be treated on the same footing as someone like Fred.'

Mr Rothwell leaned forward and clasped his hands on the desk in front of him. She had given him a little ammunition. 'I hardly think Fred's situation is relevant. You know that I'm not prepared to discuss the position of other individuals in the firm. We are discussing you. Now, I think you made a very valuable contribution with your paper at the conference, and I'm grateful for the contacts you made. But the fact remains that you are a young married woman with a family, and it is not the firm's intention to impose upon you burdensome expectations which would be inconsistent with your domestic situation.' The fact was, there was a very good chance that she would go off and get pregnant again, only he couldn't quite come out and say that.

Rachel stared at him and, despite her seething anger, laughed. 'This, if I may say so, Mr Rothwell, is extraordinary. Are you now saying that you're doing me a favour by holding me back? That I should be somehow grateful to you for not allowing me to work too hard, so that my family doesn't suffer? Don't you think that's just a little patronising? Not just towards me, but towards every other female partner in this firm?'

Mr Rothwell's own temper began to fray. 'Rachel, you may choose to distort what I say, but the fact is that the rewards which you receive from this firm are rewards which we regard as commensurate with your work and the way in which you perform it. Now, I'm sorry that this should lead to any ill-feeling on your part, but there is nothing further to be said.' He glanced at his watch. 'I have a meeting in a few moments, so you must excuse me.'

There was nothing more she could say at that moment. This was not the end of the matter, she decided, as she left his office smarting with bitter frustration. She would take this further. But what if it cost her her job, as it surely would? Well, she would worry about that when the time came. Then she thought of Oliver, of nannies, of trying to find another job and fight for her rights in some drawn-out industrial tribunal, and already she felt overwhelmed and exhausted by the dubious prospect. She longed for the evening, when she could tell Charles and find some comfort from him.

Charles and his friend Timothy had had an excellent lunch. A couple of drinks beforehand, a couple of bottles of very decent claret with the meal, brandies afterwards. They hadn't left the place till after four. Maybe going on to the pub afterwards had been over-egging the pudding, but they'd been having such an enjoyable, witty conversation that it had seemed a shame not to prolong it. Charles now felt beautifully mellow as he made his way to the station taxi rank, realising that he was certainly not in any condition to drive himself home. He was mildly astonished, through his alcoholic haze, to see Rachel coming out of the station, and then realised that, of course, she would naturally be on her way home at this hour. She smiled when she saw him.

'What are you doing here? You didn't come to meet me, did you?'

'No, my psychic powers aren't quite up to that, my sweet. I've been lunching with an old friend, and we got talking . . . The fact is, I've only just left him.' He glanced at his watch, astonished to see that it was already ten past seven.

Rachel frowned anxiously as they walked together towards the car park. 'What about Jeanette? She's supposed to go off at half-past six.'

Charles felt mildly disgruntled at the implication that since she, Rachel, was late, it was up to Charles to look after Oliver. 'Oh, she won't have abandoned him, don't worry.'

When they got in, Charles loafed happily in an armchair, squinting at Rachel's copy of the *Evening Standard*, while she put Oliver to bed. When she came down later, Charles was unpleasantly aware that the effect of the afternoon's alcohol was beginning to wear off. There was only one cure for that, he knew, and that was to keep the old level topped up. He would regret it tomorrow, he knew, but since he was due to start a serious work stint the day afterwards, he might as well behave recklessly this evening. There would be enough sobriety over the next month, when he was being nagged by producers and working flat out. He went to the cellar and fetched a bottle of wine, then wandered into the kitchen, where Rachel was putting together a chicken salad. He was glad that supper was going to be light, after that lunch, he reflected, wandering from drawer to drawer in an exasperated search for the corkscrew.

'Thanks,' said Rachel, as he handed her a glass of wine. 'I need it, after today.'

Charles circled her waist with his arm and softly kissed the side of her neck, making her shiver with pleasure. 'Tell me about it, let me soothe away your worries . . . '

She sighed, moving away from him, and set the plates and cutlery on the broad kitchen table. 'Oh, it wasn't all bad. This afternoon was quite encouraging, in fact. I left work early to look at a house in Kew. That's why I got back late.'

Charles took a healing draught of wine, and felt his alcohol level climbing comfortably back up. 'And?'

'It was very nice. Lovely, in fact. Big garden, decently sized rooms, not too far from the station and shops. The couple who are selling it have already found somewhere else and are ready to move, and I'm a first-time buyer, so it's all ideal, really . . . '

'Excellent!' said Charles, with an enthusiasm he did not feel. Of course it had always been understood that she would be leaving – hadn't it? – but the reality of it gave him a cold, bleak feeling. He took another gulp of wine and prodded moodily at a piece of chicken. ·

'Is it?' murmured Rachel, looking at him thoughtfully. Well, it was natural enough that he should be pleased. This was his home, he was used to being here alone. No doubt he was looking forward to having some peace and quiet again.

'So . . . what was wrong with the rest of it? Your day, I mean.' He did not want to talk about the house, did not want to hear her plans for redecorating, or where Oliver's nursery would be. He didn't, above all, want to think about this house after she had gone. A maudlin vision of himself sitting alone in the evenings, at this table, came to him. I could cry, thought Charles.

'The rest of the day was horrible,' said Rachel decisively. He noticed that she wasn't eating. 'You remember I told you that I found out that I wasn't being paid as much as male partners, and so on?' Charles nodded, listening absent-mindedly and gazing at her in a fond, hazy way, surprised at how randy he could make himself just by looking at her and thinking certain things. 'Well, I was pretty convinced after this conference that they'd have to take a different line, that I'd shown them I was capable of doing the job without any concessions, just because of Oliver . . . ' She sighed deeply, her voice trailing away. 'But,' she went on, conscious of incipient tears rising, 'I was wrong. They have no intention of treating me equally. You would think, wouldn't you – ' her voice shook slightly as she tried to contain a sob at the thought of the sheer injustice of it ' – that in this day and age women could expect to be dealt with on their merits, and not according to some chauvinistic . . . ' She put her face in her hands and let all the misery and frustration overwhelm her.

Charles rose in consternation and went to her, putting his arms around her and drawing her to her feet. She held on to him, her slight fit of weeping already subsiding, but Charles, ever a susceptible fellow, and now made even more so by wine, was struck to the core by her unhappiness. With the vague idea that he could cheer her up by making love to her, he kissed her tears, then her mouth, and began to unfasten most of the buttons and zips that came to hand.

'Don't worry about any of that,' he muttered. 'Forget them ... God, you are utterly gorgeous,' he breathed, as he fondled one breast and kissed her shoulder. It had always been one of Charles's weak points that he confused sexual arousal with genuine emotional feeling, and now, as she responded to his caresses and returned his kisses, glad of their comfort as much as anything, he became entirely convinced that the worst mistake of his life would be to let this woman go off to Kew and leave him. 'And another thing,' he said, gazing into her eyes and kissing her nose lightly, 'I don't want you to go. Forget that house in Kew. Stay here. Stay here for ever. I love you and I don't want to be without you. Truly. Please, please tell me you'll stay ... I want you to come and live with me. Permanently. God, how beautiful you are ...'

As he said it, Charles was entirely sincere. But then, after a day in which he had consumed two gin and tonics, a bottle of claret, two brandies, a couple of pints in the Crown and Trumpet, and a glass of Australian chardonnay, there was much that Charles might say and mean.

Rachel was too far lost in the familiar passion which Charles now aroused in her to say anything instantly. But the words sank in and, just as Charles was wondering if he was too old to make love over the kitchen table or whether it would put his back out, she replied in a happy murmur, 'Yes, of course I'll stay. I love you, too.' And Charles, as he pushed the plates aside in a clatter and lifted her on to the table, was convinced that this was exactly what he wanted to hear.

It was after eleven when the phone rang. Leo was slumped in an armchair with a book, a glass of Scotch balanced beside him, feet on the coffee table. In the past weeks he had grown accustomed to the unbroken silence of the house, and the sound of the telephone startled him. He stretched out a hand to pick it up.

'Hello?' he murmured, hoping like hell that it wasn't Murray or Fred getting themselves into a lather over some obscure point. That was the trouble with solicitors – always fearing the worst and looking round for trouble.

There was a pause before the voice on the other end spoke, and when it did, it was with a light, breathless catch.

'Leo?'

'Yes,' replied Leo. 'Who is this?'

'It's Francis.'

There was a long pause. Leo wondered for a moment whether he should simply hang up. Francis was the last thing he needed right now. He thought he'd made it clear to the boy months ago that it was all over. How the hell had he got his home number? But after a moment's hesitation he decided it would be better to speak to him.

'Francis . . . What can I do for you?'

Francis laughed, a brief, light sound that Leo had once liked and had entirely forgotten. But his voice, when he spoke, was tired and dull. 'Not very much, I don't think . . . I'm afraid this is a duty call, more than anything. I can imagine that you didn't much want to hear from me, but I'm afraid I hadn't much choice. I'm rather unwell, you see.'

For a second Leo was tempted to ask what the hell that had to do with him, and then a small, cold fear struck him. He felt his grip tighten on the receiver. 'I'm sorry to hear that,' he said evenly, waiting.

'I've got Aids, Leo,' said Francis tersely, his voicing shaking a little. 'A few weeks after – after you last came to see me, I had a test, and I was HIV positive. And now it's something rather worse.' The chill of fear which Leo had felt now seemed to numb his body like ice. He himself hadn't been tested for six months. He thought suddenly of Rachel and Oliver. Christ. Oh, sweet Christ. He closed his eyes momentarily, then heard Francis continue. 'That's why I had to call you. So that you – so that you know. I – '

'Yes, yes, I know. God, look – I'm sorry. I'm terribly sorry.' Was he? Could he care less about Francis? It was himself he was sorry about, himself he was concerned for. He could have himself tested tomorrow, but this couldn't have come at a worse time, in the middle of this case, when he needed to be at the peak of his form, concentrating on nothing other than the issues. It was a nightmare. Struggling to control the fear he felt, Leo said, 'Thank you for letting me know.' It seemed an absurd, trite thing to say. But what else was there to say?

'I just hope . . . ' Francis hesitated, then went on, 'I just hope – you know, that everything is all right for you.'

Oh God, thought Leo, add your prayers to mine, Francis. 'Yes,' he said. 'I hope so, too.'

Leo replaced the receiver and sat staring unseeingly ahead of him for a long, long time.

Chapter Twenty-five

Leo left the Harley Street clinic shortly after nine, leaving himself just enough time to get to chambers and pick up a few things before getting to court. As he swung his car away from the meter and into the traffic crawling across Wigmore Street, he could still see in his mind's eye the enigmatic features of his doctor, whom he had known for fifteen years. The man's tact, discretion and swiftness of response were worth all the money they cost – but, beyond that, there was nothing more to be bought. Leo was in a situation now where all the money in the world could not buy him the peace of mind he wanted. At least he would not have long to wait – he had been told he could pick up the results of the test at the end of the day. He had slept wretchedly the night before, and was grateful for the fact that at least he did not have to perform today. Underwood would be giving his opening address, which was bound to be short, and would then begin the examination of the expert witnesses. The crux of this case was, for Leo, his cross-examination of Capstall, and that was several days away, by which time, all being well, he should have recovered his equilibrium. If he could get the man to admit in court that he had had no business writing those risks on behalf of the Names, given the potentially over-whelming liabilities to which he was exposing them, then they were home and dry. But he knew Capstall, had seen and heard him often enough to know that this would be no easy task. He was a slithery type, glib and extremely good at giving oblique answers. Leo's mind lurched suddenly away from the case and back to his own predicament. What did any of that matter, should the result of this test turn out to be positive? At this thought, Capstall and the Names seemed to shrivel into insignificance. He tried to envisage how it would be . . . Would he be able to carry on? Would he have to ask Anthony to take over? Even as he contemplated the enormity of the possibility that the result would be positive, Leo could not imagine how he would react. It was one thing to suppose, to conjure up the demon, but until he actually stared that mortal reality in the face, he had simply no idea how he would cope. All he could do was to get through today.

The hours in court that day were long and slow and painful for Leo, but perhaps the worst part was having to behave normally, to smile and talk, to appear responsive and attentive to the day's proceedings, when all he wanted to do was to creep into a quiet lair of introspection. It was not true, he thought, struggling to pay attention to Underwood's words, that activity helped time to pass. When the ticking was that of one's own mortal clock, no amount of talk or action served to distract one from its dull, endless stroke. The unsettling rumour concerning himself and Anthony seemed trite now, a groundless piece of gossip which had, for Leo, now paled into an ironic insignificance.

'... of course, my Lord, no doubt my learned friend Mr Davies would be quick to say that this matter is one of Lilliputian proportions when compared to the larger issue of the run-off contracts...' Underwood turned slightly to glance smilingly in Leo's direction, but the faint grin with which Leo responded was no more than a muscular response, for his concentration was so destroyed that he was incapable of feeling the slightest glimmer of amusement.

At one point he glanced round towards the back of the court, wondering, as he had wondered each day so far, whether Charles would look in. But the public benches contained only the solitary figure of the loyal Freddie, blinking in a mystified fashion, and a couple of bored journalists. The thought of Charles now seemed a hollow, bleak one. How, in these circumstances, could he ever contemplate the possibility of another lover? What was it one said to placate the fates? Make everything all right, God, and I won't ever be a bad boy again, I promise. How untrue. If everything did turn out to be all right, he knew that his passion for Charles would be undiminished, and he would remain undismayed by any threat such as that which now hung over him. But if only all might be well... The sound of Sir Basil's voice and the realisation that he was being addressed brought Leo round with a start.

'Do I take it that you agree with that, Mr Davies?' There was a pause, and Sir Basil frowned slightly, aware that Leo's mind had been elsewhere. 'That the 1984 consultative document should be read in conjunction with page 104, paragraph 7?'

Leo hesitated momentarily, glancing to where Anthony's finger had flicked to the relevant page of the bundle and was indicating the paragraph in question. 'Yes, my Lord,' replied Leo after an instant's furiously concentrated thought, 'I quite accept that reading of the document.'

'Good.' Sir Basil nodded. 'We appear to be achieving some degree of consensus.' He glanced at the clock. 'Well, I think that this might be a convenient moment to stop for lunch.'

Anthony rose and began to tidy his papers together, the bustle and hum of the court rising around them, then stopped and glanced curiously at Leo, who was still seated, the fingers of one hand touching his lips, his gaze vacant and steady.

'Are you all right?' he asked in a low voice. He had noticed all morning that Leo seemed exceptionally subdued, as though his mind were not properly focused on the proceedings.

Leo took a slow breath and glanced up at him. 'Yes, yes I'm fine.'

'Fred and Walter are going to go over the deficiency figures. Do you want to come and have a bite of lunch? You look as though you could do with an hour spent away from all this.'

Leo regarded Anthony for a moment. Could he tell him? God, he longed to talk to someone, longed to unburden himself and share the suspenseful waiting. Anthony would understand. He felt a sudden, sharp surge of affection as he looked at Anthony's candid, anxious features. Whatever happened, Anthony would always be someone he could talk to. And then, if it came to the worst, he would be there . . . Leo nodded. 'Good idea.'

'Good, I'll just – ' He broke off, glancing round at Camilla, who was sorting through stacks of bundles with an exasperated Walter. 'Leo and I are just going round the corner for some lunch. D'you want to join us?' he asked her.

'Yes, I'll be with you in a minute . . . ' She turned back to Walter. 'No – it's the other one, with the yellow tabs . . . '

Leo glanced at Camilla and then back to Anthony, and after a second's delay, said suddenly, 'On second thoughts, there are one or two things I have to attend to in chambers. You two go on without me.'

He felt an unreasonable anger as he left the court. Why did that bloody girl have to come between them? After what he had told her at dinner a couple of weeks ago, he hadn't expected the relationship with Anthony still to exist. But it would appear that she hadn't yet ended it. As he crossed through the Strand traffic, Leo tried to assure himself that it was only a matter of time before Camilla and Anthony had ceased to be an item, and he could be assured of the younger man's exclusive attention and friendship. At that moment he felt it was something he badly needed. But it was not, he reflected darkly, a day for feeling sure of anything. On his way into chambers he bumped into Cameron's portly figure. 'By the way,' Leo said to him, 'I think it's about time we called that chambers meeting to discuss the new tenants, don't you?' The sooner Camilla had to make her choice – and Leo was pretty sure he knew which way she would choose – the better for everyone.

By the time Leo mounted the broad carpeted staircase to the Harley Street consulting rooms where his fate awaited him, the sense of dread which he had carried about with him all day was so much a part of him that he was scarcely aware of it as a separate emotion. It was by now a permanent state of mind, woven into his consciousness. The doctor's receptionist smiled her cold, bright smile and asked Leo to take a seat. The minutes ticked by. Leo tried to fill his mind with thoughts of Davenport's examination that afternoon of one of the underwriting experts, but they trickled away from his mental grasp like so many grains of sand. He sat, utterly blank, waiting.

After five minutes that seemed like eternity, the doctor put his head round the door and looked in Leo's direction, his smile sufficiently affable to give Leo a faint hope. When the door closed behind them both and he saw the man seat himself at his desk and then look up with the same smile, he knew in an instant that it was all right.

'Your tests, I'm glad to say, were negative, Mr Davies.'

The next few moments, whatever else passed between them, Leo was almost unaware of. He spoke and smiled mechanically, and left the consulting rooms with a sense of total unreality. Only when he reached the cold air outside on the pavement did he begin to feel human again, receptive to external influences. Rarely, he thought, had he been so consciously thankful for that physical well-being which he had always taken for granted. He thought with fleeting guilt of Francis, but the thought was eclipsed almost instantly by his own vast sense of relief, and after that he did not think of him again.

Freddie was nothing if not diligent. Over the next few weeks he attended the court every day, sitting for long, uncomfortable hours through the examination and cross-examination of streams of expert witnesses – auditors, actuaries, claims handlers, under-writers, American lawyers. In Freddie's consciousness they blend-ed into one amorphous middle-aged being of indeterminate height, usually balding, with glasses and a droning voice. What the lawyers said to this creature, and what he replied, made little or no sense to Freddie most of the time, although there were occasional spells where he could follow the gist of the thing. But each day seemed to consist largely of a dreary trawl through endless bundles of documents and lists of figures, with references to people and things of which Freddie had never heard. When, he wondered, was Leo going to get that man Capstall on the stand and demand of him why he had perpetrated his gross acts of folly in Freddie's name, and the names of countless others? That was what this case was all about. The rest of it was just so much padding. He rubbed his eyes with dry, cold fingers and tried to concentrate on what was going on, longing for the luncheon recess so that he could go and have his sandwich and cup of coffee at the tea bar round the corner on the Aldwych. Sir Basil was poring over some document in front of him, a copy of which Anthony, conducting the cross-examination, was quoting from aloud. The man on the witness stand was staring at his own copy of the document with a bored and weary air.

'This item is obviously a crucial document, Mr Cross,' said Sir Basil.

'Indeed, my Lord, it speaks for itself. If I may continue – '

'I confess to having a little difficulty with the manuscript. Can we go over that part again slowly?'

'Indeed. If I can go back to page 177, under "asbestos", the document continues as follows: "There was a review of the movement of incurreds during calendar year 1986. The assump-tion had been made that this group represented twenty per cent of total deterioration ..."'

It was no use, thought Freddie, he didn't have a clue what they were on about. He sighed and eyed Sir Basil, envying him his apparent ability to follow all this complex evidence so thoroughly, entirely unaware that each evening Sir Basil had to go home and ring up an amenable friend from the Court of Appeal and get him to explain the knottier points to him.

'I'm going up to town to see my agent this morning,' Charles told Rachel over breakfast. 'We can catch the train together.'

'You'd better hurry,' remarked Rachel. Charles hadn't yet shaved and was still in his dressing gown, and she couldn't see him getting ready to leave the house in twenty minutes. She sometimes wished that Charles wasn't quite so sloppy about things. He must be the worst timekeeper in the world, and if there was one thing she couldn't stand, it was having to wait while someone else dawdled around.

He got up from the table, but not with any particular briskness. 'Bags of time,' he said cheerfully, rubbing a hand over his chin and smiling at Oliver. Then he went off whistling to run the hot water. Rachel picked up the plates from the table and suppressed a sigh, convinced that he was going to make her late for the train. She particularly wanted to get to work on time, because she had a mass of paperwork to sort through before lunchtime, when she would be seeing Leo. She had rung him yesterday and arranged to see him briefly today. Now that she and Charles were living together, she wanted to sort things out, arrange for a divorce as soon as possible, and set herself entirely free from the past eighteen months and the misery of loving someone like Leo. She thought fondly of Charles as she picked Oliver from his high chair, reflecting on how much pleasanter he was to live with than Leo. Not quite so tidy, of course, nor so personally fastidious, but she was pretty sure, given time, that she could change all that.

Charles had found that he generally came up with some of his most inspirational thoughts whilst shaving. The task was so boring that it usually generated a free flow of creative ideas. This morning, however, he found himself preoccupied with thoughts of himself and Rachel. It was over a month since he had asked her to come and live with him, and everything had been very pleasant since. But he had begun to wonder whether she was quite in tune with his way of living. She was terribly tidy. In one way that was a good thing – at least he didn't have to scour the house for the *Radio Times* or waste time swearing and hunting for the car keys. She made sure everything was always in its proper place, the rooms were always tidy, cushions on the sofas, no newspapers littering chairs and tables. But in another way it was incredibly irritating. Charles had not realised until now that swearing and hunting for the car keys were part of a ritual for him, something almost therapeutic, and ultimately rewarding in a small way. It was a little dull to know that from now on they would always, always be in that ceramic pot on the kitchen dresser. He sighed and plunged his razor into the water, then scraped mechanically at his chin. Still, everyone had their own ways, and adoring her as he did, it must all be worth it. He just wished that he could put from his mind the casual remark which she had uttered last night, about how he should perhaps cut down on his drinking. Now that *had* worried him.

They had come at last to the day for which Freddie had waited so patiently. Admittedly Leo had had Capstall on the stand for all of the previous day, but that had been merely to take him through a variety of documents and letters, all just stuff leading up to the real issues. There had been some interesting moments, but Freddie was convinced that today they would get to the heart of the thing, that Leo would get Capstall to demonstrate to all the world what a charlatan he was, and to admit that everything he had done had been negligent in the extreme. He noticed, as he edged his way into his seat, that Basher was there, and Mrs Hunter, and Cochrane, and a handful of other Names whom he vaguely recognised. They had come today, of course, though they couldn't be bothered to show much interest in the rest of the proceedings. Freddie felt a faint pride at the thought that he, and he alone, had been up to the task of coming every day, seeing the thing through properly.

Anthony sat listening to the buzz and murmur of voices as everyone in court sat waiting for the proceedings to commence. Was he imagining it, or could he detect a heightened tension, an air of excitement that was not usually there? He glanced round, and saw that there were many more people in the public benches than usual. Everyone regarded Leo's cross-examination of Capstall as the key to their case, wanted to see and hear for themselves what the man had to say in defence or explanation of his actions. Above

314

all, they wanted Leo to get him to admit that he had acted recklessly and arrogantly in the manner of his underwriting, which had ruined so many. If Leo could do that, thought Anthony, then they would be well on their way to winning. But, of course, in the end it all depended on the view that Sir Basil took. It was hard to tell, so far, whether he was sympathetic to the Names or not. At that moment Sir Basil himself entered the court to take his place on the bench, and Anthony and everyone else rose mechanically. Sir Basil's own sister and brother-in-law, reflected Anthony, had been badly hit by Lloyd's, so it was fair to assume he would tend to take the Names' part. But one could never be sure. It would be nice, thought Anthony as he resumed his seat, to have a bit of an indication of what Sir Basil's real feelings were.

After a few seconds Alan Capstall mounted the steps to the witness stand. He was a tall, well-built man in his mid-fifties, expensively dressed, but not remarkable in any way. He looked out at the court with a bland expression, endeavouring to appear matter-of-fact, but there was no mistaking the swift, wary look in his eyes as he glanced from Sir Basil to Leo, who had risen to his feet to resume his cross-examination of the previous day. So far Leo had been the soul of smiling courtesy, but it was this very fact that made Capstall uneasy. If anything, he felt he would have fared better in an aggressive atmosphere, could have risen to a scathing challenge or outright offensive. But Leo's polite, dry manner made him feel foxed and defensive.

'Yes, Mr Davies?' said Sir Basil, when everybody appeared settled.

Leo smiled at Capstall, who did not smile in reply. 'Good morning, Mr Capstall,' said Leo easily. 'Mr Capstall, I would just like to ask you one or two more questions on the topic of the responsibility of the writing of the run-off contracts and your involvement in it . . . '

Here we go, thought Anthony, preparing to take notes. Here was the long, slow run-in. He wondered whether Leo would try to nail him before lunch, or leave it until later. All in all, it was going to be an interesting day.

For the next two hours Leo worked diligently, taking Capstall through documents and letters, harping on the topic of reasonable exposure and unquantifiable risks, pushing further and further towards the question of Capstall's own imprudent behaviour. It was all done with politeness and patience and masterly skill and, by the time the lunchtime adjournment came, Leo felt that he had his end in sight, that the pressure which he had begun to apply would show results in the afternoon. As Capstall stepped down from the stand and the lawyers began to gather up their papers, he glanced at his watch. Today wasn't the best of days for Rachel to pick, but he had said he would see her at the main entrance to the Law Courts. He thought he had a good idea what she wanted to say.

As he glanced round, he noted with a sudden flash of pleasure that Charles was there, chatting to Freddie and Basher at the courtroom door. He hadn't been there at the beginning of the day, so he must have slipped in during the morning. The rush of excitement which he felt was quite exhilarating, and he hoped that Charles would be there for the afternoon. Charles glanced across, saw Leo and smiled.

'Good stuff,' he said, as Leo approached. 'You've got the bastard looking very jittery.'

'Well, we'll see what the afternoon brings,' said Leo, trying not to let his gaze rest for too long on the features which he had come to love.

'I don't see why you have to be quite so polite to the damned scoundrel,' muttered Freddie, who had hoped to see blood by now.

'Oh, I have my methods. Courtesy and patience, you know.'

'Not what I'd give him, if I had my way,' said Freddie. 'Come on, Snodgrass, let's find some lunch. Good luck this afternoon,' he added to Leo.

Charles gave a chuckle as Freddie and Basher made off, and at the sound and sight of him Leo felt that he could do anything that day, just so long as Charles was there. Then he remembered Rachel. The pleasure of Charles's company would have to wait until later.

'I'm sorry we can't have a bite of lunch together. I'm meeting someone in a few moments,' said Leo.

Charles shrugged. 'I hadn't actually meant to be here till this afternoon. I came up to see my agent, but things got messed up. Come on, let's walk out together.'

Charles was so involved in conversation with Leo that he didn't notice Rachel at first, standing at the foot of the steps leading down from the Law Courts, wrapped against the cold in a long camel coat, the wind whipping strands of dark hair about her face. When he did notice her, he was pleased but not particularly surprised. This was her stamping ground, so to speak. He left Leo's side, and went forward and kissed her.

'You just can't let me out of your sight for more than a few hours, can you?' he said, smiling and giving her a sideways hug. Then he glanced at Leo. He and Rachel were staring at one another in a sort of frozen way. 'I don't think you know Leo Davies, do you – ?' he began, but before he could complete the introduction Rachel broke in, her face stony. She had seen too late who Leo's companion was. The situation was one which she would just have to face. But this was not the way she had wanted Leo to find out about Charles, or Charles about Leo.

'Yes, I do,' she said simply. 'He's my husband.' She turned to Charles. 'I thought you said you were seeing your agent this morning?'

'I was,' said Charles very slowly, his mind trying to absorb what she had just said. 'He had some sort of domestic crisis, so I came over to court to see how things . . . ' He let his words tail away, then looked from Leo to Rachel. Good God. So it was Leo. He was the chap who slept with blokes and shagged the nanny. Good God. He looked from Rachel's white, mortified face to Leo's grim one, and for a moment all three stood in an astonished and uncomfortable tableau.

Leo, recovering from his shock and disbelief, put it all together in an instant, marvelling at how simply the pieces fitted. The kiss, the way Rachel had spoken to Charles, mentioning his agent – that casual domesticity betrayed everything. Charles was her lover. She must be living with him, she and Oliver. It was where she had automatically gone the day that she had left him. How long had the thing been going on? he wondered. Months? How long had he been pathetically deluding himself with his infatuation, lusting after Charles, hoping? The sense of shock, of humiliation, was appalling, cavernous.

He turned to look at Charles. Charles was smiling. Charles was positively grinning. And after a few seconds in which Charles tried to contain his feelings, he positively exploded with laughter. He laughed with his whole body, throwing back his head and hooting with mirth. He laughed so uproariously and helplessly at the ludicrous situation in which he found himself that passers-by turned and looked at his tall figure, grinning slightly at the infectiousness of his laughter. Then he managed to control himself long enough to clap Leo lightly on the back and say, 'I imagine you two have a few things to talk about.' And, still laughing, he walked off, leaving Leo and Rachel looking at one another.

Chapter Twenty-six

When he came back into court after lunch, Anthony had a distinctly unsettled feeling. At lunchtime Camilla had said she wanted to speak to him at the end of the day, making it sound as though it was something serious and difficult. He only hoped she wasn't pregnant. And then Leo. He had passed Leo just after this morning's session, standing on the pavement outside the Law Courts with Rachel and Charles Beecham. He had almost stopped to say hello, but there was something about the atmosphere, the way all three were looking at one another, that had told Anthony it wasn't the time or the place. What could that have been about? he wondered. Then as Anthony had carried on across the Strand he'd heard Charles burst out laughing behind him, so he'd assumed it was all right, whatever it was they were discussing. Now, as he looked at Leo's face, he knew there was something distinctly wrong.

Leo, as he sat trying to focus his concentration on the business ahead of him, could feel Anthony eyeing him with concern. It must show, he knew. But in the light of what had just happened, it was hard to keep one's expression light and untroubled. The very worst thing – worse than the farcicality of the whole business, or the stark humiliation he felt – was the catastrophic timing. Were the fates in some sort of conspiracy against him? First those rumours about himself and Anthony which had been maliciously designed to unsettle the start of the case, then that chilling scare from Francis, and now this. He tried to rationalise it, put it in proportion. What was it, after all? Merely that his wife had found another man – which, Rachel being the woman she was, and in the light of events, was hardly surprising. So the man had turned out to be Charles, the object of his own hopes and affections. What did that signify, beyond disappointment, and an evaporation of cherished hopes? Nothing. Had it not been for the pure surprise of the thing, he might, under other circumstances, have been able to find the whole thing as ridiculous as Charles obviously had. But the thought of the love which he had genuinely borne for Charles these past few months gave him a wrench of pain. No, he must not allow it to touch him in that way, must treat the matter lightly. He shook his head as if to clear it, and was conscious of Anthony, sitting only inches away, glancing guardedly at him again. He turned to him, and saw in his eyes an expression of such candid concern that he suddenly found himself able to lean close to him and murmur in a low, conversational tone, 'Do you know what?'

'What?'

'I've just found out that Rachel is living with Charles Beecham. Our client is screwing my wife. I am being, to use that delightful expression, cuckolded.'

'Ah.'

'So if I don't look my normal self, put it down to momentary shock and confusion. She wants a divorce. It wouldn't surprise me if she marries him.'

'Oh.'

Leo sighed, then folded his arms and regarded his notes thoughtfully. 'And do you know what else?' He glanced back to Anthony.

'No, what?' Anthony was busy trying to absorb these sudden and surprising revelations.

'I rather fancied Mr Beecham. I even believed the feeling was mutual.'

'Mmm.' There was a long pause, then Anthony said, 'That's bad luck.'

Leo looked at Anthony and smiled, and suddenly felt much better. 'I like you, Anthony,' he said fondly. 'It rather helps to be able to tell you things.' There was a sudden stirring around them, and Sir Basil entered the court. Leo and Anthony rose.

'Are you going to be all right?' murmured Anthony, thinking, as Leo had, that the timing of all this could not have been worse.

'Oh, I think I shall rise above it,' replied Leo.

Anthony watched Leo tug his gown about him, fingering his notes, waiting for Alan Capstall to ascend the witness stand, and knew that in those moments Leo was trying to clear his mind of everything except the task ahead of him. It could not be easy.

Rachel and Charles were having their first quarrel, a minor one, and it was taking place outside Court Number 25. They managed to argue in low voices, conscious of their surroundings.

'But why didn't you *tell* me who he was in the first place?' asked Charles, who was not feeling quite so wholehearted about this quarrel as Rachel was.

'Because of who he is! He's the leader in your case! I didn't want you to . . . I thought you might have . . . oh, I don't know. Told other members of the committee, or something.'

'Thanks very much.'

'I didn't want to mess this case up for Leo. It's very important for him and, whatever I feel about our marriage, I don't want to wreck his career. It just didn't seem like a good idea for you to know. I was going to tell you once the case was over.'

'I think you've made me look a bit of an idiot, frankly, Rachel. I mean, I've been really friendly with the bloke the past few months – '

'How was I to know that? Anyway, you seemed to find it all screamingly funny an hour ago.'

'Well, it is a bit of a joke, isn't it? I mean, admit it.'

'I didn't like the way you fell about laughing. It seemed rather – rather heartless.'

'I can't help it if you don't happen to share my sense of humour, can I?'

She was about to make a retort, then sighed and looked at her watch. 'Oh, we'll talk about it tonight. I have to get back to work.'

'Anyway, what did you and he talk about?'

'When?'

'Today. Now. This past hour or so.'

Rachel sighed impatiently. 'I'll tell you tonight. I have to go.'

Charles shook his head musingly. 'I don't honestly think I'll ever be able to look him in the eye again, you know.' He paused for a moment, then asked, 'What was she like, this nanny of yours? Was she nice?'

'Charles!'

'I just wondered.' He grinned and pushed through the swing door and into the solemn atmosphere of the courtroom, where Leo was slowly preparing to tighten the screws on Mr Capstall.

'Tell me, Mr Capstall, would you agree that it is consistent with prudence for an underwriter to make enquiry as to the nature and extent of risks which he is undertaking on behalf of the Names on his syndicate?'

Charles slid into a seat, ignoring the irate glance which Freddie shot him, and gazed with a new fascination at Leo, whose manner, as he put this question to Capstall, was far less mild than it had been earlier in the day. Charles could imagine, he supposed, that men might find Leo attractive. Hadn't he, after all? Though not in that way, Charles reminded himself hastily. He glanced in the direction of Capstall, who looked distinctly edgy as he sought for a glib answer to Leo's question.

'I suppose so. But with the contracts we are dealing with, I assumed that the reinsuring underwriter would have done sufficient research – '

'Mr Capstall, the reinsuring underwriter is neither here nor there. It is your position we are considering here. Do you or do you not agree that it would have been prudent for you, as an underwriter, to have made enquiries into the asbestos situation?'

'Yes.'

'And did you do so?'

'Not in great detail. You see, I would always have to rely very much on the people that we were reinsuring, their knowledge of the account and the effect of asbestosis.'

'But, Mr Capstall, it was well known in the market that there were scares about asbestos – isn't that so? There were articles written about it by professors in the United States, and so on. The Asbestos Working Party had been set up. You were alerted to the dangers, surely?' Anthony watched Leo intently as the line of questioning gathered momentum. Leo's voice had a distinctly hard edge now, and all the smiling politeness had quite vanished.

'Well, my direct knowledge of asbestosis was limited – '

'Quite,' cut in Leo succinctly. 'Because you failed to make any proper enquiries. Even though there was gossip on the market, you failed to make any specific additional enquiries about asbestos with loss adjusters. Isn't that so?'

Leo's tone was damningly caustic. Everyone in court watched Capstall carefully, waiting for his answer.

'Well, whenever I asked the brokers and the reinsuring under-writers what they had done, they always told me that they had taken full account of future liabilities for asbestosis.' It sounded lame, and the entire court knew it. Underwood did not even look at his client, but Sir Basil shot Capstall a distinctly nasty look over the tops of his glasses. He had done his best throughout this case to retain his impartiality, but as he looked at Capstall now, and considered the evidence which he had heard the man give throughout the day, he could not but think with disgust of the dreadful losses which his own sister had suffered. And many others like her. And all as a result of indolent upstarts like this one, he thought.

Leo, who had put the incidents of lunchtime entirely from his mind and was concentrating solely on the witness before him, let the hollowness of Capstall's reply sink in before continuing.

'Mr Capstall, having established your imprudence in failing to make remotely adequate enquiries as to the risks which you were underwriting on behalf of the Names, I would like to put one simple question to you, and it is this.' Leo paused and then spoke with deliberation. 'Do you believe that it is consistent with prudence to write a reinsurance risk, the extent and nature of which is entirely open-ended and unknown?'

Capstall looked uncertain, fingering the papers before him as he sought to hedge Leo's question. When he replied, he attempted to keep his tone casual. 'Well, an underwriter might be invited to write many risks like that in the course of a day's trading.'

Leo smiled and glanced briefly down at the papers before him before looking up again. 'Mr Capstall, perhaps my question was not succinct enough. Let me try it another way. Would you regard it as prudent for an underwriter to write a risk where there is no finite limit on the amount of the monetary indemnity, no temporal limit on the duration of the indemnity, and where he is in possession of no reliable information as to what his potential liability as reinsurer or insurer might be?'

Sir Basil gazed sternly at Capstall, pen poised. There was a long silence. 'Answer Mr Davies's question, if you please, Mr Capstall.'

Capstall struggled to find words. His composure had slipped markedly, and Anthony noticed with interest that his loss of bearing seemed to touch everything about him – his suit, which now looked slightly rumpled, his hair, the angle of his tie. Capstall rested his hands on the edge of the rail, as if for support.

'Not – not as a matter of course. But people underwrite in different ways, Mr Davies. That's what makes a market.'

Leo smiled, and his voice when he spoke was soft. 'What is the answer to my question?'

'I think my answer would be – ' he hesitated, ' – that it would depend on how you see the market from the perspective of your view of it as an underwriter.'

Excellent, thought Leo. Capstall could come out with any waffle now to avoid a directly incriminating answer, but it no longer mattered. He knew from long experience that Sir Basil couldn't take much of the kind of answer Capstall was giving. As he had hoped and guessed, Sir Basil's feelings as he listened to Capstall's reply were those of incredulous impatience.

'Mr Capstall,' said Sir Basil, gazing severely at him, 'the question Mr Davies is asking you is whether or not it would be prudent for an underwriter to write a contract if he had no reasonable idea as to what the future might hold. What is your answer?'

'It would be . . . imprudent, my Lord.'

That answer, as Anthony, Leo, and everyone else knew, spelt the downfall of the defendants.

Sir Basil nodded and wrote. Thank you, Sir Basil, thought Leo. He looked across at Capstall, whose very stature seemed visibly reduced. Leo even felt fleetingly sorry for him. He said mildly, 'I do not know whether I can take it very much further, my Lord.'

'Excellent!' said Freddie, clapping Leo on the shoulder with a tremulous hand, his eyes bright with excitement. Lawyers were still milling around outside the courtroom, and the general feeling, after the day's performance, was that the Names were well on their way to winning. Sir Basil, by his intervention in Leo's cross-examination, had shown all too clearly how his own thoughts lay, and Freddie and Basher and the rest were delighted.

Leo smiled. He did not think he had ever had to work so hard to keep himself entirely focused amid so many distractions. 'We're not out of the woods yet,' he remarked. But even he had to admit that today had produced a decisive moment. He would be astonished if Sir Basil's judgment, when it eventually came, failed to find for the Names. All that remained were the closing speeches. He glanced at his watch. 'Anyway, if you'll excuse me, I'll have to be getting back to chambers.'

'Just a moment, Leo,' said Murray, 'I got this letter in from Dryden's today, and I thought you might like to look at it overnight.'

Leo took the document from Murray and glanced at Anthony and Walter. 'You two go on ahead. I'll catch you up.'

Grey dusk was falling on the City streets when Leo made his solitary way out of the Law Courts on to the Strand half an hour later. Street lights were already glimmering, and as he was about to cross the Strand through the roar and hum of rush-hour traffic, he became aware of someone at his side. Turning, he was astonished to see Sarah standing next to him, smiling her familiar, foxy smile.

'Well done in court,' she said. 'I came to watch.'

Leo stepped off the pavement on to the pedestrian crossing, glancing round at the traffic, Sarah in step with him. 'You're sure it wasn't Anthony you came to see?'

Sarah shrugged. 'Whatever. You make a lovely couple. I'm sure everyone there thought so.'

They reached the other side, and Leo stopped and turned to look at her, suddenly comprehending. 'You. It was you who started that rather irritating little rumour, wasn't it?' He shook his head. 'My, my. You never used to have a taste for petty revenge. Anthony must really have got under your skin.' Then he laughed, thinking how obvious it all was, really. He began to walk through the iron gate into Middle Temple Lane, his step meditative, Sarah still at his side. He glanced at her. She looked as bewitching as ever, her blonde hair tucked inside the upturned collar of her coat, framing her face. But God, what trouble she was.

'I was sorry to hear about your wife,' remarked Sarah. 'Leaving you, I mean.'

'I'm grateful for your concern,' replied Leo drily.

'You really should have married someone like me, Leo,' said Sarah, amusement in her voice. They paused by the archway into Caper Court, people brushing by them in the gathering gloom as they hurried up and down the lane. 'You know, someone who understands you. Where you're coming from.'

'And you understand that, do you?' Leo could not help smiling. 'You're one up on me, in that case. But I hardly think,' he added, 'that you could bear the monotony of my company. Like you, I'm probably best in small doses.'

'There you are. We're the same kind of people, you and I. As for the monotony of one another's company, I'm afraid that's something you're going to have to put up with as from next September. David Liphook is taking me on as his pupil.'

Leo stared at her. Was she joking? No, she might be smiling, but she certainly wasn't joking. God, if it wasn't one damn thing, it was another. Sarah knew much about him, and was lethally unscrupulous. The prospect of having her in the same chambers was not a happy one. What would Anthony think of it, come to that?

He sighed and turned to go. 'Oh well, roll on September, eh?'

She raised a hand, still smiling. 'See you, Leo,' she said. Then, before she turned away, she added, 'Do give my love to Anthony. Won't it be cosy, all of us working together?' And she disappeared down the lane among the clerks and barristers heading for their trains.

Anthony dumped his bundle of papers on the desk and chucked his robe bag into a corner. 'So,' he said to Camilla, 'what is this momentous thing you want to talk about?' He glanced at his watch. 'In fact, why don't we do it over a glass of wine?'

'I can't, I'm afraid,' said Camilla. 'I promised my mother I'd go over for dinner this evening. Anyway, this won't take long.' She leaned against the edge of her desk. 'The thing is, apparently they're thinking of offering me a tenancy.'

'They?' said Anthony with a grin, relieved that this was all it was about. 'Don't you mean "we"? I did know, actually. Aren't you pleased?'

'You knew? Why didn't you tell me?' demanded Camilla.

Anthony shrugged. 'Of course I knew. Anyway, it's not up to me to tell you.'

'You *are* my pupilmaster. Well, nominally.'

'I thought you should hear it from Cameron himself. Anyway, what is there to talk about?'

'Well ... I've just been thinking ... I'm not sure how many people in chambers know that I'm seeing you, but it struck me that it might be best if – ' She paused, stuck for words.

'If what?'

'Oh, you know ... I mean, I don't want anything to upset my chances of getting this tenancy – you can imagine how important it is for me. And I have the feeling that some people in chambers might not think it a good idea – us going out with one another, that is.'

'What people?' Anthony wondered, with a horrible foreboding, whether Camilla was trying to say she wanted to stop seeing him.

'Roderick, for instance, and Jeremy. Perhaps Michael. Even Leo.'

'Leo? I hardly think so,' replied Anthony with a faint smile. Then he suddenly remembered how Leo had once sought to make something more of the relationship between himself and Anthony, how he had said then that such a thing would, of course, spell an end to Anthony's hopes of getting a tenancy at 5 Caper Court. That had been different, naturally, but maybe there was something in what Camilla said. Maybe he hadn't paid enough attention to the way in which the more senior members of chambers might view his relationship with Camilla. He could see that she wanted to be as circumspect as possible. Was she serious, then? Was this her way of ending things?

'So – what are you saying?' he asked slowly.

'I'm saying,' replied Camilla, 'that it might be best, for the sake of appearances, if we gave it a rest for a while. Just until after Easter.'

Anthony felt relief wash over him. He crossed the room and put his arms lightly round her shoulders. 'For a moment there, I thought you were going to tell me that we were finished.' He kissed her lightly. 'Even so . . . Easter is six weeks away. And that's a long time.'

'Think of it as being in a good cause,' said Camilla. 'It's just a question of making to look as though there isn't anything going on any more. I suppose it helps that Jeremy's coming back from Indonesia next week, so I'll be moving out of here.'

'I never knew you were such a devious character,' murmured Anthony lightly.

'It's not devious,' said Camilla. 'Well . . . ' She smiled. 'Only slightly.'

'Hmm. And you're not concerned what people will think when they discover that things are not as they appeared to be? After you've got your tenancy, I mean.'

'Not in the slightest,' replied Camilla, but she thought of Leo with faint misgiving. 'So long as my work's all right, I don't think it matters, really – not in the long run. Do you?'

'No,' replied Anthony, and kissed her again.

'Anyway,' sighed Camilla, 'as from now, we're just good friends.' She glanced at her watch. 'And I'd better get going. I'll see you tomorrow.'

She picked up her coat and went out. At the foot of the stairs she bumped into Leo coming in, and was about to pass by with a murmured 'goodnight', when he stopped her.

'By the way,' said Leo, 'I was wondering – have you thought any more about what I said? About your tenancy, that is?'

'If you mean about Anthony – no, I meant what I said at dinner. I want the tenancy. I've just been explaining things to Anthony, in fact.' Put that way, Camilla told herself, it was all perfectly true.

'Ah,' said Leo. 'I see.'

There was a brief pause, and then Camilla said, 'Goodnight,' and went out. Leo stood for a moment in thought. She had seemed remarkably composed, for someone who had just brought a love affair to an abrupt end. Perhaps it hadn't meant that much to her after all. He went upstairs, hesitated outside Anthony's door, then knocked and went in.

'Hi,' said Anthony, glancing up. He was standing, half-leaning against his desk, looking through some papers. His voice sounded vaguely tired, non-committal, but he smiled at Leo. Whatever his feelings concerning himself and Camilla, clearly he was not going to reveal them to Leo. Well, they need never mention the matter. He had achieved his purpose, at any rate, Leo told himself. Camilla was no longer a threat, an intrusion.

'I wondered if you felt like celebrating, now that the hearing's over,' said Leo cheerfully. 'Perhaps a bottle or two in El Vino's?'

'Good idea,' said Anthony. He picked up his coat and switched off the light, following Leo downstairs. They paused on the steps outside 5 Caper Court while Leo locked up. As they strolled through the cloisters together, Leo suddenly remembered Sarah. 'By the way,' he said, 'I have something interesting and rather horrible to tell you.'

The lift gate clanged shut behind Freddie. He walked slowly up the dim, anonymous corridor to his front door and put his key in the lock. It seemed very quiet inside the flat after the conviviality of the pub in which he and Cochrane and Basher Snodgrass had spent the past two hours. He chucked his copy of the *Evening Standard* on to the table and wandered into the kitchen to survey the contents of his food cupboard. The choice was an unappetising one of ravioli or corned beef with Smash. But the beer which he had consumed in the pub had left him with little appetite, so he decided to make do with a cup of tea. He scraped a match and lit the gas and, while he waited for the kettle to boil, went back through to the living room and switched on the television, aware of the need of something to break the oppressive silence. Oddly enough, despite the success of their day in court, he no longer felt the euphoria of a few hours ago. He had expected that sense of elation to persist. The case was more or less won, after all. In a month or so Sir Basil would give judgment. If they were successful, there would be a few more months of protracted wrangling between the solicitors on both sides and then, presumably, the E&O underwriters would cough up. He would no longer have to live this eked-out, lonely existence. He would have a bit of money to make the remaining few years less grim. Wasn't that cause for celebration?

Freddie lit the gas fire and sat down slowly in his armchair, still in his overcoat. It would be the end of the fight. And what remained after that? He would have no more reason to socialise with the likes of Basher and James Cochrane. There would be no more little meetings with Murray Cameron and Fred Fenton, no more urgent dialogues between counsel and the Names committee. For there would be no more Names committee. No need for it. The game would be played out. A pity. He liked being on the committee. Without the committee, without Lloyd's, he was no one, really. He glanced up at the television, the mention of some familiar name attracting his attention, and for a few seconds he saw Charles Beecham's features lighting up the screen in a trailer for his forthcoming documentary. Charles, thought Freddie. He had a future. He had other fish to fry, a life to get on with. Then the kettle began shrilling in the kitchen, and Freddie got up and went to switch it off.

A few hours later, at about half past one in the morning, Oliver began to cry. His thin wail, growing more and more insistent, lanced into Charles's sleep, stirring the sediment of his dreams, probing him awake. As he stirred groggily, he was aware of Rachel slipping out of bed and going to soothe the child, and he lay back on the pillow, closing his eyes and willing sleep to rush in and

329

enfold him again. But, as always, his heart was beating fast from the sudden disturbance of his rest, and sleep was gone. Cursing beneath his breath, he got up, fumbling his dressing gown from the back of the chair. As he crossed the landing he could see a dim light coming from Oliver's room, where Rachel's soothing voice mingled with the baby's whimpers.

He went down to the kitchen, which was still warm, its subdued light enveloping the space round the broad table with a cocoon-like peace. Charles pulled his dressing gown around him and picked up his half-read copy of the *Literary Review* from the dresser. Now that he was awake he might as well sit up for an hour or so until he felt tired again. Rachel, he knew, would drift off back to bed when she had the baby settled.

Instead of reading, however, he sat staring unseeingly into the corner of the kitchen, brooding. He wished he could get Leo out of his mind, wished that the day's events had not so unsettled him. What had happened to his life? How had it changed so radically? A sudden renewed squall of crying came from upstairs, and at the sound of it Charles let out a groan. He loved Rachel, he told himself. She was here, at his invitation, already making plans for decorating and furnishing the unused rooms in the house. It was what he wanted. Of course it was wonderful to have someone in his life again, to have – to have the sound of Oliver in the night. And Rachel. Of course he meant it when he said he loved her. Her sweet, compliant body, that lovely, hesitant smile of hers which made his heart turn over. He sighed as he thought of that smile. It was the smile she had smiled earlier this evening, when he had idly suggested opening a second bottle of wine, and she had said, 'Don't you think you should try not to drink so much? I'm sure you don't really need it.'

Charles glanced at the bottle, still standing unopened by the cooker. He reached out gratefully for it, set it before him, and then turned to fumble in the drawer where he thought the corkscrew was.